THE
THUNDER

THE
THUNDER

A NOVEL ON

John Knox

DOUGLAS BOND

P&R
PUBLISHING
P.O. BOX 817 • PHILLIPSBURG • NEW JERSEY 08865-0817

Scripture quotations are taken from John Knox's own translation, as found in *The History of the Reformation in Scotland*.

ISBN: 978-1-59638-214-5 (pbk)
ISBN: 978-1-59638-546-7 (ePub)
ISBN: 978-1-59638-545-0 (Mobi)

Scroll ornament © Dave Smith, istockphoto.com

Printed in the United States of America

Library of Congress Cataloging-in-Publication Data

Bond, Douglas, 1958-
  The thunder : a novel on John Knox / Douglas Bond.
    p. cm.
  ISBN 978-1-59638-214-5 (pbk.)
  1. Knox, John, ca. 1514-1572--Fiction. I. Title.
  PS3602.O65646T49 2012
  813'.6--dc23
                                        2012012391

For my wife

Contents

1. Dead Bishop's Castle   9
2. It Begins   19
3. Flight or Fight   25
4. Bodies and Souls of Men   31
5. War Galleys   39
6. Before the Regent   47
7. Subterranean Calling   55
8. Make Haste!   61
9. Was It Real?   65
10. French Ships Use Slaves   69
11. Shattered Like Eggshells   75
12. In the Bottle Dungeon   81
13. Willful Falsehood   87
14. At Sea in Chains   91
15. Accursed Idol   99
16. Welcome to England!   109
17. Bath, Food, Bed   113
18. New Friend   119
19. Wednesday Sermon   127
20. Provoking Battle   135
21. Religion by Royal Edict   143
22. Bishop Knox?   147
23. Swaggering Unquiet Spirit   153

24. Bells and Smells 155
25. Abominable Idolatry 163
26. Muddy Berwick 171
27. Love 175
28. Knox and the King 183
29. Kings Are Mortal 193
30. Flee or Bleed 203
31. Faint-Hearted Soldier 211
32. Geneva 215
33. Faction and Disorder 225
34. Nothing to Sing 233
35. Play the Man 241
36. Simple Soldier 247
37. Bodley's Bible 257
38. Blast of the Trumpet 265
39. Scotland on Fire 273
40. St. Andrews Thunder 283
41. Cannons at Perth 291
42. War and Death 301
43. Confession and Death 307
44. My Calling 319
45. Charm and Tears 325
46. Seduction and Murder 337
47. Lost Lambs 341
48. Cousins 349
49. Another Man's Wife 357
50. Douglas the Dungman 363
51. The Assassin 371
52. Final Malady 381
53. The Fatherless and Widowed 391

John Knox and the Reformation: Timeline of Events 397

1

Dead Bishop's Castle

I WAS BORN IN A CASTLE. Hugh Douglas, Laird of Longniddry, was my father, and the only home I had known was the Douglas ancestral keep. Yet it makes too free with veracity to call it a castle. It was not a proper castle, one queens and fine ladies strut about within. In truth, it was a damp, smelly, crumbling fortified house, more akin to a vertical stone casket than a lavishly appointed bishop's castle.

Now, in late April 1547, I found myself—for good or ill—hemmed in by the fortifications of St. Andrews Castle, a proper castle, a veritable palace bedecked for a bishop, now a dead bishop. Much of the luxury of the place, so it seemed, had died with him. Cowering behind the crenellation that day, I mentally attempted to calculate the thickness and stoutness of the stones that made up the dead bishop's battlements facing the town. I breathed shallow so as to avoid the full force of the pinching odors of amassed humanity that hung palpably in the air.

The town rumbled with activity: shouting men, bawling oxen straining at their carts laden with timber and stone and with victuals for the soldiers, laden with spades and barrows, and with other things as well—cannons, barrels of gunpowder, ball, shot, and the like—ordnance, I'd heard it termed. Above all, there were the shouts and cries of men. My shallow breathing, in truth, came less from the stench and far more from gnawing anxiety at the deadly preparations surrounding me and St. Andrews Castle.

With a shudder, I turned my back on the cacophony and eased myself away from the scene. Crossing the paving stones of the inner court of the castle, I mounted a narrow stairway that led up to the battlements of the dead bishop's castle jutting into the North Sea.

As I climbed, I tried to avert my eyes from the blackened stones of the blockhouse that contained the bottle dungeon. My abhorrence for enclosed places sent a shudder down my frame. The place was a veritable hellhole, a constricting cavern into which condemned prisoners were lowered on a rope; there they crouched amongst the putrid filth of former occupants, surrounded by the foul scratching and gnawing of rats to await the rack or the stake. For Mr. Wishart, as I had often heard, it had been the stake.

I broke into a run on the last few treads, leaving the dungeon behind me. Through a notch in the wall, I squinted into the distance where the gray water met the gray skyline. I'd heard talk that the Queen Regent had petitioned the French to send their navy, thereby hemming us in by both land and sea.

Since first hearing of her scheme, I often studied that horizon, my mind troubled. But as with other days, I saw no ships bearing toward St. Andrews in the grayness—not today. Perhaps they would not come. Navies were in much demand these days, so I had been told. Perhaps the French were occupied with busting down other castles, too busy for St. Andrews.

Inching my feet forward and steadying myself with my hands against the stone battlements, I eased closer to the edge. With my eyes clamped shut, I breathed in the salty air and listened to the foamy shying of the surf. I felt a lurching of my insides as I forced my eyes open and looked down the castle wall directly into the sea. My fingernails clawed the stone edge. A gull hovered in the breeze above me, wings spread wide in flight but going nowhere. It mocked me with its screeching. Far below, and surrounding three sides of the castle, the frigid North Sea pummeled the walls. In the backwater of that pummeling, the sea churned like boiling tar in a vast caldron. My stomach did much the same.

"George!"

For an instant my heart halted—so it seemed—and then thundered back to life. I nearly sank to my knees in fright.

"George, where've you been?" asked my brother. "And do be tending of your eyeballs, lad. They're a-bulging out of your head again. I swear, one of these days you'll be making them so wide and gogglee they'll come a-popping out of your sockets like when farmer McAllister is wringing the necks of his chickens and—"

I'd heard this all before and cut him off. "Francis, if you do that sort of thing again, I'll end up tottering clean over the battlements and splitting my crown on them rocks. And if there's anything left of me, I'll be drowned and battered in the sea. It'll be all your doing, brother."

"And eaten by a haddock," he added, clapping me on the back in what he intended to be a good-natured gesture, but one that I felt nearly launched me over the wall. "You're always fretting yourself, George. Eyes goggling out of your head. That's your problem."

There was no denying what he said. For weeks now I had felt myself in a perpetual state of fretfulness.

"Now, you must come along with me," he continued. "Master Knox'll be expecting us in the chapel for our lessons."

"There's time," I said.

"Which is what you always say," said Francis. "Which is why you're always late."

"I'll not be late."

This being besieged was all a game to my brother Francis and Alexander Cockburn, our childhood friend and fellow student. To me it was no game. Dutifully, I began following him down the narrow stone stairs.

"Why did they do it?" I blurted after him.

Francis stopped and turned slowly toward me. He heaved a sigh. "If you don't ken the answer to that, you've gone daft. 'Why did they do it?' you ask. They did it because fornicating Cardinal Beaton was a monster. His vows of chastity notwithstanding, his holiness fathered no less than seven bastard offspring. If anyone in God's universe had it coming to him, Beaton did. That's why they did it."

"Who counted?"

He scowled and shook his head. "Counted what?"

"His . . . well, his offspring?"

"Brother, there you've gone and clean missed the point again," he said.

"But it was murder," I persisted. "They murdered the man. And if they hadn't done it we wouldn't be trapped in this castle awaiting the cannons of the Queen Regent to smash it to rubbish—and us with it."

He held up his hand, eyes blinking rapidly, the expression of the longsuffering elder brother coming over his face. "Now,

George, there's many a thing about this world that you, tender of years that you be, have not the slightest notion of. 'Murder,' you call it? Well, then, do you call it murder when a man orders the hanging of four husbands and fathers, whose only crime was eating a haggis during Lent? And there's public record of what I'm telling you, you always wanting proof of everything. Beaton did it January 26, 1544, in . . . in Perth, I believe it was. Do you term that 'murder,' I'd like to know? Or do you call it 'murder' when an adulterous bishop arrests a fair young mother, wife of one of the hanged men and, by his holiness's order, has her drowned in the river? Do you call that 'murder'?"

"Beaton did that?" I said. "Why would he do that to the woman? There must be another side to the tale, Francis. Always is."

"Aye, that there is. Beaton ordered her drowned because in her labor pains with her new bairn she prayed to God in the sweet name of Jesus."

"Aye, and what's so wrong about all that?"

"The drowning?" Francis looked at me like I was offspring of a haddock.

"No, the praying. What was so wrong with it?"

"Have you a mincemeat for a brain, George? There's times I wonder at you. You're supposed to do your praying in the name of the Holy Virgin, not in the mere name of Jesus Christ. So says his holiness, Cardinal Beaton, Archbishop of St. Andrews—or as was. And still would be if James Melville and the others had not broken into this castle and ended the miserable life of Cardinal Beaton. It's he, dear brother, who is the murderer."

"So, since he was a murderer," I said, "that makes it acceptable for them to murder him?"

13

"It's no murdering of him," said Francis, all longsuffering gone. "It's justice. Plain and simple justice. That's what I call it. And have you gone and forgotten what he did to saintly George Wishart?"

I knew. It was often spoken of in these besieged walls.

"While you doddle," said Francis, "I'm off to the chapel. Don't you be late."

I watched Francis until he disappeared behind a stone buttress. Master Knox himself had told us of what happened to Mr. Wishart. So important was it to him, he'd made it part of our lessons. It was January 16, 1546, when Mr. Wishart told our father, Hugh Douglas, and Master Knox of the shortness of the time he had to labor, and of his death, the day whereof he had said was approaching nearer than any would believe. Master Knox had admitted his bewilderment, and he told us how he stood off and observed the anguish of his troubled mentor. By all accounts, our tutor had for a time been wielding a broadsword and had been acting the part of a bodyguard for the preacher. Beaton and others wanted the man dead, had even hired assassins to do the deed. Yet knowing all this, Mr. Wishart demanded the claymore from Master Knox, and when he had it from him, he held comfortable conversation on the death of God's chosen children. Always a man of the Psalms, the preacher then sang a version of Psalm 51 with his followers, expressing his desire that God would be granting all of them quiet rest. And then, amidst loud protests from them all, he sent the men away from him. Master Knox told us of his great reluctance to leave the man's side. But Mr. Wishart was not to be put off, and said, "Nay, return to your bairns, and God bless you. One is sufficient for a sacrifice."

We were those bairns, my brother Francis Douglas and my own self, along with Alexander Cockburn. Alexander's father was arrested some time after Mr. Wishart and held for a time in Edinburgh Castle.

Master Knox did return to us at Longniddry—for a time, schooling us in our Latin grammar. At times in his lessons, he broke off, some hapless Latin verb suspended in its conjugation, he stroking his beard and gazing out the window in silence. We knew it was his way of being anxious about the fate of his friend Mr. Wishart. Meanwhile, in those days it was not only Latin grammar Master Knox taught us. He became most animated in his lessons when he turned to the Evangel of Jesus Christ. That's what he called it, the Evangel.

Master Knox's lessons in the Gospels fairly made my mouth water. And I was not alone. Word spread, and folks from the village took to sitting under the windows so as to listen in on his explanations of the Gospel writer, and when all was damp and dreary, they'd make their way quietly into the hall where we read our lessons.

At long last, word of the fate of Mr. Wishart arrived at Longniddry. I'll not soon forget the anguished sobs of our master when that word was made known to us.

By all accounts, it was near midnight when Beaton's foul agent, the Earl of Bothwell, busted in Wishart's door and dragged him off to the infamous Bottle Dungeon in St. Andrews Castle. In the days that followed, the bastard Cardinal tried, convicted, and condemned Mr. Wishart to death by burning. Worried that supporters might attempt to rescue him at the stake, Beaton ordered armed guards to encircle the place of execution, and he charged his cannons with grapeshot and readied them from the battlements to unleash their fury on the crowd should it become unruly at the burning. Then Beaton—it was so like the luxury-loving fool—made himself comfortable, watching the cruel spectacle from a window in his boudoir, hung with rich hangings and velvet cushions.

Master Knox was not there, as I've related, he dutifully schooling us in Longniddry. But we learned copious details of the foul deed. So loved was Mr. Wishart that eyewitness accounts proliferated throughout the realm. There was talk of little else. The story went like this. As the hangman chained the condemned man to the stake, Wishart said, "For this cause I was sent, that I should suffer this fire for Christ's sake. I fear not this fire. And I pray that you may not fear them that slay the body, but have no power to slay the soul." Then, the account goes, Wishart turned and kissed his executioner. "Lo, here is a token that I forgive thee. Do thine office." Just before Wishart expired in the flames, he turned to where Beaton reclined in the window and prophesied his soon-coming downfall. It was March 1, 1546.

As I've related, Beaton was a great fool. Wishart, who had preached throughout Scotland, and who was greatly loved throughout the realm, was now dead at the hands of a man who was now more than ever greatly damned and hated throughout the realm. What happened next, to any sane man, was as inevitable as rain drenching the moors in November.

From where I then stood musing to myself, I could just see the arch of the postern gate of the castle. That gate became the key to a scheme James Melville and several other noblemen's sons concocted to break into the castle. They knew from Beaton's philandering ways that one of his mistresses, Marion Ogilvy it was that night, would be let out the postern gate in the early hours of the morning. So it was, May 29, 1546, that they surprised the porter at the gate and entered the bishop's stronghold. Moments later, they burst into the bedchamber of the reclining Beaton. "I am a priest!" he's said to have cried. "You will not slay me!" That did nothing to cool the rage of James Melville, who called on Beaton to repent of slaying Wishart, and after calling him an obstinate enemy against Jesus Christ, ran him through with his sword. Beaton's dying words were, "I am a priest. All is gone."

If the peasants throughout the realm took the side of Wishart and rejoiced at the downfall of Beaton, Roman clerics and the Queen Regent gnashed their teeth in their determination to crush the rising. In the midst of the tension, I had heard locals in Longniddry render their homespun prophesy, "Master George Wishart spoke never so plainly and yet he was burnt: even so will John Knox be." Master Knox had been a known follower of Wishart; what's more, he had publically gripped his broadsword in the man's defense. It was impossible for those who wielded the power in the realm not to connect our tutor with the martyred preacher.

With the henchmen of the Regent at our heels, Master Knox made good his escape from their grasp by fleeing Longniddry and taking to the heather. We rarely slept in the same bed twice—I say bed, but we more often slept like beasts in holes in the ground or cradled in the heather, the rain drenching us more than one night, and we only slept dry indoors when now and then a crofter took pity upon us and invited us to huddle about his peat fire and share his humble broth. Eventually at the urging of my father, who was himself equally a fugitive, Master Knox made his way here, joining the handful of young men who, for the moment, held St. Andrews Castle.

I confess to being deeply perplexed by this strategy. It seemed rather like fleeing the fangs of the wolf by taking up residence in its lair. But I had no say in the matter, and so I found myself bound by the walls of a castle, bitter enemies encircling those walls, determined to starve us to death or unleash the fury of royal artillery and break us all to pieces.

I slept little and ill in those days, and my eyes were often wide and frightened, for which my brother Francis would chide me.

2

It Begins

Holding my breath, I cautiously gripped the iron handle on the oak door of the chapel. Why had I not greased the hinges with pig fat as I had resolved the last time? Pulling gently, I felt the door begin to groan like an old man when the weather turns foul. I gave it a quick jerk, but the groaning sprang into a mighty creaking that to my mind was as penetrating as the shattering of a clay pot on a quiet night.

I blinked in the dim light, my eyes no doubt larger than usual as I strained to see. Without looking up from the book opened before him on the table, and as if reading from its pages, Master Knox said, "And George Douglas has decided to join us for our lessons today. We beg his pardon. How inconsiderate" —he paused— "of us to commence the grand object of learning without him."

I mumbled an apology and sat on the empty stool between Francis and Alexander. My brother eyed me with late-again, I-told-you-so eloquence.

Alexander turned. "Have we met?" he asked, extending his hand. "My name's Alexander Cockburn of Ormiston. Are you new here?"

I pretended not to hear. Composing myself in what I hoped would appear a posture of yearning after knowledge, I fixed my eyes on Master Knox.

Master Knox was shorter than the average man, with black hair and keen, penetrating eyes the color of the sea on a brilliant summer day; his face, as was his nose, was long, and he had a full mouth, with upper lip slightly larger than the lower one; his beard was black as his hair and hung down onto his chest, and his eyebrows—or, shall I say, eyebrow—extended like a black hedgerow sheltering his eyes.

Though he was stern and imposing in countenance, my frequent lateness was not due to a dislike of the man or of his lessons. I must confess to caring little for Latin grammar, but our tutor more often read out a lesson from the Evangel, and then commenced an explanation of the text, one that often fascinated me. Not only me. Increasingly over the weeks, men shuffled quietly into the chapel to sit in the shadows and listen to Master Knox as he delivered these lessons from the gospel.

That day, due to my tardiness, Master Knox had already read out his text. And I had arrived as he commenced retelling the account of the followers of Jesus at sea in a storm-tossed boat and terrified for their very lives. As he spoke, it was as if the stool beneath me was tossing with the waves.

"When the disciples passed to the sea to obey Christ's commandment, it was fair weather, and no such tempest was seen. But suddenly the storm arose with a contrary flow of wind when they were in the midst of their journey. For if the tempest had been as great in the beginning of their entrance into the sea, they would have never ventured such a great danger, nor would it have been in their power to have attained the midst of the sea. Hence, we know that the sea was calm when they entered into their journey.

"Moreover, we do well to mark by what means this storm was moved. Was it by the plunging of their oars, and the force of their small boat; was it such as stirred the waves of that great sea? No, doubtless, but the Holy Spirit declares that the seas were moved by a vehement and contrary wind, which blew against their boat in the darkness. But seeing that the wind is neither the commander nor mover of itself, some other cause is to be sought after.

"We must consider what the disciples did in this vehement tempest. Truly they turned not back to be driven on land or shore by the vehemence of the contrary wind, for by so doing they could not have escaped shipwreck and death. But they continually labored in rowing against the wind, abiding the contrariness of that horrible tempest.

"Consider and mark, beloved in the Lord, what we read here to have happened to Christ's disciples and their poor boat, and you shall well perceive that the same thing has happened, does happen, and shall happen, to the true church and congregation of Christ (which is nothing else in this miserable life but a poor boat), traveling in the seas of this unstable and troublesome world, toward the heavenly port and haven of eternal felicity which Christ Jesus has appointed to his elect.

"Even so, dear lads, the raging wind blows without bridle upon the unstable seas, in the midst whereof we are in this hour of darkness."

Master Knox, as I have said, had a sternness about him, but of a kind to be differentiated from harshness, of which he had none that I ever saw. And he was endowed with a personal dignity, a sort of innate authority that demanded the attention of all about him. It was not, mind you, that he forced himself above his station—he never did such that I observed—his was the untutored authority that is bequeathed by God to but few men. And he possessed a voice like no other I had ever heard. As he spoke it reverberated off the barrel-vaulted ceiling above, growing in volume and intensity until it animated the dead bishop's chapel with life, crowding out every other sight and sound, even thought.

Or so it had seemed. Suddenly Master Knox's voice and presence were engulfed in a thundering roar that shook the chapel to its stony foundations, sending rivulets of dust and grit raining down upon us. Francis dug his fingers into my arm. Our companion Alexander, his stool having toppled, lay sprawled on the flagstones of the chapel floor.

"Will it fall upon us?" I heard myself cry.

"It begins!" cried Alexander, scrambling to his feet. "We must man the guns!"

"We're doomed if we stay in here," yelled Francis.

"It begins, indeed," said Master Knox, his voice level.

It felt far less like a beginning to me, more like an ending—the ending of the world. "Will we p-prevail?" I asked, my words choked off by the dust that hung in the air.

"George, my lad, Christ our Champion will ultimately prevail," said Master Knox. "But, yet I fear these walls shall crack like eggshells before the day of his deliverance."

There was little immediate comfort in his words. As if to confirm them, another cannon suddenly thundered. I felt its retort deep within me, and my heart trembled as I attempted to scramble for the door, chunks of stone falling with the dust and blocking my way.

"Lads, you must keep yourselves out of harm's way," called Master Knox to us. "I must go and speak with Laird Melville."

I watched his hunched figure grow dim and disappear in the dust and smoke. He'd just been speaking of unstable seas and the hour of darkness raging about the disciples. With panic rising in my bosom, I suddenly felt that it was we who were entering into that darkness.

3

Flight or Fight

UNDER SUCH A BARRAGE, I wasn't at all certain there was any place within the precinct of the castle out of harm's way, though I desperately longed to discover it if there was. After Master Knox left the chapel, Alexander took charge.

"It's no good staying here," he shouted. "Let's away."

"But Master Knox said . . ." I began.

"To stay out of harm's way," Alexander finished for me. "I'd wager there's just as much harm underway here as anywhere." He said the latter with a nod at the stone fragments and dust all about us.

Alexander made for the door with Francis at his heels, as he so often was. But my boots felt like they had lead in them. How could it be safer outside the walls of the chapel? As I watched my companions' shapes grow dim in the smoke, I nearly panicked. Just then, staying alone was more fearful to me than braving the open. "Wait! Don't leave me." I stumbled after them.

Outside the chapel, the inner court of the castle was in chaos. Men ran in all directions, seemingly without destination. There was a great deal of shouting but none of it made any sense to me. It only served to increase the o'erwhelming sense of panic in my own breast. Then I caught the words of one man as he ran past.

"None shall break through these stout walls," he boasted. I looked closely at the man; dust and smoke shrouded the scene in an unearthly vapor, but as near as I could tell the speaker appeared to be James Melville, the cause and leader of this mad enterprise.

I desperately hoped that he was correct. His words should have given me courage, but instead they made me want to laugh.

"Aye, we'll give them what for if they try," said another, this from Henry Balnaves.

In the weeks of our occupation of the castle, I had often heard men speak thus. But that was before the cannonade began. Now that it had begun, their nervous laughter, frowning eyes, and sober brows contributed much to my fears that it was all bluster, the speaking of those who deep within their bosoms desperately wish their words to be true. I have since learned that no amount of such wishing has the slightest degree of effect on the inevitable outcome of real events.

"We must return fire," said David Lindsay. "If we do not, they will believe us to be incapable of doing so. All will be lost if we be not bold."

There it was again. Brave words, but ones that gave me little confidence in our capability to resist. Were we returning fire to try to prove something to them or to drive them away? I wondered if we gave ourselves to all the boldness we could muster, if all might not still be lost. James Melville was hollering orders at the men, calling them to man the guns, attempting to bring order.

The very air seemed double charged with dreadful expectation. My own heart, I must confess, felt cold and heavy as a stone within me. I wondered if this was what the end of the world would be like.

And then an idea began forming and gaining momentum in my imagination. Why must I remain within these walls? Sooner or later, the Queen Regent's army must prevail over such zealous but ill-prepared men. I shuddered to think what would happen to us—to me—when it did.

I knew it was possible. If James Melville and his men had managed to trick their way into the castle as had Marion Ogilvy that night when she left the faithless cardinal's bedside and sneaked out the postern gate before first light, why might not I affect just such an escape from this doomed fortress? No one would blame me overmuch, young as I was, and subject to the frailties of my youth. I would then live. Remain within these fated battlements, take my stand with the overzealous enterprise of these enthusiasts, and I was sure to be hanged with the lot— and with Alexander and my brother Francis. They too would be hanged. We all would be hanged.

At that moment, I could only imagine one other way to avoid hanging. If I were blown to bits by the cannons royal of the Queen Regent, there'd be no hanging necessary. With that thought, as if aware of my considerations, another gut-wrenching volley thundered from the town. I heard the eerie whistling sound as the double cannonballs hurled themselves at the stone walls of the castle. I had thought those walls stout and impregnable—when first we arrived, before the cannons began their work on them.

"They'll crack like eggshells," Master Knox had concluded about those walls. It had troubled me the way he said it. It seemed a dispassionate assessment of the facts, rendered without a trace of fear. I often wondered to myself of the man.

And then it stopped. As abruptly as the bombardment had begun, it halted. The air reeked of gunpowder, and my eyes felt like they had hot gravel in them. While the cannons had been thundering, my stomach had formed itself into a hard knot as if for my own protection. No amount of concerted effort to relax myself would do. My ears felt as if they were engaged in one prolonged wailing, and I wondered if it would ever subside, if I'd ever hear properly again.

"What are they w-waiting for?" I asked, my voice breaking the eerie stillness. No one replied for nearly a minute.

As if he'd been holding his breath for the entire cannonade, Alexander let out a long sigh. "Let's go see," he said.

I followed behind Francis as we inched our way up a flight of stone stairs leading to the wall. The air was gritty, and my eyes filled with tears, tears that I attempted to tell myself were from the smoky air and from nothing else. Once on the battlements, Alexander cautiously peered through a notch in the wall. I held my breath. Would one of the Regent's snipers shoot him? Were they waiting for someone to do just what he was doing? Wincing, I turned away, horrified at what I might, on the instant, witness. When nothing happened to Alexander's head, we gradually joined him and surveyed the town, I the last to venture a look.

Through the dust and smoke, what met our eyes made my heart sink. Men stood near their cannons, but none readied his weapon for another volley. No one from the town, commoner or laird, was visible. No children, no dogs, no cats. Only soldiers. But they were soldiers that seemed to be at parade rest, frozen at their posts, as if made of pewter like the playthings of a wealthy boy. For reasons I could not explain, their statuesque posture, their inhuman rigidity, appeared more ominous to me than if they had stomped and shouted in defiance.

"For what are they waiting?" I heard Francis voice what I was thinking but was too hoarse to say.

"I do not know," said Alexander at last.

"What if they're toying with us?" I had wondered this deep within my bosom, but now I voiced it. "If it's terrifying us they're after," I added, "i-it's working."

Alexander slapped his palm against the stone of the bulwark. "Well then, if they're a-toying with us, biding their time, intending to affright us, we'll use their hesitation to ready a return volley. If I were in charge," he said, his teeth clenched, "that's what I'd be doing. If only I were in charge!"

"Aye, as would I," said Francis.

It was at times like these that I felt I little understood Alexander and my brother. Taking on those soldiers in a battle was the furthest thing from my desires. And being in charge— what would make someone want to be in charge of a deadly battle? Cannons, smoke, thundering, and steel and lead balls never were to my liking, still less so now that I found myself the target of such crushing weaponry. My mind returned to my early musings: Why must I remain here, awaiting the whim of Mary of Lorraine's soldiers? I knew Master Knox was correct; many more volleys like the one they had just unleashed on us and these castle walls, stout as they were, would crack like eggshells. What would it take? Days, a week, perhaps a month? Why might not I flee and live? I turned toward Francis, intending to tell him my plan, to invite him to join me in it, and Alexander, if he would. Whereas mine were no doubt wide and affrighted, Francis's eyes looked like the black orbs of a bear sizing up its prey; his jaw was set, and I read in his features a resolution, even an eagerness to be at the enemy.

I said nothing, instead champing my lower lip with my teeth. If I was to escape the madness of this siege, I knew of a certainty that I must do so alone.

4

Bodies and Souls of Men

THE YAWING IN MY EARDRUMS provided an ominous accompaniment to the stillness that remained from the soldiers and the town. A steady breeze off the North Sea soon dissipated the smoke and grit of that barrage, and if it were not for the rubble that lay here and there from the cannonballs that had met their match in the dead bishop's fortified walls, some might have forgotten that we had just sustained a deadly attack of the Queen Regent. For me, it was not so easily forgotten.

Word was passed that James Melville wanted every available man to gather in the chapel. Up until that day, we had faced little or no resistance. There were constant threats issued in belligerent communiqués, but no genuine hostilities until now.

"What's it for?" I asked as we followed Master Knox into the chapel. It felt odd to be in the place where we had school, where we had been only hours before when that first cannon had thundered against us, and where we now gathered in an anxious, boisterous company.

"We gather, no doubt, for a council of war," said Master Knox.

Though he was below the average size of a full-grown man, there was an incalculable dimension about him that made me think of him as larger in size than other men, and he had the stride of a courier. I hurried to keep pace with him. I thought of breaking my fears to our tutor, of asking him if he might give me leave to flee this place.

"It has begun," shouted Melville above the roar of voices filling the chapel. "Our cause is just. We must remain resolute, stout-hearted, and firm against the Queen Regent."

"She did little damage this day," shouted one man.

"Aye, nor shall hereafter," said another, followed by a trickle of cheering that gathered in volume, though I felt it lacked the full-throated vigor of certainty.

"Time is on our side," continued Melville. "Few castles are as well provisioned or as stoutly reinforced."

"Why, Master Knox, did they stop?" I asked in a whisper. "Could they not smash these walls to rubble in a few days, if they continued?"

"Aye, but the Queen Regent would rather not destroy her own castle," said Master Knox, his mouth close to my ear. "If she can intimidate us into capitulating, that is far more to her liking. She may need this fortress to defend Scotland against the English. Smash it all to bits, and she gains little from the victory."

His words gave me a glimmer of hope. But if no reinforcement materialized from England, it was a dim hope indeed. Eventually she would unleash her full fury on us. I feared it of a certainty.

"We have a fresh report from our delegation to Henry's court in London," continued Melville. "Which delegation has sought and secured the support of Protestant Henry to aid us in driving Mary and France from our shores. We the Castilians here at

St. Andrews are in a most advantageous position. We, by God's grace, are to be the principle instruments of her expulsion from Scotland."

"Most advantageous position?" I mused to myself on his words. I felt that our position was many things: reckless, doomed, fool-hardy. The very last thing I would term it was advantageous.

At my side, Master Knox voiced softly the words, *"Protestant Henry, is it?"*

"Henry of England has every reason to support our cause," continued Melville. "Though we none of us feel warmth from his royal halls, his distaste for others is far greater and more severe than his distaste for Scotland. The French he cannot abide on his shores. Hence, the success of our delegation and of his promised military support of our cause."

"Promised support," said John Rough, putting considerable weight on the word *promised*. "Might I say, the success of our delegation yet remains to be seen. Success will result when that promise is realized by its fulfillment, when we see Henry's navy just there—" He pointed toward the sea. "Then we shall have success."

"Aye, and is not Mary doing the very same?" said another. "Petitioning her French allies to assist her in breaking down these walls? What becomes of us if her enterprise succeeds before Henry arrives with his ships and cannon?"

There was a moment of silence followed by a low rumbling of voices at the prudence of the man's question. I felt myself gnawing on my lower lip as my eyes fell on a crack I'd not noticed before in the stone vaulting overhead.

"A consideration with which to reckon, indeed," said Melville, raising a hand for silence. "But is not that yet more incentive for

Henry to come to our aid? If the French were to launch their fleet against us at St. Andrews, Henry would be all the more compelled to drive them from his shores. His aversion to France is our surety."

"These are Scottish shores," shouted William Kirkcaldy. "They're not Henry's shores!"

"Aye, but he thinks they are," said Henry Balnaves.

"And, in our extremity, we must encourage him so to think," continued Melville.

"But is not Henry aged, sick, and dying?" said another.

"True, indeed," said Melville. "But it is a matter of English political policy to keep France from her shores. There would be not a single advisor in Henry's court who would not bow to the wisdom of such a policy, and, hence, to sending military support for our cause."

"Meanwhile, we must make preparations until English support arrives," said Kirkcaldy.

"We must return volley for volley," said Lindsay.

For the next hour the chapel thundered with shouted deliberations over manning the guns, securing powder and ball, training the men, recruiting in the town and surrounding countryside for more men to join the Castilians. And there was talk of preparing to dig beneath the walls to cut off the mining of the Regent's troops.

"They're certain to be at their digging," said Balnaves, "even as we deliberate." He stomped a foot on the flagstone floor of the chapel. "They may be beneath us at this moment!"

At this, John Rough stepped to the pulpit, lifted his hands, and called the men to silence. "The horse is prepared for battle," he said, "but victory belongs to the Lord. You've wrangled with the horse long enough. In all our preparations we must not neglect the most important thing."

Mr. Rough then began calling the men to repentance for their sins, urging them to trust in the mercy of Christ alone for their ultimate deliverance, and for temporal deliverance, should God will it. After some time, he paused, staring fixedly in my direction. There were one hundred and fifty men in the chapel. Why was he staring at me? I could not meet his gaze. My heart raced. Had he discovered my cowardice, my scheme to flee the castle, to make good my escape? How was it possible?

"Who among us has not found his way into this very chapel to listen in on the instruction that daily takes place within these walls?" continued Mr. Rough.

I was in torment at his words. Was he to publicly rebuke me for my tardiness? Had Master Knox taken my offense to Mr. Rough and was I now, here, before all, to be chastised for it? Just as I was about to cry aloud my penitence and beg for mercy for my crimes, Mr. Rough continued.

"It would be a clod and not a man who did not recognize in that instruction an extraordinary gift of God. I, for one, am no such clod. What's more, I stand here before you to make a solemn confession."

At these words silence fell over the chapel, a silence so palpable that it ceased to be the absence of something and became the thing itself.

"I have, these many weeks," persisted the chaplain, "had my sermons fortified by another's pen."

A sharp in-taking of breath rose from the men.

"I am no clod, however, and recognize with joy and gratitude when a man has been given an extraordinary gift of God. My words do not come as a complete surprise to a number of you, you who have prayed with me for this most important of decisions for this beleaguered band: the choice of her preaching minister and chaplain. Our young brother is loath to run ahead of where God has clearly called him, thereby confirming the humility so necessary for the man who would execute this holy office for the glory of Christ alone. And now on behalf of and for the eternal good of the men present in this council—"

Here Mr. Rough leaned over the pulpit and bore down upon me (as I still supposed it to be) and began to exhort with these words:

"In the name of God, and of his Son Jesus Christ, and in the name of these that presently call you by my mouth, I charge you that you refuse not this holy vocation, but that you have regard to the glory of God, the increase of Christ's kingdom, and the edification of your brethren, that you take upon you the public office and charge of preaching, even as you look to avoid God's heavy displeasure, and desire that he should multiply his graces with you."

John Rough certainly was no clod, but I was that day. It was not until I was compelled to observe the state of Master Knox at my side that I understood aright Mr. Rough's words. Master Knox did what I had seldom seen him do: he trembled, and it was no bit tremor; he shook from head to toe. His breathing became like that of a man laboring under a great sack of oatmeal, and his attempts to speak were choked off as if by the noose. I had only one other time seen what I saw next, and that was Master Knox's reaction when word of Mr. Wishart's death reached him. As then, so it was again. Tears welled up in his eyes. He made again as if to speak, but no words came forth from his lips, which were now trembling with the rest of him. Suddenly, he rose and bolted from the room. Only at these signs did it come home to my befuddled brain that Mr. Rough had been all the while looking at and speaking about and to, not myself, but to Master Knox at my side. I felt I was often thus misconstruing most everything about me.

Awkward moments followed at the reaction of our tutor to his call. To my mind, his reaction made perfect sense. By accepting the call to be chaplain of this doomed band, Master Knox would become its spiritual leader, its earthly head, and thus would find himself in the forefront of the rage of our enemy when they prevailed over us—which they most certainly would do. I too would have fled from the room in tears. I often felt that way. It seemed a most logical reaction.

When some moments later Master Knox returned to the chapel and mounted the pulpit, he was sober and composed. He opened an English Bible and read out from Daniel chapter seven. It was not the finest lesson I had heard Master Knox deliver from that same Bible, but it was a most effective salvo against the idolatry he believed infested the Roman Church.

"In Daniel's holy vision, the Pope and his kingdom are the little horn, having a mouth and speaking great things and blasphemous. The decaying Church, filled with bloated clerics, is St. Paul's 'Man of Sin' and John's 'Whore of Babylon.' And the merchandise of these money-grubbing, hireling shepherds—is the bodies and souls of the people of Scotland."

5

War Galleys

IN ALL WEATHER, fair or foul, I daily kept my vigil and climbed to the seaward wall, often squinting through the bleak grayness, the North Sea wind lashing my face and eyes. For me it had become a means of hope. One morning surely I would see the standard of King Henry VIII fluttering on the rigging of a man-of-war, the flagship of a fleet. So I hoped.

Yet were these hopes but a tint of canvas away from my direst fears. Would there be a ship, but would it be the *fleur-de-lis* of the French standard a-fluttering at its sternway, another Henry, French King Henry II, reportedly a monstrous hater of Reformation and the gospel of grace, coming to crush this castle like an eggshell—and us in it? And so were my daily vigils ones of hope, yet was it a hope saturated with profound apprehension.

The winter of 1547 was persistent and lasted well into the months in which one at least begins to hope for brief visitations of the sun, an easing of the vehemence of the winds, and a lessening of the torrents of precipitation. So, though it was May 15, I was drenched and shivering when I returned to the chapel, late again, for lessons that day.

Nearly a year had passed since the martyrdom of George Wishart, and this put Master Knox in a frame of mind to recollect and comment on the events that had brought us to this extremity, surrounded by royal troops, their cannons royal gaping at us.

He was just beginning his lesson, a sermon really, on a topic I had heard him speak of before, but never to this degree. There were five or six dozen men in the chapel to listen in to our lessons. Though this made it easier for me to slip in to lessons undetected—or so I supposed—I confess to a degree of jealousy about our tutor. He was, after all, our tutor, yet I rarely had him to myself as in the old days in Longniddry, our home.

And with thoughts of Longniddry my mind was flooded with boyhood memories: my father playing at chess with me before the fire of an evening, him teaching me to know the ways of sheep on the moorlands, and him schooling of me with the great sword, beginning my lessons with the weapon when it was fully two handbreadths taller than I. Which recollections often made my innards grumble with longing for my mother's savory Scotch broth; her nutty oakcakes, so lovingly shaped, patted down, and baked to crisp, nutty perfection; and her sweet, flakey shortbread, buttery to melt in the mouth; and her blood sausages, and smoked hams, and leg of lamb roasted 'til the meat fell off the bone. Then she had lost color in her cheeks and began walking with a stoop to her shoulders, and she coughed. At the first it was a light clearing of the throat and we gave little thought to it. Within days it became a tortured hacking that shook her whole body. I sat on my bed those nights, my hands clamped firmly on my ears in a vain attempt to block what it meant from my mind. At the last she stopped coughing, and died. This event had occurred the winter before we came to this wretched castle on this sea-battered coast. Our father consoled himself by pouring his energy into our cause, which meant for him laboring outside the castle in efforts to raise funds and men to defeat the French. My innards ached, but it was less for my mother's food and more for the tenderness of her touch on my cheek, the melodic sweetness of her voice, and the warmth of her words. I scrunched my eyes tight together and tried to form a picture of her in my mind, but it was little use. The image that formed in my mind's eye was evermore a faded one, one in which she was always moving away from me, away into the mist. When the rains fell heavy and the winds howled in the battlements, I would awaken with a start, my mind troubled at her lying still and alone beneath the sod in such weather.

There were many times when I longed to bury my face in my sleeve and weep. This was one of them; though I dared not for fear of incurring the scorn of Alexander and my elder brother. I felt at times that Master Knox would understand, yet I had little opportunity to speak alone with him, so many men pressed around him even in our lessons. It seemed unfair to me, and I desperately wanted to live in a world that was fair—at least one that was fair to me.

"Persons who, by the commission of flagrant crimes," Master Knox was saying, his voice clear and ringing with a faint echo off the stone vaulting of the chapel ceiling, "had forfeited their lives, according to the law of God, and the just laws of society. Men such as notorious murderers and tyrants might with warrant be put to death by private individuals, provided all redress in the ordinary course of justice was rendered impossible, in consequence of the offenders having usurped the executive authority, or as a result of their being systematically protected by oppressive rulers.

This was an opinion of the same kind with that of tyrannocide, held by so many of the ancients, and defended by Buchanan in his dialogue '*De jure regni apud Scotos.*'"

"Psst! Did you hear?" It was Francis, a hand cupped at my ear.

I shook my head. I'd heard nothing except the wind in my ears and the rain pelting the stone battlements of the castle—and most immediately, Master Knox's lesson.

"Balnaves has returned from another commission to London," he hissed. "He's been given the services of one of Henry's royal gun-founders, Archane de Arrain. He's the best. And England has promised 100 long handguns, and 150 longbows, and has promised to send a shipment to Holy Island—that's not so far away—of timber and stocks to mount a demi-cannon, two demi-culverins, two sakers and six falcons, and two tons of iron and steel."

Francis recited the list by memory, savoring it as if it were a passage from Virgil. I knew what longbows were, but I understood little else in the arsenal he had described. Nevertheless, it had to bode well for our cause that Henry of England was lending this much support. But was it enough? And why didn't he just send ships?

"Holy Island is many miles from here," I hissed back in his ear.

He rolled his eyes at me as if saying that I'd clean gone and missed the point again.

I added, "It must be over one hundred sea miles. If he really wants to help us, why doesn't he just send his fleet?"

"Shh. Attend to your lessons," he said, as if I had been the one who had disturbed him.

The cannons had not sounded since that first day now weeks and weeks past, and I wondered what they were doing. What they were waiting for? Had the troops of the Regent merely been sighting in their guns? The sun now shone brightly, sometimes for whole days at a time, and in the warmth of its rays I continued my daily vigil at the wall studying the sea for ships. But no matter how hard I looked, how much I strained my eyes at the horizon, all I saw was an occasional fishing vessel or a merchant-man carrying oranges from Spain or some other cargo from some other place.

I longed to be in some other place, and I spent lengthy stretches imagining myself at sea on one of those seemingly peaceful, ordinary ships, sails billowing, salt air in my face, the kindly water foaming at the bow and trailing behind in my wake, and like that wake, my troubles and fears growing smaller and then dissolving into nothingness.

On the morning of June 29, 1547, I ascended the narrow stone stair to the southeast-facing battlements of St. Andrews Castle. I had done this now daily for so many months, and without result, that I may have begun to believe there would never be a result, that since all the other days had yielded nothing, this day was somehow obligated to yield the same. I was wrong.

What first caught my eye looked like a smaller egg sitting on top of a larger egg. And those then on top of a still larger egg. A ship. But not a coastal fishing vessel or a merchant ship from Holland. It was too big for either of these. And then there was another, bearing unmistakably for St. Andrews Castle. I wanted to convince myself that they were Henry of England's ships, but I could not. The course was wrong. Henry would not come at us from that far east of south.

And then there were more of them. Many more, all bearing down upon our castle, upon us, upon me. I tried to count them. I'd always been good with numbers, but it was impossible for me to determine exactly how many, not from this distance. Perhaps when they were close at hand, within cannon shot, I would have an easier time counting them.

Suddenly it occurred to me, I'd heard no shout of alarm from the watch, the official one. My vigil on the wall had become something of a jest among the men. They called me Watchman Douglas, and ruffled my hair. There were at least twenty ships, and coming on under full sail in a fresh breeze. Getting larger by the minute.

"Sail! Sail!" I cried, my voice cracking into a girlish screech. I cleared my throat and tried again. "Sail!"

"To arms! To arms!" the watchman cried.

There was an instant's delay and then doors slammed open, and men—some hopping on one leg as they yanked on a boot, others pulling tunics over their heads—came pouring out into the inner court of the castle, all talking at once. I spotted Francis and Alexander, Master Knox striding toward the wall ahead of them.

"Under what flag?" Master Knox called up to me.

"I believe, sir, they are war galleys of France."

"How many?"

"M-more than twenty," I replied. I could barely speak, and I felt that the thundering of my heart would drown out my words when I did.

"Man the guns!" this from James Melville.

"There's a signal to parley from San Salvators!" cried William Lesley.

Melville lifted his palms in disgust. "The Regent's captain believes we need him to inform us of the arrival of the French

44

fleet?" he said. "I can little spare fighting men for a parley just at the moment." He looked hastily around at the faces that had gathered awaiting his command.

I suddenly found myself fascinated with the mineral pattern on the flagstone beneath my feet. My stomach began its churning.

"George Douglas!" called Melville.

My heart sank to my boots, and for an instant I felt certain I was going to spew my breakfast. I longed to drop beneath those flagstones into oblivion.

"George Douglas, are you man enough to bring back a reliable message? To be herald of a communiqué from the Queen Regent's commander in the town?"

6

Before the Regent

THERE COULD BE NO MISTAKING IT. James Melville had called not Francis or Alexander. He had called my name.

I don't know how it came about, but Master Knox was at my side on the instant when I had thought him some distance from me only a moment before. His arm was across my shoulder, and he bent low and spoke in my ear. "I too was and yet remain affrighted at my calling, but I was granted strength from Christ our Champion, and so, my lad, shall you be."

I little trusted my voice, but, nodding, I called back, "God h-helping me, I am." I wished I hadn't stammered, but I had never figured out how to take a stammer back, and I comforted myself with the intimate knowledge that a little stammer was nothing; in my frame of mind, my fear could have shown itself far more irretrievably.

They fitted a leather shoulder bag across my torso and gave me a tabard of the herald. "It's a trifle large for you, my lad," said William Lesley, taking a tuck in the tabard and cinching it at my waist with a belt. "But it's meant to guarantee fair play from the Regent."

Meant to? I felt my stomach rising into my mouth at his words. What if it didn't work this time? What if the Regent is weary of the nuisance of it all? I'd heard that female rulers could be more cruel than real kings. Given what I'd heard about real kings, I found it hard to imagine; nevertheless, it troubled me as they led me to the postern gate. One of the last things I saw through the gate was my brother Francis looking a bit envious. He brought his fingers up to his eyes and made as if he were closing them with his fingers. He often made this gesture to me. I blinked and tried to narrow my eyes, for the sake of the family name, if for no other reason. Alexander stood next to Francis, his arms crossed and his brow furrowed in a manner I could not well interpret. I felt that I was of all people most simple to interpret: timorous as a young rabbit. But Alexander was something other, and he often puzzled me.

The gate closed behind me with a thud, and the latch fell with a clunk, sounds that seemed to prompt a corresponding lurching in my heaving innards. I felt that thud and clunk as if they were of the magistrate's gavel and signaled the termination of my all-too short life.

Slowly I turned toward the town, St. Andrews, now occupied by the French Regent's troops. These were my enemies, and there were cannons in the Abbey tower, cannons in San Salvator's, cannons in places we didn't even know of. I felt like I'd swallowed a mouthful of dry oatmeal.

As I walked near the west wall of the castle, I heard scraping and clanking sounds. It was as if my hearing had suddenly become voraciously acute, and I was disturbed by minute sounds that ordinarily I would have ignored for their commonness or that would simply never have registered to my ears. These sounds registered.

Warily I looked at the high windows of the stone houses lining the main street, and I felt certain that there were snipers with their long guns trained on me at that moment. I began a morbid speculation about what I would feel when one of them pulled the trigger, a lead bullet rending the air as it hurled itself toward my breast. What horror would I feel as it drew closer? Would I perceive its approach? What would it feel like when it struck its mark, tearing my flesh and my ribs? I could barely breathe with these thoughts filling my mind. Would I die instantly? Painlessly? Or would I be wounded only, not killed on the instant, mercilessly surviving for agonizing moments, during which I would be forced to witness my own death throes, my own wallowing in my lifeblood? The cobblestones beneath my feet, though worn smooth with constant treading, felt sharp and angular and pained me greatly. I saw, as it were, my blood flowing in the gaps between each stone. I wanted to turn and run for my life, but I dared not. Surely the sniper with his long gun pointed at my tabard would be ordered to fire if I did.

I felt more than saw the eyes of town folks as I walked down Market Street. Were they eyes of pity? Or were they eyes that hungered for the thundering retort of a long gun, eyes eager to watch me fall and die for my crimes against the Regent and the French? I knew not.

Somehow in my distraction of mind, my feet had carried me nearer to San Salvator's. On either side of the archway leading into the inner court stood royal guards, their battleaxes crossed, blocking the gate into the college court. My head felt light, and I felt that I might at that instant spew my last meal. It had happened before.

"Halt, rebel!" they cried. I was only too ready to halt. Another soldier stepped up, blocking my way. Staring scornfully down at me, he gestured for me to lift my arms. Roughly he commenced a search of my clothing. Searching for a weapon on one such as I suddenly made me want to break into laughter. I felt certain that I would never be mistaken for an assassin. But I knew it was more than this. In the man's zeal, he touched one of several places on my torso that always made me squirm and writhe in laughter. As brothers do, Francis knew these places well and could reduce me to a giggling, flailing ball simply by feigning with his fingers to tickle me. In any event, I found myself desperately attempting to suppress my laughter. There was nothing to laugh about in my predicament, and I attempted further to control myself with the stern reality of that thought. But there it was, that quivering nerve radiating hysteria throughout my body, not to be put off. I nearly burst myself. This would never do. Here I was herald for our cause, and I was on the verge of collapsing in a heap of hilarity. The man eyed me, apparently sensing my discomfort. Though he and I both knew of a certainty that I carried not so much as a dagger, he yet again pressed his fingers into my ribcage just beneath my armpits.

It was too much. Here was my opportunity to do my part, to have an important and respectable role to play in this mad scheme, for me to stand before the commander of the Queen Regent, perhaps before Mary of Lorraine herself. And here I was about to discredit our entire cause by flinching into a mound of giggles. Yet there are some physical realities that, when they make their demands, cannot so simply be put aside. For me, it could be either a fit of laughter or spewing the contents of my stomach, or both, the one following routinely upon the heels of the other. The cruel fellow making free to search me seemed very much aware of the inexorable demands of the funny bone on one such as I. As

I attempted to meet his now mischievous gaze, I wondered if he in his younger days had had a brother subject to my hysterical ailment whom he had thus taken delight in torturing.

Just when I was about to relinquish all restraint and bow beneath the nerve-twitching demands of my ailment, a voice broke in.

"That'll be enough!" it said. "Bring him in!"

I was escorted roughly into the nave of the chapel of San Salvator's. It was a narrow hall with a vaulted ceiling soaring high above. My footsteps echoed on the flagstone aisle as I followed the brute who had tried to tickle me moments ago. Shafts of daylight slanted through gothic stained-glass windows on the west; one such shaft, larger than the rest, fell on a wooden-paneled pulpit to the right of the high altar.

In the place where the elements of the Mass would have been sat the Regent. I had never seen her before, but as I drew closer, my legs feeling like the jelly on a cold ham, I knew that this French woman had to be the widow of James V, deceased king of Scotland. And here I was about to see her, nay, to be spoken to by her, perhaps to speak myself to her. As uncontrollable as my previous urge had been, so now my terror at this encounter gripped my insides into a knot that made the Gordian knot seem as the tangled lacing on a child's slipper. Would I be able to make reply if she demanded words from me? What kind of herald could not speak? And then it occurred to me to wonder what kind of commander made a stammering youth his herald?

I halted moments later before Mary of Guise, Mary of Lorraine, the Queen Regent of Scotland—important people seemed to require so many titles. My heart thundering in my breast, I managed to observe several things about the Regent: first was

51

the pallor of her skin; her cheekbones were delicate and rather higher than other women's, but her cheeks lacked color where it seemed they ought to have it. More than that, her whole face lacked kindness. It is difficult to explain, but her features were completely devoid thereof. Her small red lips seemed pursed to her right side in a delicate sneer, and I recall thinking how much more attractive her face would be if it didn't do that. Her right eyebrow remained suspended above its fellow throughout the duration of my brief audience with her; I wondered if it perpetually remained so, if she slept with it scornfully perched so on her unconscious features.

My fears about speaking to her were unfounded. She never spoke directly to me, but to a dark-haired man at her right hand whom I at first thought to be a very tall man indeed. As I observed him more closely, however, I discovered that he wore odd silver shoes with tall heels, and that he wore his hair in a manner that made it stand high above his forehead. These features, coupled with his tilted chin and manner of looking down his lengthy nose, gave me the impression of his being taller than I deduced he would be without them. *"Ecoutez-moi!"* the Regent's courtier yelled at me as if I were a child and he a fishmonger's wife.

I believed that I had been looking at him and giving him my attention, awaiting his words. My innards churned, and I fretted that I might at any moment disgorge their contents, which made them churn the more. The Regent spoke softly to him in French, he leaning down deferentially as she did so. They assumed that I understood no French and spoke with open scorn for the Scottish lairds in the castle sending a *"petit enfant"* for their herald, *"le petit enfant avec les yeux trop grands."*

As laughter erupted in the stone chapel, I felt my face grow hot, and I attempted to narrow my eyes, eyes they thought were too large for such a small child. Francis, no doubt, would have agreed.

Abruptly halting his laughter, the Regent's attendant demanded, "What news, boy, from the renegade Castilians?"

I swallowed, groping for words to reply. It was my escort, the royal attendant who had searched me, who thus knew every plait of my tabard and its contents, who nudged me and, pointing at my leather bag, reminded me of its contents.

I drew out the letter James Melville had given me and, without a word, extended it toward the Regent. As I watched and heard the letter quavering in my hand, I wished I could be strong and brave like Francis and like Alexander always seemed to be. More titters of laughter came from the Regent's entourage.

There was still more laughter as they read out the letter, the sum of which was that the men as gentlemen, sons of nobility, were appealing for quarter, for a promise of freedom for all if they surrendered the castle to the Regent. It seemed to me they were bargaining without a cow. By the Regent's scorn, she seemed to agree. But who was I to judge?

"There is no hope for you," said the tall courtier, looking taller as he spoke. "Hence, we urge you to surrender without further resistance." At this he unfolded a letter, and with great fanfare, read it out. My heart sank at its words. With a flourish at the end of the letter, the Regent's courtier looked triumphant, or so he must have thought; it appeared merely pompous to my eyes. He refolded the letter and handed it to me. I could not help observing that his hand shook not a fraction.

Without further ado, they escorted me out of San Salvator's and sent me on my way.

I stood for a moment looking down the deserted street: to my right the rising green of the moorlands and freedom and to my left the castle. I was in precisely the circumstances I had longed to be in: out the postern gate and able to flee the castle for my life. I stood still for as long as I dared. I felt that in that instant all the course of my life, short as it was like to be, irretrievably depended. And then without making a conscious decision, I found myself turning my steps back to the castle, back to certain death and destruction at the hands of either the French navy or the Regent's footmen and artillery. We were doomed. What insanity had overtaken me?

7

Subterranean Calling

"THERE ARE T-TWENTY-ONE WAR GALLEYS," I heard my voice reading out the letter. Only moments before, I had been let back in the postern gate of St. Andrews Castle. Master Knox was the first to greet me, and he did so with warmth and with something about his manner—perhaps it was a slight sagging of the muscles in his face—that faintly suggested relief. When I reported to James Melville what I had heard and that I had been given a letter, to my horror, he asked me to read out the Regent's letter.

"The f-fleet of his Majesty the King of France is commanded by Leo S-strozzi, Prior of Capua, the finest sea captain of any navy in Europe. Each ship carries sufficient ordnance to reduce the castle to a mound of rubble." I paused. "There is no hope for you, and so we urge you to surrender without further resistance."

James Melville heaved a sigh. "Did you hear or observe anything of note?"

"Of note?" I said, racking my brain.

"Anything out of the ordinary?"

I had no idea how I was supposed to discern if something was out of the ordinary. Was siege warfare ordinary? Was meeting the Queen Regent ordinary?

Master Knox seemed to read my thoughts. He placed a hand upon my shoulder. "Did you hear or see anything that might help us in our defense?"

I began frantically to rehearse my outing. What was I looking for, I wondered?

"Take your time, lad," said Master Knox. "But do tell us all. What you may have thought was inconsequential may be of great importance. Now then, when first you left the gate."

"I heard something," I said.

"What did you hear and where?" said Melville.

"By the west wall of the castle," I said, "I heard scraping and—and clanking."

"As of spades, perhaps shovels and barrows?"

"I could not be sure, but, yes, it might have been spades and earth."

How little did I then realize the price of that bit of intelligence. James Melville and the others concluded on the instant that the Regent's miners were at their work burrowing under the castle, intending to break out in the middle of the night, kill us all, and retake the bishop's castle without utterly destroying it, something they were loath to do.

After quizzing me carefully about precisely where I had heard these sounds, our commander ordered a detail of men to begin countermining near the west wall.

"And George," he said to me, "I want you to bear a hand in this effort. Much depends upon our cutting off their digging."

My mind was troubled in the days ahead. Melville ordered every man to carry his sword, axe, and dagger with him at all times, and he doubled the watch at night. Yet did I sleep fitfully in those final days of the siege. And still the French Navy positioned its twenty-one ships of war, anchoring and re-anchoring as if readying itself for a grand game of chess at sea.

Meanwhile, not only was my mind troubled, but every muscle in my body protested at the mining. We labored first with picks and spades, clearing through sod and earth and centuries of broken stone, fragments of old pottery, rubbish, and bones. I shall always remember with horror the moment my spade struck something hard, and I fell to my knees to clear earth away with my hands. I threw it from me, shaking my hands to rid them of the contagion. I had unearthed a skull, a human skull.

William Lesley often ordered silence and had us all lie upon the ground, our ears pressed against the sod to listen. Countermining, I was to learn, is far more an art than a science. Where the enemy were digging, where they would break through, no one knew. And so we dug and we listened.

When at last we came to solid rock, Captain Lesley, commander of the countermining efforts, ordered men to set out charges of gunpowder to blast our way through the rock. "And every man," he added, "keep your weapons ready to hand."

"And what if we fail to meet them?" asked Alexander, hefting a borrow load of crushed stone against the south wall of the castle.

"What if we d-don't fail?" I said, the thought that troubled me every hour we dug. I awoke myself screaming in the night with these fears. What would it be like when we did meet them?

The next day was July 15, 1547. It was fair and warm, for Scotland. The North Sea was unusually calm, and I batted at a cloud of gnats that meandered in the still air eager to land and feast on my flesh. A seagull screeched overhead, circling for scraps of food. I felt the perspiration trickle down my chest as we gathered our spades and axes for another day of breaking stones, hauling loads. It all had seemed rather futile to me. All this work, yet they were sure to bring us to heel at the last. I had somehow thus far avoided actually entering the mine. It was a dark narrow shaft, into which only one or two armed men could squeeze at one and the same time. There was a great deal of work to be done above, clearing away barrow loads of stone and earth. I had begun to believe, much to my relief, that I would never be called upon to actually descend into the subterranean blackness of that shaft.

Until that hot morning in July. William Lesley gave out the orders for work detail. I stood waiting, expecting to hear the usual, that I was clearing rubble on the surface, or working on the gang that pulled the rope that carried the sledge up and down the shaft. After he had ordered every man by name to his post, he looked at us and said. "I need three volunteers to man the shaft." My heart nearly froze. "The shaft grows narrower, and I need young men who can make like moles, who can fit into the wee spaces for clearing of the rubble from yesterday's discharge."

Alexander unsheathed his dagger, checked its point, and set it back into his sheath with a snap. "We're your men," he said.

"That's right," said Francis.

I could barely move. Francis took my arm and handed me a spade. "I'll be with you, brother," he said as we crouched before the dark abyss.

His words were well meant, but I found greater comfort in something Master Knox had often said in our lessons:

"Only men who ken their weakness, find their strength in Christ alone." I was not entirely certain what he meant by the words, but clung nevertheless to them. With that, I lay down on my stomach and began slithering like a snake down the shaft. Leaving the bright sunlight behind, I knew my eyes would be wide and staring into the blackness. My breath came in short gasps, less from the lack of good air than from the clutching tightness in my breast. My insides revolted at the earthy stench of decay and dampness, and I felt the dirt turn to a slimy film of mud on my face and neck as it mingled with my sweat. Dimly at first my eyes began to make out the jagged stone walls of the tunnel in the pale light cast from our whale-oil lanterns.

"H-how much farther?" I called behind me. My voice sounded hollow and muffled.

"You'll know it when you get to the rubble," said Francis.

I heard the scuffling behind as he and Alexander followed me deeper into the mine, the rhythmic skidding of the sledge pulled by Alexander sounding like the low moaning of a man in pain as it scraped over the rock.

"How long does this oil burn?" I asked.

"I really don't ken how long," said Alexander. "When the oil burns out, we're finished."

I didn't much care for the sound of that, crawling back in pitch darkness. A shiver ran through my body, but still I continued deeper into the mine.

My elbows and hands felt raw from scraping against the jagged rock. Suddenly I felt a sharp pain in my right elbow, and then another.

"There's rock fragments ahead," I called.

59

For the next quarter of an hour we worked at filling the sledge with loose rock. While Alexander guided it back as the men pulled on the rope, Francis and I cleared more rock.

"It's sort of spooky down here," he said. "Think about what would happen if—"

"Let's not talk about that," I cut him off. "Look at this. The explosion left a steep drop here. I wonder why?"

"I don't know, but let's clear this rubble away and see what's there."

At this point in the tunnel the floor sloped off to the left, making it awkward to keep my footing. With our spades, Francis and I cleared more rock fragments from the end of the tunnel, collecting the pile to the left side until Alexander returned with the sledge.

We were making the scuffling and clunking kinds of noises one makes when clearing rock with spades in a mine, but suddenly I felt certain I had heard something different. "What was that?" I whispered.

"What was what?" said Francis. "Probably Alexander coming back with the sledge."

"No. L-listen."

"You're imagining things again," said Francis. "All you hear is—"

He broke off. I felt his fingers digging into my arm. My left ear was near his face, so close that I heard a gulping sound as he swallowed. And then he must have been holding his breath, for I heard only silence.

8

Make Haste!

WE LAY THERE PRONE, terrified to move a muscle. There was no denying it. The sound we had heard was not different from the scuffling and clunking sounds we had been making. But these were being made by others. By men who were close, very close, separated from us by only the remnants of shattered rock left from the last explosion. I gripped my spade so tightly that my fingers hurt.

What happened next I shall never forget for as long as I may live. We heard them talking, apparently oblivious to our presence, now only a few feet away. *"Nous ne sommes bout de bras, et puis nous allons couper la gorge."* I heard every word.

"What did they say?" whispered Francis.

Francis had never liked French and so in our studies he often asked me this question. "They are arm's length away and they plan to cut our throats." Mine was dry and hoarse as I whispered the words back to him.

"What shall we do?" I whispered. I was counting on my older brother for an answer to this. "They don't ken we're here," I added.

"I say we have but one hope," said Francis.

"What's that?"

"We take them by surprise. Here, you get behind me."

I tried to pray, to pray like Master Knox prayed. But I was too terrified to form words. I could only pray that our tutor was praying for us right then.

After a final clattering of rubble, they broke through. *"Qu'avons-nous ici?"*

With a howl that terrified me nearly as much as it must have terrified the Regent's miners, Francis fell on the men. We discovered in those seconds that, combined with the element of surprise, spades do make good weapons in a mine.

In the scuffling and grunting, Francis's lantern stopped glowing, as did the Regent's miners' lights. By the dim light of my own lantern, I saw the two men sprawled and motionless on the floor of the tunnel, blood oozed from the forehead of the one nearest me; Francis crouched over them with his spade at the ready.

"Are they d-dead?" I stammered. My stomach churned, and I feared I was about to be sick.

"Not yet," said Francis, breathing hard. "But if they so much as twitch I'll finish them off for good and all."

Lying prone in that shaft with two grown men, seasoned soldiers by the look of them, and our enemies, the men who moments before I had distinctly heard vow to cut our throats, I felt still more the child. "They're not p-playacting?" I was power-less to keep my voice steady.

"I'm ready for them if they are," he said, menacing with his spade. Motioning toward them with his head, he added, "Better take their daggers."

I crawled toward the nearest, a brute of a fellow, the stench of whose sweat and filth recoiled my stomach. What happened next sent a chill deep into the marrow of my bones. As I reached for the dagger, my lamp gave off a wheezing sound, flickered, gave a final fizzle—and went black. It is difficult to describe the torments of mind that darkness caused. With eyes no doubt wide, I groped for some hint of light. What if those men were not truly unconscious? I felt panic rising uncontrollably in my bosom.

Just when I thought I had no alternative but to unleash my panic with an unrecoverable scream, I heard another voice and caught the flicker of a lantern.

"What's all the commotion?"

It was Alexander, and by the sound of his crawling he was making for us with all speed, all speed that one can make when crawling on one's belly in a damp, dark shaft in the regions where death and darkness reign supreme.

"Make haste!" said Francis. "We got them! Two of them, but I fear they may come around and set upon us in rage. And there's more where they came from. Make haste!"

And then my heart nearly halted in its beating. I heard them. In the tunnel from which the two unconscious miners had emerged upon us. Scuffling, crawling sounds, mingled with excited voices, some French, some Scots.

"They'll not be wielding s-spades," I stammered into the darkness.

9

Was It Real?

THE RAWNESS OF MY FLESH all forgotten, elbows and fingers, feet and knees, I clawed my way back up our mine, Francis making speed ahead of me. It is remarkable how fear makes one move with such haste. I loathed the prospect of my own death at the hands of an enemy, but death by falling into the brutal grasp of the Regent's soldiers in the damp subterranean confines of a siege tunnel seemed like death and burial all in one fell swoop—a cruel way, indeed, to part this life.

Alexander must have heard them, or seen in the light of his lantern the terror on our faces, for he turned without a word and made haste to the surface. He broke into the light first, and I heard him yelling something, I couldn't make out what it was. Francis's voice joined in an instant later. I cared only for getting clear of that foul place and the hands that I felt sure were clutching after me from below.

"They've broken through!" cried Francis.

"How many?" demanded William Lesley. "And how armed?"

"We clubbed two of them with our spades," said Francis.

"They had d-daggers," I managed to add. I was never more happy to see the light of the sun, and I gulped in the fresh sea air as a man dying of thirst drinks fresh, cool water.

"But there are more coming," said Francis.

"Ready the long guns!" cried Captain Lesley. "Ready the pikes."

I could not wait to get far away from the black mouth of that siege mine. Terrified as I had been of those men who I was sure had been chasing us in the mine, I felt a twinge of pity for them. Our side had no less than a dozen men armed with deadly weapons to be employed instantly and at point-blank range when those men appeared. We stood off and watched, though I cared little for watching what I feared would follow.

I fumbled with my lantern as we waited. "Francis, my lantern's not empty of oil," I said. "So why'd it go out?"

Francis shrugged. "Mine went out in the scuffle. Why yours died, I have no idea. Bad air, maybe."

We waited. Guns at the ready, pikes poised, our men stood unflinching, waiting the onslaught of the Regent's men. But the black hole stared dumbly at us all. A quarter of an hour passed, but there was not a sight or a sound of the Regent's miners.

"Now then, you lads," said Captain Lesley, his sword drawn, his eyes never leaving the mouth of the tunnel. "Are you certain of what you say you saw?"

Staring at the black mouth of the mine, Francis nodded without saying a word. "Tell all, Francis," I said. But Francis seemed unable to speak, as if in a state of shock, or was it unbelief? And then I began to doubt my eyes. It had been dark as ink. There was their voices, what they said, and in

66

French. But then I might have merely imagined their words. Had we imagined the whole episode? Had we merely gone too long without proper air, our minds befuddled by our fears, by my fears?

"And you, young laird of Ormiston," said William Lesley to Alexander. "Are you certain of what they say they saw?"

"For my part," said Alexander, "I saw nothing. And only heard the racket Francis and George made coming toward me, their eyes goggling in fright."

I stared hard at Alexander. He grinned and feigned a courtly bow in my direction. "Tell them, Francis!" I said, tugging on my brother's sleeve. "We know we saw what we saw. They were real men. They even smelled like real men. Tell them."

"At your ease, men," said Lesley to the soldiers. "It looks as if we may have been a wee bit hasty."

Suddenly an idea occurred to me. "Show him your spade," I said.

"My spade?" said Francis, pulling his arm away from my grasp.

"Your spade. Show it to Captain Lesley. It'll have the man's blood on it. Even some of his hair. Go on, show it him."

William Lesley eyed Francis. "It would be helpful, lad, to see a bit more evidence to support your tale."

Francis brightened for an instant, and then his face went slack. "I left it in the mine. In our haste to be away, I dropped my spade."

My heart sank within me. Surely we saw and met them, Francis stopping them with his spade, and perhaps me aiding him with mine. Surely we did. His face speaking eloquently of his disbelief in our story, Lesley ordered his men to halt their vigil

67

at the mouth of the mine, to gather tools and weapons, to return to sentry duty on the ramparts of the castle.

"Did it happen, Francis?" I said, collapsing onto a mound of earth. He said nothing. "Maybe none of this is happening. Maybe it's all playacting."

If I had actually begun to believe what I was saying, what occurred in the next instant jolted me forever from my incredulity.

10

French Ships Use Slaves

WHAT I HEARD NEXT was a muffled thud, as if from a far-off crack of thunder, but one I felt deep in my innards. It was followed by a whirring that grew rapidly louder. Then a crashing and splintering of rocks, and the ground shaking beneath our feet. Next followed, in rapid succession, another and another, the ground shuddering with each blow, like a moving ocean of rock and earth. For a grim instant, I shuddered in horror at what it would be like deep in the mine when the ground was shaking thus. In the midst of the roar and quaking all about me, the sounds of dozens of men, some yelling orders, others just yelling, joined in making a chaos of sound that I shall never forget for as long as I live—which at that moment I felt would be very short, indeed.

"The French begin their barrage!" cried Balnaves.

"Every man to his cannon!" cried William Lesley. "And may God preserve us!"

"Stay close by me, lads." It was Master Knox. He had taken Francis and me each by an arm and was running with us toward the eastern ramparts of the castle. I turned and saw Alexander close at our heels. I say we were running, but it was more a frantic stumbling, with the earth moving so beneath our feet that there was no real running to be done without a great deal of lurching about. Everywhere there were men yelling and jostling, and the stench of gunpowder hung like blue acid in the air. My chest heaved as we ran, and I felt I must have more air, but each time I opened my mouth to take some into my lungs, I felt instead as if I had swallowed fire.

Once on the battlements, I found the scene stretching before my eyes astonishing beyond my ability to describe. The ships that so lately had lain calmly at anchor were now spread wide in a fire-breathing phalanx against us, their gun ports open, cannons belching flames and smoke in rapid sequence. The coordination of it all amazed me. The opening of each volley began at our far right and passed from cannon to cannon, then from ship to ship, in a staccato of thundering volleys stretching in a wide arch to the northeast. Through twenty-one ships this pattern was repeated.

The opening barrage had done surprisingly little damage to the walls of the castle. And I wondered at this. So much firepower and so little damage. The cliffs below the castle had been pounded by the opening barrage, and many cannonballs had landed harmlessly in the sea. But how such little damage to the castle?

As if reading my thoughts, Alexander yelled above the racket. "They're sighting in their guns." He paused, his face set as if reconciling some inner conflict.

"Ships roll with the swelling of the sea," said Master Knox. "They must compensate for the swell. They may be at their gunnery practice for some time," he paused.

I observed that Alexander looked away from Master Knox, his eyes fixed on the ships and the cannons.

70

"When they master the range and the sea swell," continued Master Knox, "it will be a fearful bombardment that shall shake these walls."

I could not recall seeing Alexander ever show a hint of fear at anything. When we played on the moors near Longniddry as young boys, he was always fearless. But just then in his face and in his tone, I detected that he was more than a little afraid.

"We might be useful." Master Knox was yelling to be heard above the racket, but his voice betrayed no hint of the terror that troubled my mind. "Let us lend a hand," he added.

And with that he stooped and picked up a cannonball, passing it on to the next man in line, who passed it on up to the gunners. "But we must stay together," he called over his shoulder. "I've sworn to your fathers to look after you lads, and I intend to do so."

We had no sooner taken our place in line, hefting cannonballs, when I felt my feet nearly knocked from under me.

"Ready your guns! Fire! Fire! Fire!" came James Melville's cry. What followed felt like a violent rearranging of my internal organs, so gut-wrenching was the thundering of our own cannons so close at hand. My ears whined in protest and I felt my head spinning, so that I thought I would lose my balance and fall to my harm on the stone steps leading to the bulwark where the cannons were mounted.

Again came the command, this time from Henry Balnaves, "Ready your guns! Fire! Fire! Fire!" I clamped my hands over my ears for fear they would explode with each thunderous retort. Then suddenly a great cheer rose from the men on the ramparts immediately above where I stood. Master Knox took the steps two at a time and we followed, eager to see what had prompted such jubilation.

What met our eyes was an infernal sight. A French galley near the center of their phalanx had been struck by our cannon. But it was no glancing blow easily shaken off. Apparently one of our gunners had managed to strike the ship's powder magazine. Ill-trained and unpracticed as our men were in the art of firing cannons at ships rising and falling five hundred yards to seaward of us, it had to be either the merest chance occurrence or the direct intervention of Providence that enabled such a blow to the French fleet, and so early on in the engagement. I watched in wonder as a brilliant instant of white light flashed from her ports, and then her stern and quarterdeck planking seemed visibly to swell, and then all hell erupted, the aftermost portion of the ship splintering into a ball of fire and smoke. In less time than it takes to tell it, the midships of the vessel, partially in flames, plunged into the sea. Like a human arm reaching heavenward for a lifeline, the galley's bowsprit was the last vestige of the vessel as it disappeared beneath the water.

"Hurrah! Hurrah!" cried the men, clapping each other on the back and raising their fists in the air. It was an astonishing sight to behold, and all affected so rapidly in the engagement with the French fleet. A second wave of elation spread throughout our ranks as fire from the explosion of the first galley leapt up the bow and forward rigging of the ship anchored immediately astern of the hapless vessel.

"Who needs Henry of England and his aid!" shouted one elated fellow. Others took up the cry.

"*Sancta Barbara*!" shouted one of the gunners, making the sign of the cross with his fist on his chest.

Master Knox seemed not to share in the glee all about us. "We must give God glory," he said, "not the gunner's goddess." I fear few heard him above the exuberant shouting. "They have many more ships. The fight has only begun. It is far from ended." I heard Master Knox say these words, and perhaps Francis and Alexander did as well, but few others heard him. Those who did seemed ill-disposed to heed his caution.

We watched as the French fleet, too preoccupied for firing cannons, labored to extinguish the fire threatening to engulf another of their war galleys. The men around us watched with satisfaction as two other galleys cut their moorings and towed the damaged ship north toward the sands, there to save it by beaching it for repairs. Some of our men shouted insults at the French as they managed their initial losses.

I watched as Master Knox stared out to sea, a reflection of the flames from the second ship flickering in his blue-gray eyes. "When the wind is slack," he said, almost as if talking to himself, "the French use slaves to propel their ships, slaves chained fast to their oars." He paused.

I followed his gaze. My throat burned, and I found it difficult to find my voice. "Chained so they cannot get c-clear?" I said.

Master Knox nodded.

"How many men?" I asked.

"The French generally use twenty-five oars in their galleys," he said. "With six men to an oar."

"That'd be 150 men," I said, my voice barely audible. "That ship—the one we just sank—went to the bottom with 150 slaves— men chained to her timbers, with no hope of getting clear?"

"Aye, that's so."

"W-where do they get the slaves?" I asked.

Alexander who had been staring off to sea as if he hadn't been listening, now turned. "They get them," he said, his voice rising into something akin to a shriek, "from the likes of us!"

11

Shattered Like Eggshells

BEFORE I COULD FULLY COMPREHEND what Alexander meant about the French getting their galley slaves from the likes of us, prisoners taken in battle, a new thundering suddenly drowned out the shouts and cheers of our men.

Instantly sobered by the sound, men turned their backs on the French fleet and stared wide-eyed toward the town and the artillery of the Queen Regent, so long silent. By the looks on many of their faces, our men had nearly forgotten the cannons royal of the Regent. The roaring of her guns suggested that her patience was at an end. Perhaps it was the failure of her miners to take the castle intact that now prompted her to unleash her fury. And unleash it she did.

"Man the guns!" shouted Melville above the din.

What followed in the next hours was the closest thing to hell that I care ever to experience. Death would be better, if one could be certain the afterlife was nothing like this. But I never wanted to be forced to endure again what followed on that dreadful day.

The cannons royal of the Regent, their great double-barreled mouths gaping from the west, pummeled the castle walls from the town. The sound was deafening; there was rarely an instant when cannons were not thundering. I don't know exactly when I realized it, but the French had at some time resumed their battery of the castle by sea. All around me the world seemed to be collapsing. The principle sea tower of the castle fell under relentless French bombardment; many men were crushed by its fall. By late morning, the whole south quarter of the fortification of the castle from the fore tower to the east blockhouse was pounded into rubble, indefensible. Everywhere I looked, I saw death and destruction. It was as if the judgment day had come, and the castle—what remained of it—was Armageddon. We were men hard pressed on all sides, with the French by sea and the Queen Regent by land, men doomed, with no path of escape. And no relief from Henry of England.

We did as Master Knox had urged us and kept close to him, lending aid to the wounded and dying, or rather watching as he did so. We heard the noise, smelled the stench, saw the sudden deaths of men dismembered by fiery cannonballs or crushed by tons of stone blasted into lethal projectiles that cut them down and heaped burial mounds on the instant dead. We saw men killed and buried in the same instant of time, without ceremony or remorse. Any moment I expected to be one of them, and I lamented that ever I had returned to this God-forsaken castle.

Far worse than all the hellish chaos on every side was my inner turmoil. I was terrified at what must surely happen to us when the castle fell. The Regent, after waging a long and costly siege and now being forced to destroy her own castle, would be disinclined to mercy. Her rage would not show itself in benevolence. Word was that James Melville had sent William Kirkcaldy to negotiate a peace with the Prior of Capua, commander of the French fleet. We had nothing, so it seemed to me, with which to bargain for our lives. By the look on men's faces, we knew that capitulation was inevitable. What they would do with us afterward seemed just as inevitable to me.

And then an odd thing occurred. It started as a light shower of rain, but within minutes it was the heaviest downpour I had ever seen in all my life, a life lived, albeit few in years, entirely in Scotland, a land where heavy, drenching rain is as common as wool on sheep. It was not possible to fire cannons in such wetness, since gunpowder moistened by rain does no harm. So the rain gave us a respite from the thundering of cannons, and it brought the blessing of cleansing the foul air, which had been clogged by acrid smoke and the stench of death. Soaked to the bone, we retired to the chapel with Master Knox.

"Let us commit our way to God," he said, then led us in a prayer, a calm prayer, not one, under the circumstances, that I would have been inclined to offer. His was full of hope in God, trust in the mercy of Jesus, confidence in the rule and reign of Christ over the temporal powers that raged against us, and a quiet repose in the arms of a loving heavenly Father.

Water from the heavy downpour outside found its way through many fractures in the stone vaulting of the ceiling, dripping water that echoed throughout the battered chapel as Master Knox prayed. And while he prayed, Alexander at my side seemed agitated, scuffing his feet in the dust and rubble on the flagstone floor and fidgeting with his hands and fingers. Master Knox had barely said, "Amen," when Alexander spoke.

"I have discovered a plan," he said excitedly. "If we remain here, we'll be hanged by the Regent or by the French—take your pick. Or we can look forward to slavery in their galleys—do any of us believe that is not still an execution, worse for being an elongation of agony?"

He was in earnest. I had always thought Alexander was fearless, but not so this day. His eyes darted from side to side as he spoke, and he paced back and forth in front of us as he laid out his plan.

"You know the bottle dungeon? Only the foulest prisoners are thrown in it. If we were to lower ourselves down into it, then when the Regent's soldiers discover us, we could simply tell her men that we were kept in the castle by the rebels against our will, and they eventually threw us in the dungeon, and how happy we are to see the soldiers of the Regent. I know it will work. I can think of no other course of action."

We stared at him for several moments without saying anything. He was serious, that much was clear. I wondered if it would work. Francis at my side shrugged his shoulders and nodded. We had little chance otherwise.

"Such a scheme could turn on you, lad," said Master Knox. "A far better one would be to play the man, take the path of honor, and trust the outcome to the Almighty."

Alexander scowled but said no more. After an hour, the rain halted as abruptly as it had begun. Cautiously we opened the door of the chapel and stood in the archway looking numbly on the barren rubble and muck that was the inner court of the castle precinct. I recollected what Master Knox had predicted months ago, that the castle walls would crack like eggshells. And then what?

78

"Is there any hope, Master Knox?" asked Francis. "Is there any hope that William Kirkcaldy's commission will succeed? That the Regent will show mercy?"

Alexander snorted. "The Regent show mercy? After what we've made her do to her favorite bishop's castle? I'd expect more mercy from the devil!"

"From the devil?" said Master Knox. "Never expect mercy from the devil—nor from Mary of Lorraine. But King Jesus is a king full of mercy and lovingkindness for miserable wretches such as we. Hence, we must place our hope in him alone—come what may."

12

In the Bottle Dungeon

As MASTER KNOX SAID THE WORDS, I heard a sound above us, the sound of a crushing and grinding as when a stone shifts against another stone. I glanced upward and watched, time suddenly slowing as if to the crawling of a snail. A cut stone from the archway, loosened no doubt first by the bombardment and now by the heavy rainfall, broke free and hurled itself in a shower of crumbled stone down upon us. I cried aloud in my alarm, though I cannot remember the words I uttered, and grabbed Master Knox by the arm in a desperate attempt to pull him clear.

Francis somehow managed to leap clear of the falling stones, but in my efforts to pull Master Knox clear, I found myself, with him, caught under the pounding shower of stones from the collapsing arch.

I came to my senses with Francis fairly screaming in my face. "George! George! Are you living? Speak to me, brother!" He was saying this over and over, or so it seemed to my befuddled brain. I heard the clunking sounds of rocks being tossed aside and felt him lifting me under my arms and dragging me away from the debris. Then my brother's face was close to mine, and I recall feeling a degree of pleasure as I looked up at the lines in his anxious brow and the wide, hopeful searching of his eyes, the patting of his hand on one of mine, and the tender stroking of his other hand on my cheek.

"W-where is Master Knox?" I managed to ask.

Francis blinked rapidly. He jumped up, letting go of my hand, and turned back to the pile of debris that had been the arched entrance to the chapel. I lifted myself to a sitting position, my head spinning.

"Master Knox! Can you hear me?" Francis was on his knees shouting, hurling stones like a man possessed as he tore through the rubble.

My head pounded, and I felt blackness closing in on my vision from all sides as I attempted to rise and help him. I may have crawled, but I found myself at his side just as he uncovered the face of Master Knox. His eyes were closed. Grime and grit covered much of the man's features, and I could not be sure if there was life in him. Francis cleared more debris from his cloak, and then laid his ear near Master Knox's chest, listening for the beating of his heart.

"He lives," said Francis. "But we must get him to safety. Can you help me?"

"I'll do my best," I said, lifting Master Knox's left arm onto my shoulder.

"Alexander, lend a hand," said Francis. Then he halted. "Where is Alexander?" His voice sounded hollow. Kicking at the rubble, he said, "He's not here. When did you last see him?"

"Just b-before the arch fell," I managed to say. "I think."

All about us, dejected-looking men were coming out of cover after the rain storm. Their faces were grim, and had the look as of men shuffling to the gallows. Francis stood up, cupped his hands around his mouth and shouted for Alexander. But there was no reply.

"Stay with him," said Francis. "I'll go and see if I can find out where everyone is going, and where Alexander has got to."

I attempted to clear dust and grit from Master Knox's face. He was cool to the touch, and there was a gash above his right ear, blood oozing slowly from the wound. I placed my ear close to Master Knox's chest and listened. There was life in him, but for how long?

Moments later Francis returned. "There's no sign of him," he said, scowling. "Brother, we are indefensible. Word is, James Melville has surrendered all to the French."

"W-what happens to us?" I asked.

Francis looked at Master Knox's still form and bit his lower lip. "Either they'll hang us all on the spot . . ." He paused. "Or enslave us in the galleys of the French. We can expect little else."

I felt my heart grow cold within me. I had a deep aversion to my own dying just yet, and the prospect of being hanged sent a shudder of horror throughout my young frame. Hanging was bad enough, but I couldn't get the image of the burning French warship out of my head. I kept seeing it sinking beneath the waves, galley slaves chained to her keel with no way of escape, perhaps tearing at their bonds and screaming for their lives to the bitter end.

"We've got to help Master Knox," said Francis. Again he bit his lip. "I wish I knew where Alexander has gone."

It was at that moment that a thought occurred to me. "Francis," I said, cautiously. "What about Alexander's plan? If there's no other hope, might we not try it?"

"You mean the bottle dungeon?" said Francis.

"If it's death by hanging or slavery in the galleys," I said. "Why might not we try it? It may be the only means of saving ourselves and Master Knox." I was little convinced by my own reasoning, and, looking back on it, it was indeed the scheme of a madman. Nevertheless, it seemed we had to try.

Carrying Master Knox between us, Francis and I made our way across the wreckage of the castle court to the east blockhouse that contained the dreaded bottle dungeon. A trumpet flourish sounded from the town as we dragged Master Knox into position at the mouth of the dungeon.

"What does that mean?" I asked.

"That is the herald of the French and the Queen Regent," said Francis, "coming to receive the sword of Melville and the rest. We must make haste. Help me ready Master Knox." We secured the rope sling under his arms, and he groaned softly as we lowered him through the narrow neck of the dungeon, his head lolling onto his right shoulder, his body suspended over the foul dungeon and spinning slowly as we lowered him to the putrid straw and filth covering the floor. I could barely make out his still form in the darkness.

"Now w-what?" I said. I had failed to prepare myself for the darkness of that awful place. "How are we going to get the rope back?"

"You're next, brother," said Francis. "I'll tie the rope off, then you lower yourself down and free Master Knox. I'll follow. We must make haste, or they'll be upon us."

My head still pounded, and I nearly lost my grip on the coarse rope as I shinnied myself down into the blackness of that foul dungeon. "We must be daft," I called through clenched teeth. It occurred to me that in the hundreds of years this notorious chamber had been in existence we were likely the very first men ever to have willingly lowered ourselves into that horrid place.

When my feet came in contact with the dank debris that littered the stone floor of that abyss, I felt around cautiously for Master Knox. Cautiously, I say, because I heard them—the sounds of rats gnawing and scurrying and made all the more sickening to me for the blackness that barred me from seeing.

Looking up at the bottleneck, I watched the worn leather soles of Francis's shoes gripping the rope as he slid toward me into the darkness. "Are w-we certain of this?" I said, my voice higher than I thought it ought to be.

"Ugh! It reeks!" said Francis, when he at last joined me and Master Knox in the depths of the prison. I heard and felt him pulling one end of the rope through. I grabbed his arm. "What's this?" he said.

"I just want us to think for an instant longer," I said. "W-when that rope falls down here with us, we have no way of escaping. I just wanted to make that clear to myself before you did it."

"And if we don't do it," said Francis, pulling the rope down arm over arm, "we face almost certain death."

My heart sank within me as he gave one final pull, and the chaffing of the rope on the iron bar ended abruptly in silence. Not exactly silence. There was a soft rushing sound as the rope came free, gathered speed, and fell to us. In my tormented mind, it had become a noose snaking toward me, making free to coil its taut fibers about my young neck.

"This dungeon," said Francis, digging in the straw and filth, apparently hiding the rope, "is our only hope of escape."

13

Willful Falsehood

THE NEXT SEVERAL HOURS deep in the dungeon of St. Andrews Castle were some of the most anxious of my life—at least up to that point in my life—more than I then knew lay ahead. Foremost in my troubled thoughts was the question: Would Alexander's plan work? Which always brought on the nagging subordinate question: Just where was Alexander? We occupied ourselves doing what we could to revive Master Knox, but there was precious little we could do for him; yet he continued to breathe—foul air for breathing though it was—and his heart continued its beating.

"Why did we not bring a morsel of food and some wine?" said Francis.

"A-and a light," I said.

My insides grumbled for nourishment, as Francis's no doubt were also working at doing. It was impossible to differentiate between inner rumblings caused by hunger and the inner turmoil caused by the much larger and more threatening worries plaguing my mind. "H-how long before they find us?" I asked. "And what will we say?"

In the filth and blackness, we attempted to make Master Knox comfortable—as comfortable as is possible for a man with a thump on the head, holed up in the most notorious dungeon in Scotland, encircled by scurrying rats scheming about where to begin picking our flesh from our bones, and with the French about to burst into the blockhouse above at any time. We spent the next while planning out what we would say and how we might say it when they did call down to us through the narrow neck of the bottle far above us. The more we debated and rehearsed, the more I came to believe that our plan might possibly work. No sane men would enter such a hellish place of their own free will; surely they would conclude that we had been held by the Castilians against our wills. I believe at that point we convinced ourselves that we might actually save ourselves and Master Knox from the noose or the galleys by Alexander's mad scheme. Thus, we rehearsed with care.

"No, no, George!" said Francis in frustration. "When you say it like that, your eyes all wide and goggled—"

"How do you know they're wide and goggled?" I retorted. "It's pitchy dark."

"I can feel them so," said Francis.

"But if we were really prisoners in this place," I said, "my eyes would be wide and goggled."

"Aye, but there's a wide and goggled that just tells all. The sort that makes them know from looking at you that you're lying through your teeth and feeling none too good about it either. Now try it again." I don't know how long we had been at this, but we had been so preoccupied that we had failed to check on Master Knox for some while. Perhaps it was our consciences that troubled us, but we halted as if hearing a ghost when we heard his voice.

"Where are we, lads?" he said, his voice low but clear. "And what on earth are you talking about?"

Neither of us spoke at first. "Well, sir, ah, well," began Francis.

"You were struck on the head by a collapsing arch," I said. "When we stood in front of the chapel, right after the great rainstorm. Do you recollect it, master?"

"Aye, that much comes back to me," he said. Faintly, I saw and heard him rubbing a hand over his eyes. "But how, lads, did we come to be here? If my nose doesn't mistake me, this is the bottle dungeon."

Neither Francis nor I said anything. I could imagine Master Knox narrowing his penetrating blue-gray eyes at us, and I heard the straw under his head rustle slightly as he made to nod his head. "I'm beginning to see my way clearly here," he said. "You've gone and put Alexander's scheme into effect, haven't you then?"

"Aye, so we have," we said together, I glad for the dimness so as not to be forced to look at his accusing eyes.

"Well, lads," he said, more rustling of straw as he turned on his side; I felt certain he was leaning on an elbow, straining to see us in the dark. "And you've gone and dragged me down here with you. I do hope this scheme of his works." He paused as if listening for something. "I hear Francis and George, but where's young Cockburn, then, the mastermind of this mad scheme?"

"That's just it," said Francis. "We don't have the slightest idea where he's gone. After we dragged you out of the rubble, he was just gone, and no amount of looking for him would do."

Master Knox lay back on the straw. I could just barely make out, if I didn't look quite directly at him, the outline of his features as he eyed the narrow neck of the bottle above. I imagined a frown on his lips.

"So then," he said after several moments of awkward silence. "What is it you two are plotting to say when the henchmen of the Regent come calling, as they most certainly will be doing?"

We explained to him that James Melville had surrendered the castle and told him all we had been planning to say when they discovered us in the dungeon.

"So you're scheming willful falsehood, then," said Master Knox. "All for saving of your miserable hides."

"Aye, and yours," said Francis. I felt his words came close to disrespect and that if we hadn't been enclosed in such darkness he'd never have made so bold as to say it.

But all this was cut off when suddenly we heard the clattering of a key in the gate of the blockhouse above, the puzzled hesitation as the guard found the gate unlocked, the moaning as it turned on its ancient hinges, the sickening clunk as it came to against the stone wall.

"Ready yourself, then," said Francis.

There was a striking as of flint on stone, and then a hissing, and then light from a torch flickered in the bottleneck above. Then came the ominous tread of boots on flagstones.

"You're goggling, George," hissed Francis.

I knew he was correct, but I felt that if ever there was a time for goggling, this was it, and there was to be no helping it.

14

At Sea in Chains

I HAD HEARD TELL OF BOYS whose only wish was to run off to sea. They thought of nothing but making their way to the seacoast and rendering themselves up as crew on a ship. They wanted nothing short of a life of adventure on the high seas, setting sail for anywhere far from home and Scotland. They yearned for voyaging to faraway and mysterious places, experiencing lands and peoples unknown by their fellows in Scotland, growing rich by trading, or by warfare with galleys set low in the water with gold and riches from the New World. They imagined themselves swashbuckling adventurers charting new waters, gallant captains discovering new lands, conquering and subduing barbaric nations around the globe.

My first hour at sea dispelled any such romantic notions of the seafaring life. The grueling nineteen months of my life that followed, chained to an oar on the rowing deck of the French galley *Nostre Dame*, demolished any vestige of such delusions. The memory of the galley we sank, that we sent to the bottom of the North Sea with all hands, including her 150 galley slaves, was never far from my mind in that year and a half of hell.

Things had fallen out so oddly in the bottle dungeon. Francis and I had made ready our script, but before we spoke a word, the Regent's henchmen hollered scornfully down the bottleneck of the dungeon at us, "Bold attempt!" That was all they had said, and we were bewildered by it all. They hurled down at us a stout rope with a loop tied on its end. It reminded me far too much of a noose, and I had wondered if we were being lifted up alive by a rope only to be led out and dropped by another rope to our deaths. The prospect seemed intensely likely in those moments.

Fearful that Master Knox was too weak to cling to the rope in his own strength, we lashed him to it. "Hope in Christ, lads," he said as he rose above us. Jeering at us for our "bold attempt," the Regent's soldiers hoisted each of us in turn out the dungeon. We were then marched to the sands north of the town, Francis and I practically carrying our tutor between us, where we were made to climb the boarding ladder of a ship. There was a pinching smell as of tar and smoke. We discovered in the few moments we were on deck that it must have been the very galley whose rigging had been badly damaged by fire from the single ship struck and sunk by our cannons. I at first felt grateful that they did not hang us. There were a number of times in the nineteen months that followed, however, when I wondered if hanging would have been far better.

James Melville, William Kirkcaldy, Balnaves, Lindsay, and the other lairds were brought on board with us, but they were not taken below with us. I searched the sooty faces of our men, but Alexander was nowhere among them. Perhaps there were men being taken aboard other ships.

Once below, what met my eyes in the dimness of the rowing deck was the hollow eyes and emaciated bodies of broken men,

men once hale and strong, taken in some other battle, beaten, chained, and starved, here lashed to an oar destined to propel the enemy's war galley. There was a perversity about it all that I could not ignore: Here these men—and I now with them—were to be made to use up our final strength to aid our enemy in conquering her enemies, my strength to be employed in giving more power to France. It was enough to make one despair of living.

"*Attendez vous!*" yelled a brute of a man, a whip coiled at his hip. I looked around. He was yelling at us. "*Cet homme est trop malade.*" He yanked at Master Knox as if to pull him from us. I clung to our tutor's arm more firmly. The man glared at me, fingering his whip. It was true, Master Knox was too sick to enter service as a galley slave, but what would they do with him? I did not want to imagine. Glancing back at the men leaning on their oars, I suppressed an overwhelming urge to laugh. Every man here was too sick for such a labor. Something awakened in me in that instant. I realized how absolutely important it was for me, for Francis and me, to do all we could to protect our tutor. I cannot fully explain it, but I had a palpable sense that it was my duty, perhaps my destiny, to keep this man alive, whatever it might cost me. It was an odd sensation for me since, heretofore, I had not felt myself to be of a courageous disposition. I did not feel so then. It was a sensation that seemed not to depend upon any conscious sense of courage, for I felt I had none. Yet was I resolved.

"*Il est bien.*" I tried to make my voice firm. I felt certain that if Master Knox had some nourishment and care for his wounds he would soon be well. "*Le vin et la nourriture, et de l'eau propre pour sa blessure—et tout ira bien.*" Perhaps it was my passable French that disarmed the *souscomite*. It was not my courage.

Nevertheless, I pressed my advantage, explaining that Master Knox, once recovered, would be a strong man at his oar. With a grunt of indifference, the man released his grip and shoved our tutor toward us. Next we were roughly ordered to place ourselves down on a bench. Then, amidst the rattling of iron shackles, we found ourselves chained to our place, six men to a grimy oar. The image of that sinking ship flashed in my mind as I tugged at my shackle. So this was what it felt like to be a slave. I wondered how many other men had been restrained by those same chains and forced to grip that same oar, and I wondered how long they had lasted at their final employment in this life. And then we waited. An odd thing occurred as we did so. A skin of wine and a hunk of bread were delivered to Master Knox, and a basin of water and a rag for his wounds. When I made to thank our *souscomite*, he growled at me like a beast and lumbered forward, lashing the bare back of a poor fellow at the next oar. Master Knox insisted on sharing his bread and wine with us, though I felt certain he needed it far more than we.

At last, we felt the ship lift off the sand with the incoming tide, and then with a clattering of chain that echoed throughout the hull of the ship, we weighed anchor, the *Nostre Dame* pitching with the sea swell.

"*Tirez! Tirez!*" cried the *souscomite*. The taskmaster strode down the keel aisle between the rowing benches on either side of the ship. Uncoiling his whip, he lashed at the nearest men.

"What does 'tirez' mean?" said Francis.

"Pull," I said, grunting as I did so. "Really, Francis, you ought to have attended our French lessons with more care."

We propped Master Knox between us. He seemed somewhat refreshed by the wine and bread. Thanking us for our care of him, he gripped the oar. "Hold fast to Christ, my lads, hold fast," he said, throwing his weight behind every pull. Our first day as galley slaves had begun.

"I hear wind sloughing in the rigging," said Francis, panting hard. "I thought galley slaves only rowed when there was no wind for sailing."

"She's damaged in her spars by the fire," said Master Knox.

"Where are we going?" I asked, to no one in particular.

"Like as not we're bound for France," said our tutor.

"With rigging all crook as it is," grunted Francis, "we'll be rowing the whole way."

Terrified as I felt at that moment, his words made my stomach lurch more violently within me. Then again it may not have been his words. There was plenty else to make one sick. The pitching and rolling of the vessel alone was enough for that. It was August and hot; the rowing deck grew yet more foul smelling with the heat and sweat from the laboring bodies of dozens of men. One man across the keel aisle from me suddenly coughed, retched, and then emptied the contents of his stomach on the man before him. Others did the same. Waves of ill-will swept over me at the sight and sound. And the stench was unbearable, though we had nothing to do but to bear it: the vomit, the excrement and urine that made up the contents of the bilge, the hacking and spitting. The rowing deck was alive with the sighs and moans of doomed men who knew their final energies were being expended in the most foul and inhuman of conditions—in the service of their enemy.

Days passed, mind-numbing days, ones that ran together into an unbroken sequence of cold and wet and misery. They must have been days, but reckoning was impossible. We were given a meager bowl of thin soup once a day, with a hard biscuit crawling

95

with weevils, and the water we were given to drink was brown and fetid. We had no alternative but to drink it, though we felt our innards revolting as we did so. On a few occasions we were given a thin, sour wine to drink, though it tasted more like vinegar than true wine. We drank it eagerly, nonetheless. Exhausted and ill, we spoke little. Our *souscomite* was a taskmaster we had come to refer to as Evrard. We were forbidden to speak. Evrard was a wild boar of a man who whipped first, then, if it suited him, made inquiries.

When Evrard was farthest from our oar, Master Knox would sometimes whisper aloud to us. "God is our refuge, a very present help in trouble," he would recite from the Psalms. Or he would pray specifically on our behalf, "God our Father, come to the aid of my younger brothers, George and Francis. Bear them up in your almighty arms, and grant them your enabling grace this day. May the joy of the sweet Lord Jesus, who knew suffering, be their strength today."

"*Silence!*" cried Evrard. His arm cocked back, and I watched the flick of his wrist and the business end of his whip coming like a striking adder toward Master Knox's face. I was nearest the keel aisle, and felt that involuntary urge to draw back, to get clear of his lash. But then another impulse seemed to come over me, not my own, and, on the instant, I lunged forward between Master Knox and the flying whip. Try as I did, I could not restrain myself from crying out in pain as the lash caught me full in the face. The blow cut a slash in my right cheek. I felt hot tears mingle with the blood that trickled down my face and neck. We knew better than to halt in our rowing, but Master Knox gave me a look that reminded me of my father's tenderness when he had comforted me as a child. I feared I was still very much a child.

Evrard needed no provocation to be cruel, and there was no censure of his deeds. On the rowing deck he was king, above the law, a stranger to justice, almost completely devoid of human kindness. If he was in a foul mood, he whipped men for no reason at all. And the weaker the man, the greater the severity of his lash. It was Evrard's means of clearing the rowing deck of the feeble.

Men so deprived of nourishment, warmth, sleep, cleanliness, and then beaten by the lash—men under these conditions eventually die. We had been at sea for what must have been three weeks when the first man gave up living. Athwart ship and forward one oar from where we labored, a poor fellow at the end of his strength fell forward, his arms still chained to the oar, his oar mates still attempting to move the great oar but now with the added burden of the collapsed man. It was a pitiful and grotesque sight, and Evrard seemed at first not to notice. I felt I must do something.

"*Excusez-moi, monsieur,*" I called, still pulling at my oar. "*Cet homme est malade.*"

Evrard spun on his heel, cocked his whip arm. I braced myself for the lash. Then he caught sight of the limp form hanging from the nearby oar.

I learned that day what they did with men who died or were nearly dead at their oars, how they unchained them and hauled the broken corpses to the rail, and with a heave, and wholly without ceremony or feeling, tossed the lifeless human beings into the deep. Once fuel for the French galleys, now fuel for fishes. I was sickened and horrified by it all. Would I be next? If not next, when would it come? When would I have no strength remaining in my being and give up—and die? Troubled as I was at the likelihood of my dying as that man had died, Master Knox was yet more vulnerable than I or Francis. He had entered service as a galley slave already weakened by his wound, and there had been no opportunity for recovery. When would it be Master Knox they heaved into the English Channel?

15

Accursed Idol

IT IS IMPOSSIBLE TO CONVEY our joy when at last we heard the rattling of the anchor chain and the order to stop rowing. We were ordered to clean our own filth out of the rowing deck using buckets of seawater. And we were allowed to dump great bucketfuls of water on ourselves. Over and over we dipped our buckets over the rail, drew them up, and dumped water on each other, Master Knox rubbing his matted hair and beard and expressing his gratitude in little grunts of pleasure all the while. Wretched as our situation yet remained, we felt refreshed and somewhat clean from our bucket bathing, and we felt revived by the fresh air. Best of all, we were not killing ourselves with incessant rowing. Though we remained galley slaves, we felt hope again.

"Where is this?" asked Francis, eyeing the shore.

"I heard Evrard speak of Fecamp," I said. "And the mouth of the River Seine."

Next day we were ordered below, chained once again to our place at the oar. With a crack of Evrard's whip, we began pulling on our great oars, the galley moving slowly upriver.

That evening the clatter of the anchor chain signaled the end of our labors. I caught snatches of conversation from the ship's crew.

"The city of Rouen, I think it is," I said.

We watched as James Melville and the other lairds were conveyed to shore in the captain's gig. By the look of them, they had fared much better these last weeks than we, but we wondered what was to become of them now. We slept that night in the rowing deck, but the next day we were allowed back on deck for a time. We watched as shipwrights came on board and began re-rigging the vessel, replacing her charred mizzenmast and all her standing rigging aft of the mainmast. Some of us were employed heaving the mast onboard and fitting it in its place. For several days we were allowed on deck for an hour a day but kept in shackles, presumably to keep us from attempting to escape overboard and make for shore. I often longed for that shore and freedom. Few of us could swim, but even those who could, encumbered as we were with shackles, would surely sink to the bottom of the river in the attempt. Miserable and devoid of hope as I often felt, I was in no way desiring that kind of escape.

And then the leaves began changing color on shore, and the wind increased, bringing with it cold gusts that bit into our flesh like sharpened needles. We were about to discover how difficult it was to stay alive as a galley slave of the French in the dead of winter. Again without notice we weighed anchor, the grinding clatter of the anchor chain echoing with foreboding through the rowing deck. The whip cracked, and we were ordered to row, this time downriver once again to the sea. The winds rose high and frigid, sleet and sea spray driving into the rowing deck, freezing our hands at the oar, the great vessel yawing and pitching in the winter gale. The keel and timbers of the vessel groaned and shuddered as we pulled against the seas down the coast, and I feared at times that the once stout-seeming ribs of the ship would splinter into matchwood and the ship would founder, we chained to the shattered remains of those timbers and consigned forever to the deeps. At last the seas abated as we came into the relative protection of a river estuary—the River Loire near the city of Nantes, we would soon learn—there to lay up for the long, cold winter.

More than once in our first months of captivity and slavery we spoke of where the others were taken, of what would become of the lairds Kirkcaldy, Balnaves, the Lindsay brothers, and James Melville, and of what would become of all of us. Master Knox, no matter how sick, cold, or weary, always spoke with confidence and assurance. "God will deliver us from this bondage, to his glory, even in this life." I wanted so to believe him, but what if his was a misplaced confidence?

But the question that pressed hard on my mind and troubled me, was what had become of Alexander. Alexander was like another elder brother to me. I had known him all my life. And I knew that Francis felt the same.

"The French have other galleys," said Francis. "He must have been made slave on one of the other galleys."

"Perhaps he's held in Castle Brest," said Richard Ballantyne, "or Mont-Saint Michel."

"Wherever he lies," said Master Knox, "May God have mercy upon him."

Another torment presented itself that first winter of our captivity. It somehow came over the French officers on board the *Nostre Dame* that they would take it upon themselves to reconvert us to Roman Catholicism, thereby recovering us from our rebellion. One day when the sun broke through the steely gray sky and made it not feel so bitter cold, the sailing master decided to bring all galley slaves on deck for air. They did this occasionally, and though I longed for those days and drank in the fresh air like a starving man eats a haggis, I felt a bit like a wolfhound being let out for a walk, yet kept securely on a leash.

"What is he doing?" asked Francis.

I watched the sailing master hand a painted wooden object to men ahead of us. He spoke words softly to the men, made the sign of the cross on his breast, and moved to the next man.

"I believe," said Master Knox, "he is up to some sacramental mischief. We must beware."

The officer was now speaking to the men just in front of us. I heard him more clearly. "*Vénérer la Vierge*," he murmured, extending the wooden object to the men.

"What's he yammering about?" said Francis in my ear.

"He's ordering us to venerate the image of the Virgin Mary," I whispered.

The sailing master now stood before us, "*Vénérer la Vierge*," he murmured, holding the image of Mary to Master Knox.

I feared what he would do. I was certain our tutor would not kiss the image of Mary or make the sign of the cross on himself, but I worried he might do something bold, something that might bring down the rage of the French sailing master.

"Trouble me not," said Master Knox. "Such an idol is accursed, and, therefore, I will not touch it."

The sailing master's face grew pale, and he pressed his lips together in a manner that made me cold inside. He turned and nodded toward where Evrard stood with his arms crossed and his legs spread wide. In three strides the brute taskmaster stood before our tutor. He grabbed the image of Mary roughly from the sailing master and thrust it in Master Knox's face, then, grabbing his wrist, he put the icon in his hand. *"Vénérer la Vierge!"* he growled through clenched teeth.

Master Knox looked steadily at the sailing master, lifted the image, then turned and gave it a mighty heave into the air. He flung it in such a manner that it hurtled and spun through the air a far greater distance that I believe any of us thought to be normal, almost as if it were flying. At last, far from the ship, with a tiny splash it hit the surface of the River Loire.

"Now then. Let our Lady save herself," said Master Knox. "She's light enough. Let her learn to swim."

Master Knox was no formidable man. He had not the carriage or bulk of a knight, and there was nothing fearful about him. Yet there was something else. Despite the limitations of his stature, he was a man who seemed utterly incapable of fear when faced with the enemies of God. I deeply envied that in him. Any other man who might have dared do what John Knox had just done would have had the presence of mind to be terrified at the consequences to himself for having done it. But not our Master Knox. There is an unnerving effect such fearless men have on others, as I would have many occasions to observe in the future.

Though Master Knox seemed not to share my certainty, I felt that I knew what Evrard would next do with his whip. I winced as I touched my right cheek where last his whip had cut me. Nevertheless, I readied myself to stand between our tutor and the brute when the blows began falling, as they surely must. I cannot explain my behavior, and I must confess that there was nothing of courage in it. I did wonder for an instant how much more of Master Knox's unflinching boldness my frail body could bear. I felt neither brave nor devoid of fear as I readied myself. It just seemed that this was what I must do, and somehow I felt deeply that I wanted to do it as well.

I did, however, have my eyes pinched tightly shut as I awaited the blows, and when they did not immediately fall on me, I found it necessary to open one of them cautiously and no doubt widely. There Evrard stood with his mouth agape, looking out on the river where Master Knox had flung the idol. It seemed that Evrard was yet more superstitious than most and had become convinced that our tutor had employed supernatural power to make the Virgin idol fly as he had seen it do with his own eyes. Next he fell to his knees on the deck, a look of wonder spreading over his fleshy features. The sailing master shook his head in disgust, shrugged his shoulders, and strode away to his cabin.

But as the grinding winter stretched on, the wind tearing at the ship, ice forming around the hull on the coldest days, many men fell ill. I felt myself in a constant state of shivering and longed for the great crackling fireplace in my father's house back in Long-niddry. I found myself dreaming of hot scotch broth, wool plaid blankets, and that delicious inner warmth that comes from a mug of hot spiced mead taken with loved ones about the fire. Worse yet, one night in January 1548, Master Knox fell to coughing, spasms racking his body, and he passed from burning with fever to shaking uncontrollably with the cold. I begged Evrard—we now called him that to his face, which seemed greatly to please the man—to call a doctor for Master Knox. I even tried bribing him to do it with the promise of all my father's wealth—Francis, the eldest, clearing his throat, shuffling his feet, and blinking rapidly at my words. And I reminded Evrard that the only way I could ever pay him was if we were to get free of this hellish slavery on this ship. But no doctor came.

"We must pray, then," I told Francis. "If there's to be no doctor for Master Knox, we must pray." We did pray, though I felt it was not nearly so good a praying as I'd so often heard Master Knox render. Our tutor's fever did subside, but he was not well, and sometimes coughed blood and spit it in the bilge at our feet.

At last the winter cold began to abate, and springtime brought birds into nesting grounds along the banks of the Loire. I awoke one morning to the rapid click-clicking of a white stork nesting in a tree along the riverbank and even caught sight of one in flight, its neck stretched far out ahead of it as if reaching forward in its eagerness to get where it was going. And I heard the trilling whistle of a spoonbill attracting its mate. The place was fairly bursting with new life, and it filled me with hope, hope that we would be warm, hope that Master Knox would be well again, hope that we might be freed from this miserable slavery.

Master Knox did improve, though he was never strong, and coughed more than a healthy man would do. With the spring and warmer weather also came the season of hard labor for us. Soon the anchor chain rattled once more, Evrard's whip snapped back to life—though it was never entirely dormant in those winter months—and we commenced the backbreaking task of aiding the French in their enterprises against the cause of Reformation in Scotland and England. The months that remained of our captivity were grueling, and my worries for Master Knox's health were never far from my mind. At the time, of course, I had no certain knowledge that it would end, that any of us would survive it all.

My hopes were never higher, however, than when on two separate occasions we made voyages back to our beloved Scotland.

On the second of these, as the ship lay at anchor between Dundee and St. Andrews, Master Knox became so weak with the fever and his coughing that Francis and I, and others around him, felt certain he was near the end. He lay in what appeared to be a delirium, and I feared his death was near. And I knew that then Evrard would dump his body to the haddock like so much rubbish. I shuddered at the thought. One of our fellow Scots, Richard Ballantyne it was, leaned close and asked Master Knox if he could see the shore and if he recognized where we were.

To my great surprise, we all heard him reply. "Yes, I know it well," he said. "For I see the steeple of that place where God first opened my mouth in public to his glory." He paused. A determined set came to his jaw and to his pale blue eyes. "And I know, no matter how weak I now am, that I shall not die until I shall glorify his godly name in the same place."

At his last words, I was torn. Was he indeed delirious after all? Such certainty coming from the pale, cracked lips of a man in his sorry condition seemed less like faith and more like madness. I bent low and looked more closely at his eyes. They say you can see madness in the eyes. There was a firmness about his eyes I could not comprehend. Was he, indeed, set apart for a special divine task, and was God at work preserving him through this great trial so as to fit him for that task? And was God at work preserving us—my brother and me, and God willing it, Alexander, wherever he be—with him?

Then in February of 1549, as near as we could then make out, an odd thing happened. The *Nostre Dame* dropped her anchor in another river estuary, but it was not the Seine or the Loire. Speculation ran high among our Scottish fellows. Had our skipper overwhelmed his senses with too much cognac?

"If my eyes deceive me not," said Richard Ballantyne. "This is an English river. And those are English houses on her banks."

"Seeing as how there's a war on," said Francis, "an unlikely place, indeed, for a French galley."

"*Qu'est ce que c'est?*" I asked Evrard.

He cocked his whip arm at me and growled, "*Vous êtes libre de partir.*"

"What'd he say?" asked Francis.

I comprehended the meaning of the words but was too stunned to render an answer.

"We are free to go," said Master Knox. He spoke the words without surprise or relief, as a statement of fact, and in a tone that sounded more like we had been detained overnight, rather than for nineteen grueling months.

Amidst the rattling and clanging of chains—I never thereafter heard chains making their noise without a gibble-gabbling down and up my spine—I felt I was in a dream. Was it all real? Our shackles were, indeed, removed, and we were, indeed, told we were free to go. Into the chill February air hovering over the Thames estuary, we walked off the ship, free men.

I say, walked. More properly, we staggered onto English soil, bearing Master Knox's weight between us. Up to that moment in my young life, I do not believe I have ever felt so free and giddy as I did on that blustery day in 1549. Little did I know that slavery in the galleys was but the beginning of the dangers I would encounter with Master Knox.

16

Welcome to England!

WHEN MY FEET AT LAST TOUCHED LAND—a land that shared a border with my beloved Scotland—I felt an unrelenting urge to fall on my face and kiss the slushy cobbles of that pier side. I looked around at the other men. We were in a sorry condition. To a man we were uncut and unshaven—though the latter mattered little to my chin. Our clothes were in tatters, hanging from us like the shredded remains of the garments of dead men that are left in the open. Indeed, many of the men about me looked like dead men. It troubled me greatly that Master Knox looked worse than most.

"Where is he?" This from Francis at my side, he standing a-tiptoe and pressing down on my shoulder.

I knew who he was looking for: Alexander. But among that ragged, gaunt band of men, he was nowhere that I could see.

The lairds from St. Andrews Castle came up and greeted Master Knox in turn: Balnaves, Kirkcaldy, the Lindsays, Richard Ballantyne, and other men who knew him to be their chaplain.

"I am grateful to God that he has seen fit to deliver you, one and all," said Master Knox, puffs of vapor hanging in the cold air with each word. He paused and looked slowly at their emaciated faces. "But where is James Melville?"

The men looked at one another before speaking. "He expired in the dungeon at Castle Brest," said William Balnaves.

"The first to strike," murmured Master Knox. Then after a pause he spoke more loudly. "Has no one seen my other student, Alexander Cockburn? Has anyone news of him?"

Willaim Balnaves looked at Kirkcaldy, then turned as if to speak. But his reply was cut off.

"Welcome to England, gentlemen!"

I looked toward the voice. To this day I am not certain if the speaker looked so splendid to my eyes because we, every man of us, looked and felt so bedraggled and miserable. Nevertheless, I was awestruck at his costume. He wore a tunic of sky blue with black stripes that puffed out into great billowing sleeves. Silver buttons decorated the black stripes, and below the wide leather belt at his waist his tunic seemed to billow out again into what seemed rather a ridiculous turned-under pair of short trousers. A jeweled dagger hung from his belt. His legs were covered in tight hose of a fainter strip than his tunic. He wore leather boots that turned up at the toes, and on his head, cocked so that it nearly covered his left eye, he wore a blue hat with a cluster of peacock feathers rising above. And he wore an elaborate collar ruff; it looked to my eye like a round cake with white icing, with the man's head, as it were, sitting atop the cake. It was then that I noticed several others in his entourage. And they were all clean. They were so robust looking. And their cheeks seemed so full and round to my emaciated eyes.

"I greet you in the name of His Majesty, King Edward VI," the herald shouted. He had unrolled a scroll and held it before him, yet did he not once, that I could discern, glance down at it. Chin high, he continued. "By whose beneficence you have been this day freed from your cruel confinement and slavery. His Majesty has labored incessantly for your deliverance from your popish French persecutors."

We stood shivering in the chilly February air as he continued what I believe he intended to be a warm greeting. There was much more that he said, but after I had observed the healthy luster of the cheeks of His Majesty's entourage, I could think of little else than food. Perhaps it was the cakelike ruff about his neck that made me think of it. For more than a year and a half we had eaten little other than cold oatmeal, an occasional bowl of thin fish soup, and wine that pinched the mouth, brought the water to our eyes, and set our teeth on edge. I felt that I must eat or I would die. I looked at Francis and Master Knox. Their cheeks were sunken. Their eyes were vacant and staring. Master Knox leaned heavily between myself and Richard Ballantyne, who was, thereafter, never far from our tutor's side.

Timid though I yet knew myself to be, I suddenly felt that I must do something. As the herald paused for breath and, I believed, for dramatic effect, I called out as loudly as I could. "Might we have, good sir, some warmth and food and drink?"

Where the fortitude to make such an interruption before the herald of a king came from, I have no clear notion. It likely had nothing to do with fortitude, and was more the involuntary expostulation of starvation. Nevertheless, my words acted on the others as of the bursting of a dam.

William Balnaves signaled for all of us to be silent. "We are most grateful to His Majesty, and to you, good sir, but my men are hungry, and need rest, warm baths, and good food and drink. Be assured, we are inexpressibly grateful to His Majesty for all his kindness to us. Yet are we filthy, weary, and starving, and shall be far fitter to express our gratitude when these our temporal deficiencies are allayed."

17

Bath, Food, Bed

IT IS IMPOSSIBLE FOR ME to describe fully the hours that followed. Once the herald understood the peril of our condition, he set to work with expedition for our succor. All the public houses in Chatham were requisitioned for our health. We learned that the English were expert at suspending the liberties of her subjects for the compelling interests of state. Francis, Master Knox, Richard Ballantyne, and I were given rooms in St. George's Arms.

My first impression as I stepped into our rooms was of warmth. Hot coals glowed and flickered on the grate, and the heat radiating from them worked itself into my body like a healing balm into an open wound. Though we had often felt the heat of bone-numbing exertion, I believed I had not been properly warm for nineteen long months, and I was not alone.

Next I observed a large copper kettle on short curved legs positioned before the grate, steam rising from warm water therein. And there were beds, soft and warm, and covered with great downy bolsters, and feather pillows, and fresh, clean bedclothes laid out for each of us. I restrained myself only with great effort from collapsing onto one of those beds. I must first bathe, something I had not done properly for nineteen filthy months.

And in an adjoining room, there stood a trestle table loaded with nourishment I had almost forgotten existed in the world. While Master Knox was assisted at his bath, we bathed our hands and arms and faces with warm water and sat down to eat.

"Now then, have you everything you'll be needing of?" asked the plump matron of the inn. I shall always think of the people of England as plump, robust, well-fed.

We assured her that we could not imagine needing anything more and thanked her for her kindness.

"It's really nothing at all," she said, wiping her large hands on her apron. "I'll be off, then," she said, bringing the door closed behind herself. Before we could say another word, the door burst open again, and she stuck her head back in the room. "But mind you, eat slow, now," she said, wagging her index finger at us as if we were children. "There's need for caution when your stomach's been deprived of good victuals for some time—" She broke off, eyeing us critically. Clicking her tongue at the sight of us, as if it were our fault for allowing ourselves to devolve into such emaciation, she continued, "—as it looks your stomachs all have been for some time."

Her caution was well made. I wanted to eat more than I was able to eat that day, and some things I so longed to feast upon, such as roasted pork, and steak and kidney pies, I knew I must save for another meal when my stomach could well handle richer fare. I found, however, the roasted apples, sprinkled with cinnamon, went down easily—and stayed down. And the soup, leeks and carrots, cabbage and turnips, softened by hours of simmering in the ox-bone broth, and the tender chunks of beef cut small and digestible—the soup flowed down into my stomach with healing reverence. And our hostess had laid out a steaming pot of warm, spiced honey mead; it warmed my insides and made me long for bed. When it was at last my turn in the bath—the water needing to be changed and reheated after each bath, so filthy were we all—I lowered myself into the copper bath and felt the cleansing warmth surround me. To be sure it set to washing away the filth from my body, but that hot bath at St. George's Arms felt that day as if it were doing far more than just washing dirt from my outsides. After another pewter mugful of warm mead, Francis and I crawled into bed, like we had done as children together all our lives, and after murmuring good night to my brother, I fell into a deliciously deep and long sleep, the horrors of the galleys for the moment a distant memory.

I awoke to the crowing of a rooster next morning, thin sunlight filtering through the leaded panes and lace curtains of our rooms in the inn. Our hostess clucking like a mother hen as she spread our breakfast out on the board, we ate and drank again— hot tea and flakey scones swimming in fresh creamy butter that dribbled down my hand and arm as I ate. We consumed bowlfuls of hot porridge, soaked with honey and cream, and drank more mugs of hot tea.

I was pleased to see Master Knox, though yet gaunt and pale, looking clean and better rested than I had seen him for many long months. There was life and sparkle to his blue-gray eyes that looked like he was eager to be at his calling. I wondered what that calling would now be and whether we would be long in England or whether they would send us home again to Scotland.

For several pleasant weeks we rested, bathed, and feasted. It seemed that our English hosts believed this now to be our calling, and Francis and I reveled in it. Master Knox, however, did not grow healthy and fat, as did we. He often coughed. Compared to us, he picked at his food and seemed to grow restless.

Early in March, one morning after breakfast, an event transpired that put me almost into a panic. The king's herald presented himself at the door of our chambers, greeted us warmly, asked how we fared, and then abruptly requested that Master Knox accompany him. I immediately rose to my feet, as did Francis, and we made ready to follow.

"It will not be necessary," the herald said, barring our way at the door. "John Knox and Richard Ballantyne are the only ones I am commissioned to escort."

I made as if to speak, but so sharply did Francis's fingers dig into my arm above the elbow that my words came out as a sharp squawk of pain. Master Knox placed a hand on each of our shoulders, looked kindly at us for an instant, and then was gone, the door pulled to with a thud that I felt deep inside me.

"There's a fancy carriage he's being let into," said Francis, pressing his face against the leaden panes of our window.

"Where will they take him?" I asked. "And why not us with him?"

We spent an anxious morning fretting over our tutor. "Isn't it odd, Francis?" I said. "Troubling as being with him has been, I feel like we're undone without him."

"Aye, I feel the same," agreed my brother.

When at last another knock came at our door, Francis and I stumbled over one another getting at that door latch.

"Gather your things," said a short squat man with graying hair.

"We have no things," I said.

"Well, then, come along," he said.

After over an hour of riding in a different carriage than had taken Master Knox from us, this one not so glittery a conveyance, we passed over a great bridge, and into the squawking and squalor and clamor of a great city.

"This'd be London," said Francis, awe in his voice as he gazed at the tall spires, sturdy battlements, and narrow streets of the city. "I've always thought I wanted to see London."

18

New Friend

OUR CARRIAGE JOLTED TO A HALT before a great stone church, its towers rising high above the street, statues of saints and kings staring down with rigid piety at us. Our squat escort spoke little. He led us through a gateway into an inner court and from there into the cloister of the great church, gray light filtering through the gothic tracery and casting elongated lacey shadows on the polished flagstones under our feet. From the cloister he led us into a labyrinth of narrow passages that at last opened into a large room, wood paneling and tapestries lining the walls, a great log fire snapping in a vast fireplace. Seated at a long oak table was a plain man wearing a black monk's habit. To my great relief, Master Knox and Richard Ballantyne sat across the table from the man.

"Aye, my young charges have arrived," said Master Knox, rising and standing between us, with a hand on each of our necks. "Doctor Latimer, may I introduce to you my students and fellow oarsmen, Francis and George Douglas."

The man he called Doctor Latimer rose and nodded in our direction. He then signaled for us to be seated. My appraisal of the plain man was on the instant suspended by a platter of food. It was heaped with cold meats, pork and beef, and some fowl, perhaps pheasant, and cheeses and breads—all of which sat idle on the table between the men. I shall not soon forget the tantalizing aromas wafting from that platter, tormenting me. The last weeks of rest and hearty English food had informed my stomach of all that of which it had been deprived for nineteen months, and my appetite was alive and, as it were, raging. It was only with great difficulty that I managed to restrain myself from reaching for a plump leg of that pheasant. My stomach began gnawing on my insides, and I could scarcely keep my eyes from that platter of food. We were served a pewter mug of dark ale, but I longed for food more than ale, yet was no offer of that meat immediately forthcoming.

Doctor Latimer seemed to have been engaged in giving Master Knox an overview of the entire history of England, so it at first seemed to me.

"If I may speak with candor," said Doctor Latimer. "The late king, father to His Majesty Edward VI, though the seeming architect of the Reformation of the English Church and the break with Rome and the pope, was in reality no friend of the gospel."

He broke off, thrumming the table with his fingers. "Nor have I always been so," he recommenced with a sigh. "I must confess it to my shame. At Cambridge I wrote my dissertation against Luther and Reformation ideas about the gospel and justification by faith alone, and when stirrings of Reform were afoot in Cambridge, I did my part, like the Apostle Paul of old, to hold the coats of those who were bent on crushing it. I was the gospel's most virulent opponent. Until one day, a student of mine, Thomas Bilney by name—bless the dear fellow—made to give his confession to me in the confessional. 'Forgive me, Father, for I have sinned. It has been seven days since my last confession. I accuse myself of the following . . .' so young Bilney began. I assumed I was to hear an ordinary young scholar's confession of sloth, or greed, or lust after the farmer's fair daughter. There were plenty of his sins in that confession, and I hoped to hear that he was confessing his Reformation leanings as well, for I had heard of his friendliness toward the new heresy, as I then thought of it. But it was like no confession I had ever heard before or since. The young man described his anguish of soul at his sins, how the best of his good works were shot through with evil motives, pride, and selfish ambition, how he had come to despair of any merit of his own will or work, and how at the extremity of all hope, he had seen the cross and had thrown himself on the merits of the blood and righteousness of Jesus Christ alone for his eternal salvation, *Jesu, credo*, I believe!' he cried."

At these words, Doctor Latimer fell silent, gazing unblinking into the fire for several moments. He looked so much as if he were seeing someone in those flames that I could not resist turning in my chair to inspect the logs and coals.

"And what effect had this young man's confession upon you?" asked Master Knox.

"I was smitten," said Doctor Latimer. "I learned more by this confession than in many years before. I felt as Saul must have felt on the Damascus Road, and I, the priest, became the penitent. I too confessed my faith in Jesus Christ alone. Thereafter, I joined Bilney and others in proclaiming the truth of free grace, that it is God alone who justifies helpless sinners, and he does so alone through the imputed righteousness and precious blood of his dear Son, the Lord Jesus."

The man spoke the words with such conviction and feeling that I felt I was hearing his confession as he had heard Bilney's that day. I longed for it to have the same result in my confused and bewildered soul. Doctor Latimer continued, telling of his appointment in 1530 to be chaplain to Henry VIII, and of his fears of such a tyrant, a man who used his authority so without scruples.

I was intrigued by Doctor Latimer. Though he was a scholar, a learned man, he spoke with wit and in language the common man, even children, might understand. And he spoke without restraint about the evils and superstition of medieval religion and its masterminds. "That Italian bishop yonder, the devil's chaplain" —so he referred to the pope. Then, as I had heard Master Knox so preach, Doctor Latimer spoke with feeling of the idolatry of venerating images and relics, of the idolatry of the Roman Mass, and of priests and bishops who fleeced their flocks and neglected the ministry of the Word.

"Unpreaching prelates," cried Doctor Latimer, thumping his palm on the oaken table with each syllable. "Clerics so taken up with ruffling in their rents, dancing in their dominions, munching in their mangers, and moiling in their cheery manors and mansions that they have no time for preaching. Meanwhile, the devil, the most diligent prelate and preacher in all England, deceives the weak and leads the flock into perdition."

"I rejoice to hear you speak so plainly of these things," said Master Knox. "But what of your time in court, as chaplain under the gaze of the late king?"

"It was January of 1530," replied Doctor Latimer. "I was called to be chaplain to Henry VIII. I was warned by the king's courtiers to 'speak as he speaks,' if I valued my life, that is. I spent the last few years of the late king's life imprisoned in the Tower myself. The man was ugsome. He had six wives, divorced some of them—the first with my regrettable approval—and beheaded two of them. More than 50,000 people in this his realm have reason to mourn the loss of someone who died at the whim of the king, including our saintly William Tyndale."

"Surely the king called you to his court to woo and silence you," said Master Knox. "Did you, then, speak as he speaks?"

Doctor Latimer looked sadly into the fire before answering. "Being chaplain to such as King Henry was as likely to result in my losing my head as anything. To my shame, yes, I did tread softly during my first weeks in court. 'Prudence is necessary,' I would counsel myself. But weeks of silence became months, and I grew increasingly uncomfortable about not speaking with the king about the condition of his soul.

"Then, one cold morning in November, while I was reading in the early church fathers, I came across this by Augustine: 'He who for fear of any power hides the truth, provokes the wrath of God to come upon him, for he fears men more than God.' I read on, this time from St. Chrysostom: 'He is not only a traitor to the truth who openly for truth teaches a lie, but he also who does not pronounce and show the truth that he knoweth.'"

"Aye, good men from their graves—they rend the conscience," said Master Knox. "What effect had these upon yours?"

"They made me sore afraid," said Doctor Latimer. "Their words troubled and vexed me grievously in my conscience. I, therefore, resolved to declare the truth as taught in Holy Scripture, though it would most likely cost me my life. I chose to craft a letter to His Majesty."

"A letter after what fashion?" pressed our tutor.

Doctor Latimer, nodding slowly, said, "I began it thus: 'I had rather suffer extreme punishment than be a traitor unto the truth. Your Grace, I must show forth such things as I have learned in Scripture, or else deny Jesus Christ. The which denying ought more to be dreaded than the loss of all temporal goods, dreaded more than honor, and all manner of torments and cruelties, yea, and death itself, be it ever so shameful and painful.'"

At these words, Master Knox slapped a fist upon the table and gave a sharp laugh, at which the platter of victuals before me clattered. "I do not think I would have offered King Henry so many options for his taking you off. Bold words, and boldly spoken. Carry on, man. Did you speak of the Bible, the Bible in the language of the plowman? Did you, man?"

"Eventually, yes. Though with, I must confess, trepidation," continued Doctor Latimer. "I knew well the flames to which His Majesty had consigned Master Tyndale." He paused. "A punishment of which I then so heartily approved." There was a quaver in his voice as he continued. "The selfsame punishment which his Majesty reserved for my beloved student, Thomas Bilney, consigned to Lollards Pit and burned in 1531." He looked into the fire in silence for several moments before continuing.

"Yes, I did speak of the Scriptures in English. To my best recollection, by God's grace, I spoke thus in the presence of His Majesty: 'Your Grace promised by your last proclamation that we should have the Scripture in English. Let not the wickedness of worldly men divert you from your godly purpose and promise.' I recollect one of Henry's courtiers hissing in my ear and attempting to pull me to my seat. But by God's grace, I continued. I knew that the church of which he claimed to be the head was filled with men who cared nothing for the truth of Scripture. And I told him so. 'Many of His Majesty's clerical advisors hinder the Gospel of Christ, and as they are Your Grace's advisors, appointed by your royal will, it is in fact the king by them who would send a thousand men to hell ere he send one to heaven. I pray to God that Your Grace may do what God commandeth, and not what seemeth good in your own eyes.'"

"Such fearless words before the mighty!" said Master Knox, placing a hand on my shoulder and on Francis's as well. "It emboldens us all."

"A friend in court told me after my sermon, 'We were convinced you would sleep tonight in the Tower.' I replied as I then and now again believe, 'The king's heart is in the hands of the Lord.' O, if only I had remained so fearless. Yes, in that day I cared more for the cross of Christ than for my own health."

Doctor Latimer rose from his chair and stood before the fire, poking fiercely at the coals as he continued. "Alas, it was not always so with me. Yes, I then went so far as to confront King Henry's mistaken understanding of his temporal authority over the church and urged him not to make a mingle-mangle of things by laying hold of power not his to wield, power and authority that belong alone to King Jesus."

He took a vicious stab with the poker at a log in the fire, sparks hissing and flying upward into the chimney.

"To my shame," he continued, "to preserve my life from the vicious schemes of Cuthbert Tunstall, Bishop of London and persecutor of Master Tyndale, I at last conceded to fully fourteen idolatrous practices Henry was determined to preserve from Rome."

"Including images—idols in your churches?" said Master Knox, his voice low. "So it would seem from the walls and niches of this abbey church."

Doctor Latimer nodded. "When, by God's grace, I reasserted my commitment to the gospel alone and denounced idolatrous practices, King Henry did have me confined in the Tower. I was only released after his death, when good King Edward VI was crowned."

"That was fully two years ago," said Master Knox, frowning. "Yet the idols remain?"

"And a great deal of other ugsomeness remains in this Church of England," said Doctor Latimer.

He set down the poker, returned to his chair, and looked steadily across the table at Master Knox. "Which is why, John Knox, you have been brought to London. You can in no way return to Scotland. Leastwise, not while the Queen Regent wants you at the stake. So you are here, in God's good providence, with us. If purity of gospel truth is to prevail in this our half-achieved Reformation, we must have your help."

Master Knox leaned back in his chair, his palms flat on the table. "How am I, a rough Scot, to help dandy England with her halting and limping Reformation?"

"You will preach, will you not?" said Doctor Latimer.

"I, preach?" said Master Knox, his chair legs scraping in protest as he backed himself from the table. "In your grand London?"

"Indeed," said Doctor Latimer. "Tomorrow at All Hallows, Bread Street, you will preach."

19

Wednesday Sermon

THERE WAS A LONG SILENCE after Doctor Latimer called Master Knox to preach on the morrow. My mind flashed back to that day in the chapel of St. Andrews Castle when John Rough extended the call to our tutor. It was as if a lifetime ago, so much evil had transpired. I did hope his reaction would not be quite the same as then.

In that pause, I felt one of my characteristic urges to speak out. I do not know quite where it was coming from. Certainly it was not my natural inclination to burst out, to risk being made fool of with my own tongue. Nevertheless, I seemed to persist in doing so. Perhaps, in this instance, I was driven forward by my own appetite, but in that pause I blurted out what had weighed heavily upon my mind throughout Doctor Latimer's words.

"Might not Master Knox more favorably reply," I began, "after partaking of a morsel of nourishment?"

Doctor Latimer stared at me uncomprehendingly. I stared— no doubt, eyes wider than they ought to have been—at the platter of sliced meats. Francis gouged his fingers into my arm. I have come to have permanent finger markings in the flesh of my upper arms from this the perpetual expression of the distress of my elder brother.

"We have been long confined at sea," I began.

"Do forgive our greed," said Richard Ballantyne. "Though it has now been several weeks, yet do we find great interest in, that is, need of food and drink." I believed, silent as he had been, Ballantyne's eyes had often strayed with mine to that platter.

"How inconsiderate of me," said Doctor Latimer. "The meat was brought for your refreshment, and here I have been speaking and you have been starving. Do forgive me. Now let us render thanksgiving to our God for his bountiful goodness."

I must confess, I felt Doctor Latimer's prayer over the victuals a lengthier one than was absolutely needful. It is, however, remarkable what effect hearty food and drink can have upon one's frame of mind. Within moments, in between bites of beef, portions of pork, and mugs of mead, we were talking together as if long friends. While washing down a hunk of coarse bread and sharp cheese with warm mead, I felt that all just might come to rights in the end. Francis and I might be reunited with our father and with Alexander. Master Knox might recover his health, and we all might go home to a Scotland free at last of French oppressors and fire-breathing tyrants.

We were given rooms in a narrow house on the courtyard at the side of the abbey. Next morning we were conveyed by carriage to All Hallows parish church, a gothic structure with a single square tower rising high above Bread Street. A delicious aroma of fresh baking bread perfumed the air throughout the entire neighborhood, an indescribably more appealing smell than that which emanated from most districts of London and her environs we had passed through in these days.

The nave of the church was packed with people. Most of them seemed to be clerics in black or gray or brown habits, but there were among them men of rank, in silk and hose, ruff collars, and finely stitched and quilted doublets. I felt my throat going dry and my knees wobbling. With an elbow in my ribs, and his characteristic shuttering with his fingers before his eyes, Francis hissed in my ear, "You're doing it again, brother."

I attempted to ignore him. My stomach churned. There had been no sausages with our breakfast that morning, and I was not certain whether the churning was for want of sausages or the result of my worries for Master Knox. What was he thinking of this grand place and these grand personages gathered here? I was smitten with how fancy and sophisticated English people were, and how very unfancy and unsophisticated I felt at that moment in the grand capital of England, surrounded by these strutting and important dignitaries.

There being few places to sit, most people seemed to be positioning themselves to stand facing the high pulpit. Francis made himself comfortable on the ledge that ran around the base of one of the stone columns in the nave, while I leaned against the column and readied myself to hear what Master Knox had to say.

Like the abbey, this church felt like Rome. I knew this fact would not be lost on Master Knox's powers of observation. A tall slender statue of the Virgin Mary still held her place high above the chancel, and there were saints in every niche, gazing down in stony piety on the faithful. I watched Master Knox, his eyes slowly surveying the scene, and a flush of red appearing on his gaunt cheeks. On the chancel was a draped table with golden platter and goblet, candlelight shimmering on their gilt and polished surfaces.

"Who's that?" whispered Francis in my ear, clutching at my arm again.

We watched as a man strode in white-on-black vestments to the chancel lectern. As if to answer my brother's question, a presenter's voice rang out, "The Most Reverend and Right Honorable the Lord Archbishop of Canterbury, Thomas Cranmer."

Francis gave a low whistle in my ear.

"Come, let us worship the Lord our God," said the archbishop.

So anxious was I for our tutor that I remembered but few details of the opening ceremonies that morning. It occurred to me that it was a Wednesday, not a Sunday. I had a fleeting curiosity about such a high, important-seeming church service on the Wednesday. I do recall that the service, significantly, all transpired in the English tongue. Next a psalm was lined out and sung by a presenter—also in English. At last Doctor Latimer made his way to the lectern. With plainness and clarity, he introduced John Knox to the assembly.

I felt an overwhelming urge to assist Master Knox as he walked toward the pulpit steps, worried that he might not have strength to mount them on his own. Black-robed, with an English Bible cradled in his right arm, Master Knox slowly began his assent into the pulpit. Though I knew him to be yet frail from our long captivity, it was remarkable to behold. With every step he seemed to gain strength. It was uncanny to me how such a slight and unimpressive figure could take on such might and authority with every tread. It was as if each step were a step away from himself, his weakness, his pride, his littleness, and upward to a force and might not his own. I cannot fully explain it, but subsequent events would prove that I was not imagining things. Others observed the same and drew conclusions from their observations. At last he stood before the lectern of the pulpit, opened his Bible, paused, looking out on the upturned faces in the crowd, and then began reading out his text.

> Then was Jesus led aside of the Spirit into the wilderness, to be tempted of the Devil. And when he had fasted forty days, and forty nights, he was afterward hungry. Then came to him the tempter, and said, "If thou be the Son of God, command that these stones be made bread." But he answering, said, "It is written, man shall not live by bread only, but by every word that proceedeth out of the mouth of God." Then the Devil took him up into the holy city, and set him on a pinnacle of the temple, and said unto him, "If thou be the Son of God, cast thyself down; for it is written, that he will give his angels charge over thee, and with their hands they shall lift thee up, lest at any time thou shouldest dash thy foot against a stone." Jesus said unto him, "It is written again, Thou shalt not tempt the Lord thy God." Again the Devil took him up into an exceeding high mountain, and showed him all the kingdoms of the world, and the glory of them; and said to him, "All these will I give thee, if thou wilt fall down, and worship me." Then said Jesus unto him, "Avoid Satan. For it is written, Thou shalt worship the Lord thy God, and him only shalt thou serve." Then the Devil left him; and behold, the angels came, and ministered unto him.

The nave of the church was silent as Knox concluded reading. I stole a look at the faces gazing up at Master Knox. It appeared that all eyes were on our tutor, but some looked skeptical, a few appeared even scornful. Perhaps it was his Scots-accented English tongue that put them off. My cheeks burned at the thought.

"O Lord eternal!" said Master Knox. "Move and govern my tongue to speak with verity and the hearts of thy people to understand and obey the same."

Despite his weakened condition from our long captivity, his voice echoed off the walls and vaulted ceiling more strongly than I expected. I was on the instant flooded with memories from when last I had heard Master Knox deliver a proper sermon. Surely during our slavery he had admonished and encouraged us from his vast memory of the Word of God. But it was nearly two years since I had heard him do what is properly called preaching, and I worried and fretted as Master Knox began his discourse.

"Christ Jesus was led by the Spirit to go to a wilderness, where for forty days he remained fasting among the wild beasts. This Spirit which led Christ into the wilderness was not the Devil, but the Holy Spirit of God the Father, by whom Christ, as touching his manly nature, was conducted; likewise, by the same Spirit he would be made strong, and, finally, raised up from the dead. The Spirit of God, I say, led Christ to the place of his battle, where he endured combat for the whole forty days and nights. As Luke says, 'he was tempted,' but in the end most vehemently, after his continual fasting, 'he began to be hungry.'"

"I've figured it out!" hissed Francis in my ear again.

"What?" I replied, prying his fingers off my arm.

"Lent," he said. "Wednesday fancy church doings, like this. Ash Wednesday, it is. This service begins the Lenten fast."

My heart sank. Did Master Knox know this? He continued, and what he said fairly made my heart stop beating.

"Upon this forty days and this fasting of Christ do papists build their Lent. For, say they, all the actions of Christ are our instructions; what he did, we ought to follow. Since he fasted forty days, so say they, we ought to do the like. I answer, that if we ought to follow all Christ's actions, then ought we neither to eat nor drink *anything* for the space of forty days, for so fasted Christ. We ought to go upon the waters with our feet, to cast out devils by our word, to heal and cure all sorts of maladies, to call again the dead to life, for so did Christ. This I say only that men may see the vanity of these men who, boasting themselves of wisdom, are become mad fools."

At his words, there were confused titterings and rumblings swelling about the church. I felt frantic. Were folks agreeing with or enraged at what he was saying about the papists, or were they merely amused and scoffing at his plain speaking? I could not yet make sense of these English folks. But his words sent my mind racing back to Scotland, where dead bishop Cardinal Beaton had hanged four men in Perth simply for their violation of the Lenten fast. Lent was sacrosanct to papists. I wondered if it was so to these of the Church of England. Our tutor continued, a lilt of sarcasm in his tone.

"Did Christ fast thus forty days to teach us superstitious fasting? Can the papists assure me, or any other man, which were the forty days that Christ fasted? Plain it is he fasted the forty days and nights that immediately followed his baptism. But which they were, or in what month was the day of his baptism, the scriptures do not express. Am I or any Christian bound to counterfeit Christ's actions as the ape counterfeits the act or work of man?"

Master Knox paused for breath and, in that pause, there was a deathly silence in that stone sanctuary. For an instant it was as silent as if nobody was alive in the room, or rather as if all had in-taken breath and clamped down upon it, holding it in, building up pressure. I studied Doctor Latimer's face. What was he thinking of Master Knox's words? There was a glimmering in his eyes, and the hint of a smile on his lips, but nothing more. No one needed to tell me that our tutor had said something dreadfully offensive to many Englishmen in that church that Ash Wednesday.

What would he say next, and what would the rich and powerful English do when he said it?

20

Provoking Battle

"HE MUST NOT KEN IT's LENT," hissed Francis, "or surely he'd not be speaking thus to Church of England folk."

I doubted it. Whatever I had come to know of him, this much was certain: Master Knox was not one to fashion his speaking for the proclivities of his hearers.

"Christ himself requires no such Lenten observance of his true followers," he continued, seemingly oblivious to the tension that hung thick about the church. "But he says to the apostles, 'Go and preach the evangel to all nations, baptizing them in the name of the Father, the Son, and the Holy Ghost; commanding them to observe and keep all that I have commanded you.' Here Christ Jesus requires the observance of his precepts and commandments; and not of his actions, except insofar as he has also commanded them. And so must the apostle be understood when he says, 'Be followers of Christ, for Christ hath suffered for us, that we should follow his footsteps,' which cannot be understood of every action of Christ, neither in the mystery of our redemption, neither in his actions and marvelous works, but only of those which he has commanded us to observe."

I felt he might be moving into safer ground with these Church of England people. But, no. It was clear, he intended to press his railing against Lent on this day sacred to papists, and as it would seem, to the Church of England too.

"But when the papists are so diligent in establishing their dreams and fantasies, they lose the profit which here is to be gathered: that is, why Christ did fast those forty days, which were a doctrine more necessary for Christians than to corrupt simple hearts with superstition as though the wisdom of God, Christ Jesus, had taught us no other mystery by his fasting than the abstinence from eating meat for the space of forty days. God has taken a just vengeance upon the pride of such men, while he thus confounds the wisdom of those that do most glory in wisdom, and does strike with blindness such as will be guides and lanterns to the feet of others, and yet refuse themselves to hear or follow the light of God's Word. From such deliver thy poor flock, O Lord!"

Master Knox's voice rose nearly to a shout with these words, then he proceeded to expound the real reasons for Christ's forty-day fast.

"The causes of Christ's fasting I find chiefly to be two: the first, to witness to the world the dignity and excellence of his vocation, which Christ, after his baptism, was to take upon him openly. The second, to declare that he entered in battle willingly for our cause, and does, as it were, provoke his adversary to assault him. Albeit Christ Jesus, in the eternal counsel of his Father, was appointed to be the Prince of Peace, the Messenger of his testament, and he alone that should fight our battles for us; yet he did not enter his earthly ministry till he was commended to mankind by the voice of his heavenly Father, and anointed by the Holy Ghost by a visible sign given to the eyes of men. After which time he was led to the desert and fasted these forty days and nights. This he did to teach us with what fear, carefulness, and reverence ought the messengers of the Word enter into their calling, which is not only most excellent (for who is worthy to be God's ambassador?), but also subject to most extreme troubles and dangers. For he that is appointed pastor, watchman, or preacher, if he feeds not with his whole power; if he warns and admonishes not when he sees the sword come; and if, in doctrine, he divides not the Word righteously; the blood and souls of those that perish for lack of food, admonition, and doctrine, shall be required of his hand. If our horned and mitered bishops did understand and firmly believe this, I think they should be otherwise occupied than they have been this long time."

Another general rumbling and shuffling of feet, and collective whispering of men to their neighbors erupted throughout the sanctuary. I could not help but observe frowns and dark looks among some present. Master Knox seemed in no way discouraged by their clamor, but rather he seemed enlivened by it, and his voice rose higher and stronger. He next compared the forty days of Jesus' wilderness temptation with those of Elijah and Moses.

"—who were especially commissioned to diminish the tyranny of the kingdom of Satan. For by the law came the knowledge of sin, the damnation of such impieties, specially of idolatry and such as the devil had invented; and, finally, by the law came such a revelation of God's will, that no man could justly afterward excuse his sin by ignorance, by which the devil before had blinded many. So that the law, albeit it might not renew and purge the heart (for that the Spirit of Christ Jesus works by faith only), yet it was a bridle that did restrain and stay the rage of external wickedness in many, and was also a schoolmaster that led unto Christ. For when man can find no power in himself to do that which is commanded, and does perfectly understand and believe that the curse of God is pronounced against all those that abide not in everything that is commanded in God's law to do them. The man, I say, that understands and knows his own corrupt nature and God's severe judgment, most gladly will receive the free redemption offered by Christ Jesus, which is the only victory that overthrows Satan and his power."

His words now bewildered me. I felt, indeed, the inability to obey God's law, yet did I feel it within me that I must, that God would not have me unless I made improvements, became better, labored to please him, to win his favor by my efforts. Surely there was no hope for me without improvement, and as surely he would judge me for my deeds. But Master Knox declared that the Spirit of Christ Jesus works but by faith alone. And if I understood him aright, faith is turning away from my will and merits and to the will and merits of Christ alone. Yet it seemed then so undeserved, unmerited, free and unfair. It perplexed me greatly, and I wondered if Master Knox had got it right. Undeterred, he continued.

"And so by the giving of the law did God greatly weaken, impair, and make feeble the tyranny and kingdom of the Devil. In the days of Elijah, the Devil had so prevailed, that kings and rulers made open war against God, killing his prophets, destroying his ordinances, and erecting up idolatry; which did so prevail, that the prophet complained that, of all the true fearers and worshippers of God, he was left alone, and wicked Jezebel sought his life also (1 Kings 19:14–17). After this, his fasting and complaint, he was sent by God to anoint those appointed by God to take vengeance upon the wicked and obstinate idolaters. May God grant the same, to his glory, and to the comfort of his afflicted flock.

"The remembrance of this was fearful to Satan, for, at the coming of Christ Jesus, the priests, scribes, and Pharisees had taken away the key of knowledge: that is, they had so obscured and darkened God's Holy Scriptures, by false glosses and vain traditions, that neither would they enter themselves into the kingdom of God, neither suffer and permit others to enter; but with violence restrained, and with tyranny struck back from the right way (that is, from Christ Jesus himself), such as would have entered into possession of life everlasting by him. Satan, I say, having such dominion over the chief rulers of the visible kirk, and espying in Christ such graces as before he had not seen in man, no doubt did greatly fear for his most obedient servants, the priests and prelates."

There was more rumbling at this. I winced as he referred to the church in his Scots tongue as the kirk, and I felt sure that there were smirks and jabs from the Englishmen about me at this his roughness. Yet he seemed oblivious to their scorn and persisted in his address.

"Therefore, by all schemes and craft does Satan assault Christ, to see what advantage he could have of him. And Christ did not repel him with the power of his godhead to avoid Satan's temptation of him, but rather permitted him to spend all his artillery, and did receive the strokes and assaults of Satan's temptations in his own body, to the end Christ might make weak and feeble the strength and tyrannical power of our adversary by long suffering on our behalf.

"In this manner, methinks, our master and champion, Christ Jesus, provoked our enemy to battle: 'Satan, you glory of your power and victory over mankind, that there is none able to withstand your assaults, nor escape your darts, but at one time or other you give him a wound! Lo, I am a man like to my brethren, having flesh and blood, and all properties of man's nature (sin, which is your venom, excepted). Tempt, try, and assault me; I offer you here in the wilderness a place most convenient. There shall be no mortal creature to comfort me against your assaults. You shall have sufficient time; do what you can; I shall not flee the place of battle. If you become victor, you shall still continue in possession of your kingdom in this wretched world. But if you cannot prevail against me, then must your prey and unjust spoil be taken from you. You must then grant yourself vanquished and confounded, and must be compelled to leave off from all accusation of the members of my body. For to them does appertain the fruit of my battle; my victory is theirs, as I am appointed to take the punishment of their sins in my body.' "

I felt my imagination taken up with his words. So must have those around me, for their clamor had given way to a new kind of silence. Perhaps it was the heeding kind. Master Knox proceeded.

"Hence, is it impossible for Satan to prevail against us, unless obstinately we do refuse to use the weapon that God has offered. Yea, I say, that God's elect cannot refuse it, but seek for their Defender when the battle is most strong; for the sobs, groans, and lamentations of such as fight, yea, the fear they have of being vanquished, their calling and praying for perseverance, are appropriate ways of seeking after Christ, our champion. We refuse not the weapon, although sometimes, by weakness, we cannot use it as we would. It is enough that your hearts unfeignedly sob for greater strength, for perseverance, and for final deliverance by

Christ Jesus. That which lacks in us, his sufficiency does supply. For it is he that fights and overcomes for us!"

I felt the swelling of my insides at his words, and I longed for them to be true. But were they? I felt the sobs and the groans, all that attend fear, but my mind was troubled. His words thrilled me, but were they true? Was it possible that Christ could be such a Deliverer and champion?

"O dearly beloved ones, what comfort ought the remembrance of these signs to be to our hearts! Christ Jesus has fought our battle; he himself has taken us into his care and protection; however the Devil may rage by his temptations, be they spiritual or corporeal, he is not able to snatch us out of the hand of the potent Son of God. To Christ be all glory, for his mercies most abundantly poured forth upon us!"

With that he closed his Bible, and slowly began his descent of the spiraling staircase, the last echo of his voice fading away with each step he took downward from the high pulpit. As he had seemed to grow larger as he had risen into the pulpit, so he now diminished coming out of it. And I began to fear. There had been more than hostility at some of what Master Knox had preached with such power that day. But now standing frail and below average height, surrounded by an archbishop and English prelates and nobles of every rank, what would become of him in this bewildering realm. What would become of us?

21

Religion by Royal Edict

"SAUSAGE, ANYONE?" said Francis once the carriage door had been closed on us.

I looked quickly at Master Knox. Would he think my brother's attempt at levity appropriate under the circumstances? It was Lent, after all, and our tutor had just delivered a homiletical cannonade across the bow of the required practice of Lent, one of many practices, so it seemed, retained and coddled from the medieval church.

It was Doctor Latimer whose eyes began to sparkle and whose mouth began to twitch at its edges. As the carriage jerked into motion, his shoulders began moving up and down as if he were riding a horse rather than being carried along in a carriage pulled by one. In moments, hilarity broke loose within the carriage as when water breaks through a sluice gate in a farmer's cornfield. I too joined in the laughter. We had done little laughing during the past nineteen months; there had been so little to laugh about.

"I would love a good haggis," said Master Knox, wiping his eyes. "But I suppose the English have no equivalent, seeing as they are the ones who have, over the centuries, killed or carried off our flocks, leaving but trampled oats and gut piles from slaughtered sheep for our poor race to subsist upon."

"With regret," said Doctor Latimer, "we have no such thing."

"With all this pomp and ceremony," said Master Knox, his smile fading, "your Church of England is playing ape to Rome."

"Precisely why I have asked you to preach," said Doctor Latimer. "Protector Somerset as regent holds the reins of power whilst His Majesty, good King Edward VI, remains in his minority. The regent is better than most, and clearly the moral superior of King Henry VIII (though the vast majority of men throughout human history would qualify for the like comparison with the late king). The Lord Protector has repealed laws against heresy and treason, thereby opening the way for free discussion of religious questions. And he is a man with more than average care for the peasant and commoner, more than average, that is, for one who governs."

"Then why does your Church of England continue to bear so much resemblance to Rome?" asked Master Knox.

"Because too many believe that religious change can be made by royal edict, by passing and enforcing acts of uniformity, requiring everyone to worship in precisely the same manner, the same prayers to be read, the same Scripture to be read, the same vestments to be worn, the same homilies to be delivered. One would think that true religion can be put on like a tunic."

"Aye, and a tunic can be as easily taken off," said Master Knox.

"Indeed. That is why it is so needful to have the unfettered gospel of grace alone proclaimed throughout the realm. Gospel preaching is essential, as you, by God's grace, have done today. Men's hearts are not changed by royal edict. Thus far, I fear, we have severed the cord with Rome in externals only. With the late king's acts of supremacy, he declared himself and his heirs perpetual heads of state and church, freeing him to seize all church property and wealth throughout the realm and subsume it to the state—which was his royal self. Alas, our Reformation has been wedded with the most base of unholy motives. Yet, in spite of all, there is a measure of freedom and opportunity in the land, opportunity we must now seize with all haste." He paused, a frown clouding his features. "You see, King Edward is not vigorous in health, and I fear what would befall if there were to be a premature death, God forbid. The souls of men and women are at stake. Will you help us? We need more men like you to preach the true doctrine of grace, unmoved by and unafraid of the political consequences."

My head began hurting me as I listened, and it occurred to me that there was a great deal for Scots refugees, as we were, to learn about this England and her fractured church and state. To the clattering of hooves and wheels on cobbled streets, I mused on it all as we rode on, no one speaking for several minutes.

I had rarely ridden in a carriage, and the narrow half-timbered houses flickering by at the opening made me feel as if only an observer of life, seeing it pass by me as if in frozen segments; I was detached and unaffected by it and able to race onward, leaving behind its instant sights and lingering smells.

My imagination went to work, and I pictured fragments of life as we raced by, and wondered what lay ahead for the man leading the pink and black pig by the foot, the wide woman with a basket looped on her arm, the boy about to filch an apple from a distracted street vender, the wavy-haired peasant girl clutching a red chicken under her fair arm. As we cut our wheeled swathe through their world, it was as if the carriage transported me above their time and place, leaving them behind to fend for themselves through their lives and troubles.

With a snap of the whip and a jingling of harness, wheels grinding on cobblestones, we turned and followed the embankment along the River Thames, barges and sailing craft of various sizes and configurations plying the murky waters. I watched with envy as a boy jerked a slithering yellow eel from the river; as we flashed by, I caught full sight of his grinning face—he was missing two upper front teeth—and then he was gone. With another crack of his whip, our driver turned into yet another narrow street, this one again cluttered with houses and humanity. I noticed Master Knox gazing at the snatches of life passing by, his blue-gray eyes looking intently at the people. His lips were moving.

Through the labyrinth of narrow houses, we neared our lodging and the great abbey at last came into view, towering high above the shadowed streets.

As the carriage jerked to a halt, it was Francis who broke the silence. "Now then, what about that sausage?"

22

Bishop Knox?

In April 1549, Master Knox was ordained and licensed to preach in England. He had preached before he was licensed, of course—his sausage sermon, as Francis termed it—but licensure to preach was required by the archbishop to bring all who preached under the new Act of Uniformity, all the more one such as the thundering Scot, as some had already begun to call him. When he was not preaching, he continued tutoring Francis and me, though I wonder if we didn't learn as much or more from following at his coattails.

"Now then, George," said Master Knox as we commenced our lessons one morning in our rooms near the abbey. "Read out just here."

He gestured with a long pale index finger at the open Bible on the table before us.

I dutifully read out the passage he indicated. *"In principio erat Verbum et Verbum erat apud Deum et Deus erat Verbum."*

"And in English?" said Master Knox.

Francis grumbled under his breath, "A passage fit for a bairn of half your age."

"In the beginning was the Word," I gave out with ease. Francis was correct. We had translated this passage long ago, but I assumed he was reviewing so as to build on our previous vocabulary. "And the Word was with God and the Word was God."

"Very good. Now carry on thus through the chapter," said Master Knox. "And Francis," he added, his blue-gray eyes unblinking and penetrating, "Set your mind to Paul's epistle to the Ephesians—in Erasmus's Greek. Observe Paul's copious use of the appositive."

Francis paled slightly, but he opened the leather boards of Erasmus's Greek New Testament that lay on the table. He took a deep breath, dipped his quill, heaved a sigh, and fell to.

Lessons always reminded me of my home in Longniddry where first we had met Master Knox when he became our tutor in 1543, fully six years ago. Hence, lessons filled my mind with memories of the scent of heather thatch, rich simmering broth, peat smoke from the fire, roast lamb sizzling on the spit, and the golden sweetness of baking shortbread—the smells of home, they were to my senses. I only half attended to my lesson: *"Qui non ex sanguinibus neque ex voluntate carnis neque ex voluntate viri sed ex Deo nati sunt."*

Recollections of my home in Longnidry inevitably led me to reminisce of my dear mother—the thought of whom always brought a great lump into my throat, a smarting to my eyes, and an emptiness to my insides. When I had recovered myself, I began to puzzle over the fate of my father. What had become of him after the French navy defeated our cause and the castle fell? I knew he would be anxious over our own fate—that is, if he were yet living. I longed to see him again, to feel his strong arms enfold me, to inhale the father-scent that perfumed his plaid, to hear his deep, steady voice bringing me comfort, but I feared I never would. I must confess, with such thoughts occupying my mind, I gave but little attention to the English translation of the Vulgate as I gave it out with my pen, "Who were born not of blood, nor of the will of the flesh, nor of the will of man, but were born of God."

As one line of thinking so often leads to another, so I soon found myself musing on our childhood friend Alexander; like another brother to me, he had been. What had become of him? Why did he disappear and not join us in the bottle dungeon? I had never settled my mind on that.

Though so very different in so many ways, I marveled at how brothers' minds could work so alike one another. Through the doxological bursts of Paul's labyrinthine Greek, Francis must have strayed to the same line of thinking, for he said aloud, "What has become of him?"

To which Master Knox looked up from his paper, his quill poised, and queried thus, "Of Erasmus or of Paul?"

Francis hesitated. "A-Alexander," he said. "I confess my mind had strayed to Alexander, and I could not help wondering what has become of him."

Master Knox set down his quill and turned on his stool. "I do not know for certain what has become of him."

I caught his qualifying phrase. He had said "for certain." I wondered if that meant that he had some idea, yet unconfirmed. I determined to press the point. "What *might* have happened?" I asked.

Master Knox did not immediately reply.

"Do you think him dead?" I blurted out what I had feared for nearly two years now. "Surely he would have joined us if he could have, if he had been able."

Master Knox took in breath as if to reply, but there was a sudden knock at the door, and, moments later, Doctor Latimer entered the sitting room. The two men were soon lost in conversation, from which we learned that Master Knox was expected to attend Latimer on a visit with the archbishop. Evident storm clouds were thickening on our master's brow at the prospect.

"With the archbishop?" he said, rising to pace the floor.

"He is of one mind with our cause," said Latimer. "And but for him, there would be yet less evidence of Reformation in the realm."

Master Knox halted and looked doubtfully at the doctor. "Yet he is an archbishop—*the* archbishop? The man who more than any other guides your Church of England. Is it not he who has made it policy to preserve the idolatrous trappings of Rome? I fear I may not get on well with this man."

"Yet he it is who desires to make your better acquaintance. I tell you, John, he is a friend. A friend who needs you, who seeks out your counsel."

"But for what does he need me?" asked Master Knox.

"We are engaged in a grand and important project," replied Latimer. "He very much desires your wisdom and biblical knowledge on this work."

We were never in attendance with Master Knox when he had conference with the archbishop, so it is impossible for me to offer an eyewitness opinion of the man. I can only observe the effect he had upon our tutor after discussions and collaborations with him occurred, which they did on a number of occasions over the next year.

After one such meeting he returned to us in our abbey lodgings in great agitation. "It is useless! How am I to revise and amend a document so replete with Rome on every page!"

Francis and I had learned that when Master Knox was of this temper we did well to make little intrusion upon his reflections. Mind you, we never feared in the least that he would abuse us in any form, yet when he was enraged over matters about which he cared so deeply, he was, as it were, a man on fire. Hence, we kept silent, out of his path, and did our best merely to observe.

"Lads," he said loudly, turning on us. "Do you ken me as a bishop? Do you, now?"

We assured him that we would never dream of him as such.

"Aye, we're of one mind on that, my lads," he said. "But I wonder the archbishop kens me so little. Do I seem a man to be ducking, crossing, nodding, turning, uplifting, and generally cavorting and strutting about in popish finery? Do I, lads?"

We assured him we could not envision him in any such postures or vestments.

"And, I say, kneeling?"

"Kneeling, Master?" said Francis.

"Aye, kneeling. Mind you, kneeling on our faces in prayer before our gracious heavenly Father is fitting and good. But kneeling at the Supper? It is idolatrous blasphemy, nothing less!"

He paced back and forth, saying nothing for several moments, Francis and I silent at the table. Then he halted.

"*Consummatum est!*" he cried. "So declared our Lord in his passion. 'It is finished!' But to duck and bend at the Table is to say that all is not finished. For poor English souls befuddled by a popish mingle-mangle of the gospel, the Supper thus observed remains a memorial reoffering of Christ's body and blood—base idolatry! As if God the Heavenly Father needs daily reminders of the passion of his dear Son! What is more, the strutting peacocks called priests claim that it is *sacrificium applicatorium*, a sacrifice whereby these false shepherds claim they do and may apply the merits of Christ's passion unto sinners. Saying so is proudly spoken and gives the priests the power to give or withhold peace with God at their pleasure. Though no man may move God to wrath against his chosen ones, yet would these English priests curse the simple with cross, bell, and candle."

With that he fell to pacing and we to feigning labor over our lessons. But moments later he again interrupted his own brooding.

"When I refused his offer of the bishopric of Rochester— imagine it—he proceeded to extend to me a call to the pulpit of All Hallows, Bread Street. 'The most influential pulpit in London,' he termed it."

"Aye, where you preached at Lent," said Francis, grinning. "You certainly laid the papists out with that sermon, Master Knox."

He brushed Francis's comment aside with an impatient wave of his hand. "And a royal chaplaincy thrown into the bargain. I wonder there can be any gospel truth heard by the poor simple folk of this realm. Under every steeple and on every street corner there remains so much popish deception and false doctrine." He paused, astonishment slackening his face and the water whelming in his eyes. "And they call this Reformation!"

23

Swaggering Unquiet Spirit

I SHALL NEVER FORGET the afternoon when Doctor Latimer called at our abbey lodgings with the news. He wrung his hands awkwardly and at first refused to be seated. At last he broke his news, the message he had been commissioned to deliver to our tutor.

"You have been assigned to a pulpit," he began. "And it is my duty to inform you of it, yet does it grieve me greatly to perform it."

"Carry on, man," said Master Knox amiably. "As always, you are among friends here."

"You are called to the north, to the diocese of Durham, to Newcastle, more precisely, to a place called Berwick-upon-Tweed. Do you know it?"

"Aye," said Master Knox simply. "Its infamy extends north as well as south of the border upon which it is situated. I am not ignorant of the fact that Doctor Cranmer has ordered this."

"True enough, he has. Since you were unwilling to accept either bishopric or London pulpit, he has deemed it best, shall we say, to remove you far from centers of influence. Berwick is not a place of healthy belly cheer, but a bawdy wasteland, full of feuding mercenaries from a dozen countries, and all the attendant vices thereof."

"What thinks the archbishop of me that it comes to this?" asked Master Knox.

"He terms you one of the 'swaggering and unquiet spirits, which can like nothing but what is after their own fancy, and cease not to make trouble and disquietude when things be most quiet and in good order.' So speaks the order-loving primate of you, John Knox."

"That is all?"

"Not entirely all. Of your Regulative Principle, he speaks with more than candor."

"It is not, Hugh, my Regulative Principle, as you well know. It is of the Word of God. We include in worship only that which God's Word includes in worship. Anything else is idolatry. It is as simple as that. More than candor, you say?"

"His Excellency, the archbishop, spoke thus: 'I will set my foot by his to be tried in the fire, so certain am I that his Regulative Principle is untrue, and not only untrue but seditious, and perilous to be heard by any subjects, as a thing breaking the bridle of obedience and loosing them from the bond of all princes' laws.' So spoke Doctor Cranmer, and I faithfully have rendered his words, though I, dear brother, do not share his doctrine, nor his sentiments against your person."

"When are we to depart?"

"I am the unhappy harbinger of the very conveyance ordered to carry you north," said Latimer. I believed, from the tremor in his voice, to the languor on his countenance, that it was only with the greatest restraint that he controlled his emotions. "Abrupt as it all is, I am to say that you depart this very day, and may God be with you."

24

Bells and Smells

MY PULSE QUICKENED with every revolution of the carriage wheels conveying us northward, closer to the border, closer to Scotland, to home, perhaps to be reunited with Alexander, to be reunited with our father. I could think of little else on that journey. The lovely green pastures, stone walls, ancient villages, castle walls and turrets, rivers, mountains, spring songbirds nesting along the roadside—nothing had the power to fully divert my attention from the grand object of going home, or at least closer to it. We were, as yet, unwelcome in Scotland, still under the fist of the Queen Regent, Mary of France, mother of the child Queen Mary of Scots.

We arrived in Newcastle-on-Tyne in early spring of the year, according to my reckoning. And Master Knox was received with coolness and suspicion by the local clergy and the mayor, yet were they men under authority, the authority of Archbishop Cranmer, who had sent a commission to them ordering them to have our master preach on the forthcoming Sabbath Day.

We were let out before a narrow house on Percy Street and led up a steep winding stair to an upper chamber with a gable and double window looking out on the market square below. The food was simple but hearty and was delivered to us with cheer and good wishes. In two large pots on either side of the doorway that led to our rooms grew plants called Jacob's Ladders. The proprietor of our chambers doted on these bushes, often watering, weeding, and poking at the soil. Fernlike foliage, lush and green, and rich lavender-blue flowers with yellow stamens were her reward. The prospect of passing between these two potted sentinels made me look forward both to leaving our rooms and returning again to them. Newcastle, on the whole, felt homey, and whatever the real cause, I attributed this to its getting us closer to Scotland.

Master Knox set to work preparing his sermon, with the Vulgate, Erasmus's Greek New Testament, and the Coverdale Bible opened before him. I had observed our tutor preparing sermons many times before, and I was never certain if he spent more time reading and meditating or more time praying and crying out to God for his hearers. It was a great deal of both. I also observed that he wrote little down in his hours of study.

As we walked along the pavement to St. Nicholas Parish Church on the Sabbath morning of April 4, 1550, Master Knox carried nothing but his Coverdale Bible. To my knowledge he never employed any kind of notes for his sermons, but merely opened the Bible to the text before him, read it out, and, with force and feeling, delivered his sermon.

We passed before the black gate of the castle, the cluster of bulky stone turrets looking dark and formidable. I shuddered and made effort to quicken our steps. The sight of that gate, the crenellated towers, and the stony grimness of the place brought to my mind the months of our besieged confinement in St. Andrews Castle—and of its fall under the punishing bombardment of the French. I wondered if there were a bottle dungeon within those walls. My attention was diverted when on our left the crown-like tower of St. Nicholas Church rose above the clustered houses. It was an extraordinary structure, with four delicate stone spires standing at the four corners of the square tower, from which rose the arches that supported the high central spire.

"Ships at sea have long navigated by a light placed high atop the church," said Master Knox. "Fitting, is it not?"

We agreed that it was so. "The tower looks much like St. Giles in Edinburgh," said Francis.

He was right, but St. Nicholas appeared to my eye to be lighter and more delicate. After passing through the great doors, the clustered columns and the pointed arches forced my eyes upward to the timbered arches of the roof, and the blue, yellow, and red of the armorial symbols decorating the ceiling. It was a splendid interior. Gothic arches supported by stone columns lined either side of the nave, and, as we walked toward the high altar, I felt I was going downhill. At the crossing, four enormous octagonal columns stood holding up the great tower we had seen outside. Meanwhile, there was a stirring and rustling as the church began filling up with townsfolk.

My imagination again was set to working. For nearly three hundred years, people just like the ones filling the church that morning had entered these same walls, the medieval footfalls of their steps echoing throughout the stone grandeur of the place, just as folks were doing on that day. All those people of centuries past now lay dead, the important ones entombed beneath the flagstones under my feet, the peasant faithful beneath the sod of the churchyard through which we had just passed, the outcast, cutpurse, and plague victims consigned to the refuse mound on the edge of the town. I was troubled by how little these things had changed over the centuries.

In the melancholy of my musings, I watched the stooped figure of an old woman, though feeble, walking forward with resolution, as near the high altar as she dared, her gnarled walking cane tapping rhythmically on the stone floor. We had been informed that there were Scots refugees in Newcastle who had fled across the border for their lives. Hungrily I studied the faces in the gathering congregation. Might our father not be among them, perhaps Alexander as well? What I observed, however, was a host of important-looking clerics and men and women of rank and station entering with exalted dignity, but I saw no one who looked either like Hugh Douglas or Alexander Cockburn.

In my searching, my attention was drawn to a gaunt man clothed in haphazard layers of tattered cloth. His right leg dragged uselessly behind, and he made his way with a crutch. But it was his face that captured my notice, his cheekbones protruding defiantly as if determined to penetrate the pale flesh that yet covered them. He looked past me with eyes wide and watery, a frightened expectancy in his darting glances.

Master Knox paused near the pulpit, gazing around the church. "Bells and smells," he murmured. Then with a catch in his voice, he continued, "Dear souls who've had the plaster of popery and false doctrine laid upon their wounds, yet the consuming disease rages on. Govern my lips, O Christ."

We were met by a short man, elaborately dressed in the vestments of a priest. "Greetings," he said in a breathy, drawn-out tone, one it was clear that he thought was befitting someone in his exalted station. "I am the Right Reverend Doctor Thomas Boast, priest of St. Nicholas. I am instructed to welcome you into my humble pulpit." He intoned the words with effort, a studied effort that had perhaps long ago begun as an attempt to be precise, but that had now devolved into a mannerism less concerned with clarity and more concerned with showcasing exalted self-importance. And I thought I detected in his tone and in the flush on his cheek more than a hint of resentment. "*Ergo*, I welcome you," he continued, bowing stiffly, his eyes fluttering and remaining more often closed than open throughout his introduction.

Francis and I looked at our schoolmaster. How would he react to the Reverend Thomas Boast?

"Imagine a chap named 'Boast'!" hissed Francis in my ear.

I shrugged. It seemed an odd surname, one quickly to amend, though in this instance perhaps a fitting one. Master Knox was led to a seat near the pulpit and we with him. Thomas Boast left us with a curt bow, his eyes in the closed position.

"He must be constantly bumping into things," I said in Francis's ear.

He nodded. "Aye, Master Knox'll have choice words for this tattie-peeling lot. It should be amusing."

Moments after Thomas Boast left us, the church suddenly erupted with the sounds of organ music. The organist had pulled out all the stops, and loud, rapid notes flitted throughout the church in a dizzying volley of sound. Next everyone rose to their feet and turned toward the aisle. Men and boys in white and black vestments walked solemnly down the aisle, one carrying aloft an elaborately jeweled cross, glittering in the candlelight. Following behind came another robed cleric, this one swinging a censer of incense, blue smoke trailing behind in eerie wisps.

My eyes smarted as the incense settled down in a blue layer over the congregation. Next in the procession came Thomas Boast, bedecked in elaborately embroidered vestments that glittered and shimmered as he walked. Most people crossed themselves and bowed their heads as he strode by them down the aisle. At last the entourage dispersed and the service of worship commenced. Where and when Master Knox's sermon would figure into the goings-on in that service I had no idea, nor, I think, did our tutor.

I often glanced at Master Knox, knowing full well that he would be sickened by all the trumpery going on in that house of God. The liturgy was, indeed, read in English, and Scripture was read also in the common vernacular, yet did I know the trappings of popery in it all would not please our master.

At last, with a fluttering of eyelids and an impatient nod from Thomas Boast, Master Knox made his way up the steps of the pulpit. I wondered what would follow. Never did a man seem more out of place than Master Knox in his coarse black robe surrounded by high church pomp and ceremony. But our tutor was never daunted by his roughness when amidst the high and mighty. On many occasions I observed how the loftier the audience, the more confident and bold he was in his delivery. That morning, as he so often did when he preached, he surveyed with tenderness the upturned faces of the several hundred people gathered. He then slowly opened his Coverdale Bible and read out his text, his voice clear and firm.

Next he prayed aloud, though I had heard him pray in like fashion when he thought no one heard him. Such was the way with Master Knox and praying.

"O Lord eternal! Move and govern my tongue to speak the truth and the hearts of thy people to understand and obey the same."

Thereafter, he delivered a fearless sermon—I believe that all Master Knox's sermons were, indeed, delivered without the fear of men. His sermons have been described as thunderclaps, and there is some truth in the metaphor. That morning in Newcastle Church he labored to demonstrate the vast difference between the Mass and the Lord's Supper. I must confess that prior to this sermon I continued to entertain the notion that there was little if any significant difference in the two: there was bread; there was wine; there was ceremony. Mere wrangling of theologians, so I had thought it. But Master Knox that day in St. Nicholas Church, Newcastle, thundered in ways that began powerfully to change my mind.

25

Abominable Idolatry

HE BEGAN CALMLY, in a soft, meek tone. I knew it would not remain so.

"Let no man intend to excuse the Mass with the pretext of the Lord's Supper. For now will I prove that the Mass has no congruence but is expressly contrary to the Lord's Supper, and, thereby, has taken the remembrance intended in the Supper out of the minds of the participants. And further, it is blasphemous to the death of Jesus Christ.

"First, they are contrary in institution. For the Lord's Supper was instituted to be a perpetual memory of those benefits which we have received by Jesus Christ and by his death. Call to mind in what estate we stood in the loins of Adam, when we all blasphemed the majesty of God in his face.

"Secondly, that God's own incomprehensible goodness moved him to love us most wretched and miserable, yea, most wicked and blasphemous, and with a love most perfect compelled him to show mercy. And mercy pronounced the sentence, which was that his only Son should pay the price of our redemption. Which payment being rightly called to memory in the present action of the Supper, could not but move us to unfeigned thanksgiving unto God the Father, and to his only Son Jesus, who has restored us again to liberty and life. And this is it which Paul commands, saying, 'As often as ye shall eat of this bread, and drink of this cup, ye shall declare the Lord's death till he come.' That is, you shall laud, magnify, and extol the liberal kindness of God the Father, and the infinite benefits which you have received by Christ's death."

Master Knox's words began to cut as if with a sharp sword into my very heart. I had, of course, many times sat under his teaching, but it was these his words at St. Nicholas Church that morning in April of 1550 that laid bare my soul and made me quiver within, both with terror and with longing, to know what it all meant.

"But the Mass is instituted," he continued, "as the plain words thereof and the papists' own laws do witness, to be a re-sacrifice for the sins of the living and the dead. Of which sacrifice, they claim, God is bound not only to remit our sins, but also to give unto us whatever thing we will ask. Masses are celebrated for the most diverse causes: some for peace in time of war, some for rain, some for fair weather; yea, and (alas, my heart abhors such abomination!) some for sickness of beasts. Using the false sacrament of the Mass for the obtaining of such vain trifles is a profanation of the true sacrament of Christ's body and blood, herein abused, which should never be used but in memory of Christ's death. They admit in the Mass to offering prayers that the toothache be taken away, that our oxen should not take the lowing ill, our horse and cattle not take the spavin or farcy maladies. Perverse priests! Yea, what is it for which you would *not* say Mass?"

At his words, there were rustlings that sounded like murmured agreement from many, and yet there were rumblings that could be not but the gnashing of the teeth of priests and prelates in attendance that day. Master Knox seemed little concerned with the hissing of the latter. He pressed his argument, making further the contrast between the false Mass and the true Supper.

"The Supper of the Lord is the gift of Jesus Christ, in which we should laud the infinite mercy of God. The Mass, they say, is a sacrifice which we offer unto God, and for the doing of it the papists allege that God should love and commend us.

"But in the Supper of the Lord, we confess ourselves redeemed from sin by the death and blood of Jesus Christ only. In the Mass, we are taught to crave remission of sins, aye, and whatsoever other trifle we desire, and all by the working of that same work which we do ourselves. And herein is the Mass blasphemous unto Christ and his passion. For insofar as it offers remission of sins, it imputes imperfection upon Christ and his sacrifice; affirming that all sins were not remitted by his death, but that a great part are reserved to be purged by virtue and the value of the Mass. And also it is injurious unto Christ Jesus, not only by speaking most falsely of him, but also by usurping to the sacrament itself that which is proper to Christ alone. For Christ affirms that he alone has, by his own death, purged the sins of the world, and that no part remains to be purged by any other means. But the Mass sings another song, which is, that every day, by that oblation offered by the priests, sin is purged and remission obtained. Consider, papists, what honor your Mass robs from Christ Jesus!"

There was now throughout the church a breath-gasping silence at his words. I feared that silence more than the previous rumblings. Again our schoolmaster, free of trepidation, pressed his argument.

"In the true Supper of the Lord, we acknowledge ourselves to be eternal debtors to God, and unable in any way to make satisfaction for his infinite benefits which we have received. But in your Mass, it is alleged that God is a debtor unto us for the pouring out of that sacrifice which the priest offers and dares to affirm that in the Mass we make satisfaction for the sins of ourselves and of others.

"If the true Supper and the Mass be not contrary, let men judge without partiality. They differ in practice, for in the Lord's Supper the minister and the congregation sit both at one table, no difference between them in preeminence or habit, as seen with Jesus Christ and his disciples, and in the practice of the apostles after his death. But in the papistical Mass, the priests (so they call themselves) are placed by themselves at one altar. And I would ask of what authority and what Scripture commands it so to be done? They must be clad in layers of vestments, whereof no mention is made in the New Testament. It will not excuse them to say Paul commanded all to be done with order and decency. Dare they be so bold as to affirm that the Last Supper of Jesus Christ was done without order, and indecently, wherein were worn no such disguised vestments? Or will they set up to us again the Levitical priesthood? Should not all be taught by the plain words of the new covenant?

"Prelates or priests, I ask one question: You prefer the vestments of Aaron in all things. Aaron had affixed unto his garments certain bells, which were commanded to ring, and to make sound, as often as he was clad therein. But, priests, your bells want tongues; they ring not; they sound of nothing but of the earth. The people understand nothing of all your ceremonies. Fear you not the wrath of God? It was commanded Aaron that the sound of bells should be heard, indicating that he yet lived. Yet your bells ring not."

There was rustling of feet and garments at this, and I fretted that Master Knox might have exceeded all boundaries with such a pointed rebuke. I feared what would befall if he had. Yet he, devoid of any visible sign of fear, pressed on.

"In the Supper of the Lord all were equally participants: the bread being broken, and the cup being distributed amongst all, according to his holy commandment. In the papistical Mass, the congregation gets nothing except the beholding of your jukings, noddings, crossings, turning, uplifting, which are nothing but a diabolical profanation of Christ's Supper. Now, juke, cross, and nod as you want; they are nothing but your own inventions."

Here our schoolmaster's tone became gentle, more fatherly. For a moment, at least, he seemed to have shifted with tenderness to the peasant and laboring man, the child and the old woman hearing his words.

"Finally, dear brethren, in the Mass you get nothing, but merely look on while the priests eat and drink all. It is no excuse to say that you, Christ's dear flock, are participating spiritually."

But his tender tone was but for a moment, and his rage at the priests returned. It was remarkable to see how a man so meek and frail in other respects was, when in the pulpit and fulfilling his calling, transformed into a mouthpiece of such weight and force. It was truly astonishing to behold.

"O wicked antichrists! Jesus Christ said no such thing. He said, 'Eat of this, and drink of this; all do this in remembrance of me.' Christ commanded not that one should gaze upon it, bow, juke, and beck thereto, but that we should eat and drink thereof ourselves, and not that we should behold others do the same, by which we confess the death of Jesus Christ to mean nothing to us. For when I eat and drink at that table, I openly confess the fruit and virtue of Christ's body, of his blood and passion, to appertain to myself; and I confess that I am a member of his mystical body, and that God the Father, in Christ alone, is pleased with me, notwithstanding my original corruption and present infirmities."

Again his tone grew tender as he directed his words to the common people there gathered.

"Judge, brethren, what comfort have they taken from us with their Mass. I would ask, first, if the mere sight of meat and drink does feed or nourish your body? I think we will all say, 'Nay.' And so I affirm that no more profit receives the soul in beholding another eat and drink the Lord's very Supper (as for their idolatry, it is always damnable), than the body does in beholding another eat and drink, and goes away unnourished thereby.

"But now briefly, let this contradiction be examined. In the Lord's Supper we are brought to thanksgiving for the saving benefits which we have received of God. Contrarily, in the Mass, the papist presumes to compel God to grant all that he asks of him, by virtue of the sacrifice, and so alleges that God should render thanks unto the priest that does the Mass.

"Moreover, in the Supper of the Lord, the participants humbly do confess themselves redeemed only by Christ's blood, which once was shed. In the Mass, the priest vaunts himself to make a sacrifice for the sins of the living and the dead. In the Lord's Supper, all the partakers at that table grant and confess themselves debtors unto God, unable to render sufficient thanks for the benefits which we have received of his liberality. In the papistical

Mass, the priest alleges that God is a debtor to him, and unto all of them for whom he makes that sacrifice. For he does affirm remission of sins to be obtained thereby. And in that affirmation the Mass is blasphemous to Christ's death.

"Consider now, beloved brethren: The Mass is nothing but the invention of man, set up without authority of God's Word, and, therefore, the Mass is idolatry. Unto it is added a vain, false, deceitful, and most wicked opinion: that is, that by it a man may obtain remission of sins; and, therefore, it is an abomination before God. It is contrary unto the Supper of Jesus Christ, and has taken away both the right use and remembrance thereof, and, therefore, it is blasphemous to Christ's death.

"Let no man think that, because I am in the realm of England, therefore so boldly I speak against this abomination. Nay, God by his mercy and goodness has freed my heart, hand, and tongue to confess the truth, whether in painful bonds or amidst cruel tyrants. And here I call my God to record that neither profit to myself, hatred of any person, nor affection or favor that I bear toward any private man, causes me this day to speak as you have heard; but only the obedience which I owe unto God in this my calling, that is, showing forth his Word, and the common love which I bear to the salvation of all men. For so odious and abominable I know the Mass to be in God's presence, that unless you decline from the same, you can never attain life eternal through the merits of Christ alone. Therefore, brethren, flee from that idolatry more than you would flee from death itself."

He closed his Bible and descended from the pulpit. For a lengthy moment, nothing happened. No one rose to speak, no organ blew a note, no one in the congregation made a sound or moved from his place. Silence, prolonged and awkward, reigned for several minutes.

Yet silence could not possibly be the final response to such a salvo. Our Master Knox was a master at creating a stir wherever he preached. I knew this to a degree already, yet would I learn to plumb the depths of this knowledge more fully in what lay ahead.

During the silence, Master Knox had rejoined us. It was Thomas Boast who broke the silence. He strode in our direction.

Francis gave a low whistle. "His face looks like a dragon's. I don't doubt he'll be breathing fire."

He halted before our tutor. "His Excellency," he said with a sniff, "the Right Reverend Bishop of Durham was in attendance today at your rantings. He, Cuthbert Tunstall himself, awaits you in my vestry."

26

Muddy Berwick

A GREAT DEAL HAPPENED in the hours that followed. Cuthbert Tunstall, Bishop of Durham, raged before our schoolmaster for more than hour. "You shall have every man be a babbler on the Bible and a meddler with the Scripture!" He was furious, and I expected him to strike our tutor at any moment, but Master Knox stood unflinching before the verbal assault laid on by the man.

When at last the aged bishop had so exhausted himself with his railings that I thought he might be sickening himself and going down the brae, he dismissed us curtly.

"If Archbishop Thomas Cranmer had not assigned you to preach to the God-forsaken, wretched garrison at Berwick," he said, his voice raspy and spent, "I would forthwith defrock you and banish you from ever again preaching in the realm of England!"

That very day we were bundled up like the bedclothes of a plague victim and sent away from Newcastle. For as long as we were in the company of our tutor, I wondered if it would be forever our lot to be outcasts. In a gandiegow of spring rain that turned the roadway into a muddy slough, the carriage did its best to take us yet farther north, closer to Scotland, to the England side of the River Tweed. My heart ached for Scotland, for home, and for the north.

As we jostled, bogged, and slithered along the road, Master Knox prayed aloud, "O God Eternal! Hast thou laid none other burden upon our backs than Jesus Christ laid by his Word?" There were times when I couldn't be sure if he was praying or merely speaking with us. This was one of those times. He continued, "Then who has burdened us with all these ceremonies, prescribed fastings, compelled chastity, unlawful vows, invocation of saints, with the idolatry of the Mass? The Devil, the Devil, my lads, he it is who invented all these burdens to depress imprudent men to perdition."

I ventured to ask him a question that had been on my mind these many months. "If this is Reformation England, why does so much of Rome remain?"

"Aye, the pope's name and authority is suppressed in England," he replied, "but his laws and corruptions remain in full vigor."

Cautiously, I pulled back the shutter. Drawing my cloak more tightly about my neck, I shivered at the clinging dampness. The stone arches of a bridge lay to my left, and smoke hovered over the black slate roofs of a village. Following my gaze, Master Knox leaned forward and said, "This Bishop of Durham, Cuthbert Tunstall, Lord President of the King's Council in the North," he continued, "illustrates the point. Tunstall cares a great deal for the false doctrines of Rome, but cares nothing for the Word of God alone. He's been long at it. It was Tunstall who acted treacherously with Master Tyndale, railed against his English Bible, burned piles of them at St. Paul's Cross in London, and then rejoiced at the burning of the good man himself. Yet he remains a bishop in this Reformation England."

"Berwick!" shouted the driver. Blowing and snorting, the horses came to a stand, and we stepped out of the carriage to look on the place about which I had heard many things, Berwick-on-Tweed. Not one report of the place had been good. The carriage, the horses, and the driver were plastered with mud, and it seemed that the whole village wore the same covering. Leather-clad soldiers and hooded women moved about the dingy streets. The driver hastily threw down our luggage and seemed eager to be on his way.

The pavement on which we and our luggage alighted was covered in mud and filth, and we had no sooner gathered up our bags when we heard singing—of a sort. Three men staggered toward us, blethering out the lines:

> Bring ush in good ale, and bring ush in good ale,
> For our Blessed Lady's sake, bring ush in good ale.

There were more stanzas than this, but these seemed to be the burden of the lyric. They appeared to be soldiers, but ones blootered from being too long at the cup, ones clearly in need of no more ale—good or bad—that much was certain. The man in the middle of the three was supported by the others and staggered more than his fellows. His face was bloodied and one eye was aflame and swollen entirely shut. His tunic and trousers were rent and soiled as if he had been in a brawl.

"We must move!" I shouted.

But it was too late. Looking back, I cannot be certain that it was wholly intentional, but the result to Master Knox was the same. They knocked him down, the slurring lyric of their drinking song interrupted momentarily by their uproarious laughter at the sight of our tutor face downward in the refuse on the pavement.

Attempting to rise, Master Knox said, "A warm welcome, indeed." Gray-brown slime dripped from his chin and nose.

Francis grabbed his arms, lifting him from the pavement and aiding him in the recovery of his footing.

Our tutor, hopelessly besmeared with mud, caught sight of himself in the window glass of the public house before which the carriage had dropped us. I wondered if he would rail fiercely after the drunken soldiers, as he had railed against idolatry in Newcastle, perhaps call in the magistrate and have them arrested for ill-treating him. But he did no such thing.

Wiping muck from his face, he looked up at the sign above the door and said, "Now then, lads, let's see if there's refreshment and a hot bath to be had at the King's Arms."

27

Love

In the months that lay ahead, we were to encounter a good deal more rough and coarse usage in Berwick. But our master reacted in the most unusual fashion to coarse society, ill-treatment, and abuse. London and its sophistication and political wrangling had aggravated our tutor. But here as preacher at the King's garrison, he was surrounded by common men, soldiers defending Protestant England's northern border against Scotland, a Scotland yet under the power of Catholic France. Berwick was to his taste. He preferred preaching to battle-hardened mercenaries, foul-smelling fishermen too long at the ale bench, giddy women from the brothels, the working poor, the peasant farmer hawking his turnips in the market. And to Scottish refugees who flooded the border towns, especially Berwick and Newcastle. We met these refugees with hungry expectancy, hoping to discover news of our father or Alexander, but to no avail.

After days of staying in chambers above the King's Arms in Berwick, we were driven out to the garrison at Norham Castle. Standing high atop a rocky outcrop on the south banks of the

River Tweed, Norham was an impressive fortification built centuries ago to guard England's northern border from Scottish invasion.

"Norham Castle!" shouted the carriage driver.

A short, sturdy man awaited us as we stepped out of the coach.

"Bailey's the name," he said amiably, taking up our baggage with one sweep of his great hands.

"Did you see that?" said Francis in my ear. "He hefted all our baggage as if it were nothing more than goose feathers."

Bailey's physique gave me the impression of a stone block with stout arms and legs. Not only strong as an ox, Bailey was a chatty fellow, whose age I was never able to determine. He appeared old, but in a manner that gave the impression that he had always been old and had long ago made his peace with the fact. He further elucidated his age with his accounts of battles and sieges he had survived while serving a succession of wardens at Norham Castle.

"Built in 1121 to fend off robbers and Scots," he said—then bowing slightly to our tutor, he added, "begging pardon, that is, of the present company. Bishops of Durham have long maintained these walls. Bishops are an ornery lot that come and go; while Norham's outlived them all." He led us over a drawbridge and through the gatehouse, talking all the while. Passage through the gatehouse was like passing through a tunnel; the castle wall must have been nearly twenty feet thick. I commented on such sturdy fortification.

"Stout she is," said Bailey, patting the wall as if it were an old friend. "Withstood the most recent bombardment of our northern neighbor in 1513. I was here. Saw it all. Them cursed Scots—begging pardon—leveled the massive siege cannon they call 'Mons Meg' and let fly at these walls, but to little effect, as you see. 'The most dangerous place in England,' she's called. Yet here she stands."

The gatehouse arch framed the massive Norman keep, walled by yet another fortification. Bailey led us across the outer ward, through another gatehouse, and over another drawbridge and the moat into the inner ward.

"Norham's no solitary laird's manor house. She's home to an active garrison, as you see." Bailey paused, nodding at two dozen soldiers drilling with pikes on the green of the inner ward, sunlight flashing on their helms and breastplates. Armored sentries patrolled the crenellated walls, and other men-at-arms cleaned and repaired weapons. I saw men nudge one another and cast their eyes upon Master Knox. We passed the dark glowing cave of the blacksmith, ringing with the clanging of hammers on steel.

"Bishops of Durham, as I said, think they own the place," continued Bailey, "but Norham's actually under the civil authority of the Warden of the East Marches." His head bobbed as he recited the title. "And the acting warden is Deputy Warden Sir Robert Bowes." He withdrew from his tunic a great ring of keys. Rattling through them, he said. "Aye, then, just here is your billet."

We followed our guide up a narrow winding staircase and into our chambers in the west corner of the Great Tower. A fire crackled at the hearth, and a trestle table was laid with coarse bread, cheeses, cold beef, and ale. "If you have need of anything," said Bailey, "I am he commissioned to look after you."

Master Knox asked Bailey questions about the warden, the garrison, and the region, and about preaching and divine services of worship. "Been little of that hereabouts," he said. "But you're to preach on the morrow, in the great hall, so I'm told." He turned to go, then slapped his forehead and added. "And Sir Robert's sister-in-law and niece are here at the moment and shall attend, so I'm told." With that, he was gone.

Late in the morning of the following day Master Knox was summoned to preach. The hall of the Great Tower was a large room that smelled of oiled leather, wolf hide, candle wax, and dried heather. Carved wooden timbers, blackened with centuries of smoke, held up the roof, and the walls were hung with tapestries of hunting themes and grape harvests. Guarding the walls stood shiny suits of armor, with swords, halberds, lances, and battleaxes on display throughout. Above the vast fireplace at the west end an eight-point stag trophy presided over the room. There were long tables and chairs and cushions set out on the stone floor. A gray wolfhound sprawled before the fire, and servants carried platters of meat and pots of ale to the tables.

"Is it to be a banquet or a sermon?" said Francis.

Master Knox was introduced to Sir Robert Bowes, Deputy Warden of the castle and garrison, and to his brother Sir Richard and his wife and daughter. Sir Robert set my spine to tingling. He studied us through gray eyes, narrowed in slits and devoid of feeling; his cheeks were sharp, his skin pale, and his iron gray hair hung in oily strands past his shoulders. On either side of the man sat his relations. Sir Richard was a distracted man, playing often with his fingers, his listless eyes gazing at nothing. It seemed obvious that Sir Robert was the master of the affairs of this extended family.

Elizabeth Bowes looked like she had once been an attractive woman but was now weary of life. She had developed the habit, so it seemed, of glancing anxiously at her husband; she reminded me of a frightened hare. I couldn't help feeling pity for her. Marjory, their daughter, was another matter altogether. I believe this might have been the first time in my short life that I began to become aware of the intriguing qualities of the fair sex. She was five or six years my senior, by my reckoning, which would make her about twenty years of age. She wore a blue silk gown, and from under her lace wimple hung long wavy auburn hair. Something about the way she sat, her shoulders squared, her chin level, and her dark eyes sparkling with life as if she had discovered a humorous side to an otherwise cheerless existence. I must confess, to my mind, she seemed perfect in her every feature.

Francis placed a well-aimed jab at my ribcage and whispered, "Your eyes, brother," and he winked with his fingers in that annoying manner of his.

Sir Robert called out in a voice that reminded me of gravel being dumped from a barrow, "Well, man, let's get on with it." He made no effort to conceal his scorn for preaching, or was it scorn for the sort of preaching he anticipated from our tutor?

Unruffled, Master Knox bowed slightly and strode to a lectern before the fire. From where we sat on the floor, I amused myself by moving slightly to the left, thereby aligning the trophy buck so that he seemed to perch atop our tutor's head.

"By God's grace," began Master Knox, "I declare Jesus Christ, the strength of his death, and the power of his resurrection."

While he preached I studied the faces of the Bowes family. Sir Richard continued drumming his fingers. His brother, Sir Robert, knew the routine and settled back in his chair, his eyes drooping, his mouth sagging. Before Master Knox had finished reading out his text, the man's breathing became heavy and regular, giving off the sounds of a highland cow after a long morning of grazing on the moorland. With a slap of our tutor's palm on the lectern, Sir Robert's snoring was abruptly stifled in a snort. The wolfhound whimpered, and the warden clamped his teeth, sat up, and scowled at our master. Fully awake now, his face grew red with anger the longer he listened.

Elizabeth and Marjory's attention to our master's sermon could not have been more contrary to the men's. Their expressions were of someone discovering, after diligent searching, a long-forgotten treasure, or perhaps the solution to a vexing dilemma.

"Everlasting death," continued Master Knox, "has had, and shall have, power and dominion over all who have not been born from above. This rebirth is wrought by the power of the Holy Spirit mercifully creating in the hearts of God's chosen ones an assured faith in the saving promises of God revealed to us in his Word. By this faith all who are poor in spirit may grasp Christ Jesus with the graces and blessings promised in him. Be freed today from this everlasting death. Repent and lay hold of Christ and his promised grace in the gospel."

When he had finished his sermon, Sir Robert growled something incomprehensible, though I felt certain it included something about a "runagate Scot." And then he stomped from the hall, his wolfhound glancing our way and growling at his heels. Sir Richard rose and followed his brother from the room.

The reaction of mother and daughter, however, was entirely of another kind. As the men disappeared from the room, the women seemed to bloom into life, and for more than an hour, we sat at table with them, Francis and I partaking liberally of beef and cheese and washing it down with Norham ale, mother and daughter making earnest inquiry of Master Knox.

"How is one to come by this r-rebirth, as you have termed it?" asked Elizabeth.

"And be forever freed from this everlasting death?" asked Marjory.

As Master Knox answered their questions, I felt as if I were in the company of intensely parched and thirsting souls.

Bailey, whose duty required him to attend upon these conversations, murmured at my side, "I've never heard such good news afore."

In the months that followed, Master Knox preached often before the soldiers of the garrison. They first shuffled into the chapel in a begrudging manner, some of them hostile, disruptive, even threatening. One big fellow would collapse into a chair, thump his boots onto the seat in front of him, and, on the instant, feign sleep and a flatulent snoring. Master Knox, however, had a unique ability to pass over their belligerence, even to tame or divert it, and preached with fellow-feeling and winsomeness, and somehow he managed to convey all this with inexplicable force and authority.

"Remission of sins comes only of the mere mercy of God, without any deserving from us or any work proceeding from ourselves. As Isaiah recorded of God himself, 'I am he who removeth thine iniquity, and that for my own sake.'"

It was remarkable to behold the effect our tutor's words had upon the battle-hardened soldiers of that garrison. And he was called upon to preach in the Great Hall, sometimes several times in the week. Acts of Uniformity that required observance notwithstanding, Sir Robert rarely attended divine services, begging to be excused for some pressing civil duty. His brother Richard was more often there in body, though he seemed a man with little interest in divine things; the blandness of his features made me wonder if he had interest in anything. But Elizabeth and Marjory were never absent and often continued in lengthy conversation with Master Knox after the sermon and service had drawn to its conclusion.

Over these months Francis and I began to observe a change in our master.

"Have you seen the way he looks upon Marjory?" said Francis, after we had attended one particularly prolonged conversation.

"Aye, perhaps a wee bit," I said. "Though I cannot discern what it is."

"That, my brother, is because of your age and inexperience."

"Aye, and when you g-go and say things like that to me, I've noticed that your eyes begin f-fluttering like Thomas Boast's do. It's a sort of manner of uplifting of yourself, brother. I think I may now rechristen you, His Excellency, Francis Boast."

"Aye, and you're a fine one to speak about *my* eyes."

We tussled back and forth in this fashion for some minutes. It was nothing new to us.

"By my reckoning," continued Francis, "Master Knox is thirty-seven years of age, or thereabouts."

"Aye, so he is. And just what does that have to do with anything?"

"Wee brother," he said, shaking his head in a fashion that seemed to indicate he had not met another living human being so manifestly ignorant of the world and its ways. He continued, speaking louder and drawing out each syllable, "It means he's of the marriageable stage of life."

"M-marriageable?"

"Aye, marriage. Man, woman, love, marriage, the bedchamber, children, family. You ken it: marriage. Anyone can see it on his features."

"See what?"

"It's as obvious as looking through the portcullis of a castle," he said in exasperation. "The man's in love!"

28

Knox and the King

WHILE MASTER KNOX CONTINUED preaching the gospel
to the garrison at the Great Hall of Norham Castle and at the
parish church in Berwick, political unrest fomented in London.
In the autumn of 1551, word reached the Berwick garrison that
trouble had erupted amongst the court advisors to young King
Edward VI. In a bold political stroke, on October 16, 1551, John
Dudley, Duke of Northumberland, challenged and overthrew
the Regent, Edward Seymour.

"A *coup d'état*," I said.

"A coup de what?" said Francis.

"A hostile seizure of power," said Master Knox, slapping a fist
into his palm, "which will without a doubt result in the execution of the ousted regent. How will Reformation prevail in this
benighted land amidst such base, treacherous fellows!"

The next day Master Knox received a letter from Hugh Latimer, which stated that the archbishop had arranged for our tutor
to preach again in Newcastle. On All Saints Day, 1551, under the
frowns of Thomas Boast and the mayor of Newcastle, Master

Knox again climbed the steps of the pulpit of St. Nicholas Church to preach.

"By this palace revolution," declared our master, "the devil and his ministers intend the subversion of God's true religion by that mortal hatred among those who ought to have been most assuredly knit together by Christian love."

He roundly condemned the *coup d'état*. "This ungodly breach of charity is the handiwork of wicked and envious papists who have used the Duke of Northumberland as their pawn to weaken and destroy Reformation and most certainly to bring about his own destruction. By this treachery, the hedges, ditches, towers, and winepresses in this vineyard of the Lord are broken down, and shall bring forth no good and lasting fruit. This away-taking of the Duke of Somerset, once Regent of Edward VI, shall mark the decline of the Protestant cause and shall weaken the whole realm of England."

I feared that when our master's words came to the ears of the court in London, there might be yet another away-taking—this time of the life of Master Knox himself. In the anxious months that followed, I daily feared that Sir Robert would break in on a sermon while our tutor preached at the Great Hall in Norham, or that a sergeant-of-the-guard and his troop would break in on a chapel sermon and drag our master away in chains. And that would be the end of him.

Meanwhile, during these months I began to take more notice of Master Knox and Marjory Bowes. I confess at that stage in my young life I was never as clearly aware of the mysteries of love and marriage as my brother claimed to be. Yet, even I could not remain entirely ignorant of their growing attachment. An inexplicable momentary suspension of the conjugation of a Latin verb in our lessons, *amo, amas, amat, amamus* . . . his words trailing off, and an instant of sublime tenderness reflecting in his blue-gray eyes; or any number of other lapses in concentration or the fractional suspension of a word or phrase.

No soldiery burst in on a sermon, but one day in June of 1552, word arrived from the court in London that Master Knox's presence was imminently required. I feared that this bode ill for our fate. We once again made the long journey by coach. With every bone-jarring lurch of that conveyance, I felt myself carried nearer destruction. I fretted that Master Knox was sure to be called up on charges of treason for his bold denunciations of Lord Dudley. I worried still more that Francis and I would be implicated with him. Once again, I wondered at the wisdom of our association with the man. We had thus far been nearly destroyed with him after the burning of John Wishart in our perilous flight from Longniddry, nearly destroyed in the siege and down-falling of a castle, and nearly met our end in the grueling deprivations of the galleys. What awaited us in London—and we insanely carrying ourselves to our own destruction of our own will—it all tortured my imagination. Yet Master Knox behaved as if we were embarking on a holiday; he highlighted the scenic beauty we passed by on the journey, read aloud from the New Testament in Latin, Greek, and English, propounding on the intricacies of creating a precise conjunction of meaning in the three languages, and he prayed, always aloud, and long, and with feeling.

"Are you not afraid?" I blurted at last.

"Afraid?" he said as if the word was unfamiliar to him, not to be found in his catalog of vocabulary.

"Aye, the Duke of Northumberland—he chopped off the head of his friend. What might he do to you—to us?"

"We are in God's hands, lads. Not in the duke's."

His confidence notwithstanding, I puzzled over whether it would be hanging, beheading, or the stake for Master Knox—and for us. The final ruts we passed through on the road as we drew near to London each felt like the foreshadowing of my plunge into the abyss.

When we at last arrived in London, and after several torturous days of anxiety, we were summoned to appear before the new regent, John Dudley, Duke of Northumberland. I was nearly faint with dread. But to my astonishment, he greeted Master Knox with cordiality and proceeded to appoint him royal chaplain to His Majesty, Edward VI, and invite him to preach before the king at Westminster Abbey on the forthcoming Sabbath Day.

"It's like a giant tomb," said Francis in my ear as we followed Master Knox into the great abbey church.

I swallowed and felt a quavering down my spine at his words.

Nudging me in the ribs, he hissed, "Your eyes."

We were led past the nave, through the elaborately gilded altar screen into the quire. The ribbed vaulting of the ceiling seemed higher than that of any other church I had been in, and our footfalls echoed throughout the stony magnificence of its walls, arches, and clustered columns. A robed verger with drawn sword motioned for us to be seated in the first row of three tiers of carved oaken pews, the designer of which had apparently given no thought to comfort, but configured them to absolutely demand an upright posture of the sitter. In fact, we were compelled to sit so rigidly upright that I felt I was being prodded forward. I suppose this forced all in attendance into a posture that appeared to be yearning and attentive. Across the aisle and to our right stood the pulpit.

There were some sixty or seventy people gathered, all of them bedecked like peacocks in silk and satin and lace, the men wearing small collars, silk hose, trunks, and doublet, clearly all of the upper crust, as it were. How Francis and I came to be among such exalted company, I have no explanation, though no doubt our master who was to preach had seen to our being included and similarly dressed in the latest London fashion.

The carved pews rose in three tiers, facing each other on both sides of a central aisle. Rows of candles were mounted on each tier to give light for our reading out of the liturgy. The flame of the candle poised above my place suddenly flickered.

"Hail to His Majesty, King Edward VI!" called the harbinger.

I had not heretofore seen a king. The Queen Regent of Scotland I had seen, but never a genuine king. Ermine fur flecked with black streaks lined his doublet, which he wore widely off the shoulder and open, giving the impression that he but carelessly threw on the garment. On his head, tilted at a slight angle, he wore a flat cap, adorned with delicate jewel work, a white feather drooping over his left ear. His red hair was neatly trimmed and seemed to create a precise frame around his pale face. His blue eyes were serious but sparkled as if he had just looked upon some splendid thing that had left some of its splendor behind. His eyes and face lacked the steely luster of command that I had expected to see in the eyes of a king, and his mouth looked like he was perpetually on the verge of whistling a melody. My inspection of his features was made more easy since, to my horror, he was gazing in our direction.

Francis's elbow came sharply into my ribcage. "He's looking our way," he said without moving his lips. "The King of England's looking at us!"

It was, indeed, true. I nodded, and the king returned the nod with a smile. He had an extraordinary presence. According to what we had been told, Edward was very much unlike his father in matters of religion and Reformation. Contrary to his father, he believed the pure doctrines of Christ and his gospel and cared little for temporal power. There was something about his manner and posture, as I observed him that day, that compelled me to believe this.

Master Knox sat calmly by us while the liturgy was being read out by the archbishop, Thomas Cranmer. The service had been underway for some minutes when Master Knox placed a hand on my neck and the other on Francis's. Drawing us toward him, as was his manner, he whispered, "The Roman order, but in English."

At last it was time for our master to mount the pulpit and to preach. Odd it was, to my mind, but every time he was to preach before the mighty, as he surely was that day, my heart pounded out of its place, my palms grew clammy, my stomach rumbled, and my face became instantly hot and beaded up with sweat. I glanced about the quire at the silken brilliance of the exalted company therein gathered, and I could not help but feel the incongruity of Master Knox. Though I could detect nothing of this on the young king's expression, many of his courtiers' faces betrayed with a sneer that they thought him unworthy to stand before their greatness. The human face is remarkably eloquent of the soul. This was by no means the feature of all present. There were merchant families whose wealth and stature had secured them a place in the first rank of London society, notably the Locke and Hickman families, who were devoted supporters of true Reformation and, hence, of our master.

But Master Knox, as he laid open his Bible on the lectern, gave not the least sign that he felt their scorn. He bowed slightly toward the king and read out his text. "Give the king your justice, O God, and your righteousness to the royal son!" And then he proceeded, in his earthy, forceful manner, to expound the psalm verse by verse and phrase by phrase. Though we had heard critics term him the Thundering Scot and labor to portray him as a preacher more akin to a maniac than a minister of the gospel, this sounded oddly in our ears, we who had heard him preach more often than any. He was indeed bold, free, and devoid of all fear in his delivery, yet did he often plead with the weak, encourage the frail, and tenderly chide the halting in his ministrations from the pulpit. His manner that day before the young king of England was more that of a tender father, at times comforting, at others, gently rebuking, and still at others, urging with command and force.

"Sire, you are not unaware of how much danger kings and princes are in. The exalted height to which kings have been elevated more often dazzles them with their own greatness, amuses them with their own prerogatives, and at the last makes them forgetful of the heavenly kingdom, and of Christ the King over all kings and kingdoms. But I doubt not, sire, that God by his grace has so warned you against this evil as to preserve you from it. It is indeed a great thing to be a king, and still more, king over such a country. Nevertheless, sire, I have no doubt that you reckon it incomparably greater to be a Christian, that is, a grateful subject of the King of kings. It is an invaluable privilege that God has vouchsafed to you, sire, that he has made you a Christian king, to serve as his lieutenant in ordering and maintaining the kingdom of Jesus Christ in this his and your realm of England."

I glanced often at the young king's pale face during the sermon. He sat upright, leaning forward in his throne, his eyes intent on Master Knox as he listened. Our master preached as if there were no one else present, as if they sat companionably before the hearth in the family room, just he and the king. His words were respectful but not fawning, substantive but never erudite and exalted, simple but never condescending. He spoke as I had heard my father speak at times to me in my youth. In that sermon, my heart once again ached for home.

After Master Knox concluded his sermon and again sat at my side, the archbishop commenced the institution of the Lord's Supper. Master Knox was agitated. "The popish Mass, but in English," he murmured. When it came time to receive the elements of bread and wine, the lectionary indicated that we were to assume a kneeling posture. His face the color of a ripening tomato, Master Knox did not kneel; seeing this, neither did Francis and I.

"Kneeling springs from a false opinion," he explained to us after the service. Becoming more agitated as we walked through the cloister, he recited and briefly expounded Scripture texts to support his argument. At last, before the door of our chambers, he turned and said, "Kneeling permits the idolater to continue in his idolatry."

Master Knox was called on not infrequently to preach before young Edward. Which meant that Francis and I found ourselves in exalted company with Master Knox several times in the chapel and halls of Windsor Castle and the grand splendor of the royal residence at Hampton Court.

After one such sermon, as we parted for our chambers, Master Knox breathed a weary sigh and said, "King Edward is a young man so godly in disposition toward the truth of God's Word, that to my knowledge none of his years did ever match him in Christian virtue." Though I believe he intended no insult to my brother and me with his words, yet did I feel a prick at his observation of the young king.

Steadying himself in a doorway, he sighed again and said, "The last trumpet is blowing within the realm of England and therefore ought everyone to prepare himself for battle. For if the trumpet should altogether be put to silence, then shall it never blow again with like force till the coming of our Lord Jesus." He paused, his face pale and his brow furrowed in thought. "If only in this benighted realm such a king were lord of his own royal will. As it is, he is surrounded by a multitude of wicked men, guilty of crimes so manifest and heinous that the earth could not hide the innocent blood, neither yet could the heavens behold without shame the craft, the deceit, the violence and oppression that universally have been wrought by these men."

Yet the young king often called for our master to preach. And I, being thus in the vicinity of the king, sitting in his royal presence as he listened to our master preach, I believe that I become rather intoxicated by the privilege. I confess that I was tempted to believe myself vicariously growing in importance with each encounter. But little did I then realize the extraordinary encounter we were about to experience.

29

Kings Are Mortal

EARLY IN APRIL OF 1553, I cannot recollect the exact date, Master Knox was called to Westminster Abbey, there to preach for Edward. We had no way of knowing that it would be the last sermon he would preach before the young king. Ever fearless before the mighty—usurping regent John Dudley in attendance, and double-dealing clerics strutting in great abundance—Master Knox stepped boldly into the pulpit and read out his text.

"He that eateth bread with me hath lifted up his heel against me." Though weak in body—only that morning he had awakened groaning at pains in his insides—his voice rang out with clarity and vigor in the royal abbey church. "It is commonly seen in history that the most godly princes have had officers and chief councilors who are manifestly most ungodly, conjured enemies to God's true gospel and traitors to their princes. If David and Hezekiah were deceived by traitorous councilors, how much more a young and innocent king?"

My old fears returned at his words that day, and my stomach grew turbulent. I was certain that our being with Master Knox would land us that night in the Tower, and after that?—I did not care to think more on our fate.

But quite the contrary was the case, for on the morrow we were escorted into the turreted grandeur of the royal residence at Hampton Court. This, in itself, was not so new a thing for us. In fact, at the royal chapel of the court our master had delivered several sermons before the king, and it was ordinary for us to attend him at these his royal sermons. What so astonished me that day in April 1553, however, was that we had been invited, by the king himself, to dine in the royal hall, with His Majesty himself.

As we passed the trimmed yew hedge and entered the arched gateway into the castle, my mouth felt as if I had been cutting and stacking dried heather thatch throughout a long, hot summer day in Longniddry and without a drop of water. And I knew, without Francis reminding me, that my eyes were in the process of lunging from their place.

"Who would have thought it?" murmured Francis at my side. And then, as if as an afterthought, he added, "Try not to drop your knife."

"Aye, and don't you gl-glug in your cup," I said back. "Mother always scolded you for glugging."

"And you for picking of your teeth with your knife." His fingernails were gouging into my arm again. I tried shaking him off. "What do we say?" His voice sounded high-pitched, bordering on the hysterical. After our imprisonment in the galleys, Francis could not always be counted on for courage. I had come to know this, whether he had acknowledged it to himself or no.

"'Your Majesty,'" I said. "When in d-doubt, just say 'Your Majesty.'"

"Aye, then," he said, nodding.

We followed a page who led us through the massive kitchen, savory aromas of rich broth and roasting beef seasoning the air. I say massive, because everything was large beyond imagining. It made me feel disproportionately small, as if I had stepped into a world where men were of a considerably greater size than in my world. The kettles for cooking looked as if they could hold an entire beef—head, hooves, the lot—and the cooking forks, spoons, and knives seemed more suited for giants to wield at table than for ordinary men and women. There was a clamor underway; perhaps we had entered the kitchen at a bad moment.

"You'll pay for your indolence!" shouted a man wearing a white frock stained with grease and blood. He stood before a broad gothic fireplace, wide enough for four carthorses to pass through abreast. I took the fierce-looking fellow to be the chief cook. With face red and puffy, the cook menaced a servant with a wooden spoon. Whimpering, the boy cowered behind a rack of copper pots hanging from stout oaken beams. With a cutting backhanded stroke, the cook swiped at the boy. "*Gong, gong!*" rang the blow as the spoon glanced mercifully off the pots instead of the servant's head.

I had little opportunity to pity the boy, for we were hurried on through a passage that opened into the great hall. By this time in my life, I had had experience of great halls, but this one—with its intricate, stone-carved, fan-vaulted ceiling and high buttresses, its magnificently detailed tapestries, its gothic stained-glass windows, and the multicolored light flashing and shimmering on rows of heraldic banners hung high above—this great hall surpassed all others.

Silk-clad servants scurried about a grand table, loading it with food for the midday meal; the table was as wide as a cottage and

195

as long as a carriage pulled by three teams of horses, yet was it dwarfed by the roomy magnificence of the place. I could not help staring at the platters of roasted pheasant and the shiny brown crackling of roasted suckling pig, its mouth clamped firmly on a roasted apple. There were bowls of fruits, some of which colorful orbs I had never seen before in my life, and golden-crusted pies, and a larger fowl that I believe to have been a roasted swan. Servants readied themselves for the royal event with carving knives and forks, and pitchers of ale and wine. My stomach churned with an awkward combination of midday adolescent hunger and a yet deeper rumbling at the exalted company with whom we were about to dine. At that moment, I did very much fear I might ruin all with being sick in my plate.

Master Knox, Francis, and I were escorted to three chairs at the near end of the table. Unaccustomed as I was to having my chair positioned for me by a footman, I nearly fell onto the floor. As it was, I bungled the tender back of my heels rather painfully on the chair in that seating.

"Do try not to humiliate the family name beyond recovery," said Francis in my ear.

Near a large fireplace set with a cheery fire, a man plucked at the strings of a lute, while two others played recorders; as the polyphony accelerated and the recorders swelled into their upper register, the music multiplied itself, reverberating throughout the stonework of Wolsey's Hall, for so we had learned the place to be called.

Suddenly, the music was interrupted by the king's harbinger. "Hail to His Majesty, King Edward VI!" he cried.

The great oak doors at the far end of the hall opened as if of their own accord. We rose to our feet. Flanked by attendants, into the hall walked the young king. He walked in a precise way, as if thinking about each step. He smiled our way as he neared his place. Two courtiers aided the king as he took his seat in a chair at the head of the far end of the table.

Master Knox was introduced and asked to commence the meal with a prayer of blessing. When we were seated again, our plates were loaded with food, the music recommenced, and the meal began.

I stole glances at the king as I ate, but tried not to stare. My mother had always instructed us not to stare. His face seemed more the color of well-kneaded bread dough than when we first had seen him, and I noticed that he scowled at his plate and ate little, though not for want of cajoling by his attendants. An older gentlemen, the physician, hovered around the young man in a manner that I believe I would have found annoying, though the king seemed gracious and appreciative, insofar as we could determine much about him from so great a distance.

"That is his Majesty's physician," said Master Knox softly.

He need not have spoken softly. The table was so long that it would have been impossible for the king to hear anything we said without raising our voices considerably above the ordinary register for speaking at table.

"It's less like dining with someone," said Francis, his ale cup poised to conceal his mouth, his words sounding hollow in the cup, "and rather more like watching an animal feed at a zoo."

Though the king had nothing like the manners of a beast at the zoo, from the far end of the table, more than two dozen yards away, it was as if we were not actually dining with him, only dining in the same large room with him, at the same large table. That was all. I jabbed my knife into the leg of swan on my plate.

"Something's happening," said Francis.

I halted in my chewing. He was right. The king had risen slowly to his feet. His physician and attendants scurried around him like fawning hounds to their master. He waved them off, and, smiling, he walked the length of the table, coming slowly toward us.

I tried swallowing the bite of swan I had been chewing, but it felt suddenly dry and lodged stubbornly in my throat. The king came nearer, his retinue scolding like old hens at his heels. I felt my face reddening. I grabbed for my cup. It would simply not do to erupt in a fit of gagging on my meat. Not before a king. And there was always the possibility of my spewing. I had been prone to spewing as a child. I was not at all aided by Francis's fingers cutting off the circulation in my arm. For an instant, I had the urge to bolt to my feet and flee the room, before worse befell. The king was now very close, and he smiled more broadly.

"Forgive me for allowing so great a distance between us at table," he said. "May I?" He gestured toward the place next to our master and directly across the table from my brother and me.

Francis and Master Knox rose to their feet. "Your Majesty is most welcome," said Master Knox.

"Your Majesty," said Francis. Three or four times he said it, "Your Majesty."

Meanwhile, I yet wrestled with the hunk of swan leg in my throat. It felt as if the fowl was yet living and wreaking its final revenge on my digestion. I took a pull of ale from my cup and swallowed. My eyes—no doubt grown wider than their usual— watered terribly.

"Your M-Majesty," I stammered, my voice sounding like toads in a bog on a summer night. But I felt greatly relieved. I had managed not to spew, and the swan leg had passed, and I could breathe again.

Once seated, the young king became almost chatty with us. "I have little society with others near my age," he began, "what with my lessons with good Master Sidney, duties of state, ceremony, and diplomacy pressing upon me."

He spoke as if these were simply the facts of his life, and there was no hint of resentment in his tone. As near as I could judge, the king was very near my own age, indeed, perhaps my senior by no more than months. For a while he addressed questions to Master Knox, theological ones about the gospel, ones that very much pleased our master, and which he answered with clarity, always directing the young king to Holy Scripture.

"It is my calling, Your Majesty," said Master Knox, "publicly to preach the gospel of Jesus Christ, and to feed the flock, which he hath redeemed with his own blood, and has commanded the same to the care of all true pastors." With feeling, he urged the king to exert his royal efforts to expunge idolatry still rife in the land, and to protect the purity of the English church from error, new or old, and to do all to encourage the faithful proclamation of true doctrine in the realm.

"We must call a fig a fig, Your Majesty, and a spade a spade." Edward listened, his eyes attentive on our master. "Your Majesty must not fear, nor be thrall to the flattery of men."

"They freely speak of my illness," said the king, leaning in closer and speaking in guarded tones. "And many speak openly of my impending and premature death."

Master Knox scooted his plate aside, swept the crumbs away with a hand, and opened his Bible. Tenderly he explained to the young man the gospel, how Jesus was crucified and died, and was buried, and was raised to life, the Victor over death.

"And he did all this, dear King, for our salvation. He alone by his death is the redeemer of God's elect. Place your hope by faith in him alone, and he by his perfect life is your righteousness on the day of your death, be it sooner or later."

The young king glanced at the musicians and gave a slight movement of his hand. On the instant, the musicians stopped their playing, and all his courtiers fell silent. The fire had burned down to glowing coals. It was odd in a room so immense to feel a silence so complete. Master Knox then read from 1 Corinthians 15, his voice the only sound that reverberated through the ancient stones of that magnificent hall.

> Christ has been raised from the dead, the firstfruits of those who have fallen asleep. For as by a man came death, by a man has come also the resurrection of the dead. For as in Adam all die, so also in Christ shall all be made alive. But each in his own order: Christ the firstfruits, then at his coming those who belong to Christ. Then comes the end, when he delivers the kingdom to God the Father after destroying every rule and every authority and power. For he must reign until he has put all his enemies under his feet. The last enemy to be destroyed is death. For "God has put all things in subjection under his feet." But when it says, "all things are put in subjection," it is plain that he is excepted who put all things in subjection under him. When all things are subjected to him, then the Son himself will also be subjected to him who put all things in subjection under him, that God may be all in all.

Master Knox paused, gently explaining the text to the king. I studied the young man's face. The king could not be a year older than I was, and as much again younger than Francis, and yet here he was talking and speaking candidly with Master Knox of his own dying, and as if it were soon to be at hand. A different sort of choking sensation came to my throat, and I felt the water whelming up in my eyes. Our tutor continued reading, but now commenting freely as he did so.

"I tell you this, dear king: flesh and blood cannot inherit the kingdom of God, nor does the perishable inherit the imperishable. Behold! The trumpet will sound, and the dead will be raised imperishable, and we shall be changed. For your frail perishable body, O king, must put on the imperishable, and this your mortal body must put on immortality. When the perishable puts on the imperishable, and the mortal puts on immortality, then shall come to pass the saying that is written: 'Death is swallowed up in victory. O death, where is your victory? O death, where is your sting?' The sting of death is sin, and the power of sin is the law. But thanks be to God, who gives us the victory through our Lord Jesus Christ. Therefore, my dear king, for however many days God has ordained for you, be steadfast, immovable, always abounding in the work of the Lord, knowing that in the Lord your labor is not in vain."

Master Knox paused to allow the sacred words to have their effect. After a moment he said, "Is not that, dear king, a comforting chapter?"

We talked with the king well into the evening. "You must stop all this 'Your Majesty' business, my friends," he said with a laugh. "When we are alone, the three of us, I am Edward to you—or, if you please, you may call me, as my nurse used to do, Eddie." We laughed together at the idea, knowing we could never manage to refer to him as such. Edward proved to be a masterful chess player, and prevailed over Francis in a close contest that lingered well over an hour. After which, he bested me in but five moves. We parted that evening feeling we had made a lifelong friend in His Majesty.

So it was that when a courier brought the news to our chambers on July 6, 1553, that King Edward VI, our royal friend, had passed from the mortal into the immortal, we felt an indescribable emptiness. After the first hours of sadness at the news, it seemed impossible not to take stock of our position: Our mother was no more; we had heard nothing from our father in over five years and knew not whether he lived or died; our beloved Scotland remained under the cruel heel of France and the pope; the fate of Alexander our friend remained a mystery; we were exiles in an odd country, now with incalculable dangers on every side.

The king, our friend, was dead. What lay ahead for England? There had been wild speculation on that score. The future, indeed, appeared bleak for England. But what lay ahead for us?

30

Flee or Bleed

EDWARD'S BODY WAS STILL WARM when John Dudley, determined to keep his power over England, set in motion a scheme, which, as events would prove, was doomed from the start.

I have come to believe that the only rival to the convolutions of English politics is the vaulting ambition of the human heart. News was spreading throughout London that the Holy Roman Emperor, Charles V, King of Spain, had previously entered into secret negotiations with Edward's father, the late Henry VIII. The Spanish emperor had exerted pressure on Henry of England to confer the crown, should his son Edward VI die without heir, upon his cousin Mary, offspring of Henry by his first of six marriages, his union with Spanish Catherine of Aragon.

And now sixteen-year-old Edward had died, unwed and, indeed, without heir. Two months before the king's death, in a costly act of desperation, scheming Regent John Dudley, Duke of Northumberland, had wed his son to Lady Jane Grey, great-granddaughter of Henry VII. Dudley made public a document signed by Edward, contradicting Charles V's claim, declaring Lady Jane Grey his successor to the throne. Dudley promptly crowned the fourteen-year-old devoutly Protestant girl Queen of England. Her coerced and ill-fated reign was to last but nine days. Mary Tudor came on with a vengeance to seize her rightful place on the throne of England—and to restore her realm to Rome and the pope, at all costs. First to be arrested were Lady Jane Grey and her husband. They were thrown in the Tower of London to await Mary Tudor's royal will.

I was deeply anxious in those days after Edward's death. While many protestant preachers were fleeing for their lives to the continent, Master Knox devoutly believed he was needed to shepherd his flock, now more than ever. What is more, he counted all of England as his flock. He returned to Berwick, and preached again at Newcastle, but loyalty to Queen Mary Tudor was growing. Men like Tunstall had been waiting for decades for a return to the Roman fold. Mary was their deliverer. As more clerics rallied to support the new queen, hostility toward men like Knox mounted. Yet did he refuse to flee.

"Perhaps the time has come," I said one evening in our chambers. We were staying at a public house in a small village in Buckinghamshire. Master Knox had preached that day in the parish church and was yet down the street in the market square conversing.

"For what?" said Francis, his mouth full of bread and Stilton cheese.

"It's one thing for Master Knox to fulfill his calling," I said, "at the risk of his own life. It's quite another for him to fulfill it at the risk of ours. Don't you think?"

He stopped chewing. "Has it come to that?"

"I feel more certain every day. Here in Buckinghamshire many common folk want to hear the evangel that Master Knox proclaims. But you saw our reception in Newcastle, and London's in

Mary's grasp, men switching horses daily, and no safe place for any principled Reformer."

"We can't go back to Scotland," said Francis, chewing slowly. "Things'll be worse there than ever. It's not just the Queen Regent who wants men like our master to burn. Mary Tudor of England wants it now too."

"There's always Germany," I said.

"Aye, but we have no money for passage."

That evening as we sat down to meat with Master Knox, I determined to speak with him about our plight. We bowed our heads and he offered a prayer of gratitude and blessing on the victuals, as was his habit. His praying concluded in this fashion. "Seeing that we are now left as a flock without a pastor, in civil policy, and as a ship without a rudder in the midst of the storm, let thy providence watch, Lord, and defend us in these dangerous days, that the wicked of the world may see that as well without the help of man, as with it, thou art able to rule, maintain, and defend thy little flock that dependeth upon thee."

When he'd finished praying, Francis looked at me and shrugged his shoulders in resignation. I was determined to press the issue. In my mind, to delay would lead to the stake.

"Master Knox, you agree that these are dangerous days, then?"

"Aye, indeed, they are," he said, his spoon poised over a bowl of thin broth.

"Many are fleeing to Germany," I continued, "or Strasbourg, or to Geneva."

"Aye, and I don't blame them for it. Yet what of our flock, the sheep, lad, who need shepherding?"

"But surely you've heard how many who professed are return-ing to Rome? The Duke of Northumberland turns his coat and claims that he had always remained loyal to the pope and the Roman church. There are daily reports of many saving their skin by reconverting to Rome. You, Master, may soon be the only Reformer left in all England—alive, that is."

"Aye, lad, your fears for me are indeed commendable. But you must know and believe that if we were but one man in all the world, not just in England, one man with God is always in the majority."

I knew in my heart that if it were, in fact, but one man, Master Knox himself alone, I would be less anxious than I was. "But Master Knox, it would not be a sin to flee, to preserve your life so that you can one day proclaim the evangel in Scotland. This would not be a sin, would it?"

He rested a hand on my shoulder before replying. "Sometimes, George, I have thought it impossible to remove my heart from the realm of Scotland, that any realm or nation could have been equally dear to me. But God I take to record in my conscience, that the present troubles in the realm of England are more grievous to my heart at this moment than ever were the troubles of Scotland."

His words irritated me. Scots were supposed to resent and despise the English, but not so our master. At his words that evening, I despaired of fleeing for our lives. Yet was I loathe to lay down my life for Master Knox's calling. I felt I understood his message, and did partly believe the evangel and could explain it to any who asked it of me, but I doubted I could die for it, at a stake, with burning faggots consuming my flesh. I doubted this very much indeed.

I believe that would have been the end of it and we would have stayed on at Master Knox's side until he was taken, and we with him. But Queen Mary Tudor played a new hand and made as if to extend an act of toleration to Reformers. I doubted the sincerity of toleration from her in any package. Yet our master was determined to believe her, and so we set off for London, a setting off that I desperately feared would lead to our end. My innards churned and grumbled violently on that journey to London. In my anxiety I was on the very precipice of spewing for hours on end, yet I could not entirely find it in myself to leap from the carriage in a wild and forsaken countryside and flee for my life, though I thought often about it, as the carriage wheels rumbled ever closer to the capital where Mary reigned supreme.

We had lodged in London but days when word came of John Dudley's beheading, and close on the heels of the news, the arrest and imprisonment of Thomas Cranmer, Nicholas Ridley, and our master's dear friend, Hugh Latimer. In returning to London, it appeared to me we had laid ourselves bare before the very teeth of the lioness.

"They're held in chains in the Tower," said Master Knox. He had collapsed on a stool when he rejoined us in our chambers. He looked weary and held a hand hard at his middle, his face blanching in pain. "Mary makes as if to recover them, to be kind to them, to win them with friendliness, gifts, advancements. But I do not now believe her. Perhaps this toleration of hers is a sham, a ruse to gather in and destroy us all." He was silent for a moment. "I have written to them encouragement to persevere under trial, as did our Lord and Master on our behalf in the gospel. Hugh has returned a letter."

It was then I noticed the crumpled paper in his fist. "What does it say?"

He opened the letter with a sigh. "Put simply, it says: Flee. Doctor Latimer urges me to flee England, and without delay.

He claims he is not doing so in the interest of my life, but in the interest of the gospel of grace alone. 'And for the sake of your bairns,' he adds." I wondered if we would yet be called his 'bairns' when we were old and gray, should we live that long. "He orders me to preserve my life—and yours—and thereby preserve the Reformed gospel." His voice trailed off.

"You are in pain, master?" I said.

He nodded. "The pain of my head and stomach troubles me greatly." His voice was low and strained. "I daily feel my body decay. Unless this pain ceases, I fear I will become unprofitable."

"Is it not from the Lord?" I said. "Your friend urges you to flee to preserve the true doctrines of the Reformation, and you are too ill at present to remain and be profitable. Master, Doctor Latimer is correct. We must flee now or we will all die."

"What is to become of my flock?" he said, his voice barely audible. "What will become of those who have been brought to hope in Christ by my preaching and influence? What kind of shepherd forsakes his lambs into the bloody hands of such a wolf?"

I felt certain that his mind was troubled about many people, but I wondered if he was not chiefly troubled about his obligations to Elizabeth and Marjory Bowes. He had never spoken directly to us of the matter, but Francis and I had speculated that perhaps there had been a betrothal, that he was bound to Marjory. Her father, Elizabeth's husband, Sir Robert, would most certainly take his stand with Mary Tudor. There was no question on the matter. I did not blame Master Knox for his anguish and his feelings of responsibility and obligation at what might descend upon them.

"Master, there are those who are safe as they are." I felt I could not openly speak my meaning without offense, yet did I venture further. "Speaking in theory, in such times as these, a daughter of landed gentry is safe. Contrarily, a wife of one charged to decry idolatry in the realm, a wife of a preacher of Christ's evangel—as such a wife, might not she stand in greater peril in these times?"

He fixed his eyes on me in a level gaze, and for an instant I feared I may have overstepped. Then he drew in breath and sighed.

"How am I to pay for our passage?" His hands shook as he unlaced his money pouch and upended it, a few coins rattling on the oaken table board. "I have but ten groats in my pocket, barely enough to buy bread. Completely insufficient to secure passage to the continent. I know not where any more are to found."

"God will provide," I said, words I had so often heard from our master's lips. Pulling myself up to my full height, I continued. "I shall make inquiries and book us passage on the next merchant-man I can find."

He cast his eyes over me from head to foot. "Pray. Earnestly, we must pray," he replied. "Indeed, God alone must provide."

I felt a twinge of offense at this our exchange. Yet the ground I felt I had gained lessened the sting. Heretofore, I had given little credence to what Master Knox spoke to us about providence. Most things for which he credited providence, I believed would have come about in the ordinary course of events. But in the succeeding hours, I was forced to become more of a believer in his providence. Dangerous as were the times, I was to find that Master Knox had genuine supporters—and not of the Duke of Northumberland variety, who at the first blush of opposition revert to crossing, ducking, and genuflecting.

I knew I must act, but I confess, I had little notion of how to go about doing anything for our deliverance. The next day, I walked the docks along the Thames, searching faces, conversing with tarry seamen, wheedling for information. All I gathered for my efforts were suspicious looks and gruff rebuttals. I returned at dusk, forlorn and dejected, worried that I had stirred up a hornets' nest, brought down trouble on our position. What was certain was that I had done nothing to secure our deliverance. In such a frame of mind, I entered our chambers that evening.

"This arrived for Master Knox," said Francis, holding a sealed envelope above his head. "Master lies in bed, groaning with his old malady."

I lunged for it, grabbing it from his hand.

"Addressed to Master Knox, it is," he cried.

Ignoring him, I tore it open. It was, indeed, addressed to John Knox from Mrs. Anne Lockhart. Shamelessly, I read its contents. Abandoning scruple, Francis read over my shoulder.

He whistled. "God has provided."

"It pays to have wealthy friends," I said. "The Locke and the Hickman families it is. In peril of the queen as are we. Aye, they too must flee."

"Aye, and we to accompany them," said Francis.

"With all speed," I said. "We must ready ourselves and Master Knox. There is little time. We embark on the morrow at the turning of the tide."

31

Faint-Hearted Soldier

THAT JANUARY NIGHT IN 1554 my stomach and I rediscovered that the English Channel was no place to be in the dead of winter. Clutching the rail, my fingers numb with cold, I attempted to keep my feet on the listing deck as the tiny fishing cog moaned in the gale. Sleet seemed to penetrate my cheeks and forehead, and when the vessel plunged into the depths of a briny trough, breaking seas crashed over the bow, drenching me to the bone. So miserable was I that I began to long for the relative protection of the rowing deck of that French galley on which we had been enslaved. We were the last to be allowed to board this single-masted cog and, as there was no place below, were forced to weather the passage on deck. I do not recall feeling the elements so foul and ferocious as on that night. The screaming and howling of the wind in the rigging made me imagine the cries of tormented spirits in the underworld. England and her white cliffs had rapidly disappeared in the falling darkness; I wondered if I would ever see her shores again. We were engulfed on all sides by tempestuous blackness. Would we survive the night and see the shores of France in the morning? If so, would I ever cross this narrow turbulent sea again to see my home and Scotland? It was a night of terror and torment, one I hope never to experience again.

At long last, "Land ho!" came from the sailor on watch at the masthead. His voice was raw with relief. Moments later, through the bleak grayness of dawn, I too saw land. The foamy seas had begun to abate in their fury. When at last I placed my feet upon the shore in Dieppe, I was overcome as never before with the urge to fall on my face and embrace the earth most intimately.

Under the able care of the Locke and Hartman families, we were sumptuously warmed and filled in a seaside pension. It was remarkable to me how healing was a crackling fire and a hot mug of mulled wine after such a passage. As we thus recovered ourselves, Anne Locke asked our master for some word of encouragement after such a crossing. There in the low-beamed shore-side inn, Master Knox unburdened his own soul at our flight, sometimes speaking to us and at other times addressing his words to God in most earnest and familiar prayer. Such was his manner.

"By God's grace, may I come again to battle before all this conflict be ended. Haste the time, O Lord! At thy good pleasure, that once again my tongue may praise thy holy name before the congregation—if it were in the very hour of death." Unblinking, he stared into the coals; I felt certain he was thinking of those left behind, in chains, and fearing what awaited them was flames and martyrdom at the bloody hands of Mary Tudor. He continued.

"Albeit, in this my flight, I have appeared to play the faint-hearted and feeble soldier, yet my prayer is that I may be again restored to the battle. And blessed be God, the Father of our Lord Jesus Christ, I am not left so bare without comfort, but my hope is to attain such mercy that if a short end be not made of all my miseries, by final death, which were to me no small advantage, that yet by him, who never despises the sobs of the sore afflicted, I shall be so encouraged to fight that England and Scotland shall both know that I am ready to suffer more than either poverty or exile for the possession of that doctrine and that heavenly religion whereof it has pleased his merciful providence to make me, among others, a simple soldier and witness-bearer unto men."

I felt a twinge of responsibility for our having fled, and, hence, for our master's anguished sentiment that his act of fleeing for his life was equally an act of cowardice, and I grieved to see the torment in his eyes as he prayed. He looked like a man adrift in a storm, clutching for some scrap of flotsam on which to lay hold. I never saw a more honest man in prayer.

After some days, we continued our perilous journey. In the gray light of dawn, with freezing rain pelting down upon us, we clamored into a carriage that would convey us across France and—if all went well—to the safety of Switzerland.

"I fear that Mary of England may prove to be a most pernicious persecutrix," said Master Knox as the carriage lurched to life. "The king of this benighted realm of France, however, has been tormenting and burning our brethren since 1512." He then solemnly began reciting names, French names, dozens of them, and villages and cities, and dates upon which these souls had been martyred. "And but months ago in Lyon, five students of John Calvin from Geneva, Martial Alba, Peter Scribe, Bernard Seguine, Charles Faber, and Peter Navihere, met their end at the stake."

My old fears returned, and I felt my stomach hardening into a knot as the carriage took us ever deeper into the murderous realm of France. I believed our father had meant it for our good to consign us to the care of Master Knox. Yet had we encountered great dangers in his company. From an open shutter in the carriage compartment, I gazed numbly at bent backs and pale faces in the flash of village life we were at that instant passing through. What calamities lay ahead for us on this journey?

"For us, "continued Master Knox, "these Frankish roads we traverse are dangerous ones, indeed."

32

Geneva

THOSE DAYS CROSSING FRANCE seemed like months. I believe I was in a constant state of anxiety, my stomach so on the verge of spewing that I rarely felt like eating, and when I did I but picked at my bread and cheese and took but small sips of French wine.

More than once we were warned in the night of lurking perils. It seemed that there were those who somehow mysteriously knew of our master, some prepared to take great risks for his safety, while others were bent on his destruction. I was astonished at this, and could not then explain to myself how such intelligence could be transmitted across a narrow sea and disseminated throughout a hostile land, and all so rapidly.

One night in Burgundy as we slept at a hospice on the Rue de Paradis, in the village of Beaune, we were abruptly awakened by stones at our window. *"Fuyez à la fois!"* There was no time to lose. We were urged to flee at once or be taken by agents of Francis I, sworn enemy of all Reformers. Leaving behind some of our things, with all haste, we resumed our journey through that anxious night.

I cannot describe my relief when at last we crossed from France, and the lands of the Duke of Savoy, into Switzerland and Geneva. My first impressions of this land of John Calvin took my breath from my lungs. Behind us lay the muddy roads, torrential rains, darkness, and the treacherous agents of a regime determined to crush Reformation at any price. All this had been palpable in the air we breathed while in that realm. But as our carriage halted before the arches and columns of the city hall near the crown of the city overlooking Lac Leman, rimmed by the fortress of the Jura Mountains, at that instant sunshine broke through the clouds. The city seemed to sparkle with brilliance. I hasten to add that while in Geneva we often saw long, cold winter days, bleak and gray, yet on that morn Geneva seemed to shine as a city on a hill, radiant with light and beauty. For the first time in a very long time, the knots clutching my insides seemed to begin loosening, and I drank in the mountain air as a man long deprived of such delicious freshness.

As we wound our way up the narrow cobbled streets, along with many people speaking French, I heard others speaking in German, in Dutch, in Spanish, in Italian—men and women, boys and girls, whole families—as well as in other languages I had never before heard. It was a populous city, but amidst the bustle there was less jostling than other places. There was a cheerfulness and humanity about the activity of the place, less pulling apart, less a sense that folks were striving with one another, and I never once heard cursing, not on that first day or the many days to come. I am aware that any who should hap to read this account may not believe my words to be accurate ones; nevertheless, as eyewitness, I shall persist in recording precisely what I observed and the impression it had upon my mind.

After we had been given our rooms, a messenger brought an invitation to dinner. I wondered if my insides were ready for eating; the word "dinner," however, had prompted something inside me that made me feel that I might enjoy a morsel of meat. Once again we took to the narrow winding streets of the city.

"Where are we going?" I asked. We rounded a corner, the street descending steeply before us.

"To dine with an important man of this city," said Master Knox. "Aye, with perhaps the most important man in Europe."

"With John Calvin, then?" I said.

"Aye. We dine with John Calvin."

"Have you never met the man before?" I asked, wondering how it was that our master was known to such an important fellow as to be so promptly invited to dinner.

"I feel as if I have," said Master Knox, "for I have read in his books. But, no, I have never laid eyes on the man."

We had heard our master speak of Calvin with great veneration. And I believe that I expected him to be a great tall fellow, broad in the shoulders, with a strong brow and sturdy chin. So when we were welcomed into his home by an attendant, I was alarmed to see a frail figure of a man, with a wisp of a beard, pale, hollow cheeks, and tears flickering in the candlelight upon those cheeks. I felt awkward at our entrance and longed to turn and leave the poor man to his distress. Whatever might have been its cause, I did not want to add to it by our presence.

"We have arrived, Doctor Calvin, at an inopportune moment," said our master. "We shall return at another."

I was relieved at his words, and turned eagerly toward the door.

"Forgive me," said John Calvin, carefully folding a letter and rising to his feet. "I am most gratified, John Knox, at last to make your acquaintance. We have heard much of your labors in England."

Master Knox introduced us as his pupils, sons of Laird Hugh Douglas, the mention of our father always striking me with a pang of longing and of bewilderment. Calvin introduced to us a young man attending him, Theodore Beza, and another, his companion, the servant who had met us at the door; by the iron gray hair at his temples, I reckoned his servant close in age to Calvin, though more robust. We were seated, and food was laid out before us.

After Calvin asked a blessing we commenced the meal. Francis, who never seemed to have his appetite truncated by circumstances, fell to with vigor. It was a cheese soup, of a sort I had never yet seen or tasted. Francis wrenched off a hunk of bread and plunged it into the thick soup. I watched his eyes flutter as he chewed. It was an annoying habit of his but one that at that moment commended the victuals and made my stomach growl with hunger. Hesitantly, I tore off a piece of bread and dipped a corner in the cheesy broth. I learned later that the unique flavor came from a local blend of Gruyeye and Emnenthaler cheese, garlic, and dry white wine. I dipped my bread in more deeply. Cheese dangling from my fingers and chin, I now tore at another hunk of bread.

"Forgive me," explained Calvin. "I have been reading a letter from a bookseller in Rouen, Bartholomew Hector, a student of our Academy. I fear so for his safety. He has written to report on another student, Dionysius Vayre, who has labored tirelessly in smuggling French Bibles and other prohibited books into France."

Calvin paused. No one spoke. I elbowed Francis, who was about to dip his bread, and withdrew my own hand from the cheese pot.

"My dear Vayre," continued Calvin, "he was seized, arrested. There was little pretense of a trial. They sentenced him to die by burning. Thrice they lifted him up and lowered him down again into the flames. During his ordeal and before his end he made to glorify Christ in word, though they had partially removed his tongue. The French, they do this, you know, so as to silence the dying testimony of Christ's servants. It was agents of His Majesty, King of France, who plotted his end and denounced him. O, my dear son, Vayre."

He broke off, composing himself only with great effort. I could not help observing Calvin's companion and servant, who lowered his pale forehead onto his tremulous hands and slumped in his chair at the news.

Hearing the name of this man, a former student of Calvin's, and seeing Calvin's grief at his death left me numb. I wondered at men who could make their living by scheming to betray and denounce other men. How much was such a man paid for his services? A still deeper unrest descended over me that evening. Were there such men in Scotland? Had my father been denounced? Were there men in Scotland who would turn upon their fellowman to save their own skins? I feared that I knew the answer to these questions, though I hated that answer. Still more troubling to my mind: Vayre had been a student of Calvin, as were Francis and I of Master Knox. Calvin's words that first night in Geneva sounded in my ears as an eerie requiem that pressed down on my conscience like a great marble tombstone on a grave. I had no more appetite for that delicious cheese soup that night.

The next morning we accompanied Master Knox to hear our first of many sermons preached in Geneva. It was a late-February morning, the mists hovering over Lac Leman, spreading to the east of the city. The church of St. Pierre was a sturdy structure, Romanesque, with few of the delicacies of the abbey church in Westminster or the parish church of St. Nicholas in Newcastle. No crown-like spire, no flying buttresses, no vast stained-glass windows. Yet high atop the hillside overlooking the rooftops of the city and the stretching expanse of the lake, it had a magnificence that transcended other places of worship I had seen. It is difficult to describe objectively, but there was a palpable atmosphere about Geneva as if the place were a gateway to a new and alluring world, a world that I felt pulling me in, compelling me forward, tugging at my sleeve, but one I was at a loss fully to comprehend.

Up the narrow cobbled streets we walked. Master Knox set our pace, and he set a slower one than usual that morning. His shoulders were stooped, and I had heard him as he seated himself for breakfast catch his breath at some internal stabbing of pain, his old malady apparently upon him again. When this was the case, my own innards began making their protestations. I hoped that Geneva might prove to be a health-giving climate. Perhaps here his ailment would diminish and bodily strength would be restored.

I shall never forget my first time passing through the polished panels of the west doors of St. Pierre and entering the twelfth-century simplicity of the place. Stone vaulting, supported by grand columns, rose above us, as in many such medieval churches I had been in. I immediately noted, however, that this place of worship was fundamentally altered in one important respect. I knew this would be a great delight to our master. It was free of nearly all images; there were no clusters of candles burning before statues and shrines to saints; there was no smoky incense hovering about the capitals of the thick columns or curling its way in and through the circular candle lighting suspended high above and giving light to the nave and quire. There were no elaborate mural paintings of apocryphal scenes garishly decorating the walls. There was an unadorned, undistracted splendor about the place.

This simplicity was not lost on our master. He halted, gazing about the vast interior, a faint smile playing at the corners of his mouth. Perhaps he was equally smiling at the enormous crowd that had gathered to worship and to hear preaching. There was hardly a place to stand and nowhere to sit. People from every walk of life had pressed into this ancient hall to hear Calvin preach the gospel, women and children and whole families joining in the worship of God. Master Knox had told us of how, for some years, people had converged on Geneva from all over Europe, many to find refuge in this place of freedom, and to find truth in the unfettered proclamation of the gospel of grace. So he had told us. A reverent expectancy hummed throughout the place.

We were greeted warmly and handed a book, a Psalter, for singing.

"It would be all in French," murmured Francis.

"Here you will learn French," said Master Knox firmly. "Like it or not, you will be very much in the dark if you do not master the language in Geneva. What is more, you'll understand nothing of Doctor Calvin's sermon today, or any day, for he will deliver it in French."

"*Vous tous qui la terre habitez,*" we were led in singing, Francis haltingly, indeed, and grumbling at my side. After singing Psalm 100, John Calvin, his Greek New Testament under his arm, walked to the pulpit. He was thin, slightly stooped, and he hesitated for a brief moment at the foot of the carved circular stairway. I wondered how many times he had ascended that pulpit.

He had first done so nearly twenty years ago, so our master had explained. And those had been turbulent days, indeed, ones that led to an early banishment from the then licentious city. Reverently, he mounted the pulpit stairs. When at last he arrived before the lectern, he set his book down, opened it to his text, then gazed out over the upturned faces of his flock there gathered before him. In our time in Geneva, I seldom if ever saw Calvin smile broadly and certainly not laugh hilariously, but there was something about his slender features that conveyed—and that quite clearly, to the attentive observer—pleasure. So though it might not be strictly accurate to say that he smiled, it was manifest that he looked with pleasure upon his flock. Rude though it may have been, I turned to look at that flock. Their faces reminded me of guests when first they enter and see the banqueting hall adorned for celebrating, and the table laden with food and wine. Surely the faces of friends and family pulling their chairs up at a feast, gathering to celebrate in the great hall, would look just like this, so I mused.

"We owe to the Scriptures the same reverence which we owe to God," began Calvin. Small in stature though he was, his voice was clear and penetrating, and rang with force off the ancient walls of that cathedral. "We owe this because the Word of God has proceeded from God alone. And it must, therefore, have nothing of man mixed with it. When the Word of God is faithfully preached in your hearing, dear people, it is as if God himself comes into the midst of us. May he do so this day.

"Hence, we must all be pupils of the Holy Scriptures, even to the end; even those, I mean, who are appointed to proclaim the Word. If we enter the pulpit, as I have done this day, it is on this condition, that we learn while teaching others. I am not speaking here merely that others may hear me; but I too, for my part, must be a pupil of God, and the Word which goes forth from my lips must profit myself; otherwise, woe is me! The most accomplished in the Scriptures are fools, unless they acknowledge that they have need of God for their schoolmaster all the days of their lives."

Master Knox nodded his agreement at our side. At times during that first sermon I thought our master might break out in shouting, so delighted was he with what he was hearing from the lips of Calvin. "And this from the Theologian of the Reformation!" he whispered in our ears at one point. Through our long tutelage with Master Knox we had grown accustomed to his manner of placing a hand upon each of our necks, drawing our heads to his, and speaking into both our ears at once. He now had to pull our heads down toward him as both Francis and I had grown taller in stature than our master. It was a habit of long standing, and, one that he would yet be doing when we became fully grown men, though I often wondered then at the prospect of our becoming so. "Lads, we are privileged to feed from the gifted hand of a truly humble servant of Christ."

33

Faction and Disorder

THOSE FIRST MONTHS IN GENEVA began to open my eyes, a poor metaphor in my case, as Francis would no doubt affirm. Calvin preached or taught four or five times in the week. We rarely missed any of his instruction. He called upon our master to preach from time to time. But with such gifts and graces to hand, Master Knox happily deferred, preferring to listen to the preaching of Calvin.

We sat in on the lessons taught at the Academy, all these conducted in Latin. We found ourselves surrounded by educated men from throughout Europe, Hungarians, Germans, Italians, Spaniards, Frenchmen, and, to be sure, other English speakers and Scots. It was in these contexts where we witnessed the remarkable gifts and erudition of the Reformer of Geneva. I say erudition, but never was Calvin pedantic, parading his learning. Nor did he employ his learning as a club to intimidate those who differed with his teaching, and graciously answered questions with respect and generosity. Nevertheless, he shared our master's understanding of doctrinal truth and the necessity of purity for the sake of the gospel.

"I know how difficult it is to persuade the world," said Calvin one hot afternoon in July, "that God disapproves of all modes of worship not expressly sanctioned by his Word. The opposite persuasion which cleaves to them—being seated, as it were, in their very bones and marrow—is that whatever they do has in itself a sufficient sanction, provided it exhibits some kind of zeal for the honor of God. But since God not only regards as fruitless, but also plainly abominates, whatever we undertake from zeal to his worship, when it is at variance with his command, what do we gain by a contrary course? The words of God are clear and distinct; 'Obedience is better than sacrifice.' And 'in vain do they worship me, teaching for doctrines the commandments of men.'"

"You are then affirming, Master Calvin," said a young man, "that mere zeal, that sincerity in worship is not sufficient."

"Not when that zeal contradicts God's Word," replied Calvin. "Anything not expressly commanded in worship introduces an invention of man into the worship of God. The zeal, or good will, or sincerity of the worshiper, commendable though it may be, leads to idolatry, which obscures the one, true, and living God, the grand object of that worship."

There was considerable discussion the remaining of that afternoon. When nearly an hour had elapsed, our master posed the question: "What of monarchs that zealously intrude upon the worship of God in their realms? Who impose vain worship and denounce the true worship of God. Are they to be obeyed?"

"Most certainly they are not," replied Calvin.

"Aye, but then are they to be rightly resisted?"

Calvin did not immediately reply. "To disobey and to resist are not one and the same. God himself has ordained civil authority, and 'whosoever resisteth them, resisteth God.' And we are clearly instructed to 'honor the king.' Nevertheless, when monarchs overstep their boundaries and tyrannically impose their wills upon the people of God and his church, the church must stand her ground against them."

"And when the tyrant monarch will not relent at such standing of ground," said our master, "what then?"

"I believe I know of whom you speak," said Calvin.

"Aye, Mary of England, of the Spaniard's blood. She it is of whom I speak. She who bends every nerve to restore idolatry and bloody persecution in her realm. Had she . . . had she been sent to hell before these days, then should not her iniquity and cruelty so manifestly been made known to the world."

"Brother Knox, your zeal is commendable," said Calvin. "But we have already established that zeal alone is not enough. By your words you come dangerously close to advocating the assassination of the queen. Hot-headed youths have acted on less provocation than what you herein have given. God alone is sovereign and disposes of men and women, and kings and queens, sending this one to hell and that one to heaven by his sovereign choice. It is he who ordains all, including the days of such a persecutrix plaguing his church."

I had never heard anyone rebuke our master in such a manner, and I half expected a salvo of thunder from him for reply. But I was mistaken.

"My good hope is," said Master Knox, "that one day Christ Jesus, that now in England is crucified, shall rise again in despite of his enemies, and shall appear to his weak and sorely troubled disciples (for yet some he has in that wretched and miserable realm), to whom he shall say, 'Peace be unto you. It is I; fear not.'"

Though it was clear that Calvin felt our master was sometimes over rash in his pronouncements, a genuine affection developed between them, and many an evening was spent in earnest and hearty conversation and discussion with the Genevan Reformer. On one such night, Calvin asked Master Knox to consider a call from a refugee congregation in Germany. "In Frankfurt am Main, a band of English have written me asking for you to consider accepting a call to be their pastor."

"But Frankfurt," said our master. "Is not that in the realm of Charles V, Holy Roman Emperor, and hence, Roman Catholic, loyal to the pope—and to Mary Tudor of England?"

"Officially so, yes," replied Calvin. "But it is an independent-minded commercial center—not unlike Geneva when first I arrived. I was in my youth and inexperience nearly devoured by the tearing wolves of this place. There is considerable freedom in Frankfurt, however, and the congregation has secured the use of the Church of White Ladies for their worship. All that is needed is a pastor and preacher."

So it was that we found ourselves in a carriage bound for Frankfurt am Main, Francis grumbling all the way. "Now it's German I must learn."

Master Knox had not preached more than a fortnight in Frankfurt, and it was clear that there was a vocal minority of the English refugees who had a decided preference for the *Book of Common Prayer* in its high church prescriptive worship. Our master was no high churchman; I believe I had learned the art of understatement while in England. He attempted to introduce the *Genevan Order of Service*, simple, unadorned, Christ-centered, without *hocus pocus*, priestly vestments, incense, or strutting pretense. The faction would have none of it.

"O, my decaying carcass," I heard our master murmur often in those months in Frankfurt.

It was clear to Francis and me that things were not going well. The peace and order in Geneva had spoiled us—and perhaps had spoiled Master Knox. None of us dared speak of it in the privacy of our chambers near the Church of the White Ladies, but we all of us knew our thoughts on the matter. Yet things went from bad to worse.

In February of 1555, our master spent long hours at the candle drafting another order of service, a book of common order for worship that he hoped would be first biblical and then accessible to sincere worshipers of God. After seeing him one evening, face-down and asleep on the parchment he had been writing upon, spent candle wax on his sleeve and hair, I spoke to Francis of it. We determined to lend him our assistance—if he would have it.

The next morning I summoned my powers. "You have labored, Master Knox, now these many years for our knowledge and learning. You weary yourself into the night at your work. Though we have yet many deficiencies, might not we assist you in your labors?"

He hesitated but an instant, then set us to work that very morning. I was to act as scribe and write out in draft a portion of the order of worship he had as yet but made only a raw outline. Mine was to be a model for prayer of confession, and I formed my words as best I could from the hundreds of prayers I had heard our master offer:

"Wherefore, O Lord, we have sinned and have grievously offended against thee, so that shame and confusion belong to us, and we acknowledge that we are altogether guilty before thy judgment, and that if thou wouldest entreat us according to our demerits, we could look for none other than death and everlasting

229

damnation. For although we would go about to clear and excuse ourselves, yet our own conscience would accuse us, and our wickedness would appear before thee, to condemn us."

Generously, I am sure, he praised me for my efforts, and then demonstrated his amendments to it. "And what of those in our realm who have not the English?" he said. "What might we do for their edification? You lads have the Gaelic. Render the same in the Gaelic tongue."

Francis and I were thus set to the task of making drafts of Master Knox's order of worship not only in English but also in the Gaelic, after this fashion, ". . . *fa do rinde find, agas gurab find oibrighthe do lamh, & gurab tii ar naodhaire, agas ar nard bhuachaill . . .*"

After several weeks, when we presented an English draft of our labors to the congregation, the majority expressed appreciation, even delight. But the faction took no pleasure in our labors. They raged on against our master.

After one service, during which the faction had refused to participate in the worship, his voice heavy with weariness, our master said, "It is a miraculous work of God that he has chosen to comfort the afflicted by an infirm vessel, and that God has somehow raised me up to suppress such as fight against his glory."

This was, in fact, an accurate description of the two sides in the Frankfurt congregation. I believe there were many more who supported Master Knox than who opposed him there. Yet did the faction growl and hiss at him, finding every possible reason to assail him. I believe some of the English simply disliked him for his Scots tongue.

Determined to have their way, the faction turned to politics. They brought their grievances against Master Knox to the city authorities in Frankfurt, accusing Knox of treasonous speech against the emperor's relative, Mary Tudor. They finally prevailed against the council by threatening to bring charges against the city before the emperor. The faction insisted that a man who called their queen "Jezebel" ought to be banished from a city in the empire. They intended to force the city officials to dismiss him. The council requested that Master Knox not preach for a time; he submitted to their wishes in this. But this was not enough. Though our master was not in the pulpit, yet did the faction refuse to worship under the same roof with him.

It was, on the whole, a trying time for our master, and for us. He paused in our lessons one morning. "I see the battle shall be great," he said. "For Satan rages even to the uttermost. I have been fighting against Satan, who is ever ready to assault. Yet though Satan appears to prevail against God's elect, yet he is ever frustrated of his final purpose."

I found it more bewildering, however, that warring against Satan in this case meant being at odds with those in the church, others who professed to be Christians, yet who did rage violently against our master and his ministry.

"Let me get this correct," said Francis. "The faction is made up of English refugees, protestants who fled Queen Mary's persecutions. That's why they're here. Yet they now claim offence when you, Master Knox, call a spade a spade. That's how it is, then?"

"Aye, that seems to be how it is," said Master Knox. "But I have here a letter from Geneva."

"From Master Calvin?" said Francis. "Read it to us."

"The relevant portions I shall read," he said. "Doctor Calvin rejoices that we have in the management of the dispute been more courteous than the English. He nevertheless exhorts me to

231

appease those with rankling feelings or a lurking grudge, and to cultivate a holy friendship with the faction." He paused, a smile coming to his pale lips. "Aye, but here's the best part. Calvin invites us to rejoin him in Geneva. He desires that I should take up preaching and pastoral duties among the English-speaking refugees in Geneva."

"I'll get our things," said Francis, pushing his chair from the table. "George, you order a carriage."

34

Nothing to Sing

ON OUR LAST NIGHT IN FRANKFURT, Master Knox called a number of friends and supporters to our chambers. We were like herring in a pickle barrel; there were fifty people in our tiny rooms. He delivered a message to a sober and affectionate gathering on the death and resurrection of our Lord Jesus, and on "the unspeakable joys Christ has prepared for God's elect, though they may in this life suffer trouble and persecution."

On the morning of March 26, 1555, we set off by carriage to Mainz and from there by river barge south on the Rhine River, baronial fortresses standing guard on either side of us. In Basel we continued our travels by carriage. It was an uneventful journey, during which my eagerness to return to Geneva grew with every passing hour. Our carriage made a short stop in Lausanne to take on another passenger. At last we made our way along the roadway to Geneva, sunlight reflecting off the pale trunks of plane trees lining the lakeshore, their branches aglow with a verdant transparency as they were about to burst into leaf. And then the roadway turned and before us in full view laid the city, the spire of St. Pierre rising high above the lake and the old city.

At these sights, I was overwhelmed by a sense of relief. Geneva had become a haven, a place of refuge from the Queen Regent's attempts to absorb Scotland into the maw of France, from the Spanish subjugation of England, and from the petty infighting of English peers in Frankfurt. From the way Francis and Master Knox strained to see the features of the city coming more clearly into view, I saw that they felt much the same as I.

Once we had settled again in our chambers, we were warmly greeted by Doctor Calvin. He wasted no time, and took us along to the Auditoire, the fifteenth-century building hard by the cathedral where our master would shepherd his English-speaking flock, preach the gospel, and prepare his congregation for their hoped-for return to England or Scotland.

That first Sunday back in Geneva, I scanned the faces of those gathered for worship. I always did this in every place Master Knox led us, ever hopeful to see my father's face and perhaps Alexander's. They were not there. But there were faces I did recognize: Richard Ballantyne, the Lindsay brothers, a young Scotsman named William Kethe, and others. Our master began the service using the order he had so carefully drawn up in Frankfurt, we attending him in this labor. When he led us in confessing of our sins before God, a prayer I had helped to write, I will not deny that I grappled with heaping the sin of pride upon my many other offences.

"O Lord, thou art our Father, and we be but earth and slime; seeing thou art our Maker, and we the workmanship of thine hands; since thou art our pastor, and we thy flock; thou art our Redeemer, and we are the people whom thou hast bought; finally, seeing all this, because thou art our God, and we thy chosen heritage, suffer not thine anger so to kindle against us, that thou shouldest punish us in thy wrath, neither remember our wickedness, to take vengeance thereof, but rather chastise us gently according to thy mercy.

"True it is, O Lord, that our misdeeds have inflamed thy wrath against us. Yet since we call upon thy Name, and bear thy mark and badge, maintain rather the work that thou hast begun in us by thy free grace, to the end that all the world may know that thou art our God and Savior. Thou knowest that heavy souls, and comfortless, the humble hearts, the consciences oppressed and laden with the grievous burden of their sins, they who thirst after thy grace, they shall set forth thy glory and praise."

The vaulted Auditoire where we gathered filled with English voices joining in prayer and worship with heart and passion. But singing was another matter altogether. The versified psalms for singing in Geneva were written in French. Though there were those of us who knew sufficient French to participate, English was our native tongue. I knew that Master Knox longed for all our worship to be in English. Genevan psalms had been set to lively melodies by Louis Bourgeois, a gifted musician commissioned by Calvin and the consistory of Geneva to write new music appropriate for singing in worship. I could not help envying our French brethren these melodies to which they could sing the Psalms in their own language.

One of the things I so loved about Geneva were the discussions, vigorous and lively, sometimes heated. Nearing the end of a morning of instruction at the Academy, I observed one such discussion between the fugitive court poet Clemont Marot, Louis Bourgeois himself, and John Calvin. Others entered the discussion, including our master.

"Although music serves our enjoyment rather than our need," said Calvin, "it ought not on that account to be judged of no value; still less should it be condemned."

"I should hope not, indeed." This from Louis Bourgeois the composer.

"There is scarcely anything in this world," said Calvin, "which can more turn or bend hither and thither the ways of men than music."

"Hence, you agree, Doctor Calvin," said Bourgeois, "that music is most profitable."

"Indeed, music can be made profitable to men," said Calvin, "if only it be free from that foolish delight by which it seduces men from better employments and occupies them in vanity."

"Yet, when rightly employed," said Bourgeois, "music is a great aid to men in the worship of God, is it not?"

"'Make a joyful noise to the Lord, all the earth; break forth into joyous song and sing praise!' So sang the psalmist," said Calvin. "Herein is the mysterious strength of music: it has a secret and almost incredible power to move hearts."

"But what of poetry?" It seemed to me fitting that Clemont Marot posed this question.

"When melody goes with poetry," said Calvin, "every bad word penetrates more deeply into the heart. Just as a funnel conveys the wine into the depths of the decanter, so venom and corruption are distilled into the very bottom of the heart by melody."

"But when melody is matched with worthy poetry," said Marot, "with sacred poetry, and a sincere heart, then all is well?"

"Danger may still lurk. We must beware lest our ears be more intent on the music than our minds on the spiritual meaning of the words. You must remember this, Louis, as you craft your music. Songs composed merely to tickle and delight the ear are unbecoming to the majesty of the church and cannot but be most displeasing to God. Augustine heartily approved of and was brought to tears by music, yet did he recognize its perils."

"In what place does he so approve," said Marot, "and after what fashion does he render his approval?"

Any who had been but a short time in Geneva would know what Master Marot was wheedling for by such a question. We had sat enough times in these months under Doctor Calvin's tutelage to know that the man had an astonishing gift of memory, behemoth in proportion. On more than one occasion we had observed him, with no book open before him, recite lengthy passages, cross-referencing them with others, both in Holy Scripture and in the vast theological canon of the Early Church Fathers—all by memory. It was enough to take the breath away to observe it.

"A passage from Augustine's *Confessions* comes to mind," said Calvin. "He expressed it in this fashion: 'How plentifully did I weep in those hymns and psalms, being touched to the very quick by the notes of the church so sweetly singing.' But observe how he hastens to add strong caution, directing us back to the content of the poetry itself. 'When it happens that I am more moved by the song than the thing which is sung, I confess that I sin in a manner deserving punishment.' So said Augustine, and so must we beware of these dangers, dear brothers, in our use of music in worship."

"But we are agreed," said Master Knox, "that we are not now replacing the exclusive use of Latin with the exclusive use of French in worship? What is sung must be in the native tongue of the worshipers; we are agreed?"

"Most assuredly agreed," said Calvin. "Just as Holy Scripture must be read and preached in the common vernacular of the people for their understanding, so what is sung must be in the language of their hearts. For you, John Knox, that is English."

"Yet have we no psalms to sing in English," said Master Knox.

"Then you must create them," said Calvin. "You must raise up poets from among your flock, but not ordinary poets. You need men with literary skill, men who understand the gospel of grace, who are students of the Scriptures, and men who have been gloriously subdued by our Lord Jesus Christ. These are the men you must find."

I could not help observing one of our number on the periphery of this discussion. He said not a word throughout this exchange, but young William Kethe was nothing short of enraptured. I am justified in employing such elevated language, for the man's face gave off a sort of illumination and there was a luster in his eyes. It was the sort of look a boy has when he discovers a broken sword hilt or the iron point of an arrow on an old battlefield.

For several weeks we managed singing, or rather chant-ing, psalms as they appear in English prose, but it was far from ordered, and still further from beautiful music. I was forced to conclude that merely reading the psalms would have been more conducive than our mangled efforts at singing without either metered poetry or musical settings. During one service, I could not help observing William Kethe, close at my side, a short white-feather quill in hand, furiously setting down lines. I leaned nearer to observe what it was he wrote, but he leaned away, feigning distraction, and hastened to cover the paper with his sleeve.

For some months, all went well for us in Geneva, during which time, Master Knox daily engaged for nearly an hour in letter writing. Though we were not always privy to whom he wrote or to the content of his letters, he did write to his flock in Berwick, to congregations in Buckinghamshire, and in London. And I saw with my own eyes more than one letter addressed to Marjory Bowes, Norham Castle.

Then a letter arrived for Master Knox, from Scotland. He lowered himself into a chair, and what color there was in his face faded as he read.

"What is it, master?" I asked.

"This letter tells of great news," he said, once he had found his voice. "The gospel has spread widely throughout the land, so they say. The letter was penned by John Erskine of Dun, with adjoining signatures from David Forrest, Elizabeth Adamson, and many others of the Scots nobility. Together with them, many influential men of the merchant class, along with hosts of common folk, have forsaken idolatry and long for the true doctrines of the gospel of grace."

"These are indeed good tidings," said Francis. "Why then do you grow pale, master?"

"They urge me to return to my beloved Scotland, there to preach and lead Reformation."

"But is it safe, master?" I asked. "I, as you, long for Scotland. But the Queen Regent lives and remains determined to crush men such as you who preach the truth. And Mary Tudor of England yet lives and ravages her country with persecutions. You, master, are not well regarded by tyrants. Is it safe for you to return just now to face not one, but two such tyrants?"

"I feel a sob and a groan," he said, "willing that Christ Jesus might openly be preached in our native country, although it should be with the loss of my wretched life."

I felt that old gnawing in my stomach. He might happily render up his life. But what about ours?

"There is another letter," he continued. "This one arrived more than a week ago. From Berwick-on-Tweed. Norham Castle, as a matter of fact."

"And?"

"Sir Robert Bowes has died." Master Knox rose and paced to the window, his back to us. He seemed suddenly fascinated with the variety of life in the market square upon which our chambers looked. It was a common enough looking street to my eye, yet I marveled at the extent to which it captivated his attention. At last, without turning toward us, he continued. "Elizabeth Bowes informs me that her husband, Sir Richard, has agreed to the marriage."

"The marriage?"

"Yes, the marriage. Sir Robert, who so virulently opposed the union, is dead, and Sir Richard has given his consent."

"To the marriage?" I said.

"To the marriage," said Master Knox, his back still to us.

"If I may be so bold," said Francis. "Who is marrying whom?"

He turned, his expression the same as if he were untying the knot of a syllogism. "John Knox is marrying Marjory Bowes."

35

Play the Man

So it was that late in October 1555, Francis and I found ourselves once again gripping an oar, this time that of the jolly boat of a Dutch merchantman. Master Knox was behind us at the bow, no doubt eagerly straining to see the coastline in the graying gloom of dusk. Rain pelted us, drenching us until I could no longer feel that I had skin. My hands had ceased to be cold, and I only knew by seeing them so before me that they yet clasped the oar. At least we were not chained to our oars, our feet shackled in the putrid hold of an enemy warship. I bent my back and pulled on my oar, such considerations giving me a degree of consolation, though but a little degree.

Awaiting the descent of darkness, the skipper had sailed close to shore under shortened canvas. The vessel had been hove to, while hooded and silent seamen had lowered the jolly boat and stood off as we made our way to shore. It was uncanny how intimately the skipper knew our rugged Scottish coastland. He seemed to know every rock and shoal. As near as we were informed, we were making landfall somewhere between the Firth of Forth and the Border. After that, the ship would set sail for the continent and we would be left to fend for ourselves in a hostile land.

My feelings upon arriving back in Scotland after nearly six years of my life away from my homeland were various indeed. I felt in turn thrilled at the prospect, and longed to be reunited with my father, if he lived, to see my home, to wander the moors above our ancient fortified house in Longniddry, to sup on broth, haggis, blood sausages, oatcakes, rye bread, and shortbread. And then I remembered that Master Knox was a wanted man, a notorious traitor to the Queen Regent and her realm—and we along with him. And then there was England to the immediate south, Queen Mary, now wed to Phillip II, King of Spain, eager for our master's blood. As the bow of the jolly boat struck the gravel on the shore, my innards rumbled turbulently, and I more than half expected to see the mouths of cannons royal gaping at our arrival, the shouts of soldiers, chains and prison.

What followed was a lonely nighttime tramp up the moorland and through the bogs to the northern border of the River Tweed, an early morning river crossing, and refuge at last in Norham Castle. Master Knox, for all his frailty of body, was intrepid in spirit beyond the scope of ordinary men. Astonished at his vigor in such hours, Francis and I were forced to prod each other on to keep up with the man. Exhausted, in the wee hours, we were welcomed by Marjory and her mother Elizabeth at Norham. Fed and warmed by the fire, we were left to recover our strength with sleep.

When we awoke well past midday, Master Knox was up and at his books.

"I am to preach on the morrow," he explained, his face flushed and invigorated.

Like a hawk fleshed on its quarry, Master Knox set to on his mission. In as many days in Berwick, our master preached no less than three times, possibly four. "In the midst of Sodom," he told us with satisfaction after one such sermon, "God has more Lots than one and more faithful daughters than two."

We had observed that our master spent a good deal of time those days with the two faithful daughters, Elizabeth and Marjory Bowes, his first converts in Berwick. Francis and I speculated, though we had no intimate knowledge, that arrangements were being discussed for the marriage. During these days, letters arrived from Edinburgh. Erskine of Dun, David Forres, and, by their accounts, dozens of merchants and guildsmen from the city, scores of people, were urging our master to make his way to Edinburgh with all speed.

Master Knox later referred to his "slothful coldness" at his neglect of the flock in Scotland, but the expedition which these letters energized in him was remarkable to behold. We were intercepted near Dunbar by a man named Syme, a burgess of Edinburgh, who had come, at great risk to himself, to escort us safely into the city.

I had been both excited and anxious at the subterfuge of these our nighttime prowlings about the countryside, but as we came into the very city where the Queen Regent held court and made her home, the Regent who had leveled her cannons at us in St. Andrews, into the capital city of a country on whose throne she was determined by all necessary means to enthrone a French monarch, the excitement vanished into raw inner turbulence.

I wondered at the intrepid man at my side. How could he walk down these cobbled streets, the Queen Regent only yards away in her palace at Holyrood? How could he do so and all so unafraid? Perhaps something in my manner betrayed my mind to him, for he leaned near, his hand upon my neck, and gently pulled my head down toward his. "I too quake, and fear, and tremble," he said. "Hence do we hope in God."

Oddly his words were like oil on the troubled waters of my heart, and I felt that if this little man at my side could find strength to overcome his fears in such an hour, I ought also to walk more boldly at his side.

Syme halted before a narrow house that seemed, in the shadows cast by the lamplight, to be in need of a buttress to prevent it from falling into the street. "Make haste. We are here," he said. Hesitating at the open door, he looked both ways down the street, pulled the door to, and set the latch in place.

What met us at Syme's home on the Royal Mile, we were astonished to see. The place was fairly packed with people, more than that night at our parting from Frankfurt. Some of them seemed familiar to my eye, and judging by the warmth of their greetings, Master Knox was acquainted with many of them. Common folk of the town were present in considerable abundance, and others: David Forres, old friend and convert of George Wishart; Erskine of Dun, also one who had been a friend and supporter of Wishart; fellow preacher John Willock; and there was the elevated personage of the head of the Edinburgh merchants himself, chief officer of the city council of Edinburgh, the Dean of the Guild. In all there must have been more than sixty people, a veritable panoply of Scotland, crammed within the four walls of Syme's house.

Master Knox looked on the gathered assemblage in silence, composing himself with effort to speak to them. "If I had not seen what I see before me this night, here in my own country," he began, "I would not have believed it."

I stole a look at those wedged into the parlor of Syme's home. Candlelight illuminated their faces and flickered warmly in dozens of eyes. I do not exaggerate to describe that congregation as fervent. Careless of the great risk they were taking, they were a collection of people earnestly thirsting after what Master Knox had come to distribute to them.

"It hath pleased God," he continued, "of his superabundant grace, to call me, most wretched of many thousands, back to my beloved Scotland to freely distribute the bread of life as of Christ Jesus I have freely received it." Again he paused. I detected a watery glint in his eyes as he looked at the souls before him. "I feel a sob and a groan," he continued, "longing for the day when Christ Jesus will openly be preached in this our native country, although it should be with the loss of my wretched life."

I suppose it was not possible for that large of a gathering to be long kept silent. Night after night we were led to one house after another, there to dine, and there for our master to preach. Word was out. In every gathering, Francis and I hungrily scanned the faces for our father. Perhaps aware of the extraordinary force amassing against her, the Queen Regent, at first, made no move to halt these gatherings. I took little comfort from her delay.

We had not been in Edinburgh a week when a letter arrived for Master Knox. It was from England—from Oxford, to be precise. A faithful merchant remaining in England had penned the letter. It reeked of smoke, and contained tragic news for our master. He freely sobbed, drenching the parchment with his tears.

On October 16, 1555, Doctor Latimer and Doctor Ridley had been forthwith burned at the stake before Baliol College. The letter recounted Doctor Latimer's final words to his friend before their deaths: "Be of good comfort, Master Ridley, play the man! We shall this day light such a candle, by God's grace, in England, as I trust shall never be put out."

Master Knox paced the floor as he read the letter, but he paused after these words, thrusting the parchment into my hands. The man's signature had been underscored by a finger covered with black soot. I do not recall up to that point in my life seeing a man so torn with warring emotions. Master Knox's cheeks were wet with tears of pity and grief, but his eyes flashed with a rage—a holy rage, I believe it to have been—no doubt directed against the Queen who would destroy the life of such a man.

When at last he trusted himself to speak, he said, "After the death of that most virtuous prince, of whom the godless people of England for the most part were not worthy, Satan now intends nothing less than to extinguish utterly the light of Jesus Christ within the whole Isle of Britain." His voice became fierce as he continued. "God's hot displeasure shall descend upon that idolatress Jezebel, mischievous Mary, of the Spaniard's blood, cruel persecutrix of God's people."

He was fairly shouting as he concluded this denouncement, collapsing into a chair when he had spent his indignation. For some moments he sat motionless, his face buried in his hands.

But there was to be no time for mourning. The months we spent in Scotland on this adventure passed like a sudden squall at sea: violent and tumultuous, then as suddenly at an end.

36

Simple Soldier

NIGHT AFTER NIGHT our master was led to yet another house in Edinburgh where yet again people had gathered to hear him preach the gospel to them. Difficult as it is to believe, the extraordinary became the ordinary in these days, and I had little to do but to marvel at what I heard and saw. It left me exhausted, yet it was not I doing the work of preaching.

As clandestine night led on to clandestine night, I became increasingly anxious. Where was the Queen Regent? When last we had been in this Scotland she had unleashed cannon, and war, and prison upon us. Why did she not attempt to halt Master Knox from preaching? When would her patience be exhausted? When would she unfurl her fury?

I was not alone in these my fears. After nearly a month of moving from house to house in Edinburgh, Lord Erskine conveyed us north to his manor house in Dun. Raw winds savaged the sycamore trees and swept down the moor as we hastened from the carriage into the impressive stone structure. The entire manor was a whir of activity, and the main gate and outer courtyard bristled with great sword and halberd, men-at-arms stationed to defend the manor—and our master. Once within the walls, we were now not entirely surprised to find therein a host of people from throughout the surrounding countryside—from earl to commoner—gathered to hear our master preach. I was astonished to see his "decaying carcass," as our master referred to his frail body, so replete with vigor in these days. I was at a loss to explain how it was possible for such as he to be so manifestly empowered for relentless days of preaching and anxious nights of flight and vigil. The essence of his message remained passionately unaltered:

"By the brightness of God's Scriptures we are brought to the feeling of God's wrath and anger, which by our manifold offences we have justly provoked against ourselves; which revelation and conviction God sends not of a purpose to confound us, but of very love, by which he has concluded our salvation to stand in Jesus Christ."

It was impossible to hear his unfolding of the evangel of Jesus Christ—almost daily in these months—without being profoundly moved. I said unaltered, and so it was, yet I did begin to notice something of a change in our master's message. As near as I could discern—and Francis concurred—the difference lay now in his determination to establish congregations, formed in each house in which he preached.

He declared that a church was no church that taught and practiced another gospel contrary to that which is expressly taught in Holy Scripture. Perplexed, a man named Arbugkill replied, "You will leave us no church."

"It is no true church we have at present in Scotland," replied Master Knox. "The Church of Jesus Christ does not fight against the Word of God; it fights for the true doctrines of the gospel. Of the church of Rome—tyrannically ruled by 'that Italian bishop yonder, the devil's chaplain,' as my dear brother Hugh Latimer termed him—if you will be of that congregation I cannot hinder you. But as for me, I will be of no other Church but that which has Jesus Christ for pastor, hears his voice, and will not hear the voice of a stranger."

Lord Erskine kept us on the move. He was of the opinion that if Master Knox preached widely throughout the realm it would have the twofold benefit of making him harder for the Queen Regent and her bishops to apprehend; still more, the wider his sermons were heard throughout the land, the more widely would be the evangel of Jesus Christ spread to the people in every valley and burgh in Scotland. Thus, we rarely slept in the same bed more than a single night, and often Francis and I had no proper bed at all. In these our desperate wanderings I was more than once reminded of our months as fugitives before joining the Castilians at St. Andrews Castle, long ago. Everywhere we traveled, in Ayrshire, in Angus, we searched for our father and Alexander.

One of the most remarkable things about these gatherings was the social range of those in attendance. In Lothian, as guests in the manor house of Sir James Sandilands, Knox was attended upon by the highest ranking lords of the realm, two of them later to be regents: James Stewart, Earl of Moray, and his uncle Erskine, Governor of Edinburgh Castle, later to be Earl of Mar. It was amongst the exalted company in Sir James Sandilands' house that we at long last gained our first news. We knew it not at the first, but Sir James proved to be near kin of Alexander—his grandfather, in fact. Once we learned this, we asked Master Knox if he would arrange an interview with him. Barely able to contain our excitement, we begged Sir James for information.

At our questions he at first remained silent, rising from his chair in his study and turning his back on us. "I have no certain knowledge of young Alexander's whereabouts." We waited expectantly as he paused. "Though it has come to my attention that he is, in fact, alive."

He raised a hand to silence our exuberance at his words. "And that he is in Scotland. And that he pursues a course of study. Beyond that I know little else."

"With respect, sir," I said. "Alexander has been our companion since birth. When the castle fell, we were separated from him. It has been close on nine years since we have seen him. Forgive our exuberance, but can you tell us nothing more?"

Whether he could not, or would not, we were never certain, yet nothing more were we to learn from him. I felt a mingling of gladness at the news; it gave me hope that we might find still more news of our father. Sir James ended our interview, and we left his study.

Our travels next took us into the regions of the Locharts of Bar, the Campbells of Loudoun, the Chalmers, the Wallaces, and Andrew Stewart, Lord of Ochiltree. Francis and I felt that we were touring the castles of all Scotland in these days: everything from the fortified keep of the minor laird to the grand fortification of Loudoun Castle, reminiscent of when our master had preached at Windsor Castle before Edward, the king, our friend. These meetings were as the reunions of old friends, though I do not know for certain that Master Knox had met any of them in person until then. We learned that these country families were converts to Christ by the preaching of John Rough and George Wishart and, for his love to these men, our master was keen to minister to their converts.

Then in May of 1556, though the Regent dismissed Knox as a mere knave, her bishops made to act against him—and against us. Word arrived in Ayrshire that he was to appear before a council of bishops at Blackfriars Church in Edinburgh.

"Och, aye. You must not go," said Erskine of Dun with feeling. The Earl of Loudoun emphatically agreed, as did nearly every man in the company.

After quietly hearing their protests, our master said, "Yet I love to blow my Master's trumpet." He explained that it was for this that he had returned to Scotland, and was he to refuse such an offering? To defend the evangel of Jesus Christ before the most influential assembly of the clerics of Rome in the land? It was an opportunity not to be passed over. "Our Captain, Christ Jesus, and Satan, his adversary, are now at open defiance, their banners are displayed, and the trumpet is blown on both sides for assembling their armies."

"That is all good and well," said Erskine. "But it is most certainly a trap. You will be surrounded by dozens of men determined to halt your preaching. Make your way to Blackfriars alone, John Knox, and you will burn."

All the men of the company agreed, urging our master to reconsider. I felt very much like joining in their protests. Yet in my heart I never for an instant believed that we would not be packing our things and making our way to Edinburgh at first light. We knew our master better than they.

"Fear not for this decaying carcass," he said. "One man with God is always in the majority."

The assembled lairds were resolved. They determined that it would not be one man who would stand trial in Edinburgh. Dispatches were sent throughout the countryside that night.

They had their effect. When we arrived at the West Bow of the Royal Mile two days later, an assembly of lairds and commoners from throughout the realm had converged on the capital. Knox entered the city surrounded by hundreds of supporters.

Astonished, the bishops scrambled to recover themselves. There was no peaceable way they could seize John Knox, not surrounded as he was by such an array of followers, including nobles and parliamentarians, flanking their preacher. But things grew still worse for the clerics. One of their own number, Bishop Dunkeld, a professed follower of the evangel of Jesus Christ preached by Knox, warmly invited our master and his entourage to lodge with him. Hastily the other bishops withdrew their summons and cancelled the trial they had planned at Blackfriars. Under the protection of Bishop Dunkeld and the Lords of the Congregation, as the nobles faithful to the evangel had begun to call themselves, Knox preached openly for ten days, under the scowl of the clerics, and under the bewildering—and, as events would prove, momentary—indifference of the Queen Regent.

There was great exuberance in those days, as if the Reformation had won, had achieved its triumph. As a result, more than in our previous visit to Edinburgh, Francis and I felt free to move openly about the streets of the city. Everywhere we asked if anyone had knowledge of Hugh Douglas our father and Alexander Cockburn our friend.

"Douglas?" mused a laboring man, removing his tam and scratching his balding head. "Och, aye, there were a man o' the name Douglas."

We could barely believe our ears and accosted him for more information.

"I were repairing stone in the castle, I were," he said, eyeing the rooftops in thought and twirling the point of a trowel in his palm. "Aye, indeed. There were a man of the name o' Douglas there. I donna ken if he were Hugh Douglas. Just Douglas." He tapped at his head and waggled a finger in the air about his ear. "Gang gyte, he were, and months ago it were. I ken nothing more of him."

It was almost worse than learning nothing. Douglas was not an uncommon Scots name, as we knew. And this man seemed not the most reliable of sources. It did not seem possible that the man described was our father. Dejected, we returned to the bishop's lodging. There we found Master Knox seated in our chambers, reading a letter.

"From Geneva," he said. "William Whittingham and the faithful from Frankfurt have reissued now an urgent call for me to return and be pastor of the English-speaking congregation in Geneva."

"Will you go?" asked Francis.

He made no reply.

"Scotland welcomes you here," I said, not entirely certain what else to say.

"Aye, at the moment," he said. "Yet it is a calm before the storm. There's great unrest brewing between the Lords of the Congregation, now a growing political force with which the Regent must reckon, and there is the matter of her young daughter, Mary of Scots, to wed the Dauphin of France, thereby handing the realm over to a French monarch. On the other front, Mary Tudor, of the Spaniard's blood, schemes a union of Catholic Scotland with her idolatrous England, thereby forging a union with Catholic Spain. It makes the head ache to think of it all."

"What will you do?" I asked him. Yet was I asking myself what I would do, what Francis would do? How long did our obligation to Master Knox, and his to us, extend? I wondered if he puzzled over this question. Our father had charged him with our care, but that was more than ten years ago, and no word from our father for most of those years. I had passed my twentieth year, and Francis was two years my senior. Here we were back in Scotland, and, for the moment, in any event, in a lull of quiet.

"There is another matter," he continued. "Scotland's bishops, against all justice and equity, have pronounced against me a most cruel sentence, condemning my body to fire, my soul to damnation, and all doctrine taught by me to be false, deceitful, and heretical. They could not have issued this condemnation against me without the approval of the Regent. Be certain of it, she will not long remain inactive. By God's grace, I fear not their flames, yet do I fear that at this moment if they succeeded in consuming my flesh in those flames, many other preachers would be consumed by it as well, zealous and plain-speaking William Harlow, John Willock, John Grant, John Patrick, Walter Milne, and others. I fear that once the burning begins it shall extend throughout the realm, and many of Christ's dear under-shepherds will die. The Lords of the Congregation agree. Therefore, I believe that my departure at this time will do the greatest good for Reformation in Scotland. By God's mercy, we shall return again to Scotland in his good time."

He sat for some moments in silence. With a sigh, he methodically folded the letter from Geneva and continued. "There is another matter. I do have obligations in England, and have, therefore, been much in prayer about the matter. I have dispatched a letter and escort to Berwick. I am sending my family on to Geneva. Where I intend to join them."

Where he intended to join them? "And what of us?" I asked.

"Your father gave me charge of you," said Master Knox. "He made no stipulation as to the duration of that charge. You're both men and capable of caring for yourselves. Yet your father's words extend as far or as near as you believe them now to extend."

I could not discern from his words whether this meant that he wanted it to extend further or not. Perhaps he was longing to be rid of us, now that he had his wife, his family obligations? We were of age. I looked at the slight pale figure before me. Physically, there was more need of our caring for him than he for us.

"By your leave, Master Knox," said Francis. "The Lord of Dun has spoken with you of his offer to me?"

I could not believe my ears. Francis had said nothing to me of this. "W-what offer?" I managed, but they were not heeding me.

"He has spoken of it to me," said our master.

"With your blessing," said Francis, "I intend to accept his offer and enter his service as secretary."

"You have my blessing, dear Francis," he said. "Go in peace."

I believe my old habit of gazing wide-eyed might have reasserted itself in these moments. I know that the churning of my insides had commenced afresh. I did not know what to say next. I simply stared from my brother to my master.

"There is a most important project underway," he continued, now giving his attention to me. "I would be most gratified, dear George, if you would accompany me back to Geneva, there to engage in that work as my assistant. It is an essential labor for the evangel in this our realm and that of England as well."

37

Bodley's Bible

I HAD NEVER BEEN APART FROM my brother, never from my earliest recollections. As I said my farewell to him, I felt that I was severing something of my own self in that parting. I'll not deny it: I shed tears enough to launder my tunic.

We embarked at Leith under fair skies. The ship was no sooner clear of the Firth of Forth when Master Knox began telling me more of the project that lay ahead in Geneva.

"The work is already underway," he explained. "'Faith cometh by hearing,' so wrote the apostle, 'and hearing by the Word of God.' God has raised men up in the English congregation in Geneva to effect a translation of the Word of God from the Hebrew and Greek into our English tongue. It will be a version for the laird to read out in his hall to his family and servants, but more than that, for the lowest crofter to open with his work-hardened hands and read to his family at table, and to give gospel cheer to the heart of the ancient widow."

I wondered at this. In my experience, I'd never met a crofter or a widow who could read anything, leastwise the Word of God.

"Common folk must know Holy Scripture," he continued, laying a hand on my neck. "It is the flocks' only protection from deceitful shepherds, who rise up to seduce the ignorant. This Bible shall be produced for the sheep, with commentary and instruction on how to read and interpret its meaning according to the evangel of Jesus Christ. Rome has championed long enough the kingdom of the law. The Word of God will restore the kingdom of grace to the hearts of those who hear. This Bible shall be an apparatus, a complete course of study, as it were, in the evangel of grace, therein revealed. It shall include introductory summaries, an index, historical overviews, maps, cross-references, and thousands of notes to guide the common man in reading the Word of God to know the gospel of God."

He paused, steadying himself with a hand on the ratlines and the other on the rail of the ship. Looking at our wake, he gazed back at the Scottish shore. I followed his gaze and watched the craggy outline of the Bass Rock, yet visible astern. A fresh breeze filled the canvas and thrummed in the rigging, the ship heeling to leeward. Seaman shouted and heaved as they trimmed sail for France. With every rising and falling of the vessel, the shimmering haze of July made work to obscure the rock, at last enveloping it into the mainland fading behind us. Before us lay Dieppe and another journey by coach across treacherous France, and then Geneva. I wondered when we would again see Scotland's shores.

I at last broke the silence of those moments. "And, Master Knox, what is to be my task in this labor?"

"As you aided me on the Book of Common Order, so you shall do on the Bible."

"You have as yet taught me no Hebrew," I said. "And my Greek would not fool a hoplite. I pity the crofter that must make intelligence of my efforts."

He laughed. "Hence, this project shall serve more purposes than one. With you at my side, I shall continue to discharge your father's commission given to me for your instruction."

On the remainder of our journey to Geneva, I found my mind anxious about our living arrangements. Master Knox was betrothed and legally wed to Marjory Bowes. He would no doubt set up house with the young woman and her mother, a domestic arrangement that left little place for the likes of an overgrown student such as I was. I had for nearly ten years shared chambers with Master Knox and my brother. Surely that arrangement would be altered in his new circumstances. I felt in those days like a fractured curling stone kept around to prop the door.

Once in Geneva, I discovered that William Whittingham had arranged everything. I was to be housed on the main floor of a large house near the Auditoire, there to live with William Kethe, Thomas Sampson, William and Thomas Cole, and other single English and Scottish fugitives of the male gender, a sort of ships-hold living arrangement. Meanwhile, Master Knox and his new family were to set up their new life together on the floor above us.

I came very soon to know the various moods of my master in his footfalls, transmuted through oaken beams and floorboards above my head. I knew when he was energized by his studies by the weightier fall of his heels; I knew when he was preparing a rejoinder in debate by the clipped spinning of his toes as he paced back and forth above me; I knew when he was full of new domestic joys by the lightness of his tread and the vigor of his laughter; I knew when he was troubled and unable to rest by the weary shuffle of his feet late in the night; I knew when his old malady was upon him by the absence of his footfalls; in their place was the light shuffling of his wife's feet coming to and fro from his bedside as she ministered to his need.

Daily I labored at my studies and at my occasional contribution to the work of the Bible. Where we gathered each morning was a vaulted hall in the old monastic buildings hard by the cathedral. My first task of the morning was to set a fire and warm the room before the others arrived. After that, I commenced the trimming of candlewicks, the cutting of quills, the topping off of inkwells, and the setting out of blank parchment. I grew fond of the scent of that room, of the mingling of burning beeswax, carbon ink and paper, and rich calf leather. And there were books, some of them more than a span thick, stacked on three rows of tables in the hall. Leather-clad tomes they were: the Hebrew Old Testament, the Greek New Testament, volumes by Augustine and the Church Fathers, newer books bearing such authors' names as Martin Bucer, Ulrich Zwingli, Martin Luther, and Doctor Calvin himself. Master Knox was joined in the labor by Miles Coverdale, William Whittingham, Anthony Gilby, with frequent assistance and encouragement from the young Greek scholar and colleague of Doctor Calvin's, Theodore Beza. I came to feel that I knew these men, as scholars, to be sure, but as men of the evangel of Jesus Christ, as my master affectionately termed them.

John Calvin made frequent, if not daily, appearances, and was often consulted on the translation of difficult passages and for guidance in wording commentary on those passages. I was astonished at his ability to cross-reference a text to other places throughout the vast pages of Holy Scripture, all without the benefit of immediately consulting those texts, done from his memory alone.

Perhaps for this very purpose, it was he who urged us to begin adding numerical designations to the verses in the chapters of each book of Holy Scripture, thereby making easier the "analogy of faith," as he termed it, the comparing of Scripture with itself, the only method of ensuring accurate interpretation.

"The Word of God, George, it is most important that you understand," Master Knox would say to me, "is one Word, unified, consistent with itself, without error or contradiction. If we are to understand its doctrine aright, we are not at liberty to interpret one passage in a way that is inconsistent with the evangel of Jesus Christ, the pure doctrine of grace, elsewhere revealed in its glorious fulfillment."

There were others laboring at this important work: a man called John Foxe, affectionately called "Father Foxe" by some of the others; John Bale, William Kethe, Christopher Goodman, Thomas Wood, and my flatmates Thomas Sampson and William and Thomas Cole. It was an array of humanity thrown together by the providence of God: exiles, fugitives, and refugees, men with whom I spent many hours of labor—delightful labor, I must confess, labor in which I came to find satisfaction and pleasure.

Often in those days when tensions began to mount over the meaning of a particular text, when tempers flared, and dark looks began to appear on faces, it was Master Knox who would pour the oil of gracious prayer on the troubled waters of warring scholarship. "This is thy Word, O God, and we are but thy servants in our labors. Come to our aid in this hour. Illuminate our minds and our hearts by your grace to understand thy Word aright." So he would pray in this fashion.

I learned that it was John Bodley, wealthy English scholar, past supporter of my master in his ministry in Frankfurt, who had so desired Master Knox's presence on this effort. And it was he who was the principal financier of the work. As such, he was daily in the Bible hall, proofreading, amending notes, verifying cross-references, and generally taking great delight in our labors.

At last, Master Knox set me to the task of writing initial drafts of commentary. For a time I labored, with unable pen, on the early chapters in the book of Exodus. He revised and amended my work, and by his explanations for doing so, I came to a new level of comprehension of the history therein recorded. "Then Pharaoh charged all his people, saying, 'Every man child that is born, cast ye into the river, but reserve every maid child alive.'" To this verse late in Exodus the first chapter, my master added the commentary, "When tyrants cannot prevail by craft, they burst forth into open rage."

Hence, Master Knox felt my efforts might be better served if I were to labor with the men at work on the New Testament. With but minor revision of my efforts I assisted in crafting notes on the epistle of 1 John, this from the second chapter: "They went out from us, but they were not of us; for if they had been of us, they should have continued with us. But this cometh to pass, that it might appear, that they are not all of us." To which Master Knox assisted me in commenting thus: "That they should not be terrified that a redeemed soul could irretrievably stumble and fall back, first he maketh plain unto them that although such as fall from God and his religion had place in the Church, yet they were never of the Church; because the Church is the company of the elect which cannot perish, and therefore cannot fall from Christ. So then the elect can never fall from grace."

It was not possible to be unaffected by my daily labors, immersed as I was in Holy Scripture and the evangel. But it was here in Geneva that I began more deeply to wonder if I was one of those who merely had an outward place in the church. Or was I truly of the company of the elect who cannot perish, who cannot fall from Christ?

Amidst these anxieties, I came to notice a change in Master Knox's domestic life. His wife Marjory, who with her mother often refreshed us with pots of tea in our labors, come less to the hall. And when she did, her complexion was that of the parchments on which we wrote. She would halt and stand poised, swallowing. On one occasion, she hastily set down her tray and fled from the room. Master Knox was attentive to her, more so than ordinarily.

I was bewildered by it all.

38

Blast of the Trumpet

In 1557, the New Testament of the Geneva Bible, as it was now titled, was complete. I could not help feeling some small measure of pride at my part in the effort, though I knew that my role was miniscule compared with that of the scholars and preachers whose great gifts and learning had brought it about.

So where my own contribution failed me, I took pride in that of my master, who had played such an important role in laboring over and delivering this Bible for the common man, as he often termed it. In that same year, Master Knox had his part to play in yet another laboring and delivering. Marjory seldom left the floor above where I stayed with the other young men. And for several months I heard hasty footsteps in the morning, and if it violates no prohibition, I record that I also heard the most copious retching sounds.

I am, I confess, somewhat ignorant of matrimonial and domestic affairs. Master Knox took pains to teach us many things in his tutelage of my brother and me. He did not, however, inform me in any clear fashion as to such matters. Growing up without a mother, a wandering fugitive, confined in a castle under siege, chained to an oar in a French war galley, fleeing for my life from female tyrants—none of this had prepared me for what followed.

Mysterious to my crippled understanding as it was, Marjory had been pregnant and now managed to deliver a man-child into the world. A rather noisy one, as I was to find out in the nights to follow. Through the beamed ceiling above my bedchamber, I was often awakened by the weeping and wailing of that man-child, Nathaniel Knox by name. In the months that followed, as the little man gained more composure, the retching recommenced, and within a year Marjory managed the same feat, and another man-child, to be called Eleazar Knox, was brought into the world, with very much the same cycle of midnight wailing.

Meanwhile, Master Knox continued his labors on the Old Testament of the Geneva Bible, and on preaching, and letter writing with the Lords of the Congregation back in Scotland. Though from the redness in his eyes, and the slowness of his step, he sometimes looked like he had been deprived of sleep by the now two products of his domestic life, there was a manner about him that I could ill define. He seemed settled and contented in ways I had not observed in his manners before. His happiness in his wife and two sons notwithstanding, he had lost nothing of the thunder of his oratory when he stepped into the pulpit. In fact, it appeared to me that family life and the obligations of wife and children had increased his zeal for the free proclamation of the evangel in his beloved Scotland.

One morning as he prayed before we commenced our translation efforts, his voice rose to a crescendo and he fairly cried, "O Lord, give me Scotland or I die!"

That afternoon when Doctor Calvin entered the translation hall, his face seemed more gaunt than usual, his cheeks more sunken, and I observed that his eyes stared as if seeing past what was before him. He made few comments on our work, and whereas it was normal for him to offer no fewer than half a dozen references when asked for aid in cross-referencing a text, he offered only one when asked for assistance. I was near at hand when Master Knox inquired after his health.

"I am sore afflicted," said Calvin softly. "By God's mercy, my affliction today is not of my body." He gestured with a hand about the hall. "Look around you at these men. For more than twenty years I have seen men such as these come and go. They come and learn the doctrine of grace alone in Christ Jesus alone, and then inflamed with holy zeal for that gospel they return to the land of their birth." Again he paused, stroking his cheek in thought. "There they return—so many of them—to be martyred for Christ. So it has been with my beloved Bartholomew. A bookseller in Turin, Bartholomew Hector's crime was aiding in the distribution of the Old Testament in the Waldensian dialect. According to a recent letter I have received, the Parliament of Turin under orders from Pope Paul III has ordered his arrest, mock trial, and imminent burning."

Doctor Calvin's servant was standing next to me as his master related this sad news. "He was denounced by a royal agent," said Calvin. "O, how much less evil would there be in this world if men were not such lovers of money." No audible sound came from Calvin's servant at my side, but it was as if a tremor had shot through the man's body. And then he moaned. So deep was his moaning that it was more felt than heard, an anguished upheaval of some inner torment. I wondered if the man at my side had known this Bartholomew Hector, perhaps had been a friend of his, and I turned to inquire of him. But when I saw the look in his eyes, a look as of a man on the rack, I thought better of it and said nothing.

Soon thereafter Calvin with his servant left the hall. Our translation work now suspended, there was talk of Catherine de Medici, the cruel Queen Mother of France, and her schemes to wipe out all Huguenots, as the French protestants were called, from that benighted realm. Theodore Beza, who had heretofore been silent, made this observation, "It belongs in truth to the church of God to receive blows, such as do our brethren in France and elsewhere, but the church is an anvil that has worn out many hammers."

All this troubled me greatly. If we were ever able to return to Scotland, what would become of Master Knox—and of me? Was this Bartholomew's fate to be ours?

This news refreshed every violent nerve in my master's mind against tyrants who inflicted such blows on the church and her under-shepherds. And he often discussed these things with others, particularly renewing his inquiry with Doctor Calvin. Whereas news of martyrdom inflamed my master with sobs and tears and an irrepressible desire to return to Scotland, my reaction was quite the contrary. I had been happy here in Geneva, learning many things, making a contribution, so I believed, and making new friends. Yet it was not to be denied; Master Knox was determined to return.

News from Erskine of Dun and the Lords of the Congregation was not good. The Queen Regent, whose wrath had long slept, had now awakened herself with a fury. "Therewith," wrote Erskine, "every man put on his steel bonnet." The image of the patron saint of St. Giles Cathedral had been torn down, thrown in the North Loch, then raised and publicly burned on the Royal Mile. Incited by the bishops, the Regent had had enough. There was an open declaration of war on all preachers of Reformation; anyone who harbored the same was subject to the stiffest penalties the law allowed. One unlearned preacher, zealous Paul Methuen, a former baker by trade, so infuriated the Regent that she condemned him to death without a trial, and, for good measure, pronounced the same against my master's friend John Willock. A clowning effigy of Master Knox had been hoisted up at the Mercat Cross and set ablaze by the Regent's order. And then news arrived from St. Andrews that Walter Myln, an aged priest of eighty and two years, a poor man who had fearlessly gone about the Kingdom of Fife proclaiming the good news of the evangel of Jesus Christ, had been tried and convicted of heresy. In April, by order of the archbishop, he had been sentenced to burn.

Indignant at the news, my master asked me to assist in penning an epistle directly to the Queen Regent herself. He proceeded as follows: "The eternal providence of the same God, who has appointed his chosen children to fight in this transitory and wretched life a strong and difficult battle, has also appointed their final victory, by a marvelous fashion; and the manner of their preservation in their battle is more marvelous. Their victory stands not in resisting, but in suffering; as our sovereign Master pronounces to his disciples that in their patience should they possess their souls."

Then, changing course, he continued with a more confronting argument, punctuated with fuming parentheticals, which I have faithfully set down.

"Considering that this their blasphemy is vomited forth against the eternal truth of Christ's evangel (whereof it has pleased the great mercy of God to make me a minister), I cannot cease to notify as well to your grace, as unto them, that so little am I afraid of their tyrannical and surmised sentence, that in place of the picture (if God impede not my purpose), they shall have the body to justify that doctrine which they (members of Satan) blasphemously do condemn."

When he had completed the entire letter to his satisfaction, he forthwith had me address it to the Regent at Edinburgh Castle, set his signature upon it, and sent it by courier to Scotland. Meanwhile, Bloody Mary Tudor, south of the River Tweed, continued to vent her rage against Reformers in England. By 1558, the number burned by her authority had reached 280 souls. I could see it in my master's eyes, that fierce, blue-gray flashing, and I could see it in the set of his jaw. He spoke with Doctor Calvin often, who observed, "Government by such a woman is a deviation from the original and proper order of nature. Such a rule is to be ranked, no less than slavery, amongst the punishments consequent upon the fall of man."

My master was resolved. He asked me to meet next morning to assist him in a treatise he must write. He had more often these days asked me to take down what he said. Perhaps it was failing eyesight, or perhaps he had come to recognize that his greatest eloquence lay in speaking from his heart. In any event, he had me to his private study. When I entered his study, he was in prayer, and as was his custom, he was praying aloud. "Repress the pride of these bloodthirsty tyrants; consume them in thine anger according to the reproach which they have laid against thy holy name. Pour forth thy vengeance upon them, and let our eyes behold the blood of thy saints required of their hands. Delay not thy vengeance, O Lord! But let death devour them in haste; let the earth swallow them up; and let them go down to the hells. Amen."

When he rose from his knees, he greeted me. I sat down, re-cut my quill, readied a parchment before me on the table, inked my pen, and waited.

"I love to blow my Master's trumpet, as you know, George," he said. "And blow it I shall. This day we shall blow it against Bloody Jezebel, Mary Tudor, and all of her ilk. We shall call it: *The First Blast of the Trumpet Against the Monstrous Regiment of Women*. Now then set down what herein I speak."

I penned the title, and set down the date, 1558, and he commenced.

For neither may the tyranny of princes, neither the foolishness of the people, neither wicked laws made against God, neither yet the felicity that in this earth may hereof ensue, make that thing lawful which he by his Word hath manifestly condemned.

Wonder it is how abominable before God is the empire and rule of a wicked woman, yea, of a traitorous and bastard. We hear the blood of our brethren, the members of Christ Jesus, most cruelly to be shed, and the monstrous empire of a cruel woman we know to be the only occasion of all those miseries. It is a thing most odious in the presence of God, and her officers must study to repress her inordinate pride and tyranny to the uttermost of their power.

This too he sent by courier to Mary Tudor's court in London.

Meanwhile, work on the Geneva Bible was nearing comple-tion, and Master Knox was showing signs of impatience, eagerness to be back in the fray in his homeland. There was no hiding it for the man. I had come so well to read his moods. I knew that we would be returning soon to Scotland. It was what would happen to us when we did so that troubled me.

One week later, after listening to Calvin deliver a sermon from Psalm 93 in St. Pierre, Master Knox, with Marjory, his mother-in-law, and his two toddlers in tow, paused on the steps of the great church. Gazing out over the city, with wonderment on his face and in his tone, he said, "Here exists the most perfect school of Christ which has been since the days of the apostles on earth."

The next day, all Geneva was astir with the news. It is fair to suppose that all Europe was astir with the news: Queen Mary Tudor of England was dead.

39

Scotland on Fire

UPON HEARING THE NEWS of Mary's death, my master immediately dispatched letters to William Cecil. "The man is worthy
of hell for his horrible defections from the truth during Mary's
bloody reign," he said as he wrote. I wondered if he was thinking
of Hugh Latimer and Nicholas Ridley; what had time-serving
Cecil done to deliver them? "Cecil and all cowardly, unprincipled
men like him shall be as the chaff which the wind driveth away for
his dissembling." True it was that Cecil had altered his allegiance
more than once, and that he had reconverted to Rome throughout
Mary's five-year reign. Master Knox sent him letters to give to
newly crowned Elizabeth, bold letters, filled with fearless words,
calling her to expel idolatry from her realm, to give free rein to
the evangel of Jesus Christ, to bring back the exiles to her realm.
"Only humility and dejection of herself before God shall be the
firmity and stability of her throne."

So concerned was my master with England that for a time I
wondered if he did not prefer returning to preach in England more
than Scotland. Perhaps it was that his wife and mother-in-law

were English. Perhaps he felt that if he could preach the pure doctrine of the evangel in England that Scotland would follow, but that it was not likely to work the other way around. In any event, with all speed he gathered his family, and I with them, and made for Dieppe, there to wait developments.

Meanwhile, we learned that the Lords of the Congregation, the nobles of Scotland, were poised and ready to throw off the Roman yoke once and for all, along with any who opposed them. In solidarity with the lords, common peasants wrote ballads in mockery of friars and bishops: "The blind bishop, he could not preach, for playing with the lassies," they sang. And they boldly placed placards giving notice to monks and friars to deliver over the monasteries and lands to the genuine poor. The aging Queen Regent, fearful that her power was slipping from her grasp, accused the preachers of stirring up the realm and ordered them to appear in Stirling on May 10, 1559, to answer for their crimes.

We learned all this in letters while we waited. It was during this in-between time in our lives, a time of homelessness, so it felt in my bosom, that another letter arrived. This one from my brother Francis. It commenced chattily enough. Then his tone altered. He had fallen in love, it said, and was betrothed. Not knowing how long I would be in exile in Geneva, it continued, he had gone forward with the marriage. His new wife and family were people of Newcastle. With the death of the late queen, he went on, they had returned to Newcastle, there to live. He assured me of his undying love and relinquished his claim "to our father's lands and estate in Longniddry, when and such time as they fall to you, dear brother." Once again my heart was flooded with that mysterious blending of emotion, joy at his happiness, and sadness and longing for our father, for our home. I assuaged my emotions by crafting a congratulatory epistle, wishing him joy.

While we waited in Dieppe, Master Knox was not idle. I had come to believe that it was not possible for him to be so. He ministered among the oppressed Huguenots of that town and region, preaching often in their houses and barns and, on one occasion, in a remote cave. When not at this labor, he worked on a treatise responding to Anabaptist objections to the doctrine of predestination and further refined his understanding of what the Bible taught about the roles of civil and church authority. Impatient as he was during this time of waiting, I believe these his studies and ministry would prove to be of great benefit in the years ahead.

At last the Lords of the Congregation were resolved. In order to stand effectively against the Regent, they must have a spiritual leader, one all Scotland would follow, one endowed with vigor, authority, and power, one who loved Scotland and wanted her free of French oppression, but one who loved the evangel of Jesus Christ above all. So said their letter to John Knox, commissioning him to return and be that man.

Forthwith, we arrived on the shores of Scotland on May 2, 1559, with Marjory, her mother, and the boys. Master Knox's faithful friend John Syme made arrangements to care for Marjory, the two boys, and Elizabeth Bowes. I seldom witnessed my master in emotional turmoil; he was little subject to flights of superficial feeling. Yet the night he parted from his wife and children, I saw anguish upon his features like never before. "Indeed do I feel a sob and a groan," he said in his manner of speaking and praying at one and the same time, "longing that the evangel of Christ Jesus might openly be preached throughout this troubled country. It may be so at the loss of my wretched life, but, O Lord, may it not be so at the loss of my dear ones."

During the two days we passed in Edinburgh, I studied every face and feature that I saw on the streets, searching for my father or Alexander, but to no avail. On the third day, we traveled to Dundee with Erskine of Dun, the Master of Lindsay, and several others of the gentry.

"I see the battle shall be great," said Master Knox to an assembly of supporters. "And I am come, I praise my God, even in the brunt of the battle. My fellow-preachers and I have a day appointed to answer before the Queen Regent. I intend, if God impede not, by life, by death, or else by both, to glorify his Holy Name, who thus mercifully hath heard my long cries. Pray that I shrink not when the battle approacheth."

Word was out that John Knox had returned to Scotland; the Regent made a public proclamation forbidding him to preach in the realm. I knew that no such proclamation, whatever the penalty, would alter his course. In every town we passed through, more joined our procession, gentry of all ranks, students and scholars, merchants and tradesmen, peasants and crofters. It was beyond imagining.

May 10, the day the Regent had ordered the preachers to appear before her in Stirling, came and went. The Lords of the Congregation felt it was not wise so to honor her command, and urged John Knox to forbear appearing. At their insistence, we gave Stirling a wide berth and carried on to Perth. On Thursday, May 11, we arrived at St. John's Church, Perth, where a great crowd had gathered to hear Master Knox preach.

With a North Sea crossing only days before, bone-jarring travel by road, and condemned and hunted by the Regent, my master's old malady was reasserting itself. Nevertheless, he rose to the pulpit with authority and commenced preaching. No portion of the church was not occupied—but not all by friends. There were friars in gray and black cowls present, and papists wearing priestly vestments and dark looks. By their whisperings and gestures of contempt, I feared what might ensue. Yet did none of this deter my master.

"Mark, papists, and consider how Satan hath blinded you; you do manifestly lie, and do not perceive the same. You do blaspheme God at every word, and can you not repent? They say the Mass is an applicatory sacrifice, a sacrifice whereby they do and may apply the merits of Christ's passion unto sinners. They will be layers on of plasters! But I fear the wound is not well ripened, and that therefore the plasters are unprofitable. You say you may apply the merits of Christ's passion to whom you list. This is proudly spoken. Then you have the power to make peace with God for whomever you will at your pleasure?"

A stirring rippled throughout the congregation at his words.

"Paul to the Romans says no one can lay a charge against God's elect. No man can give or withhold God's grace. God himself saith that there is none who may move his wrath against his chosen. And here ought you to rejoice, brethren: neither the pope, nor his priests, nor bishops may cause God to be angry against you, although they curse you with cross, bell, and candle; so may no man compel him to love or receive any but whom it pleases his infinite goodness.

"But you make free to distribute the counsels of God? Advise you well. The nature of God is to be free, and enthralled unto nothing; for although he is bound and obliged to fulfill all that his Word promises to the faithful believers, yet that is neither subjection nor thralldom; for freely he made his promise, and freely he fulfills the same."

Words like "thralldom" and "freedom" had their effect on that congregation that day.

"Prove to me from Scripture alone where God made his promise unto you papist priests that you have power to apply, as you say, the merits of Christ's passion to all and sundry who count out their money to you for that purpose? Does God take any part of the profit that you reserve? Alas, I have compassion upon your vanity, but more upon the simple people that have been deceived by you and your false doctrine."

Next he described how God hates idolatry and how his servants, the prophets of old, ordered the destruction of idols. He concluded with a passionate call to turn from falsehood and error in repentance and true saving faith and to find mercy in Christ's merit alone.

At his final words, there was a thundering of hooves and a scattering of small stones as a rider reined in his horse before the west door of the church. Erskine of Dun strode in the door. He must earlier have left our party as it grew in size, for I had thought him still with us.

"By your leave, John Knox," he called, breathing heavily from his ride. "I have urgent news. The Queen Regent, enraged at your failure to appear in Stirling, has declared you and all preachers of Reformation, and any man who assists, comforts, receives, or maintains you, a rebel and subject to the punishment of rebellion."

Suddenly the church filled with racket as hundreds of people spoke at once. While order was suspended, and Master Knox spoke with Erskine and other lords, a priest of St. John's, either intensely courageous or intensely daft, made for the table on the chancel.

Hastily he spread a white covering upon it and laid out the candlesticks, chalice, and other appurtenances of the Mass. He then produced a plaster image of the Virgin Mary. Placing his hands together, he bowed low before it, kissed it, and then reached for the chalice. Holding the cup of wine in both hands and lifting it heavenward, the intrepid priest chanted, "*Hic est enim calix sanguinis mei.*"

"This is intolerable!" cried a boy's voice. Boldly, the young man made his way toward the altar and the priest. "When God by his Word has plainly damned idolatry, shall we stand and see it enacted before us?"

The priest's face became red with anger. He turned and struck the boy full in the face with the back of his hand. The boy cried out. Then, casting about as if looking for something, the lad bent over, then threw an object at the idol. What he threw, no one seemed to know. It may have been a stone, or it may have been a candlestick or the chalice. But the image toppled, hitting the flagstone floor with a crash. That crash ignited something in the crowd. In an instant there was a living, shouting mass of people surging forward to the altar.

"We must stop the rascal multitude!" called Master Knox.

But there was to be no stopping them. The linen table-covering and a tapestry hung before the pulpit were lit with the candles; flames leapt upward, maddening the crowd into a frenzy. Men hoisted boys onto their shoulders, who then began yanking and reefing at images until they broke free and tumbled to pieces on the floor. A woman screamed as a statue of St. John nearly fell on her child. Women and children started running to flee the chaos that had erupted throughout the church. In hopes of diverting the damage of the mob, one lord, Sir James Croft, drew his sword, and others followed suit. At that point many left the church. But word soon arrived that the mob had spread out to the nearby monasteries of the Black Friars, the Grey Friars, and the Carthusian Abbey, crashing images and breaking the accoutrements of the Roman rite.

When at last the renegades had spent their fury, Master Knox lowered himself wearily onto the steps of the church.

I knew his malady was upon him, and at such a time when strength was so greatly needed. "The Queen Regent," I ventured to observe, "will be none too happy about this."

"Aye, indeed, she will not," replied Master Knox. "I am uncertain as yet what God shall further work in this country, except that I see the battle shall be great, for Satan rageth even to the uttermost."

No sooner had he spoken the words than a young laird arrived on horseback from Edinburgh. His horse was all sweat and froth, and the man himself could barely speak, so spent was he from riding.

"The Regent," he began, blowing hard, "levies troops from Stirlingshire, Lothian, and Clydesdale. She marches on Perth with her French army. John Knox she has declared outlaw and enemy of her rule, along with any who teach his doctrine or heed his message, though she termed it 'his rantings.' The chief enemies of Jesus Christ who advise her, the Abbot of Kilwinning and Matthew Hamilton of Milburn, throw faggots on the fire with the cry, 'Forward upon the heretics! We shall once rid the realm of them!' So is their resolve, and my message."

"Do James Stewart and Argyll march at her side?" asked Erskine of Dun.

"Aye, they do."

"If those two lords turned against her," said Sir James Croft, "the breach would be complete. The greatest part of Scotland's nobility would stand against her."

"If God turns the hearts of kings whithersoever he chooses," said Master Knox, "He can turn the hearts of mere lairds." And then he led the assembly in prayer for the same.

When I observed him after the "amen," a new fire had returned to his eyes. "George, get the writing materials set out," he told me. We reentered St. John's, and I wrote as he dictated.

"In the name of the Congregation of Christ Jesus within Scotland," he began. The missive was directed to Mary the Queen Regent, and her foreign bishops, "the generation of antichrist, the pestilent prelates, and their shavelings within Scotland." He proceeded with strong words for the vacillating nobility. "You who have sometime professed faith in Christ Jesus with us and yet have left us in our extreme necessity, stay yourselves and the fury of others from persecution of us, till our cause be tried in lawful and open judgment, or at least look through your fingers in this our trouble." He declared the Congregation to be the true church in Scotland and invited all true Scots to join the church by faith in Christ Jesus. He concluded with a defiant salvo. "If you chose to fight against Christ and his church, you compel us to take up the sword of just defense and to call on the princes and councils of every Christian realm to come to our aid against you."

My heart melted within me as I wrote. His words sounded like those of Jeremiah and the prophets of old—many who came to violent ends. It was nothing short of a declaration of war, and I was tempted to suggest revision, or even insert the same. Yet I did not. When it was read out before the assembled lords, they replied with hearty shouts of defiance. Soon men had cut lengths of rope and tied them in nooses about their necks.

"They show their resolve," said my master. "If they fail in their defiance, they carry their own noose about their necks; if they triumph, it is ready to hand for their enemies' necks."

Erskine of Dun ordered his men to fortify the city and ready ordnance for defense. My old worries returned, and with them the turbulence in my insides. Wherever Master Knox went, close on his heels followed trouble, strife, and sword. Here I was again, at his side—flanked by hauberk and cannon.

"If the Regent can raise an army," said Erskine, his jaw set, "so can we."

40

St. Andrews Thunder

"WE ARE GRAVELY OUTNUMBERED. And the Regent's army stands but fifteen miles from Perth. Chatelheraut commands nigh on 8,000 soldiers, mostly French."

It was Monday, May 22, 1559, when this intelligence arrived. Our numbers were fewer than 5,000. But there was heartening word. Lord Glencairn and the lairds Boyd, Ochiltree, and Gadgirth, with John Willock for preacher and an army of 2,500 men, were on the march from Glasgow. I cannot explain it, but Master Knox was enlivened by it all, never missing an opportunity to deliver the Word of God to the amassing soldiery at Perth. And in the midst of all, he prayed.

"Let thy mighty hand and outstretched arm, O Lord, be still our defense; thy mercy and loving-kindness in Jesus Christ, thy dear Son, our salvation; thy true and holy Word our instruction; thy grace and Holy Spirit our comfort and consolation, unto the end and in the end. Amen. O Lord, increase our faith. Amen."

And we waited. There was word that Montrose, with an army sympathetic to the Regent, would converge at Perth by week's end. Then on Wednesday, the Earl of Argyll and James Stewart, under a flag of truce, entered the gates of Perth. "We must beware of placing our trust in princes," I heard Master Knox murmur at my side. Those two Scots lords received many a dark look as they reined in their steeds and dismounted before St. John's. Yet was it a promising sign that the Regent had sent in Scots lords to parley rather than her French army to crush, bombard, and destroy.

But I could not make out why she hesitated, and spoke my fears to my master. "Why does the Regent not descend upon us?" I asked. "She has power enough."

"She fears England," said Master Knox. "Though my *First Blast* has blown from me all my friends in England, yet is Queen Elizabeth dead set against a French monarch on the throne of Scotland—not on her island. And the Regent knows this. So she must be very cautious."

Negotiations commenced warily, the lairds loyal to Reformation, Lords of the Congregation suspicious of these peers who had thus far taken their stand with the Regent and the French. At last, on Sunday, May 28, 1559, an agreement was struck: John Knox and the preachers, and the Lords and their army, would withdraw from Perth, and the Regent was constrained to agree not to occupy it with French troops. The aging Regent by this concession seemed to be losing her resolve; she had placed John Knox under the ban, but when she had the chance, she feared that his support was too great to seize him. The real victory at Perth was still more significant: both Argyll and James Stewart defected from the Regent and joined the Lords of the Congregation, bringing in their train hundreds of men-at-arms. Our side saw all this as a victory, and there was great rejoicing as we marched out of Perth.

We traveled now mounted on horseback, the men of rank about me armed with musket, pike, and sword. My eyes kept straying to the sword at the hip of the man riding next to me. I was troubled in mind about what awaited us in St. Andrews. Perhaps in times such as these, I mused within myself, I ought to consider acquiring such a weapon.

Word followed us from our rearguard that a tragic incident had occurred in the town of St. Johnston after our departure from Perth. The Regent had sent her French soldiers into the town as her vanguard. Parading their strength, her troops fired their hackbuts, six or seven volleys into the unarmed people going about their business in the streets. At the first discharge of the guns, men shouted and women screamed and fell to the ground. Still the French poured in their volleys. It was not possible for such violence to miss its mark. A lad of but ten years, Patrick Murray by name, was struck and killed. His father, the laird of Murray, was beside himself at the death of his son. Word of the foul deed followed us and spread throughout the countryside. The Regent's words when she saw the boy were also widely noised throughout the realm: "It is a pity it chanced only on the son and not also on his father." Her mockery of the boy's death further infuriated Scotland against her.

"Let cruel rulers devise and study till their wits fail," cried Master Knox at the news, "how such a kingdom may prosper. Even so shall these tyrants, after their profound counsels, long devices, and assured determinations, understand and know that the hope of hypocrites shall be frustrated, that a kingdom begun with tyranny and blood can neither be stable nor permanent, but that the glory, the riches, and maintainers of the same shall be as straw in the flame of fire!"

Master Knox's words, inflamed with zeal and righteous indignation, and energized by the magnitude of his inexplicable force of character, had a profound ability to move those who heard him. And always he prayed. His prayers and words seemed to express for all of us our own grief, our indignation, and our hope.

Though stalked by the Regent's army as we marched, Master Knox halted to preach in many of the towns we passed through on our way to St. Andrews. In the towns of Craill and Anstruther, after he "distributed the bread of life as of Christ Jesus I had received it," his hearers rose up and began smashing the idols of popery that adorned their churches. I was growing accustomed to this violence.

"Certainly idolatry must be dissolved," said Master Knox as we rode on to St. Andrews. "But I long for it to be done peaceably, the monasteries restored to their intended purpose as places where the love of Christ Jesus is shown to the poor, the sick, the widowed, and the orphaned. Churches must be converted from idol worship and restored to the true and proper worship of God. Yet must idolatry be destroyed."

Gradually the spires of St. Andrews came into view on the skyline before us. There was a change in the air; in place of the earthy aroma of heather and peat came the briny scent of the sea. I was not entirely prepared for the flooding of memories that the sights and sounds of that city would bring. I had been a boy in those days, a wide-eyed, terrified lad, fearful of his own shadow. As we came into the city, our horses' hooves clopping on the narrow cobbled street, echoing off the houses that formed a stone wall on either side of our company, I recalled the last time I passed over that street. Wide, staring eyes and pale faces appeared and then disappeared in the windows of the houses as we passed.

On our left rose the tower of St. Salvator's chapel, where I had been herald of the laird James Melville to the Queen Regent. My stomach began lurching as it had twelve years before. Coming into view at the end of the street was the castle. I say the castle, but it was the skeletal ruin of a castle, its west-facing gable rising precarious and naked into the blue sky. It was as if I could once again hear the cannons royal thundering and crashing against those once-sturdy walls.

"Here is the spot," said Master Knox, dismounting with a low moan and dropping to one knee. "Here is the place where fornicating Cardinal Beaton ended the life of holy Master Wishart."

To our left rose the impressive spires of St. Andrews Cathedral. At sight of that grand church, I recalled Master Knox's words as we lay chained to our oars on the rowing deck of the galley, all of us fearful that he was near death. Master Knox looked north and east out to where our French galley had been anchored the last time we had seen this place. I knew he was recollecting that desperate time and his words that God would raise him up to preach the evangel of Jesus Christ in this place where first he had been called to preach. I felt that we were caught in spherical alignments, wonderful and strange, as we dismounted and made to enter that magnificent cathedral.

"John Knox!" cried an emissary. He was not alone. From the north side of the cathedral appeared no fewer than twelve armed soldiers, no doubt in the pay of the bishop. "His Excellency forbids you to enter his cathedral. He forbids you to preach in his seat or anywhere in the Kingdom of Fife or any place that falls within his jurisdiction."

"And if I do obey God rather than your pestilent master?" said John Knox calmly.

"You do so at peril of your life," the emissary replied, his chin thrust in defiance. But I detected a hint of fear in his darting eyes as he spoke the words. "He has positioned one dozen culverins against you. The Primate, His Excellency, Bishop of St. Andrews, declares that you will be shot upon sight if you attempt to preach here or anywhere in his diocese."

At this James Stewart, Erskine of Dun, Sir James Croft, the Earl of Argyle, and other lords called a council. At the first they were of a mind to withdraw. "You make too plain a target, John Knox, up there in that high pulpit."

"I cannot, in good conscience, delay preaching," replied my master, "if I am not detained by violence."

"The bishop of St. Andrews is a cruel beast," said Argyll. "We cannot ensure protection of you from his devices."

"Appear to preach in that pulpit, John Knox," said Erskine, "and I fear you make sacrifice of your own life, and perhaps thereby of our cause."

"As for fear of danger to my person," replied my master, "my life is in the hand of him whose glory I seek, and, therefore, I fear not their threats. I desire the hand and weapon of no man to defend me."

For more than an hour, Scotland's nobility discussed the prudence of John Knox preaching at the cathedral, the discussion at times growing heated, and becoming something more of an altercation. At last my master spoke again.

"I take God to witness that I never preached in contempt of any man, nor with the design of hurting any earthly creature, but to delay to preach next day, unless forcibly hindered, I cannot in conscience agree. In this town God first raised me to the dignity of a preacher, and from it I have been reft by French tyranny, at the instigation of the Scottish bishops. The length of my imprisonment and the tortures which I was forced to endure, I will not recite at present, but one thing I cannot conceal, that in the hearing of many yet alive"—at this he looked my way—"I expressed my confident hope of preaching again here in St. Andrews. Now, therefore, when Providence, beyond all men's expectations, has brought again me to this place, I beseech you not to hinder me."

His words prevailed, as they so often did in these days. When I followed Master Knox into the medieval splendor of the nave of that cathedral next morning, Sunday, June 11, 1559, I had no clear impression in my heart that my master would survive that day. I took the archbishop at his word. They would shoot him. And they had no scruples about shooting any who came between him and their long guns. I knew this without a doubt.

My stomach was contorted in knots as he rose and made his way to the pulpit. Each step he climbed tormented me. I held my breath. Was there nothing I could do to prevent it? I knew that James Stewart had commissioned armed men throughout the cathedral, but it was a massive building, with vast columns and arches, and niches, and vaults, and crannies aplenty. An assassin might take his pick where from to shoot and kill John Knox in such a place.

Higher he climbed. There was no one in that place who could not see him without obstruction. He was a target indeed. I was nearly frantic. Master Knox, however, placed his Geneva Bible on the lectern, opened it, calmly faced the vast congregation that had gathered, and read out his text. "And Jesus went into the temple of God, and cast out all them that sold and bought in the temple, and overthrew the tables of the money-changers, and the seats of them that sold doves, and said unto them, It is written, 'My house shall be called the house of prayer,' but ye have made it a den of thieves."

His oratory began calmly enough. But as he expounded the text and began to make comparisons with the thieves occupying the temple in Jesus' day and the priests and bishops in this day, he became more vigorous. He seemed to grow in stature, and there was an extraordinary force behind his words that astonished me, who had often heard him preach in these years. I knew him to be a man frail in health, given to malady, weak in constitution. Yet here he was thundering with an energy not to be understood save by the empowering of divine unction.

At last he came to his final words. "The merchandise of these money-grubbing, hireling shepherds—is the bodies and souls of the people of Scotland!"

41

Cannons at Perth

ST. JOHN'S PARISH CHURCH in Perth had its ornament, to be sure. But it had nothing in the way of idols and images to compare with St. Andrews Cathedral. For centuries it had been a pilgrimage site for those coming to venerate the alleged forearm of the apostle, and in those centuries, rival bishops had expanded its collection of relics, its statuary in stone, its painted images of saints, its gold and silver plate, and its gold-entwined vestments and miters. There was no end to its splendors.

When Master Knox concluded his sermon in St. Andrews Cathedral that fateful day, I knew what would happen next.

Honesty forces me to confess that as I watched the multitude destroying centuries-old stonework, and images crafted in intricate stained glass, I confess I wondered if there was some other way. Perhaps with care and time, these symbols could be reduced from idols to mere works of art, kept in another place, appreciated on an entirely different level? But must they be destroyed? Must the rascal multitude, as my master termed them, be released to do their violence on glass and stone and gold? Was there not some other way?

When we had secured Master Knox in safe lodging and set guards at the door, I made bold to broach the subject with him.

"When images have long been consecrated by a people to the worship of idols," he replied, "I cannot see a way to preserve, or a reason to preserve, the monuments of that idolatry. There are immortal interests at stake, George, that are far more valuable than the preservation of these monuments as mere human art. I cannot see it any other way. Do we maintain the trappings of idolatry, or do we remove them forever? It is chiefly by the splendor of its temples and the sensory magnificence of its order of worship that Rome captivates the senses and the imaginations of the multitude, but to what end? To their temporal enslavement and eternal damnation. The popish church falsely erects splendid idols and fabricates a magnificent strutting rite, but it does so at the cost of the bodies and souls of common folk—men, and women, and children—deceived thereby. George, I care little for the riotous mob's destructive frenzy, but there is far too much at stake. If the eternal welfare of the people of Scotland must come at the price of stone tracery and statuary, then so be it. What is more, we should not expect the prelates and their priests and friars to go away forever. The surest way to keep the rooks from returning is to destroy their nests."

For the next three days, Master Knox preached in the cathedral. So persuasively did he expound the evangel of Jesus Christ and the pure doctrine of his grace that the provost, the baillies, and the vast majority of the inhabitants of St. Andrews were of one mind in destroying the idolatry of the old rite and establishing Reformed preaching and worship in the churches throughout the city. More images were demolished, shrines were stripped of the gold and precious gems, and bloated, hireling clerics were driven from the monasteries.

"Though sworn to poverty," said my master, "these monks have lived like kings. I have never seen such lavish domestic fittings but in a duke's castle. There's enough salt beef to feed the town, smoked haddock fillets, pickled herring by the ton, and barrels of ale and wine—the finest French wine! Poverty, indeed! These be not Grey Friars; they are Grey Thieves! Let us, without delay, in the name of Jesus Christ, charitably distribute all to the poor throughout the city."

And then he turned and looked me full in the face. My heart sank. At the first I recoiled at this responsibility he extended to me. But as I traveled from house to house and croft to croft in those days, I was profoundly moved. So vast was the disparity between the luxury and opulence of the monks and friars and the austerity, simplicity, and abject poverty of the people of the town and surrounding countryside, that I was astounded. More than that, I felt the heat rising with indignation in my bosom. And, yes, I wanted to break something in that indignation. I wanted to break the bonds of false doctrine, of priestcraft elitism and hypocrisy, of the chains forged by careless bishops that shackled the minds and hearts of the ignorant poor in Scotland. Looking back upon it, I believe Master Knox commissioned me for this diaconal duty as a precise means of furthering his instruction of me. He never stopped teaching me. And I began in that duty to understand more of his instruction. A doctrine of justification based in the minutest part upon man's merit of will or good works, ironically, so it seemed to me, makes men into self-indulgent, greedy, hoarding, money-grubbing idol worshipers. Conversely, the true evangel of Jesus Christ transforms men and frees them from the bondage of idolatry and self-worship, frees them and fills them with extravagant gratitude for grace received, and with an over-flooding generosity to extend that grace and love to their needy neighbors.

Meanwhile, all combustible apparatus of the old rite, garnered from the cathedral and the monasteries, was heaped high upon the very site where holy Walter Myln had been martyred, and a great bonfire was ignited, the flames leaping heavenward. The smoke smarted my eyes as it billowed thick and black above the funeral pyre of the worthless cult it represented. Within the next days and weeks, much the same ensued at the towns of Cupar, Lindores, Stirling, and Linlithgow.

Meanwhile, more men joined the ranks of the Lords of the Congregation. From every corner of Scotland appeared lairds with their clan soldiery accompanying, lords of distinction and rank among them. Ruthven rode out from Perth with several hundred men of horse, as did the provost of Falkland.

"Men appear," said my master, "as if they have rained down from the clouds."

Yet the Queen Regent was far from giving up. Too much, for her, was at stake, and she had no intention of handing Scotland over to the "runagate Scot," as she and her kind now termed my master. Her indignation was published abroad with her vow "utterly to destroy all men, women, and children who defect to the new heresy, to consume the same by fire, and to salt their towns as a perpetual desolation." Her resolve gave me the grulie shivers.

The battle lines were drawn. It appeared that it was to be a fight to the death for Scotland. At sunset, word arrived from one of our scouts: "The Regent's French army has pushed her outposts to within ten miles of Cupar. She means to cut us off."

At this intelligence, the Earl of Argyll and James Stewart hastily rallied one hundred men of horse, marched on Cupar, and, before the Regent's troops could get there, occupied the town. The report was clear: hers was a far superior force—that is, in numbers. Perhaps to redeem themselves from their earlier vacillations, Stewart and Argyll were determined to prove their solidarity with the Lords of the Congregation and with John Knox.

More men-at-arms poured in to join our cause. It was nothing short of astonishing to behold. On the morning of June 23, 1559, Stewart and Argyll had been reinforced by Ruthven's cavalry and pikemen from Fife and Angus. Heavy mists obscured the field at Cupar Muir that morning. One of the Regent's French commanders, Monsieur d'Oysel, began a scheme to encircle the cavalry of the Congregation. But when the mists began dissipating at midday, d'Oysel saw a vastly greater force than anticipated readying artillery against him. He was little expecting a pitched battle and apparently lacked the stomach for it. We learned later that dispatches had arrived from Paris suggesting moderation and tolerance and urging the Regent to avoid the arbitrament of arms over matters of religion. D'Oysel did the only prudent thing. He raised a flag of truce and deferred to the Regent and a Parliamentary council for terms of peace.

Three days later, on June 25, we arrived in force at the walls of Perth. In all the maneuvering of these weeks, with weapons small and large all about me, yet had I not heard and felt the thundering of artillery. My last experience of French artillery had been twelve long years ago when St. Andrews Castle fell to the Regent and her French allies. The memory of that fall was like lead in my bowels.

The soldiery of the Regent holding the town, in shameless violation of the last truce, began the assault, and our men readily returned the bombardment. I had forgotten how gut-lurching the thunder of cannons was, and how nauseous was the stench of saltpeter in my nostrils. Volley after volley roared into the night.

The strain of these days was beginning to wear on John Knox. I won't deny that they had their effect upon me as well. Word of our predicament had reached Geneva, and it was in these days that he received a letter from John Calvin; I read it aloud to him. "We are astonished at such incredible progress in so brief a space of time, so we likewise give thanks to God whose singular blessing is signally displayed herein."

My master dictated his brief reply through my pen. "I am prevented from writing to you more amply by a fever which afflicts me, by the weight of labors which oppress me, and the cannon of the French which they have now brought over to crush us. He whose cause we defend will come to the aid of his own."

The next days passed like a whirlwind. The French were expelled from Perth by our force, while the main body of the Regent's army made to occupy the strategic bridges crossing the Firth of Forth. Once again, Stewart and Argyll beat her to the catch. Meanwhile, Erskine of Dun and his company of horse escorted John Knox, myself accompanying, to Scone. After my master preached, his hearers stripped both the Abbey and Palace of Scone of idols, Master Knox doing his best to restrain the mob from fully venting its rage at the Regent's clerical favorites and her commissioned overlords of the city.

Again I was sent to distribute the papists' hoards of food and wealth to the deprived poor in the town and region. There was no lack of rich food and wine, nor was there a lack of hungry, naked poor to receive gratefully the same from my hands. I encountered at a humble dwelling a poor matron of Scone who stood watching the flames of the Abbey burning. Tears streamed unheeded down her leathery cheeks, and I supposed her to be lamenting the fall of the grand gothic structure around which her town had stood these many centuries. But she clutched at my hand and looked into my face with her feeble eyes, and with a tremor in her voice she said these words to me.

"Now I can see that God's judgments are just, and that no man can save where he will punish. Since I can remember, for these many years, this abbey has been a den of whoredom. I cannot tell you how many wives have been adulterated, how many fair virgins have been deflowered by the filthy beasts housed herein, but especially by the wicked man they call bishop. No man who knows what I know of these men would be offended at the burning of this abbey and bishop's palace this day."

Hearing the words of such as that dear matron in Scone that day gave me a clearer understanding of what was at stake. Such encounters, of which there were many, began to work on my heart, and I came to find great pleasure in the fulfilling of my calling.

Then came the decisive move of the Lords of the Congregation. After securing the bridges, Stewart and Argyll, with Ruthven and Rothes, marched with several thousand men-at-arms on Edinburgh, the stronghold of the Regent. Glencairn, Morton, and other lords boldly converged with troops on the capital.

Baffled as she felt her power slipping from her grasp, and bewildered at the suddenness of this reversal, the Queen Regent fled to Dunbar. There she was joined by her commander, d'Oysel, whom, our intelligence claimed, was at his wit's end, his troops hungry and mutinous after fleeing before a rabble army of Scottish lairds and moorland farmers. Meanwhile, the French ambassador in London sent urgent dispatches across the channel. But Paris was in turmoil. King Henry II had been impaled in a jousting tournament and had died. Sickly, fifteen-year-old Francis was hastily crowned King of France. The French ambassador petitioned for Francis and his young wife Mary to join her mother in Scotland and take her place as Queen of Scots. And then Francis II died, leaving Mary of Scotland an eighteen-year-old widow.

June 28, 1559, Master Knox was led in triumph down the Royal Mile in Edinburgh. Great crowds lined the street, a thundering of shouting and rejoicing rising from their lips. James Stewart and the Lords of the Congregation escorted John Knox into St. Giles, the High Kirk of the city. For the first time of many, my master stepped into the pulpit of St. Giles. He looked out on a sea of eager faces there amassed to hear him preach the evangel.

It was a people's gathering that day, with little regard for rank and station. There were lairds in harness, girded with leather, steel, and sword, and there were crofters of the flock and sod, wearing homespun tunics and coarse breeks. There were women of status in silk and satin dresses of French and English design, and there were women of the moorland croft in earasaids, the wool folds of this outer dress wrapped about the shoulders, cinched at the waist, and flowing down to the ankles. There were children, many children: boys in tunic and jerkin, and little girls in the full-covering earasaid, bonnie miniatures of their mothers.

As I scanned the congregation, there was one face that caught and held my attention. Surely this man was not my father. But why had his features so arrested my attention? This man wore the coarse tunic of a peasant, and was of the lowliest of peasants, so it could not be my father. Still, there was something familiar about the man, though the church was so filled with people I never did get a fully unobstructed view of him. So much time had elapsed. I began to despair of ever finding him.

John Cairns, reader of the common prayers, gave a call to worship. After a pastoral prayer was offered, the service proceeded with singing, psalm-singing in English. The ancient vaulted church swelled with the amassed voices of that gathered assembly. I believe it was this moment when I ceased to be an observer of these events. I was now a full-throated, unabashed participant. It was impossible for me to be otherwise. My cheeks were moist with the overwhelming spirit of that singing. We sang as if the restraint and confinement of centuries had suddenly been burst asunder, the erroneous forbiddance against singing praises in our Scots tongue at once thrust aside, thrown off. Now the psalms burst forth from our collective voices, hundreds of people singing, high and low, rich and poor, young and old. But it was singing that came not only from voices, but more from hearts fairly swelling and rising, hearts overcome and joyfully subdued by grace, bursting with praise and gratitude.

> That man hath perfect blessedness,
>> Who walketh not astray
> In counsel of ungodly men,
>> Nor stands in sinners' way . . .

I wondered that the stained glass, sparkling with summer light, did not shatter at the fullness of our singing that day. When the last strains of that singing fell silent, a hush descended upon the congregation as John Knox mounted the pulpit. It was as if every man therein gathered held his breath in anticipation of his words.

"O brethren, is not the Devil, the prince of this world, vanquished and cast out? Hath not Christ Jesus, for whom we suffer, made conquest of him? Hath he not, in despite of Satan's malice, carried our flesh up to glory? And shall not our Champion return? Stand with Christ Jesus in this day of his battle, which shall be short and the victory everlasting! For the Lord himself shall come in our defense with his mighty power; he shall give us the victory when the battle is most strong."

Ten days later, July 7, 1559, the congregation of St. Giles High Kirk, Edinburgh, chose John Knox to be their pastor. "It hath pleased God," he said to his new congregation, "of his superabundant grace, to make me, most wretched of many thousands, a witness, minister, and preacher." But he hastened to make plain to them who the true pastor of St. Giles was always and ever to be. "I will be of no other church except of that which hath Christ Jesus to be pastor, which hears his voice and will not hear a stranger."

Hemmed in behind and before, St. Giles lay between Holyrood Palace at the east end of the Royal Mile, and the fortress of Edinburgh Castle at the west. The Queen Regent and her French army controlled both strongholds. Victory for Reformation was far from wholly achieved. The Regent was not about to hand Scotland over without a fight.

42

War and Death

IN THE MONTHS AHEAD, Scotland was locked in mortal combat, with two warring factions each determined to have its way, neither willing to compromise the girth of a whisker. The Regent occupied the port at Leith with French troops, and the Cannongate on the Royal Mile was held by her army. She swore violence against John Knox and all who protected him, offering bags of gold to any man who would shoot and kill him. Worried sick for her husband and the boys, Marjory was beside herself. There was little sleep to be had in those days, my master sleeping fewer than four hours in twenty four. Even for one such as I, for whom proximity to Master Knox and trouble had become a commonplace, even I found myself distressed in those days at the threats surrounding him—and us.

The threat of French invasion was imminent. By January 1560, the French invasion fleet, commanded by Monsieur d'Elbeuf, battled the tempests on the North Sea, awaiting a break in the weather to enter the Forth. Meanwhile, a small contingent of men of the Congregation, commanded by Stewart and the Earl of Arran, were surrounded by four hundred French and the cavalry of d'Oysel, and nearly annihilated. All seemed lost. I have rarely seen Master Knox so full of sorrow and discouragement. Fresh news of cruel wars and persecutions waged against the Huguenots in France left him in the grip of still deeper dismay. He claimed that nineteen months of slavery in the galleys did not compare with one of these many days of open warfare and uncertainty.

And still they came on against us. In March the French nearly sacked Glasgow, then they marched across the countryside to Leith, trampling and plundering all the farms and villages along the way, leaving rape and pillage in their wake, and hundreds of poor crofters and their families destitute of food and shelter. My heart ached at the news.

Meanwhile, much to my master's distress, the Lords of the Congregation felt it expedient, under the open hazards of war and the imminent threat of harm to his person from the Regent, that with all haste John Knox be gotten out of the capital. Such was his aversion to their scheme that I feared they would be constrained to bind him with ropes and carry him over their shoulders. They at last were forced to use the security of his wife and sons as a ploy to extricate him from the capital.

In the midst of violence on every hand, intrepid preacher John Willock, under the nose of enemy troops, stepped boldly into John Knox's pulpit and encouraged the beleaguered masses to stand fast in Christ's gospel, come what may from the Regent and her army. When news of this reached my master, he said, "Our dear brother, John Willock, for his faithful labors and bold courage in the battle, deserves immortal praise."

While in our exile from Edinburgh, my master came more and more to the conviction that without an English alliance, without

Elizabeth of England sending gold to support a Scottish army to defend the country against French invasion, our cause, at least on a political level, was sure to fail.

Circumstances force me to admit that John Knox, in spite of other powers he so clearly possessed, was not a very good politician. Perhaps he lacked the gift of prevarication seemingly required for such a role. Nevertheless, he was a man who knew what was needed and had the boldness and the bluntness to demand it. "Unless without delay," he wrote to Elizabeth's two-facing advisor, William Cecil, "money be furnished to pay our soldiery, we will be compelled to seek the next way to our safety. In the bowels of Christ Jesus, I require you, sir, to make plain answer what England may lippen to!"

Perhaps realizing that John Knox's strengths lay elsewhere than politics, the Lords of the Congregation set him to work writing a history of the Reformation, as an apology for and defense of their actions against French rule in the person of the Queen Regent. And they urged him to commence training preachers like himself in the pure doctrine of the grace of the evangel of Jesus Christ.

I observed in these days of our exile in the countryside that Marjory was strained and pale. I believe she slept little in the night, for I heard sounds of her movement about the house. She ate little, and when she spoke her voice was thin and frail. Much of the care of his sons, Nathanial and Eleazar, fell to my master. I assisted where I could.

Meanwhile, when all seemed at an end, the English did act. Perhaps Master Knox was not such a bad politician after all. A fleet of seven English warships appeared in the channel. In February, Stewart, Ruthven, Balnaves, and other lords were summoned to a council in Berwick, where a treaty was signed. Though she disliked John Knox and his blasting trumpets intensely, Elizabeth of England disliked the French still more. There was nothing of true religion described in that treaty, to my master's distress, but in it England committed itself to expelling the French from Scotland—and then agreed to withdraw her armies as well. Forthwith, more than 8,000 English soldiers marched across the border into Scotland. Now we were a country occupied by not one but two enemies of ancient standing.

Meanwhile, I daily labored at assessing the plight of the needy and infirmed in Mid-Lothian where we resided; the task was formidable, made more so by the ravages of war. I was placed in charge of wealth seized at monastic houses and abbeys in the region—a dragon's trove—and of its distribution to widows and orphans, and those with infirmities of the mind (idiots, they were termed by most), and those who were lame and crippled. There was a curious correspondence between the vast wealth of the abbeys and monasteries and the host of poor and lame in the realm. I confess that I wept at sight of the deprivations of their condition, and when I wasn't weeping, I found myself enraged at the bloated clerics, who had robbed and abused these forgotten ones. On deeper reflection, however, I was forced to admit that my rage was more often than not merely an extension of my pride, my self-righteous notion that one such as I would never have treated these needy ones as the monks and friars had been doing for generations. No, not I. Yet how little had I thought or cared for them until now?

At last word arrived that a parliament had been summoned in Edinburgh. And with that calling, John Knox was urgently commissioned to return to the city. I feared for Marjory's health, and I saw the lines of worry furrowing my master's brow. On April 23, 1560, John Knox entered the nave of St. Giles High Kirk. There was nothing of the rejoicing of the first triumphant gathering in that place on this day. A tattered band made up the congregation that morning, a band with ashen faces and wide vacant eyes. The psalm-singing was tremulous and low. Master Knox entered his pulpit to preach to a people whose hearts were quaking and faltering. And so he prayed.

"Seeing that we are now left as a flock without a pastor, in civil policy, and as a ship without a rudder in the midst of the storm, let thy providence watch, Lord, and defend us in these dangerous days, that the wicked of the world may see that as well without the help of man, as with it, thou art able to rule, maintain, and defend the little flock that dependeth upon thee."

He then proceeded to preach a sermon of the most tender exhortations I have heard him deliver. "And yet amongst the extremity of these calamities so wondrously has Christ's kirk been preserved that the remembrance thereof is unto my heart a great matter of consolation. For yet my good hope is that one day or other Christ Jesus, that now in this realm is crucified, shall rise again in despite of his enemies, and shall appear to his weak and sorely troubled disciples to whom he shall say, 'Peace be unto you. It is I. Fear not.'"

Yet was there more of war than peace in these days. At the port of Leith, a combined English and Scottish force commanded by Sir James Croft made great but disastrous efforts to expel the French from the fortifications of that town. Though there was a moment in the battle when it appeared that the west and east blockhouses of the fortress had been taken by our side, the French rallied and drove the allies from the town, with great loss of life.

Upon our retreat, the French stripped the bodies of our dead and laid them out against the wall, leaving them to putrefy in the sun for many days. The Regent's elation at the news and at the sight of the dead bodies of her enemies was noised abroad throughout the realm. "Now I will go to the Mass and praise God for that which my eyes have seen! Yonder is the fairest tapestry that ever I saw. I would that the whole field betwixt Edinburgh and Leith was strewn with the same stuff."

When John Knox learned of her mockery and mirth, he was indignant. "God shall avenge the insult done to his image bearers, not only on the godless and furious soldiers, but on she who rejoiced to see it."

Perhaps his words were fulfilled on June 11, 1560. With great effort I attempted to quell my own rejoicing at the death of another human being. Though as word spread throughout the city that the Queen Regent had breathed her last, I am forced to confess that I felt more than relief; yet my near-elation was mingled with sober reflection on the frightful reward awaiting someone so monstrous in policy as she had been.

The implications of her death were legion. France had in no wise abandoned its plan to absorb Scotland. Many feared that the Regent's scheme was now augmented. Her death could mean the soon return of her daughter, eighteen-year-old Mary Queen of Scots, married to the Dauphin of France. Then, on July 10, word arrived from Paris that Henry II, King of France, had been killed in a jousting tournament. His son the Dauphin had been crowned Francis II, King of France. The implications were stunning: Francis's young wife, Mary Queen of Scots, was now the queen of France. Speculation ran wild, and fears mounted throughout Scotland.

43

Confession and Death

HOSTILITIES WITH THE FRENCH suspended at least for the moment at the death of the Regent, the Lords of the Congregation, while grieving their losses, assembled in the Great Hall of Edinburgh Castle, John Knox and the preachers attending. It was a fresh, sparkling summer morning; the elaborate fireplace in the hall lay idle. The great chamber was a miniature version of Wolsey Hall at Hampton Court where we had dined with Edward VI, but it was, nevertheless, stately and armorial in its cruder northern splendors. Below the blackened timbers of the high ceiling, the wood-paneled walls were lined with standing suits of armor, soldiers of a dying era frozen in time, and with displays of polished breastplates, pikes, and two-fisted broadswords. I felt the room humming with anticipation, like bees gorging on heather, yet there was in the air a hesitant rustling of uncertainty.

On August 1, 1560, the Great Council of the Realm, a body established by the Lords of the Congregation, convened the parliament, Lord Lethington presiding. Though there were in attendance scattered delegates favorable to the Regent and the French, and those of the Church of Rome, including the bishops of St. Andrews, Dunblane, and Dunkeld, there were clearly many more of Scotland's nobility favorable to Reformation. Lesser barons of the realm, most of whom favored Reformation, who had not been summoned to a parliament for over a century, were gladly welcomed at this one.

An early consideration of the parliament concerned Scotland's money. One of the final efforts the Regent had made to cripple the growing support for the Congregation in Scotland was to corrupt the money, to tamper with its value, thereby to destroy the common wealth of the people. She did this by the printing of unauthorized currency, diluting of the supply of money so that it became less and less valuable. Parliament commenced by seizing the printing irons from the palace, thereby making such devious thievery of the people more difficult for future monarchs.

There was a feeble attempt on the part of the bishops to question, in absence of a monarch, the very legality of the parliament. After some deliberation a majority voted to proceed. Next a supplication from the ministers was read out, and after much debate, the parliament commissioned the ministers.

"We do charge you," began Lord Lethington, "to draw in plain and several headings the sum of that doctrine which you would maintain, and would desire this present parliament to establish as wholesome, true, and only necessary to be believed and to be received within the realm."

It was everything John Knox had hoped for. With a flush of color on his cheeks, and an expectant vitality sparkling in his gray-blue eyes, he rose and led several preachers from the hall. After his fashion of lunging forward without regard for his own life or health, the next four days were spent in the most concentrated and diligent labor I had ever observed. John Knox had chosen five other men, all of the name John, to assist him in the work: John Winram, John Spottiswoode, John Willock, John Douglas, and John Row. I rendered assistance by trimming candlewicks and ensuring an ample supply of paper, ink, and quills. On several occasions my master asked me to read a draft with a view to correcting any mistaken verbiage and suggesting wording that might make the meaning more clear. John Knox and the five other Johns created in those four days what they called the Scots Confession. If I may offer my opinion, it was the most remarkable achievement I had heretofore witnessed. In the confession, John Knox laid with blunt eloquence a biblical foundation for theology, worship, literacy, and preaching in Reformation Scotland. I was asked to proofread their wording on a chapter entitled "Of the Kirk," one that at first confused me with its use of the word "catholic."

> As we believe in one God, Father, Son, and Holy Ghost, so we firmly believe that from the beginning there has been, now is, and to the end of the world shall be, one Kirk, that is to say, one company and multitude of men chosen by God, who rightly worship and embrace Him by true faith in Jesus Christ, who is the only Head of the Kirk, even as it is the body and spouse of Christ Jesus. This Kirk is catholic, that is, universal, because it contains the chosen of all ages, of all realms, nations, and tongues, be they of the Jews or be they of the Gentiles . . .

I believe my master may have chosen carefully what passages he designed for me to read during those four days. I was now nearly five and twenty, and yet he never stopped instructing of me. I felt a thrill in my soul as I read how the Spirit of the Lord

Jesus takes possession of the heart—my heart—by regeneration, and how this gracious work of God changes affections and purifies desires—my affections and my desires.

> The cause of good works, we confess, is not our free will, but the Spirit of the Lord Jesus, who dwells in our hearts by true faith, brings forth such works as God has prepared for us to walk in. . . . For as soon as the Spirit of the Lord Jesus, whom God's elect children receive by true faith, takes possession of the heart of any man, so soon does he regenerate and renew him, so that he begins to hate what before he loved, and to love what he hated before.

Next he set me to read a passage from the magisterial confession that showed me how powerless I was to do anything, but how full of power is the Lord Jesus, by whose strength alone I am enabled to gain victory over my sins.

> But the Spirit of God, who bears witness to our spirit that we are the sons of God, makes us resist filthy pleasures and groan in God's presence for deliverance from this bondage of corruption, and finally to triumph over sin so that it does not reign in our mortal bodies. But the sons of God fight against sin, sob and mourn when they find themselves tempted to do evil, and if they fall, they rise again with earnest and unfeigned repentance. They do these things, not by their own power, but by the power of the Lord Jesus, apart from whom they can do nothing.

When at last the confession was completed, and John Knox's clear, penetrating voice rang out through the great hall as he read it before the assembled parliament, I studied the faces of the barons and bishops. So persuasive where the Reformed doctrines expounded, and so soundly were they elaborated that few made any objections; the few objections proffered were so flimsy and fallacious as to dampen not the enthusiastic support of the majority. On August 17, 1560, the Scottish Parliament, the Great Council of the Realm, and the Lords of the Congregation approved the Scots Confession with an overwhelming majority voting in its favor. Roman Catholicism and all its idolatrous practices were made illegal, and Reformed worship and practice were established as the law of the land.

Though the bishops left the assembly still grumbling about the legalities of a parliamentary decision enacted in absence of the queen, these were days of great triumph for the cause of the evangel.

"The young queen most certainly will return to take up her scepter," said Master Knox after the adjournment of the parliament. "That is sure, but we shall now hand her a *fait accompli* of the true doctrine of the evangel of Jesus Christ when she does."

There were a great many decisions made before that adjournment, including the care of the poor, of widows, of orphans, of the elderly, of the cripple and infirm, of those with infirmities of the mind. Decisions were arrived at regarding the seizure and distribution of all property of the old religion, churches, monastic buildings, and manses and glebes for the housing and support of the new preachers.

Hence, in early September, 1560, John Knox was given the house at Trunk Close for his home, and I assisted him in moving his family and meager possessions into the tall, narrow old house. Marjory had not recovered her strength from the days of flight and warfare, and was exhausted and confined herself in bed. Nathaniel, now three-and-a half, and Eleazar, two-and-a-half, however, thought it was all a game, a new adventure. Squealing with delight, they clamorously explored every nook and cranny of the big old house.

Master Knox preached twice on Sundays to a swelling congregation that pressed hard against the ancient walls of St. Giles, and he taught at least three times during the week. A young and flourishing church, fresh and vigorous, prone to all the excesses of its budding adolescence, exerted constant demands on my master's time. Though able young men clamored to join him in his ministry—James Lawson, John Craig, and many others like them—there was a great shortage of pastors and preachers for the burgeoning congregations throughout the realm. It was a time of great excitement, even euphoria, yet was it a time of equally great exhaustion and weariness.

As the golden days of harvest and plenty gave way to the chill and darkness of early winter, John Knox exerted himself between the demands of his young family and the ministry of the church. When I knew him to be on the knife-edge of exhaustion, he tenderly cared for Marjory, and even snatched what moments he could to play with his energetic sons. And the greater the demands on his time, the more he prayed; long and anguished were his prayers for the infant church and for his beloved wife.

November was dark, and the rains fell in torrents, running in muddy rivulets along the street gutters of the Royal Mile. While the church grew stronger in these weeks, his wife grew weaker. I did what I could to assist him in his extremity. I knew that he slept little and ill, and I often worried for his health. He would charge forward with mammoth vitality, and then he would come up short, his old malady upon him, and he near the point of collapse.

One evening, under the scowl of blackening skies, I intended for us to make a dash from the kirk to avoid a drenching that was sure to descend any moment. To my frustration, my master's steps were labored and heavy as we walked those few blocks from St. Giles to Trunk Close. I worried we would be caught out, and I feared the outcome of a soaking on his weakened condition. Three blocks to the west, I could see the rain already falling, pounding on the cobbles like the surf on a jetty, and gathering speed as it soaked its way up the Mile. Cold rain drops stinging my face, I grabbed him by the elbow and hastened up the steps and into his house. Once in the sitting room, he collapsed onto a chair; he pressed his fingers hard against his temples.

"You are in pain?" I said.

"Aye, the pain of my head and stomach troubles me greatly," he replied. "Daily I find my body decay. Unless my pain cease, I fear I will become unprofitable."

"You must take some rest," I told him.

Before he could reply, a low moan came from the bedchamber above us. He looked up and rose slowly to his feet. "I feel a great heaviness descending upon me." Halting at the foot of the narrow stairway, he turned. "Would you lend a hand with the boys?"

I heard his steady voice through the timbers of the floor above. From his inflection and intonation, I knew him to be praying. Then there was a long pause. His voice resumed. I moved to the bottom of the stairway. He must have left the door ajar, for I could hear him now reading to his wife, his voice slow and tremulous with feeling.

313

The Lord is merciful and gracious, slow to anger, and plenteous in mercy. He will not always chide: neither will he keep his anger forever. He hath not dealt with us after our sins; nor rewarded us according to our iniquities. For as the heaven is high above the earth, so great is his mercy toward them that fear him. As far as the east is from the west, so far hath he removed our transgressions from us. Like as a father pitieth his children, so the Lords pitieth them that fear him. For he knoweth our frame; he remembereth that we are dust. As for man, his days are as grass: as a flower of the field, so he flourisheth. For the wind passeth over it, and it is gone; and the place thereof shall know it no more.

Squeals and giggles interrupted my listening. I hurried into the boys' bedchamber and did my best to ready them for the night.

"Why does nae Mama ready us for our beds?" asked Nathaniel, his voice muffled as I pulled his nightshirt over his black, curly head. "I like it better when she readies us for our beds."

"Oatcake," said Eleazar. "I want oatcake."

"Your mother needs her rest," I said.

"All she does is rest," said Nathaniel.

"She's very ill," I said.

"Is she going to die, is she?" asked Nathaniel.

I tucked the bolster about his shoulders. "Since the Fall, we all of us are going to die sometime," I said, groping in my mind for a way to explain such weighty matters to a lad of not yet four years.

"I don' nae want her to die," he said, tears swelling in his wide blue-gray eyes and spilling down his ruddy cheeks. "Not just yet."

I prayed with the wee lads, they nibbling on oatcakes. I prayed as I had so often heard their father pray. The boys had seen the surgeon come and go for many weeks now, his face more grim after each visit. It was impossible to conceal from them the peril of her condition. For a time I sat in the room below where their mother lay in her bed. When there had been no sounds from her room for some time, with dread, I climbed the stair, careful to avoid the treads that creaked the most. Softly I knocked upon the door. There was no reply. I pushed it open. On his knees at her bedside, my master's face was buried in his arms, and he was motionless. Marjory's face was the color of new parchment, and it appeared almost transparent; her mouth was open and her breathing was soft and shallow. He still held a frail hand in his own, but in his exhaustion he had fallen asleep at her side. I touched him on the shoulder.

"You must go to your bed and rest," I said in a whisper. "I shall watch. I will call you if there is any change."

I took hold of his arm as he rose to his feet. He bent low and softly kissed her. Gazing at her for a moment, he stroked her pale cheek, and left the room.

I positioned myself in a chair so that I could see Marjory's face. The single candle quavered, casting crisscrossing shadows from the four-posted bed on the ceiling beams. I attempted to ready myself for a long night.

Then a sound from the street below caught my attention. I got up and went to the window. A dusting of snow had fallen earlier in the day, and now the cobbles of the Royal Mile were hoary with frost, looking like the backs of a vast mob of sheep. It had been a gray, bone-chilling December day, and now full darkness had descended over the city. The lamplighter moved methodically down the street, pausing to light the lamp nearest the Knox house, leaving a frosty glow illuminating his path.

There was the sound again. It was the ponderous clomping of hooves, not the proud, high-spirited tread of the warhorse. This was the weary, patient plodding of a work animal, and it was followed by the rickety clatter of cartwheels on the street. Dark and bulky, the beast and its burden came into view, making their way to the Netherbow. The beast was led by a lone man hunkering against the freezing haar mist in a tattered plaid. Even at a distance, I believed that I could make out the poor fellow shivering with the cold. The vapors of his breath glowed as if icy clouds were shrouding his head and stooped shoulders. He was a dungman, and his cart was mounded high with muck from the street. I mused on the irony of the man's calling. Here was a man whose only relief from the blasting winter cold was his daily intimacy with the lingering bodily warmth left behind in the foul excrement of the many beasts that traveled the streets of the city. I watched the steam rising from the dungman's cart like foul smoke from a smelting furnace. Poor fellow, I thought. What a night to be long at his labor. I hoped he had a warm fire, a hearty meal, and perhaps a loving wife and children awaiting his arrival from his calling. But I confess, I shuddered at the prospect of such a vocation, at the persistent and intractable stench that was his life, and I pitied the poor wife married to a man with such a calling.

The fellow and his beast disappeared from view, and I turned from the window and sat down. I studied Marjory's face for any sign of improvement. The surgeon had come earlier in the day. After listening to her heart and breathing, and fingering her wrist, he had risen from her side. Frowning, he had laid a hand on my master's arm. "There is nothing more I have skill to do for her. John Knox, you must prepare yourself."

316

"I hope he is wrong," I said softly to myself. I picked up Master Knox's Geneva Bible from the bedside table and thumbed its pages. He was always urging me to read this book. "If you look for the life to come, of necessity it is that you exercise yourselves in the book of the Lord your God. Let no day slip without receiving some comfort from his mouth. Open your ears, George, and he will speak even pleasant things to your heart. Learn of his gracious goodness whose mercy has called you from darkness to light and from death to life." So he often said to me. I bent close to the candle. In the dim light, I read, "O death, where is thy sting? O grave, where is thy victory? The sting of death is sin; and the strength of sin is the law." I paused, remembering when last I had heard Master Knox read these words; it was the last time we saw young Edward VI, our friend. I read on. "But thanks be to God, which giveth us the victory through our Lord Jesus Christ."

I closed the book. John Knox's wife lay perfectly still. The only sign of life was in the shallow wheezing of her breath. It filled the room with an eerie cadence: a flitting in-drawing, a soft gurgling, a hesitation, and a thin clattering of exhalation. And then with effort, it began again. This persisted without change for a great while. It nagged maddeningly at my conscience. I felt helpless. I desperately wanted that haunting rhythm to desist, but I feared what that might mean. I wished I could do something. I wished I could pray as I had so often heard my master wrestling with God in prayer. But I found no words.

Try as I most earnestly did, I found my head nodding onto my sleeve. Drawing in breath sharply, I attempted to keep myself more vigilant. At last, I knew I had succumbed to slumber when I felt myself nearly falling from the chair, and I awoke with a start. What sound had awakened me? I rubbed my eyes and reached for the candle, now little more than a mound of spent wax, the remainder of the wick spluttering softly.

Cold fingers began gripping at my heart. That spluttering was the only sound in the room. I hastened to Marjory's bedside. The haunting pattern of her final breaths had ended. She was gone. And I must awaken John Knox with the woeful news.

44

My Calling

GRAVES IN SCOTLAND are stubborn digging in winter. And it was murky overhead. I was determined to see that John Knox did not linger at the graveside, thereby exposing himself to the droukit elements and the hazard of a chill that might take him off. I fretted over his health, and I fretted over how we were to manage without a woman in the house. I had no clear idea.

John Knox had received the news of his wife's passing without murmuring, though he was no heartless stone. I had come to know him well; there was no want of feeling at his loss. In his praying, which I confess to have listened in upon, I heard him humbly pouring out his heaviness at the death of his left hand and his dear bed-fellow. And he earnestly petitioned his Heavenly Father to provide for the care of his sons.

As I bungled about attempting to form and implement a plan for caring for the boys, urgent news arrived from Paris. Sixteen-year old Francis II, king of France and husband of the Regent's daughter, Mary Queen of Scots, had been suffering the complications from a rotten inflammation of the ear. On December 5, 1560, it took the young king off, and he died of it.

319

"I am not alone in mourning my sweet spouse," said Master Knox at the news. "There is comfort in that."

Subsequent events revealed the irony of these two individuals, John Knox and Mary Queen of Scots, being bereft of their spouses only days apart. Little did we then know that in but a short time the iron wills of the fresh widow and the widower would stand off, each wrestling for the bodies and souls of Scotland.

Sorrowing in his bereavement, yet did John Knox step into the pulpit at St. Giles next Lord's Day and preach the evangel of Jesus Christ to thirsty souls. William Kethe and more fugitives from Geneva had now returned, and continued their work of versifying the Psalms for congregational singing in English. That Lord's Day we sang from Psalm 23, and there was great comfort in the singing of it.

> Yea, though I walk in death's dark vale,
>   Yet will I fear none ill:
> For thou art with me; and thy rod
>   And staff me comfort still.

I was gratified to see that Parliament had approved the Book of Discipline and that our Book of Common Order, crafted in Frankfurt, was to be the order of worship for St. Giles and the Reformed church throughout the realm. It was from this that John Knox led his congregation in prayer.

"Honor and praise be given to thee, O Lord God Almighty, most dear Father of heaven, for all thy mercies and loving-kindness showed unto us, in that it hath pleased thy gracious goodness freely and of thine own accord to elect and choose us to salvation before the beginning of the world . . ."

His voice was a mingling of weariness and passion, and in his preaching, gazing with watery eyes, he paused at times longer than the cadence of his usual delivery. There were a mere eight ministers to assist him in his task of preaching the evangel, and I feared that the labor would kill him. It was essential that ministers, elders, and deacons be trained, ordained, and installed in the congregations throughout the realm. Papistical religion had been expelled in more than 1,000 parishes throughout Scotland, and Master Knox desperately needed able men to minister to the souls in those congregations.

I came firmly to believe that God raised up John Knox and uniquely equipped him for leading Reformation in these days. There were ministers of more prestigious learning than he, as he who had never formally completed his university studies humbly acknowledged. And there were those far better connected to nobility than was John Knox, as he happily owned, being raised up from obscurity as he had been. But troubles though there were in the adolescence of the new church, none questioned that it was God who had raised up John Knox, powerfully anointing him as irrefutable leader of the kirk. Yet for his health's sake, I often wished it were not so.

"God raised up simple men in great abundance," he was to say of Reformation in Scotland, and it was no false modesty. He considered himself the prototypical simple man God had raised up. And so all men followed him. Perhaps they did so in part because he cared so genuinely for the widow and poor in Scotland. Much of his wrangling in these days with the General Assembly of the nobility was over failure to properly provide for the poor laborers of the soil, for the afflicted indigent, and for care of ministers so they were not forced to live a beggar's life.

Forthwith, nominations were being made for the leaders at St. Giles, including the office of deacon. And to my astonishment, my name was proffered. Within a few short weeks I had been examined, prayed over, presented to the congregation, voted upon, and elected, and, with the old rumblings and lurching of my innards, came at last to my ordination.

From the pulpit of St. Giles, Master Knox read out his text. "And in those days, when the number of the disciples was multiplied, there arose a murmuring of the Grecians against the Hebrews, because their widows were neglected in the daily ministration. Then the twelve called the multitude of the disciples unto them. Wherefore, brethren, look ye out among you seven men of honest report, full of the Holy Ghost and wisdom, whom we may appoint over this work."

Honored to serve as I genuinely was, my new diaconal role further complicated the management of the house at Trunk Close, and the managing of Nathaniel and Eleazar. I was needed to visit the infirm and widowed, to arrange for regular provisions of food and wine, and fuel for the fires of those incapable of providing for themselves. Though seeing the miserable neglected circumstances of the needy saddened me, on the whole, it was a joyous activity in which I, for the most part, derived great pleasure. My calling did, however, require me to be away from the immediate care of the boys. My immediate solution was to bring them along in tow as I visited the needy.

Master Knox wrote to Elizabeth Bowes in Berwick tenderly consoling her and urgently asking for her assistance, if she was at all able, with her grandsons. He cared for the lads with tenderness and affection, though the demands of the kirk upon his time were enormous. He threw himself with still greater abandon into his calling, preaching five times weekly at St. Giles, training young men for the ministry, and wrangling with parliament over policy. He was determined that all Scotland's children would grow up learning to read from the Geneva Bible. And he wasn't content unless it was all children: the poor along with the rich, lasses along with lads, all children from the lowest croft to the loftiest turret throughout the realm. There were never enough hours in these days for proper grieving.

On April 23, 1561, a letter arrived from John Calvin. I read it aloud to him after our supper. "May the Lord always stand by you, govern, protect, and sustain you by his power. Your distress for the loss of your wife justly commands my sympathy. Persons of her merit are not often to be met with. But as you have well learned from what source consolation for your sorrow is to be sought, I doubt not but you will endure with patience this calamity."

John Knox received the consoling letter from his friend and mentor with gratitude, and a fresh recollection of his loss. Yet there was no time for mourning anew. There were the boys to consider, the care of their daily needs, their learning. And there was always the kirk.

And now not only the kirk and lords—there was the young queen, come to take up her kingdom. After being denied passage through England, Mary Queen of Scots arrived at the port of Leith in late August 1561, along with a doting entourage of young French nobles and fawning papistical clerics. It was gossiped that she had wept all the way from Paris. But were they tears of mourning for the death of her husband, or mourning for her departure from the luxury and decadence of Paris and the French court? Speculations ran the gamut. Some said she was like her mother and would come like a fury and break Scotland all to pieces. Others felt more certain that she would make ready use of her charm and beauty to coddle influential nobles to her side to affect a renewed alliance with France and the restoration of Roman Catholicism in her realm.

On August 24, her first Sunday in Scotland, a French priest Mary had brought in her entourage conducted Mass at Holyrood Abbey. The following Sunday, almost within sight of the abbey at St. Giles, John Knox responded. "One idolatrous Mass is more fearful than if ten thousand armed enemies landed in a part of the realm."

Next morning there was a sharp rap on the door at Trunk Close. I opened to a courtier who reminded me of the dress and manner of the men the Regent had surrounded herself with. "Her Majesty, Queen Mary, summons John Knox—" He broke off, eyeing me disdainfully from head to toe. Then, feigning bewilderment, he said, "There is one residing here of the name of John Knox?"

I assured him there was. Curtly the courtier announced that John Knox was to appear in Queen's Court on the morrow, Tuesday, September 2, 1561.

45

Charm and Tears

I CONFESS THAT IT WAS with considerable anxiety that I attended John Knox to the palace next morning. Tradesmen and housewives were all a-bustle in the street going about their daily duties, but we walked in silence, I for one feeling like I was on my way to the scaffold at the Grassmarket. I glanced out of the corner of my eye at John Knox. Though he was short in stature, his sturdy forehead, fierce gray-blue eyes, chiseled nose, and flowing beard gave him the fearless air of a Hebrew prophet. From my reading of Holy Scripture, however, I knew that when prophets stood before queens it all came to no good for the prophets.

We had walked for less than ten minutes when the splendor of the queen's palace loomed above us. If one's importance and power are measured by one's dwelling place, then Queen Mary was infinite in both categories. My master's humble house at Trunk Close was no hovel, but her abode was a castle of vast opulence, designed to diminish all who entered its gates. I gazed in wonder and not a little terror at the great stone turrets rising with might on either side of the arched portal we were about to pass through. I'd seen the palace, of course, from the distance, but had never before passed into its resplendent inner precincts.

Master Knox must have read my thoughts. "I too quake and fear and tremble," he said, reaching his hand up to my neck. "George, it's times like these you and I must remember that though the queen is a great one in man's eyes, and though this grand palace is splendid in man's estimation, we are on God's side. And were we but one man, when that one man stands by grace with King Jesus and his evangel, that man is always in the majority."

I nodded my agreement, taking comfort in his words, yet not trusting my voice to speak without betraying my still lingering anxieties. Once inside the palace, the splendors only increased. After waiting for a considerable time, in which I began to feel that this young queen was neglecting us by design, a page at last entered the outer hall and said, "Is there a man called Knox present?"

It was a dark, wood-paneled chamber we entered, one with muted tapestries depicting royal hunting parties and triumphal parades with knights in full armor, looking cavalier and powerful, so it seemed to my wide, staring eyes.

It was my first of many sightings of Mary Queen of Scots, and I must say I had not armed myself adequately for it. There's no other way to say it. She was lovely, young, slender, vivacious seeming, sitting almost carelessly on her throne upon a dais with a canopy of deep red silk draped above her. She wore a circlet of gold in her dark hair, which was highlighted with intricacies suggestive of the colors of autumn leaves; the cut of her embroidered garment was charming, designed to awaken in the transfixed gaze of the viewer a precise estimation of the contours of the physical proportions beneath it. A coquettish smile played at the corners of her heart-shaped lips. I may have in those moments added to my old propensity of staring eyes a slack-jawed gaping of the mouth. The young woman completely unhinged my senses. It was in this moment that I felt a steadying hand of Master Knox upon my neck, and glanced at him. He was unheeding of her allurements and bowed shortly and with respect.

What occurred next acted as a much-needed cold slap in my face.

Her smile twittered as if she were restraining herself with great effort from breaking into laughter. She leaned close to a young advisor and said, *"Ma mère craignait les prières de cet petit homme plus d'une armée de dix mille hommes?"*

Titters of laughter rippled about the room. It was apparent that she believed John Knox knew no French. All my fascination at her turned on a sudden to indignation. So she thought it a ridiculous thing that her mother had feared the prayers of John Knox, the little man, more than she had feared an army of 10,000 men? I felt the color rising in my cheeks. There was a great deal this little queen needed to learn about John Knox, and I was on the verge of blurting out her first lesson. I felt again a hand of my master upon my neck.

Fuming with anger at her, and perhaps at myself, I heard little of their first exchange. But when I was of a frame of mind to heed the conversation, John Knox was speaking with respect and clarity on the error of persisting in adhering to the old rite when it is manifestly against the evangel of Jesus Christ.

"If your grace shall consider that ever from the beginning, the multitude has declined from God (yea, even in the people to whom he spoke by his law and prophets). If you shall consider that the Holy Spirit in Holy Scripture declared that nations, people, princes, and kings of the earth have raged, made conspiracies, and held councils against the Lord, and against his anointed Christ Jesus. Further, if you shall consider the question which Jesus himself does move in these words, 'When the Son of Man shall come, shall he find faith in the earth?' And last, if your grace shall consider the manifest contempt of God and of all his holy precepts which this day reign without punishment upon the face of the whole earth, as in the prophet Hosea's day, 'There is no verity, there is no mercy, there is no truth this day among men, but lies, perjury, and oppression overfloweth all, and blood toucheth blood.' If deeply, I say, your grace shall contemplate the universal corruption that this day reigns in all estates, then shall your grace cease to wonder 'that many are called, but few are chosen.' And you shall begin to tremble and fear to follow the multitude to perdition.

"The universal defection, whereof St. Paul did prophesy, is easy to be espied, as well in religion as in manners: The corruption of life is evident, and religion is not judged nor measured by the plain Word of God, but by the custom, will, consent, and determination of men. But shall he who has pronounced all the thoughts of man's heart to be vain at all times, accept the counsels and consents of men for a religion pleasing and acceptable before him? Let not your grace be deceived. God cannot lie; God cannot deny himself. He has witnessed from the beginning, that no religion pleases him except that which he by his own word has commanded and established.

"The truth of God's Word itself pronounces this sentence, 'In vain do they worship me, teaching for doctrines the precepts of men.' And furthermore, 'All religion which my heavenly Father has not planted shall be rooted out.'"

To her credit, the queen had remained relatively silent, with an occasional whispered council with one of the youths attending upon her. These whispered intimacies were most often with one whose name we soon learned was Pierre de Boscosel de Chastelard, who flirted with the queen more shamelessly than the rest.

There was one courtier whose face I had not yet seen clearly; he seemed to hang behind the rest, his face concealed in the shadows. I peered more closely into those shadows. On a sudden, I knew the man. It was Alexander Cockburn, my childhood friend and fellow student—Master Knox's student. The instant of elation I felt at the long last discovery of my friend suddenly plummeted, like a stone dropped from a tower. Why was he here?

Through these my cogitations, John Knox had continued speaking to the queen. But at last she had had enough of listening. She cut him off.

"But yet you, John Knox, have taught the people to receive another religion than their princes can allow. How can that doctrine be of God, seeing that God commandeth subjects to obey their princes?"

"Madam," replied John Knox, "as right religion took neither original strength nor authority from worldly princes, but from the Eternal God alone, so are not subjects bound to frame their religion according to the appetites of their princes. Princes are oft the most ignorant of all others in God's true religion, as we may read in the histories, as well before the death of Christ Jesus as after. If all the seed of Abraham should have been of the religion of Pharaoh, to whom they were long subjects, I pray you, Madam, what religion should there have been in the world? Or, if all men in the days of the Apostles should have been of the religion of the Roman Emperors, what religion should

329

there have been upon the face of the earth? Daniel and his fellows were subjects to Nebuchadnezzar and unto Darius, and yet, Madam, they would not be of their religion; for the three children said: 'We make it known unto thee, O King, that we will not worship thy Gods.' Daniel did pray publicly unto his God against the expressed commandment of the king. And so, Madam, you may perceive that subjects are not bound to the religion of their princes, although they are commanded to give them obedience."

A flush came to her cheeks, and she leaned forward and said, "Yes, but none of these men raised the sword against their princes."

"Yet, Madam, you cannot deny that they resisted, for those who obey not the commandments that are given, in some sort resist."

"But yet, they resisted not by the sword?"

"God, Madam, had not given them the power and the means."

"Think you that subjects, having the power, may resist their princes?"

"If their princes exceed their bounds, Madam, no doubt they may be resisted, even by power. For there is neither greater honor, nor greater obedience, to be given to kings or princes than God hath commanded to be given unto father and mother. But the father may be stricken with a frenzy, in which he would slay his children. If the children arise, join themselves together, apprehend the father, take the sword from him, bind his hands, and keep him in prison till his frenzy be past: think you, Madam, that the children do any wrong? It is even so, Madam, with princes that would murder the children of God that are subjects unto them. Their blind zeal is nothing but a very mad frenzy, and therefore, to take the sword from them, to bind their hands, and to cast them into prison till they be brought to a more sober mind, is no disobedience against princes, but just obedience, because it agreeth with the will of God."

Mary had arisen to her feet as their exchanges had become rapid and more heated. She now stood speechless, turning on her heel and pacing, halting and staring back at John Knox, then pacing again. All this she did in silence for a quarter of an hour, no man speaking but in guarded whispers during the interlude.

During the interlude after my first recognition of Alexander, my mind had been in torment. Why was he here amongst the queen's entourage? How had he come to be so? How could he have been with us and now take the side of Mary Queen of Scots? Like a flash, a comforting thought came to mind. Perhaps he was a spy, planted here by the Lords of the Congregation, taking great personal risk for the cause of truth and the evangel of Jesus Christ. I so wanted to believe this, though I had no sooner began forming the notion than I knew it could never be true. Meanwhile, the queen had recovered her voice.

"Well then," she said at last, "I perceive that my subjects shall obey you, and not me. They shall do what they want, and not what I command; and so must I be subject to them, and not they to me."

"God forbid that ever I take upon me to command any to obey me," replied John Knox, "or yet to set subjects at liberty to do what pleaseth them! My travail is that both princes and subjects obey God. Think not, Madam, that wrong is done you when you are required to be in subjection to God. It is he that subjects peoples under princes, and causes obedience to be given unto them. Yea, God craves of kings that they be foster-fathers to his Church, and commands queens to be nurses to his people. This subjection, Madam, unto God, and unto his troubled kirk, is the greatest dignity that flesh can get upon the face of the earth; for it shall carry them to everlasting glory."

"Yes, but you are not the kirk that I will nourish," she said, her temper raising the pitch of her voice. "I will defend the Kirk of Rome, for it is, I think, the true Kirk of God."

"Your will, Madam, is no reason. Neither does what you think make that Roman harlot to be the true and immaculate spouse of Jesus Christ. Wonder not, Madam, that I call Rome a harlot. For that Church is altogether polluted with all kind of spiritual fornication, as well in doctrine as in manners. Madam, the religion of the Jews which denied and crucified Christ Jesus, was not so far degenerate as the Church of Rome is declined from the purity of the evangel which the Apostles taught and planted."

"Well," said the queen, "my conscience does not agree with yours."

"Conscience, Madam, requireth knowledge; and I fear that right knowledge you have none."

"But I have both heard and read," she said, a tremor in her voice that sounded more like emotion than anger.

"So, Madam, did the Jews who crucified Christ Jesus read both the Law and the Prophets, and heard the same interpreted after their manner. Have you heard any teach, but such as the Pope and his Cardinals have allowed? You may be assured that such will speak nothing to offend their own estate."

"Well, you interpret the Scriptures in one manner, and they in another. Whom shall I believe? Who shall be judge?"

"You shall believe God, that plainly speaketh in his Word; and further than the Word teacheth you, you shall believe nothing. The Word of God is plain in itself. If there appear any obscurity in one place, the Holy Spirit, who is never contrary to himself, explaineth the plain meaning more clearly in other places, so that there can remain no doubt, except unto those who obstinately will remain ignorant."

What happened next sent me again into a bewilderment of emotions about that intriguing woman. First her face and neck began to develop faint blotches of red. Then her chin began to quiver and a tremor disfigured her lips. Next she buried her face in her skirts, and burst into tears.

In a torrent, her courtiers fawned upon her, fanning her face, shooting dark looks at John Knox, cooing and clucking at her like mother hens with their chicks, offering her cake and chocolate.

When the vehemence of her sobs had subsided into sniffles and little hiccups, John Knox, with tenderness, made an effort to console her. "I never delight in the weeping of any of God's creatures. I can scarcely well abide the tears of my own boys when my own hand corrects them."

We were hastily escorted from her presence, and led curtly to the gate of Holyrood Palace, spewed out of her presence like Jonah from the great fish. We had walked in silence for perhaps the distance of a jousting course. I could not contain myself.

"Did you know?" I blurted.

He halted, looking intently at me. "Alexander?" he said with tenderness as if speaking of one of his own sons. "I feared it," he said slowly. "I did not absolutely know it."

"W-what happened? Why did he do it?"

"I can only speculate," he said. He proceeded to offer an explanation for what had occurred while we were in the bottle dungeon those many years ago when St. Andrews Castle fell to the Regent and the French. It was simple really; and it made sense. Fearing for his life, Alexander had betrayed us to the Regent.

333

"But why?" I asked.

"He was afraid. He wanted to live."

"And so, he exchanged our lives for his own?" As I said the bitter words, I felt rage and hatred whelming in my bosom.

He placed his hand upon my neck as he had done since I was a boy. I felt a twinge of guilt as we walked on. Surely Alexander's betrayal was as great a blow to my master, his tutor, as it was to me. Yet did he have far greater pressures exerting themselves upon his heart and energies. Mine was a private grudge; on John Knox had been laid the wrongs done to the bodies and souls of the kirk, of an entire nation.

"Be not the unforgiving servant, George," said my master. "Alexander's crime against you—against us—is far less than the sum of our high crimes against a holy God."

I would be long in gaining victory over my bitterness at Alexander, but it began that day at his words.

That day's audience at court was to be the first of five private audiences John Knox would have before the queen. He said nothing more that day as we walked the short distance to Trunk Close, but I knew from the creases in his brow that he was not at all certain what to make of the effect of his words upon her.

We soon found out. She must have concluded from that interview that there was to be no subduing of the thundering Scot, John Knox, by the subtler method of her feminine charms. Forthwith, she made a proclamation forbidding the General Assembly of the kirk to meet without her express summons.

Perhaps her charms were more successful with members of the nobility. Some of the Lords of the Congregation were inclined to permit her to have her Mass said in the privacy of her chapel at Holyrood Palace. After all she was the queen and what harm to the realm could come from a private mass now and then in the privacy of her own palace? And some were even inclined to submit to her supremacy over the Assembly of the ministers and elders of the kirk.

But not John Knox. "Take from us the freedom of assemblies," said he, "and she takes from us the evangel of Jesus Christ!"

46

Seduction and Murder

As INTRIGUES, DECEIT, adulterous scandal, and murder became commonplace in Mary Queen of Scots' court, John Knox would contribute little to her downfall. She proved more than capable of bringing her own ruin down upon herself. Yet did she appear to make efforts to reconcile with the Protestant majority in her realm. She appointed William Maitland and James Stewart, Earl of Moray, to be principle advisors. John Knox cautioned both men that their appointments might merely be a scheme to charm them. They would not be the first to be so deceived. And through them Mary could work to win over more of the Lords of the Congregation to her policy.

It required little imagination to conclude that woven into her policy was a master plan to become queen of England. Elizabeth was her cousin, an unmarried cousin, and it made sense to Queen Mary that an alliance ought to be forged leaving the throne of England to her, should Elizabeth never wed and die without an heir. Meanwhile, whom the queen of Scotland would marry became the speculation and manipulation of all Europe. Her first marriage to Francis had been a cold, calculated, political arrangement entirely; though he was king of France, he was sickly and uninspiring, and she spent no time mourning after his death. Would it be the idiot heir to the Spanish throne? Or Elizabeth's favorite, Robert Dudley, proposed by the Queen of England as a counter ploy to keep her royal eye on her cousin? There were dozens of possibilities. For a frivolous widow of eighteen, suckled in a court with the sexual morals of a pig sty, and now surrounded by groveling admirers, these seemed to be adventurous days, indeed.

While casting her eye all about her, Mary chose a favorite of the English court. When Henry Darnley, great grandson of Henry VII, came to Scotland, Mary was smitten. He was a charming dancer, and she called him the properest tall man she ever saw. She immediately began negotiations to gain the support of Spain if she should marry Darnley. She would use him to strengthen her connection to English royalty and to be a means of recovering both England and Scotland for Rome. Forthwith, the two were secretly wed in the apartments of a courtier, David Rizzio, at Stirling Castle. When word got out, the Scottish Parliament was enraged. The monarch was not at liberty to forge alliances by marriage without the approval of the nobility of the realm. To make matters worse, nineteen-year-old Darnley seemed ill-content with being a mere consort, and began seeking coequality with his queen that he might be crowned King of Scotland.

At the news, Master Knox was enraged. "Have you, Lord Darnley, for the pleasure of that dainty dame, cast the psalm-book into the fire? The Lord shall strike both head and tail."

In 1566, at Edinburgh Castle, the queen gave birth to a child, a son she called James. Perhaps Mary Queen of Scots was not destined for marital bliss. Darnley was suspicious of his wife's

338

favorites, especially her Italian secretary, David Rizzio. In March of 1566, Darnley hired murderers to enter the queen's chambers and put an end to Rizzio before her horrified eyes. They stabbed him fifty-seven times, and her chamber ran with his blood.

In November of the same year, while at Kelso Abbey, the queen gave voice to her distress at her marriage to the man who had murdered her lover. "If I must live on wed to such a man, I shall end my miserable life." A new favorite of hers, the Earl of Bothwell, understood her meaning precisely.

Forthwith, on February 9, 1567, Darnley fell suddenly and suspiciously ill and lay sick in bed at a house at Kirk 'o Fields, outside the south wall of the city. In the middle of the night, all Edinburgh was aroused by a thunderous explosion. The house in which Darnley was believed to be had suddenly exploded. Next morning, upon investigation of the rubble and surrounding garden, workers found the body of Darnley and his page. They had both been strangled. Few doubted who was behind the murders. In April, the Earl of Bothwell divorced the wife he had recently married, and in a staged abduction of the queen, took her off to his castle at Dunbar. Some days thereafter they returned to Edinburgh, where they were married before Mary's Catholic priest, she claiming it was all against her will.

Not only were the sordid goings on of Mary odious to the ministers of the kirk and John Knox, and to the Lords of the Congregation and Parliament, but even her Catholic support-ers were disgusted by it all. The Council of Trent had recently resolved to clean up the abuses in the Roman Church, especially the rampant immorality of its clerics and prominent members. And there was the matter of her divorce. Murder was one thing, but the pope could not sanction a Catholic monarch who had so flouted the church's stance on divorce.

Feeling her power slip from her grasp, as it had so recently from her mother's, Mary and Bothwell fled the capital and hastily raised an army of border clansmen. Met by a superior force led by Lord Morton, she surrendered, and was led before an angry and jeering crowd into Edinburgh. Sympathetic lords moved her to Lochleven Castle, where she seduced a laird's son into arranging for a horse and aiding her escape. Again she attempted to raise an army but met more than her match near Glasgow, and was forced to flee again, on horseback and alone, across the border into her cousin Elizabeth's England, hoping beyond hope for aid from the one she had been scheming to overthrow. Elizabeth could ill afford to have such an unruly neighbor queen on the loose, even if she was her cousin. Mary was made prisoner and held under guard till the end of her life.

Meanwhile, the Lords of the Congregation forced Mary to abdicate. On July 29, 1567, her nine-month-old son was crowned James VI of Scotland. John Knox preached the inauguration sermon at St. Giles. In August, the Earl of Moray was proclaimed Regent to the infant king.

Said he, "God has mercifully delivered Scotland from a proud mind, a crafty wit, and an obdurate heart against Christ and his truth."

It appeared that God had, indeed, stricken both head and tail.

47

Lost Lambs

WHILE MARY QUEEN OF SCOTS wore herself out scandalizing Scotland, I marveled at the wondrous work of God's grace in the hearts of his people. There had been but eight ministers to preach and pastor in a thousand congregations when first the trumpet blast of the evangel of Jesus Christ sounded throughout the land. And I feared that such a burden of labor was like to kill John Knox. I'm convinced that it would have. But God raised up simple men with passion for the evangel in great abundance in those days.

John Craig, recently returned from Protestant Germany, a man of conviction and courage, faithful to the evangel of Jesus Christ and an able preacher, was appointed to share John Knox's preaching burden at St. Giles. "In the cause of Christ's Evangel," John Knox charged Craig, "be found simple, sincere, fervent, and unfeigned." Craig commenced preaching half of the time in April of 1562. I thrilled at the prospect. Perhaps now my master could rest, recover his health, take some time for himself.

I could not have been more wrong. Whatever time he gained, alas, was to be absorbed ten-fold in arbitrating political unrest, the sordid intrigues of court—as I've already described them—and the vacillations of nobility.

When the dark, sclutter days of the winter of 1564 gave way to a brilliant sparkling day, well in advance of full of springtime, I felt I had to get Nathaniel and Eleazar out of the house.

"Don't forget your plaids, lads," I called. "Aye, it's sunshine at the moment, but you never can tell."

Nathaniel was now six and Eleazar was a strapping lad of nearly five years. I knew it would do them some good to go for a tramp, and I knew it would do me some good too. We set off down the Royal Mile, out the Netherbow, and past Holyrood Palace. The towers and turrets of the palace pointed to a sky that was an intense blue, with white flocks of clouds scudding across it. I only wished I could have persuaded the boys' father to join us. With the thought, I felt a twinge of guilt. He labored on while I recreated with his lads. And there were matters of the diaconate that I could be, ought to be, attending to.

I pushed the thoughts aside, gripped a pudgy hand in each of my own, and set off up the path of the dun of Arthur's Seat. It had been ages since I had tramped to its lofty summit, and my heart was elated at the prospect. We left the clamor of the city behind us, and before us lay the turfy freshness of the hills. The pathway followed a rising ridge with prickly gorse bushes on either side, now flowering a brilliant yellow. Bees hummed in and amongst the flowers, and corbies guffawed at us from their nests in a sycamore tree that sprawled on the low end of the ridge.

Tearing free of my hands, the boys chased after a pair of early spring lambs frolicking on the hillside. Kicking their tiny hooves and flicking their tails, the pair of lambs cavorted with the pair of lads. I dropped the sack in which I had prepared our lunch, and joined them.

"Can we take 'em home wi' us?" cried Eleazar. "I've always wanted my own lamb."

"Aye, there's one for each of us," said Nathaniel. "And we've spare rooms enough."

"That'd be stealing, then," I said. "And the Apostle tells us to steal no more, but work with our hands so we have the means to share with those in need."

Just then from around a gorse bush an ewe appeared. Bleating angrily, she broke into a run, her heavy fleece flouncing in the breeze as she gained momentum. Lowering her head, she came at us with her curled horns at the ready.

"Och, not only does the evangel forbid it, their mother forbids it too!" I yelled. "Run for it, lads!"

I snatched up our lunch, took their hands again, and we carried on up the pathway, the ewe nuzzling her lambs to assure herself we had done them no harm. Above us loomed the craggy summit, patches of cloud standing out brilliant white against the deep azure sky. My heart swelled within me so that it fairly ached with the beauty of it all. And to my mind sprang one of the Psalm versifications inspired by those men in Geneva. As their father had done when I was but a lad, I made to tutor my two charges, here in singing of the Psalm.

> The little hills on ev'ry side
> Rejoice right pleasantly.

With flocks the pastures clothed be,
　　The vales with corn are clad;
And now they shout and sing to thee,
　　For thou hast made them glad.

There was no one about to be troubled by our singing, so we lifted our voices with abandon, the boys cavorting like wild spring lambs as we sang. At last, our energy spent, we collapsed in a heap on the sod to recover our breath.

"That one's a billy goat," cried Nathaniel, pointing at the clouds.

"Aye, so it is," I said, tilting my head and squinting.

"And that one's a lamb," said Eleazar. "And there's another, and another."

"They're all like lambs," said Nathaniel, laughing. "That one there's an old man with a great white beard."

"Aye, and perhaps they're all old men with great white beards, then," I said. "Let's up and away to the top."

Higher up we climbed, at last coming to a wide shoulder that formed a high meadow that stretched around the base of the summit. The lush green of the meadow was speckled with close on a hundred sheep, many of the heavy with the promise of lambing season, and there several lambs already dropped and staggering about the meadow. Arms flaying the air, Nathaniel and Eleazar chased another pair of lambs for a quarter of an hour.

"Follow me, lads!" I called to them. "We'll have our wee luncheon on the top."

The final pathway to the summit was steep and rocky, and I took care to keep a tight grip on the lads' hands.

"I can nae go another step," said Eleazar, flopping onto the path, his lip quavering.

With a grunt, I hefted him onto my shoulders, grateful that he had made it as far as he had. He rested his chin upon my head, and clutched an ear in each of his hands.

"Tell us a tale," said Nathaniel, following close behind me up the trail.

"Alright, then," I said, breathing hard with the weight of the lad on my shoulders. "There were nine and ninety sheep spread out on the hillside, a-feeding on the spring grass. But there was one—like that wee lamb, right there, frolicking close to a precipice."

"What's a precipice?" asked Eleazar, tugging on my ear lobes.

"It's a rocky place, lad, like you see all about us just here."

"Foolish lamb," said Nathaniel, stretching his neck to see down the craggy face. "He ought to ken better than to lose his self on a precipice."

Holding one of Eleazar's ankles, I took a firm grip on Nathaniel's collar. "Och aye, so he ought to do. But the good shepherd, he left the nine and ninety sheep and searched night and day, clamoring over the most treacherous terrain, searching every vale and hill—"

"And prec-pice-pice," added Eleazar.

"—Aye, and precipice," I continued, "until he had found the one lost lamb, and he rescued him from peril. Ah, here we are at last."

I lowered Eleazar onto a soft clump of heather. The boy was groggy with weariness. In moments he had curled into a ball, closed his eyes and fell into a slumber. I tucked his plaid in about him against the soughing breeze. Nathaniel helped me spread out our wee feast on a flat rock. We offered our thanksgiving for the same, and commenced eating.

345

High atop Arthur's Seat the air was sweet, scented with heather, and patches of purple were showing through cracks in the rocky mount. The capital spread out below us. Wisps of smoke from dozens of cooking fires rose over the stone dwellings as hundreds of folks, high and low, went about their business in those homes and on those streets. I felt blissfully detached from it all, at least for these moments.

"They're like wee ants," said Nathaniel munching on an oatcake. "And there's an ant-horse pulling an ant-sized cart."

From our vantage point the city and our struggles for the pure evangel against the forces of queen and parliament suddenly made more sense. There stood the sturdy ramparts of Edinburgh Castle on the far end, and on the other, the fairyland turrets of Holyrood Palace. I studied the intricate crown-spire of St. Giles rising above it all. Caught in the middle of those two strongholds stood the kirk, and in its pulpit my master John Knox, buffeted and wrenched to pieces in the middle. It all made more sense.

"What does it mean?" asked Nathaniel.

I thought he was following my own thoughts and began to try and explain to the lad the convolutions of the struggle we were caught in: the Reformation, the Lords of the Congregation, the queen and the French, and the bishops and the Roman pontiff, and the decaying religion that had held Scotland in bondage for centuries.

"Nae, I mean the tale you told us," he interrupted. "The one about the shepherd and the wee lost lamb."

I recovered myself. "Well, as you ken, it was Jesus who told that tale," I said.

"Aye, I ken that. But what does it mean? Eleazar, now he'd be being the lost sheep some of the time, now would nae he be?"

I looked at the ruddy cheek of the sleeping lad, his heart-shaped lips parted, the trickling of drool wetting his arm, his steady breathing.

"And you fancy yourself one of the good sheep, don't you?" I said.

He stiffened. "Aye, then," he said shortly.

"But it was Jesus, lad, who said that he came to seek and to save that which was lost. If you do nae ken yourself to be lost, then, you'll never know the sweet grace of the rescuing embrace of Jesus."

"Och, then. But who are the nine and ninety sheep?"

"They're all of us," I said, finding my way as I spoke. "We all of us think we're not so lost a sinners. We all of us imagine ourselves to be righteous, deserving residence of God's green pastures. It's not till we're brought to see ourselves in peril on the precipice of eternal ruin that we can be rescued by the Good Shepherd himself."

I hadn't noticed that Eleazar had stretched himself and sat up. He snatched up a cold leg of mutton and was gnawing on it. But at my words, he began humming a tune, waving the mutton leg in rhythm with the melody. We joined him with the words.

> The Lord's my shepherd, I'll not want.
> He makes me down to lie
> In pastures green: he leadeth me
> The quiet waters by.
>
> My soul he doth restore again;
> And me to walk doth make
> Within the paths of righteousness,
> Ev'n for his own name's sake.

When we'd finished the Psalm, I tried to explain to the lads. "You see, it's all the Good Shepherd's doing. You've heard your father preaching the evangel of Jesus Christ. That's what it all means. Jesus alone is the one who makes us lie down, who leads us, who restores us, who alone makes us walk in the path of his righteousness. It's his righteousness alone, and it's his precious name alone that does all this. That, lads, is the evangel your father wears himself out proclaiming to everyone."

After allowing them to mull it about in their young hearts, I rose and said, "Now, we must make haste. If we miss the fishmonger at the market—och, then, no supper."

48

Cousins

MY FEET ACHING from the long tramping, I was, nevertheless, invigorated by our day away from the crowded city. We walked through the kirkyard of the Abbey of the Grey Friars on our return and then to the West Bow and the Grassmarket. I needed to buy some food for the Knox larder at Trunk Close. The day had stretched on, and I feared we might be too late. The market was thinning out as the day drew to its close, but I was arrested by the voice of a young woman.

"Three groats for a dead fish!" she cried. "You're no fishmonger. You're a thief."

The young woman had her hands upon her hips. There was fire in her eyes, and a flush upon her cheeks. I had an instant of thinking that there was something vaguely familiar about the lass. She tucked a strand of wavy red hair behind an ear, smoothed her embroidered dress, and continued.

"I'll give you a half-groat for it—not a farthing more," she said, her chin jutting at him defiantly.

"Lass, this is a fine specimen of a haddock," said the fishmonger meekly. "I'll take nothing less than three groats for him."

"You might just as well thump me on my pate and rob me," said the girl. "I'll give you one groat, and that's double the value. Och, it smells, and it's all scaly and slimey."

"Madam, it is a fish," said the man.

And so it went till at last they made their bargain. I too wanted to pay less than the asking price for fish, but this girl struck me as ruthless, hard bargaining, and more than a trifle pushy in her manners. What is more, I could not help noticing that she was dressed and had the carriage of the upper crust, at least a laird's daughter. The lass paid not a copper more than the one silver coin. And then she did an odd thing. Her manner changed entirely. She turned with a smile upon an old stooped woman who had been waiting in line at the fishmonger's stall. So distracted by the young woman I had failed to recognize the widow Murray. Only last week I had been to her hovel on the edge of town; she was always humble and grateful for the bread, or blood sausages, or wine that I delivered to her on behalf of Christ's kirk. I took pleasure in dolling out to her fine wine, wine fit for a duke, wine seized from the cellars of the monks at Grey Friars Abbey. Widow Murray was a dear.

"This, my dear woman, is for you," the young woman said to the widow, as if she were speaking to a duchess. Then she turned to the fishmonger. "And how much for that fat one there?"

His face reddened. "Lass, you'll be a-paying three groats or I'll close up my stall." He braced himself for her rejoinder.

She flashed him a smile. I confess, it was a lovely smile. "I'll take it," she said simply.

"You'll what?" said the astonished fishmonger.

"I'll take it at your full price—three groats," she repeated. "On condition, that you'll make a solemn covenant before God and these witnesses—" She raised her voice, and looked about the crowd. "That this dear woman pays never a farthing more than one groat—one groat—for the finest, fattest haddock in your stall."

The perplexed fishmonger nodded his consent. And, one at a time, she dropped three silver coins into his hand. Then she gathered up her fish, touched the widow on the sleeve, and turned to go. Mouth agape, the man weighed the silver coins in his hands.

As she turned, the girl caught sight of Eleazar upon my shoulders and Nathaniel at my side.

"What fine young lads!" she said with delight. From within her shopping basket over her arm she produced two squares of shortbread. "With your father's permission," she said, "you lads look like you're needing a morsel to sustain you till suppertime."

Crumbs scratched at my neck as Eleazar munched on her offering. As I completed my shopping, I found myself catching sight of the young woman. She was before me at the sausage makers, and I saw her buying a loaf of bread while I purchased a crock of pickled cabbage. I wondered what she paid for a loaf of bread. I paid exactly two groats for a smoked haddock.

I pushed the girl out of my mind as we walked toward home down the Royal Mile. I intended only to poke my head in the kirk and perhaps persuade John Knox to come home early, take some supper, get some more rest. But as I entered there were five or six young men seated in the south transept of St. Giles, John Knox seated before them.

My mind flashed back to my youth when my brother Francis, Alexander, and I had sat before Master Knox. I used to feel jealous of his attentions to us. There was no place for that now. He often said that he'd rather spend fifteen hours interpreting a text of Holy Scripture with young men preparing for the ministry than an hour doing anything else. This appeared to be one such earnest discussion. I was about to go, when the words of one of the young men arrested my attention. I lingered, the boys weary and fidgety at my side, I hoping it would not be prolonged for fifteen hours, but eager to hear their debate.

"But will not such teaching loosen the reins of lusts?" asked the young man. "If we instruct the ignorant that salvation is entirely an unconditional free gift—they'll be no restraint on manners and behavior. Law is smashed and Antinomianism shall prevail."

"Do you imagine that any of us can earn God's favor by keeping God's law?" said John Knox. "Do you imagine that salvation is mostly of God's grace, mostly of Christ's merits, but that we must be his partners in our own salvation, then?"

"But you cannot deny, Master Knox, that huge tracts of Holy Scripture address the members of the visible kirk as responsible partners in covenant with God, whose destiny is determined by our faith and our obedience or lack thereof."

At the young man's words, I saw the vitality of John Knox's convictions rising up in him, his forehead seeming to become more broad and set, his eyebrows overshadowing his features like dark clouds before a tempest; his eyes flashed like lightning, and his in-drawing of breath seemed as if it would burst forth like thunderclaps in his reply.

"Every papist, man, would agree with you," he said. "The only way huge tracts of Holy Scripture say such nonsense, however, is if you make a mingle mangle out of law and gospel, that is, if you get the cart of good works before the horse of electing grace. You must not separate the things that God has joined together.

The cause of good works, my friend, is not our free will, but when the Spirit of the Lord Jesus, whom God's elect children receive by true faith, takes possession of the heart of any man, the Spirit regenerates and renews the man, so that he begins to hate what before he loved, and to love what before he hated.

"If you make the believer's good works, his sanctification, a condition of his justification, you mistake the evangel and make man's faithfulness a means of meriting or of maintaining the salvation of God. If we determine our destiny by anything in us, faith, faithfulness, obedience, free will, good works, anything by which we partner with God, then you must say, as the papists say, that God has come down to save the just. But Jesus the Son of God came not in the flesh to call the just, but to call sinners, surely not to abide in their old iniquity, but to true repentance, true dying to sin. The Christian's hope of mercy and forgiveness before God is not in his faith and obedience, but in the redemption that is in Christ's blood alone, by which alone a man's imperfection has no power to damn him, for Christ's perfection is reputed to be his by the regenerating and renewing of the Spirit which alone engenders faith in us, faith which he has in Christ's blood. God has received already at the hands of his only Son all that is due for our sins, and so cannot his justice require or crave any more of us. There is no other satisfaction or recompense required for our sins."

"You said the same today on the mount," said Nathaniel as we left the kirk and walked home.

"Did I?"

"Aye, you said Jesus came to seek and to save the lost," continued the boy, "the lost, like the wee lamb on the precipice. It was the same as father was speaking of."

353

"Aye, so it was," I said.

Several times over the next weeks, I saw the haddock lass, as I at first termed her. Then I came to call her in my mind, the generous lass. At last I learned her name.

"I'm Margaret Stewart, Lord Ochiltree's daughter," she told me.

Our meeting this time required more coordination than merely meeting at the Grassmarket where everyone in Edinburgh came and went. It came about as I carried a sack of oats upon my back to the door of the widow Murray's home. My back felt like it was about to crack in two as I heaved the sack onto the floor of the cottage. And there she was, chatting away as if the elderly widow were a lady in court. And she'd not come empty handed. There was a plump turnip on the table, a basket of duck eggs, a fresh-baked pan loaf, and the lass was arranging a lovely bouquet of tulips in a crock vase as she chatted.

When her errand and mine were accomplished, we walked back into the city together, she doing most of the talking.

"And where are your wee lads today?" she said, as if only on the instant noticing that they were not with me.

"They're at home," I explained. "And you should know, they're not my lads. They're the sons of John Knox, my master."

She laughed. "So I discovered after our first meeting. I saw you with them at the kirk, and they resembling our dear pastor as they do. No, I ken it now. You're not their father."

The next day as I halted in my lessons with Nathaniel—we had commenced his study of Latin, now under my tutelage as I had been under his father's—to stir a pot of broth, and then to put to soaking the boys' breeks and tunics, a thought began forming in my mind.

Margaret Stewart was a generous-hearted lass, cared for children, looked after widows of her own accord. When I had questioned her about her visitations on the widow, she had replied, "I'll not leave the poor dear with but a dish o' want." Such a benevolent lass, why might she not be put into service here at Trunk Close, to care for Master Knox and the boys? Perhaps I could form a scheme whereby she and John Knox might meet. I could not think of a more amiable woman to care for the boys, be a housekeeper, and generally arrange things for him, for us.

I made free to speak with Margaret about it the very next time I saw her.

She looked troubled at my suggestion, and her usually cheerful countenance fell. "John Knox and Her Majesty the queen, they're not on the best of terms, then," she said, weighing her words carefully.

"Aye, indeed they're not," I said. "I wish you could have seen and heard his last interview with Her Majesty. He's a man who speaks the same way to every man. He never flatters the mighty, nor ever insults the lowly. He calls a fig a fig, and a spade a spade, does he. The fact of the matter is, I believe he speaks with far more tenderness and generosity toward the lowly, unlike most in the realm. He's a man, is he, that neither fears nor flatters any flesh."

"So you've met the queen, then?" she asked. There was a lilt of incredulity in her tone, and she tossed her head in a manner that rather made me think she doubted that one such as I could ever have been welcome in a queen's presence.

"I have indeed," I said, with more enthusiasm than I had intended. "Have you, Margaret, ever met the queen?"

Her eyes grew wide as if the prospect was too wonderful for her to imagine. "Ding me daft," she said, curtseying. "I'm in the presence of Lord Muck himself." She was toying with me, and it was beneath her to do so. I was about to rebuke her for it. But before I could do so, she continued.

"Met the queen?" she repeated, blowing a long strand of her hair that had trailed onto her cheek. "What are you yammering about? Och, man. She's my cousin!"

49

Another Man's Wife

MARGARET WAS GETTING UNDER MY SKIN, if I may use the metaphor. Cousin of the queen? Well, I determined to keep her unfortunate bloodline in the suburbs of my proposal to John Knox. I was uncertain how my master would react to the information. But I felt certain the queen would never consent to her cousin entering into domestic service with her chief nemesis in the realm.

What transpired in the next weeks rather made my head to spin. Facts force me to acknowledge it, and denying of it would be a sham: Margaret was a lovely young woman, all the more so for her frank, unpretentious manner. So unlike her cousin, she was a lass who was seemingly ignorant of her own charm and attractiveness.

No man, unless he was a stone, would be unaware of her qualities. Master Knox proved to be no exception. He was a widow of fifty years, sickly, consumed with his calling, a willing slave of the kirk, his ministry, and the poor souls of all Scotland. He was a man desperately in need of domestic assistance. I felt certain I could convince him to take Margaret into our home at Trunk

Close, not as a servant; that would have been beneath her station, though she had the heart thereof; I supposed it would be more as a domestic administrator of our affairs.

And so I made bold to propose the matter and introduced Margaret to him. I chose to do so after morning worship at St. Giles. I made her promise to stick close, and waited until after he had greeted the last of those who had gathered to hear him preach. The boys clamored at her skirts in excitement as we waited. For an instant I wished she had not worn that dress. It was a lovely blue, which brought out the color of her eyes, and the manner in which the dressmaker had achieved its shape worked with considerable advantage upon her own. And why did she have to have such lovely hair, the wavy strands hanging about her fine cheek bones, and why did she toss them aside with such carelessness? I wished she were stout, in her forties, with thinning hair, and perhaps missing some of those beautiful white teeth. A wart or two upon her delicate nose would have helped. It was maddening. I would abandon the whole scheme. And I would have, but it was too late. He stood before us.

I have already recorded that John Knox was not unaware of the loveliness of this singular young woman. I am forced to confess that my first thought was not for him to fall in love with her and marry the girl; she was of an age to be his daughter. But to be the man's wife? She was more fit to be my wife; she was yet ten years younger than I, and more than thirty years younger than he. It was all moving so rapidly. I felt I had lost control. Perhaps she would not have him. Or perhaps her father would object. Or the queen herself might attempt an intervention against the union.

I had had stirrings of late. I had had thoughts of considering the possibility of musing on the prospect of taking a wife. I had even written Francis. I had made bold to ask him about family life, children, home, domesticity. It was five or six letters exchanged before I spoke more directly and asked him searching questions about marriage, about a woman, his wife, their life together. There was so much I did not understand about these matters.

And then my real battle began to rage about me. In some way that I could not understand or explain, those stirrings in my bosom turned upon me with vengeance. And for a time I thought I was like to be ruined by what those desires became in my mind, and in my heart.

On March 26, 1564, John Knox and Margaret Stewart were wed at St. Giles. The groom was a stooped man of fifty, aged beyond his years, who looked like his head and innards were troubling him more than usual that day. The bride was fair, and young, and lovely beyond my ability to describe, and anyway, the describing would do no one any good, leastwise myself. I wondered if there were yet another such fair cousin in the family. I ought not to have attended.

His marriage was so like my master. Controversy followed him wherever he trod. When Mary Queen of Scots learned that John Knox had married her cousin, that her cousin had married John Knox, and that they'd done so without her consent, even without seeking her consent, she was furious. His critics leapt to the chance. Here was a widower in his fifties going off and marrying a lass who had but seventeen years.

I confess that I spent many a dark night travailing with my soul in these days. And I was tempted to join his critics, to rail against him on the high street. But I did not. Instead I found myself almost daily assaulted with temptation. It was monstrous. I tried everything. I raged against it. I attempted to deny it. I spent hours at a time telling myself the most vicious lies against Margaret Stewart, now Margaret Knox. And when I had spent my fury I would awaken in the small hours of the morning, alone with my desire for her, for another man's wife; yet not just any other man. It fairly drove me to madness.

I began to believe that undergoing such temptation and warfare was itself a grievous sin, a black stain within my heart, unpardonable. And at the lowest ebb of the temptation I was entertained with thoughts that temptation of this magnitude could never be resisted without at last surrendering to its all-consuming urging.

I could be very wrong in the assumption, but I believe that neither John Knox nor his wife knew of my anguish. Then in a sermon my master was preaching he, if I am correct, unknowingly gave me great comfort and encouragement in my battle. He began as he so often did by directing us away from his words and to the eternal truth of God's words.

"The person of the speaker is wretched, miserable, and nothing to be regarded; but the things that are spoken are the infallible and eternal truth of God, without observation of which, life never can nor shall come to mankind. God grant you, beloved people of God, in all your temptations continuance to the end."

He then took us to the days when Jesus' ministry was inaugurated after his baptism. "There remains yet to be spoken of, the time when our Head was tempted, which began immediately after his baptism. Whereupon we have to note and mark, that albeit the malice of Satan does never cease, but always seeks the means to trouble the godly, yet sometimes he rages more fiercely than others; and that is commonly when God begins to manifest his love and favor to any of his children, and at the end of their battle, when they are nearest to obtain final victory."

And then he commenced a thundering salvo against the enemy.

"O cruel serpent! In vain do you spend your venom. For the days of God's elect you cannot shorten! And when the wheat corn is fallen on the ground, then does it most multiply."

I found great comfort in this. My Lord Jesus had been tempted in every way, yet without sin. He was my righteousness, and as my righteousness, I could take strength from his triumph over temptation and sin. Yes, his perfections fully absolved me of all of my imperfections, yet did he continue that work in me begun by his grace. I had died with Christ my Head, and had been crucified with him, and I was raised up with him by the regenerating power of his Spirit at work in me. There was no charge that could be laid to God's elect.

I threw myself more completely into my duties, and they were seemingly endless duties, of caring for the poor and needy in this benighted city. It was ironic to me that under centuries of the teaching of justification by faith and works, there had been so little good works done to relieve the great afflictions of the infirm and indigent souls in the extremity of need throughout the realm. Outward obedience motivated by fear of punishment under law had done nothing to alleviate such suffering. The evangel of Christ alone and his love for the poor in spirit, only his loving the unlovely, the leper, the blind man, the deaf, the mute, the demoniac—only his love could constrain me to love the needy. I saw them every day, and my heart was heavy. Yet was it also full of joy, joy in loving as I had been loved.

Meanwhile, as I delivered food, repaired door hinges, replaced roof thatch long neglected, I began to look for another living situation for myself. John Knox ever extolled the importance of daily searching of the Scriptures for God's sweet promises. And I found therein encouragement to make no opportunity for the flesh to fulfill its lusts thereof.

I had no idea that in the course of my calling, I was about to make a discovery that I had long ago abandoned hope of ever making.

50

Douglas the Dungman

IT HAPPENED ONE EVENING as I came wearily back to Trunk Close. My back ached, and I had nearly fallen and broken my neck while attempting a repair on a thatched roof that morning. Coming toward me was the dungman. His horse's head was low, placing one fetlock hoof in front of the other. I had seen him often in the years since that cold December night when Marjory had died. But we had never spoken. I confess that the reason for this, if I am to be honest, is that I simply could not abide his odor. I can't say for certain that it was the man's odor, for his cargo being dung forever smelled of dung. Hence, I had always assumed that so did the man.

But I was prompted to speak to him that evening, and so I hailed him as I drew near. He had halted his horse without a word, and was engaged in his calling of forking up dung from the street and lobbing it into his cart. I had an instant of hesitation. Perhaps he needed no conversation that day. With a deft motion of his fork, he scooped up a mound of dung, and, without looking, flung it into the cart. It was skillfully accomplished, and I wondered if he ever missed.

I was now closer to him than I had ever allowed myself to be in the past. There is another matter that had troubled me about the dungman, and that was the matter of his name. "Douglas the Dungman" he was called by everyone in Edinburgh. I had known it for years now. But being my surname, common though it was, his having of it made me uneasy. Why not "Donegal the Dungman" or "McDonald the McDungman" even. Anything but Douglas.

I was suddenly flooded with memories of that early visit to Edinburgh when the stone cutter had told me of the man he had seen in Edinburgh Castle. "Gang gyte," he had said of the fellow, twirling a finger about his ear.

"Good day to you," I managed to say as I stopped myself near him.

He looked at me with vacant eyes and said nothing. Nor did he move on.

Perhaps he was incapable of hearing and speaking, the thought suddenly occurred to me. I was probably not alone in my aversion to him, and I wondered if anyone ever attempted to speak to him. Shifting my stance uncomfortably, it occurred to me just how important his calling was to the health of the city. I envisioned in those moments the Royal Mile heaped with foul-smelling horse dung. Day after day, more horse dung rising in the streets. How fetid and diseased the place would become. I wondered how much the city council paid the man. I felt a twinge of guilt that in my role as deacon I had never inquired, never even thought to do so, and had never thanked him for his service.

"Thank you," I said. "For what you do for our city, I thank you for it."

He stared and said nothing.

I continued. Perhaps I said more to him because he said nothing in reply. "Have you ever wondered what this place would look like if you missed one day of your calling here on the Royal Mile? And if you lay ill in your bed for a week's time, the place would be heaped with . . . well, with dung."

Standing as I was a cart-length from the man, and wondering if he was deaf, I spoke loudly. Several people walked by, giving me a wide berth, and eyeing me as if I was standing on the street corner shouting at a lamp post.

Still the man did not move on. I attempted to speak with him further. "And your family, does your labor provide sufficient income for your family?"

No reply.

"I certainly hope it does. It should, you know, as important as your calling is. Can you imagine the disease that would run unchecked throughout the city? All that dung and all these people coming into such close contact with it. Surely it would not be good for the health of the community. That is, if you didn't engage so faithfully in your calling."

I paused for breath. He made no reply. I felt like a daft limmer speaking to him thus. With a clomp, his horse stamped on the cobbles, then shook its bridle impatiently.

"I've come to believe that there is no calling that is not . . ." I hesitated, eyeing the mound of dung in his cart. In this instance, I wasn't certain if I really believed what I had so often heard John Knox say, and what I had often heard John Calvin speak of when we lived in Geneva. I tried again. "I'm convinced that every calling is a sacred one. That our labor is a gift from God to us, that in it we serve God and our neighbor if we do it cheerfully from the heart and for his glory. Wouldn't you agree?"

I felt that perhaps it was better not to ask him questions. It was easier to speak to him when my words required no verbal response from him. Yet the more I spoke the more I was determined to find out about the man.

Heretofore, I had stood a cart length from the man as I spoke. I took several steps closer. My eyes smarted, and I felt my insides heaving at the stench. I swallowed hard, and tried once again. I now saw the man's eyes, the curve of his nose, his bone structure, the texture of his skin, though his chin was covered with a graying beard. He leaned on his pitchfork, and his work-hardened hands, one atop the other, grasped the stock of the implement of his trade. He continued to stare at me, making no move to pass on. I took a step closer. When first I had seen him and he had looked back at me, his eyes had been vacant, emotionless, blinking only occasionally and returning to their dispassionate gaze. But there was something in them now. I could not be sure what it was.

I knew in my own soul that something had awakened in my mind as I looked more closely at the poor fellow. Had he been here all along, but I too repulsed to know him? Could this be my father? How had he come to this condition? He was a laird, had a fortified house in Longniddry, cultivated lands, sheep, and cattle. Why was he forking dung on the Royal Mile? Perhaps it was all a mistake. Had I so wanted to discover my father that I had come to this: convincing myself that the dungman was he?

"They call you 'Douglas the Dungman,'" I said. "Why do they call you by that name?"

There was no verbal reply, but he shifted his weight from one foot to the other at my question. And that odd flicker came into his eyes again. I took another step nearer the man.

"If you are not able or willing to speak, can you give me some sign, a shaking or nodding of your head, a signal with a hand, that you understand me?"

I made the request more out of desperation than expecting any meaningful reply. So when he gave a slight nod of his head, I felt my heart lurch within me. He had heard and understood.

"Do you ken your full name?" I asked.

He looked steadily at me then slowly nodded his head down and up.

I was terrified to ask the next question, but I knew I must. "Are you Hugh Douglas?" I asked, "Hugh Douglas of Longniddry?"

There was now a tear globbing in his right eye. Slowly it broke over his lower eyelid. Slowly it made its way down his cheek, leaving a clean furrow in his soiled skin. His head went up and came down.

It was now my turn to feel the water in my eyes and coming shamelessly down my cheeks. There were tears in both of his eyes now, and haltingly he lifted a hand toward me. It was a filthy hand, blackened with dung and labor. I stepped closer to him. All the vacancy in his face dissolved into full recognition. I had not seen him for eighteen years. I wondered which of us had most changed in that time. I forgot the soiled work tunic, the dirty hands, the matted hair and beard, the stench, the mound of dung behind him.

"My father," I stammered. He held me in his arms, and I heard the first sounds from his mouth as he began sobbing.

When I had composed myself sufficiently to attempt speaking again, I asked, "Where do you live?"

He turned and gestured down the Royal Mile in the direction of Holyrood Palace and Arthur's Seat.

"Do you have sufficient food and fuel for warmth?" I asked what I had asked so many people.

He nodded. And then he turned and led his horse and cart full of dung down the Mile. I watched him until he disappeared from view at the Netherbow.

My life took on a new purpose in the days that followed this encounter with the man that must be my father. I determined to find out everything I could about him. I hunted down the stone cutter. I showed my father to him. He confirmed that Douglas the Dungman was the same man he had seen in the dungeon at Edinburgh Castle.

"Did nae I tell you?" he said. "He'd gang gyte. He is nae right in the head. But I'm glad they've freed the poor man and that he's got a job to do."

I felt some days of rage at Mary Queen of Scots, at her mother the Regent who had imprisoned my father, at the foul, bloated bishops, at the pope and all the falsehood and evil he had perpetrated, and I felt renewed anger at Alexander. It was men like him who turned on their fellow Scots to save their own worthless necks.

But I felt no better for my rage against the world. None of that would help my dear father. I asked him if he would show me his dwelling place, and he allowed me to follow him past the palace and up an incline overlooking the city. There was an old hermits' chapel with a small stable. It was a stone structure in the gothic style, but the stained-glass windows had all been broken out during the iconoclasm, and my father had covered them over with oiled sacking to keep out the wind and weather. It was dark inside, and smelled—as everything about him smelled—of dung. But he did not live like an animal. He had neatly arranged a table, and a chair with a broken leg that he had carefully mended. He had a bed made of heather and sacking. And there was evidence of him making efforts to keep the place clean and free of rubbish.

"Father, I will help you repair the windows," I said.

He nodded. His beard was so heavy that I never saw his mouth, but I could tell when his cheeks rose under his eyes that he was smiling. But he never spoke. I wondered what deprivation he had undergone in his years in that dungeon. And I wondered if he had had flickers of recognition of me in those years before I knew him.

When the Lord's Day arrived, I hiked up to his chapel house and took him with me to St. Giles. It was the first time I had been to public worship with my father since I was a boy. During the Psalm singing he wept, his shoulders heaving as he listened. I believe when he recovered himself he was making efforts to join in the singing, but no sound came from his throat.

John Knox walked slowly into the pulpit. His face was the color of spring lilies, and he winced on the last steps of his climb. I wondered for how much longer he would have strength to preach. As he opened his Geneva Bible on the lectern, I caught sight of Margaret. "O cruel serpent! In vain do you spend your venom," I murmured to myself. My father looked from me to the woman and back to me.

"Father," I whispered to him. "May I come live with you in the chapel?"

51

The Assassin

John Knox greeted my father warmly, prayed earnestly with him, and sent me with his blessing to live with my father. "For God's mercies freely given are like the handling of the most sweet and delectable unguents, whereof we cannot but receive comfort by their natural sweet odors." So said John Knox while grasping the hand of my father, the city dungman.

It was a tearful parting for me. For twenty years, I had rarely been out of John Knox's presence for more than a few hours. Dangerous as my life had been with him, he cared for me like a son, and he had taught me everything I knew. I was blessed in my calling as deacon, for I was daily at the kirk, where I saw him often. There were some months, however, when he was away from Edinburgh. He traveled to St. Andrews and for a time he was in Newcastle.

During these years I could not from time to time help seeing Margaret, the wife of John Knox. And she was well. She was a great aid to my former master in his writing, and helped him as his eyes grew dim by reading aloud to him. Nathaniel and Eleazar, whom I still took for tramps up Arthur's Seat and for rides on my father's pony, were well cared for by their new mother. I was grateful to see that she was attentive to her husband when his old malady descended upon him. I have never seen a woman more faithful and longsuffering. While doing all this, wonder of wonders, she gave John Knox children too. First, Martha was born in 1565; then Margaret, her mother's namesake, was born in 1567, the year the shameful queen was forced to abdicate the throne; and in 1570 she gave birth to little Elizabeth.

These were years of growth and progress in the kirk, but they were not for the most part years of peace and tranquility in Scotland. They were years of laborious building for John Knox: training ministers, planting schools, and sometimes fighting bitterly with the queen and strong-willed nobles who opposed Reformation. I suppose John Knox, my master, was like the prophets of old in this too: some hated and feared him and others deeply honored and respected him. But John Knox was not a man to be moved by either.

He told me one evening as I walked him home, he leaning heavily on my arm, "I distribute the bread of life as of Christ Jesus I have received it. I seek neither preeminence, glory, nor riches. My honor is that Christ Jesus should reign."

Meanwhile, I who had not known my father for twenty long years now had a great deal of discovering to do. Those first months living with my father in that broken-down hermits' chapel did not solve all my problems. I never truly became accustomed to the stench, though I discovered ways to help my father launder his clothes, and reserve clothes that would never come near the object of his daily labors. And we began spending what time we could repairing and improving the quaint little chapel. We pooled our financial resources and bought window glass and learned to cut and fit it to the shapes of the gothic tracery. And we repaired the roof with thatch we harvested ourselves from the heather that grew on the slopes of Arthur's Seat. After considerable experimentation, we managed to brew our own heather ale from the same source. From the hermit's chapel, the view was exceptional; we looked out over the city and the palace. Perhaps it lacked a woman's touch, but over the next years it became home to us both.

My father and I became very conversant with one another in these years, and I loved him dearly. He yet remained mute, but we came to understand one another in ways that required concentration on my part and attentiveness to him. I cannot fully express the joy of our eventual discovery that he was capable of relearning to read and to write. Whether he would ever recover his speaking, I did not know. But once he was able to write, I began spending a great deal of money on paper and ink. He had very much to say to me, but he spoke—that is to say—he wrote little of his imprisonment.

Soon it was clear that it was intensely important to him to know what had happened to me in the long years of our separation. He seemed to want to hear my voice, but he was not satisfied if he did not think I was giving him every detail. And always he wrote down my words; he wrote them as I told them, from my vantage point upon the events. He developed a manner of twirling his quill pen, then setting it down slowly. He would then fold his big hands and fix his gaze upon me. Slowly he would shake his head at my inadequate words, and then he would pick the pen up again. I came to know that this meant he did not believe I was telling him everything—everything. He wanted to hear what I said, and what others said, and what Master Knox preached and wrote. But he was not satisfied with the mere words spoken. He wanted to know my thoughts, my fears, my longings. It was at times laborious and exhausting to me to recollect so minutely these often painful things, but it seemed essential to him to know everything that had transpired, and everything about me. Over these years of telling him the story, and he penning the words, I was enabled to assess the fearful events that had made up my life with John Knox for twenty years. Telling my father these things—and I believe he understood this far better than I—acted as a healing balm upon my soul.

And we went regularly to hear John Knox preach at St. Giles. My father began taking down his sermons as best he could, which required still more paper and ink—and feathers. I believe my father's writing alone may have depleted the population of geese throughout the realm. I recall watching John Knox prepare his sermons. "I did ever abstain to commit anything to writ," he had told me, "contented only to have obeyed the charge of Him who commanded me to cry." So it may be that my father's efforts at taking down in writing those sermons has left behind the only written record of what Master Knox actually preached.

One of the last sermons I heard him deliver at St. Giles—we nearly had to carry him into the pulpit—was written down by my father.

"The same eternal God and Father, who of mere grace elected us in Christ Jesus his Son before he laid the foundation of the world, appointed Christ to be our Head, our Brother, our Pastor, and the great bishop of our souls. But because the enmity betwixt the justice of God and our sins was such that no flesh by itself could or might have attained unto God, it behoved that the Son of God should descend unto us, and take himself a body like our body, flesh of our flesh, and bone of our bones, and so become the Mediator betwixt God and man, giving power to so many as believe in him, to be the sons of God; as himself does witness, 'I pass up to my Father, and unto your Father, to my God, and unto your God.' By which most holy fraternity, whatsoever we have lost in Adam, is restored unto us again. And for this cause, are we not afraid to call God our Father, not so much because he has created us, which we have in common with the reprobate; but because he has given to us his only Son to be our brother, and given unto us grace, to acknowledge and embrace him for our only Mediator."

My master, indeed, loved to blow his Master's trumpet. Wherever in the Word of God he preached, he was never far from Christ. His words always rose into singular beauty and passion when he held before us the sacrifice of the Savior.

"Hence, he has given us his only Son to be our only Mediator, because Christ was to undertake the punishment due for our transgressions, and to present Himself in the presence of his Father's judgment, as in our person, to bear our penalty in our place for our transgression."

John Knox's voice rose to near ecstasy. "God's electing love in the redemption of Christ did triumph and purchase to us life, liberty, and perpetual victory. If we are to be truly humble, if we are to be ravished in admiration of God's goodness, and so moved to praise, we must know and believe the doctrine of eternal predestination.

"The doctrine of God's eternal predestination is so necessary to the church of God that, without the same, can faith neither be truly taught, neither surely established. And, therefore, we fear not to affirm that just as necessary as it is that true faith be established in our hearts, and that we be brought to unfeigned humility, and that we be moved to praise Him for his free graces received—just as necessary also is the doctrine of God's eternal predestination.

"There is no way more proper to build and establish faith than when we hear and undoubtedly do believe that our election consisteth not in ourselves, but in the eternal and immutable good pleasure of God. And that upon such firmity alone it cannot be overthrown, neither by the raging storms of the world, nor by the assaults of Satan; neither yet by the wavering and weakness of our own flesh. Then only is our salvation in assurance, when we find the cause of the same in the bosom and counsel of God."

When the sermon ended another deacon informed me that the widow Murray was failing rapidly. He had family obligations that afternoon, and so I hastened to her bedside, Nathaniel Knox accompanying me as errand boy if needed. Now that he was coming of age—he had close on twelve years by this time—he often joined me in this capacity, to my delight. I sent him for clean cloths, water, and perhaps some broth. Breathing hard, he returned within a quarter of an hour; his stepmother Margaret Knox had sent along the broth.

"The dear woman's going down the brae," I said to Nathaniel. "Yet, lad, it could be a long vigil. Run along home to your mother, then."

Widow Murray could no longer speak, but she could listen. I made sure she had a cool cloth on her fevered brow, and I read to her from the evangel. "I am the Way, the Truth, and the Life . . ." I held her hand in mine for hours that day. It was speckled with age, calloused with labors, boney with the veins standing out in sharp relief. I stroked her frail hand and her forehead, speaking softly with her of heaven, of eternal joys awaiting the righteous, of Jesus the Righteous One in whom alone the Christian hoped. The room grew dark. The broth became cold. I made to get up and light a candle, but there was a tiny press upon my hand from her fingers. I remained at her side in the dark, speaking to her, speaking to her Heavenly Father. I had to lean close to hear her faint breaths. And then without a tremor she no longer breathed. Her hand grew cold in mine. I rose, passed a hand across the dear woman's pallid cheek, and prayed that I would be more faithful in loving the poor and lonely as Jesus had loved me. There was no one to inform. She had, to my knowledge, no living family, none to mourn her passing, but the kirk, the family of God. It was enough.

As I walked along the Royal Mile in the darkness, I felt that I had been close to eternity, that by being at her bedside as she crossed the narrow sea into the stupendous wonder of the heavenly land, I had caught a glimmer of that place. I felt warmed and blessed, and small and grateful, all at once. Stony St. Giles stood dark and somber against the night sky as I passed by it, and the Mercat Cross, a hub of activity in the daylight hours, stood rigid, bear, and vacant.

In my comings and goings, when I felt my weakness come upon me with thoughts of Margaret troubling my peace, I would often take another pathway home to avoid the feelings that were aroused when passing by the house at Trunk Close, her house. I nearly did so that night, but thoughts of the widow dying peacefully in the arms of Jesus as she so apparently had done distracted my mind from lesser things. I kept my feet upon the Mile.

Through an upper window of the Knox house, I saw the glow of a candle on the side table, and my master's favorite chair, where he often sat to read before bedtime. Its back was to the window, and I wondered if he was seated therein at that moment.

I had been walking along the pavement close to the houses that form an unbroken stone wall along the mile, when the sound of footfalls came to my attention. Edinburgh is a bustling city by day, but generally of a chilly night there would be but few folks out and about. But there it was again. I came to a stand nearly opposite the house so as to listen better. The wind had begun to rise and there was the creaking sound; I guessed it was the iron sign affixed above Fountain Close just before me.

Then I saw him. I assumed it was a man, though dark as it was, it was difficult to tell. There was a movement at the black entrance to Fountain Close, that much I was certain of. Making my way as silently as I was able, I drew nearer to investigate. Perhaps it was only a stray cat on a rat hunt; I'd best leave it to it if it was; the city could do with fewer rats.

But there was a sound. A distinct sound unlike any I had ever heard a cat make. My blood ran cold. I knew there was nothing that made that sound but the thing itself. It was a tense metallic click, the cocking of a weapon. It may have been a hackbut, but I felt more certain that it was a pistol. And then I saw a pale glow of a match, and in that glow, the unmistakable profile of a man—forehead, nose, and chin. So intend was he on his mission, he was oblivious to my observation of him. I watched him slowly raise the pistol to his eye.

I followed the direction of his aim. Suddenly it all made sense. The man was aiming at the second story window of the house at Trunk Close. My heart went fair jeelit—cold as ice. To my horror, I felt certain that this man was about to shoot John Knox.

I wish I could say that, on the instant, in hazard of my life, I leapt to stop the man. But I did not. For a fraction of a second, I considered what would happen if the man fired, if he hit his mark, if John Knox was that mark, and if the gunman succeeded. My foul longings rose like the scum on a glaur marsh.

At one and the same instant, I cried out savagely, "Cruel serpent!" and lunged at the dark shape. At that same instant there was a click, a hiss, and a deafening retort. Then shattering glass. And the clattering of the pistol on the pavement. I felt the man crumple under me, the breath rushing from his lungs as I landed on top of him.

He grunted, and we scuffled briefly, but he was so winded by my assault upon him, that he had little ability to resist. The dark street burst into life. Windows opened, and there was shouting. Apparently someone was running while carrying a lantern, splashes of light jerking against the pavement and stone walls.

"What's this!" cried a man, grabbing me savagely by my collar. "What have you done?"

Eerie shadows bobbed against the wall at my right. I looked up at the man. He was blowing hard and his eyes shown wide; light from his lantern played on his fleshy cheeks. He held his light aloft.

"I-I've done nothing," I said. "But this rogue fired a pistol at my master."

What happened next nearly turned my heart to stone. The body of the assassin under me convulsed; he struggled and made to turn. In the flickering illumination of the lantern, I saw his face. I knew this face.

"Alexander?" I gasped.

52

Final Malady

IT WAS ALEXANDER. There could be no mistake.

I recoiled from him as if he had plague. Wrenching myself free of the man with the lantern, I rose to my feet. Looking down at Alexander, I felt myself torn between wanting to snatch up his pistol and shoot him through his miserable head and turning and getting forever clear of such a pestilence.

"Do not let him escape!" I cried, my voice like gravel.

I staggered across the street and pounded upon the door till my fists were bloodied. "Master Knox! Open to me! Margaret! Does he live? Open the door!"

At last I heard the fiddling of the latch. Her face was ashen, and she had wee Elizabeth on her hip, the child weeping like a prophet.

"Does he live?" I cried.

"H-he lives," she said, a tremor in her voice. "He lives."

Taking the treads three at a time, I ran up the stairs. The lead ball had shattered the window, and shards of glass littered the floor. On the table, a candlestick had been knocked over. Flames had been extinguished, but there was splattered wax already hardening where it had spilled on the table.

From the shadows next to the broken window, John Knox spoke. "I was not sitting in my usual place," he said. He was looking out on the excited crowd talking all at once on the street below.

"You are unhurt, then?" I asked.

"Aye," he said. "But had I been seated here, as is my custom—" he broke off, placing a finger through a bullet hole blown through the chair. "I would, indeed, be in a bit of a mangled condition."

Sighting from the broken window and the hole in the chair, I envisioned the flight of the ball. I went to the table and picked up the candlestick. The lead ball, or what remained of it, was imbedded into its filigree.

"God be praised," I said, and meant it.

"You were on the street?" asked Margaret, who had joined us. She swayed and cooed gently to calm the bairn.

"Aye," I said. "I'd been with the widow Murray; she expired about dusk."

"Poor dear," she said. "But it must have been you, then, who battled the gunman to the pavement."

I felt the warmth rising in my cheeks. "I did nothing," I said shortly.

"Och, nothing," she said, handing her husband the baby and squaring herself before me. "What I saw with my own eyes tells another tale," she said, blowing a wisp of hair from her face and placing her hands deliberately on her hips. "Och, you must've hurled yourself on the murderer like a madman."

"I must away," I said. I fear I spoke all too curtly. "My father will wonder what has kept me."

"And who was the rogue?" persisted Margaret.

I hesitated. They stood awaiting my reply. Would it not break Master Knox's heart to know that one of his own had attempted to end his life so? Would it not?

I attempted to speak. But I could find no words. I turned and bolted from the house.

"Have a care," said John Knox, his face blanching with pain, "for my decaying carcass."

It was Sunday, November 9, 1572. Several months had elapsed since the attempt on his life, and his health had deteriorated rapidly in those months. After much ruminating within my bosom, I was resolved: I would never speak to him about the identity of the pestilent assassin that night. Perhaps he already knew. Somehow he had known of Alexander's previous betrayal of us when hiding out in that foul bottle dungeon a lifetime ago. I confess, I lay awake at night imagining the most prolonged and torturous end for such as he. But I knew that Master Knox would not be so engaged. Nor would he approve of my unforgiving fantasies. That much I knew right well.

On that foul Sunday morning in November, Richard Ballantyne, John Craig, two other men, and myself, had rigged a chair to carry him in. It was a dreich morning, with gusts of wind sending the rain in slanting fury upon us like waves of drenching specters. His old malady was on him in force; his ashen face winced as we hoisted him in the improvised chair.

"It's dumping auld wives and pike staves," called John Craig above the din of the weather, and breathing heavily with the effort of carrying him. "You ought not to be out in this."

Come weather and decaying carcass, I knew that nothing would deter John Knox; he was determined to preach that day. As we made our way down the Royal Mile, doing our best to stay in the lee of the elements, I feared that such transporting of him, in his weakened condition and in such foul weather, would kill him. Though we covered him with an oilcloth, there was no keeping out the rain when it came on with such determination. At last we entered St. Giles, water trailing on the flagstones, and lowered him and his chair in a puddle before the pulpit. He made as if to rise, and I believe he thought he could climb the many steps into the pulpit. In this, our wills proved stronger than his, and we restrained him from his design.

We did not absolutely know it, though I believe we all feared it would be his last sermon preached to his beloved flock at St. Giles, as it indeed proved to be. His voice began weak and tremulous. I feared that few would hear his words.

"It was God our Father's own incomprehensible goodness that moved him to love us most wretched and miserable, yea, most wicked and blasphemous, and it was love most perfect that compelled him to show mercy."

A hush fell over the sanctuary as folks strained to hear his words. It seemed that his voice grew stronger. At his words, my mind was in turmoil. If he knew of Alexander's foul deed—and I felt sure he did—yet would he, like his Savior, forgive? I was certain of it.

"And mercy pronounced the sentence," he continued, "which was that his only Son should pay the price of our redemption, a price we ourselves inflicted upon Him. Make no mistake, you and I it was who were his betrayer, his denier, and his executioner, we in rage hanging Him upon the tree as payment for our great transgressions. And how could such a payment not but move us to unfeigned thanksgiving unto God our Father, and to his only Son Jesus, who has restored us again to liberty and life? For which we are constrained to laud, magnify, and extol the liberal kindness of God our Father, and the infinite benefits which we have received by Christ's death."

It was remarkable to behold the power of the very gospel he proclaimed as it overwhelmed and enlivened his own frailty—and as it tempered the unforgiving high winds rending my own heart.

"Blessed be God, the Father of our Lord Jesus Christ. I am not left so bare without comfort, but my hope is to attain such mercy, that if a short end be not made of all my miseries, by final death, which were to me no small advantage, that yet by Him, who never despises the sobs of the sore afflicted, I shall be so encouraged to proclaim that pure doctrine, and that heavenly religion, whereof it has pleased his merciful providence, to make me, among others, a simple soldier, and witness-bearer, unto men."

I believe that all present at that last public sermon of John Knox felt that he was saying farewell to his flock. We carried him back to his house at Trunk Close. His body trembled as we lowered him onto his bed and covered him with blankets against the chill. In the days of excruciating pain that followed, so many friends and supporters gathered at his bedside, it was as if he were holding court.

"The time is approaching," he said one evening to those who had gathered, "the time for which I have long thirsted, wherein I shall be relieved of all cares, and be with my Savior Christ forever."

One of those present was yet besmeared with mire from his long ride. James Lawson of Aberdeen, who had been appointed and called to succeed John Knox as minister of St. Giles, fearing he would arrive too late, had nearly killed his horse getting to Edinburgh.

"And you, Mr. Lawson, fight a good fight," said my master, his voice low. "Do the work of the Lord with courage and with a willing mind; and God from above bless you and the church whereof you have the charge. Against it, so long as it continueth in the doctrine of the truth, the gates of hell shall not prevail."

His breathing was becoming more labored. I had seen death before. From where I remained in the shadows, not trusting myself to speak, my chest felt like someone had laid a cannonball upon me. Margaret was never far from his side, and as much as the weight of her impending loss could be seen upon her anxious brow, she graciously served the almost endless stream of friends and supporters who came to pay their respects to her husband. But there was one evening when she stood with hands on her hips before a room crowded with grown men.

"He must rest," she said in her intrepid manner. "And you must go to your homes." When none of them made immediately to part, she added, "At once!"

On Monday, November 24, 1572, he refused food or drink, and it seemed that the pain had eased. "Margaret, my dear," he said, "Read where I cast first my anchor."

She took up his Geneva Bible and turned its pages. Leaning toward the candle, she read. Her voice rising and falling in an enchanting lilt; I had not before realized how much her voice was like the most lyric of music.

Christ has been raised from the dead, the first fruits of those who have fallen asleep. For as by a man came death, by a man has come also the resurrection of the dead. For as in Adam all die, so also in Christ shall all be made alive. But each in his own order: Christ the first fruits, then at his coming those who belong to Christ. Then comes the end, when he delivers the kingdom to God the Father after destroying every rule and every authority and power. For he must reign until he has put all his enemies under his feet. The last enemy to be destroyed is death. For "God has put all things in subjection under his feet."

He lay so still with his eyes closed while she read that I feared he may have fallen asleep—or worse. But when she finished reading, his eyes fluttered open; he smiled, and said, "Is not that a comfortable chapter?"

He dozed fitfully for an hour, and then awoke with a measure of alertness and energy. He asked to hear a sermon of his beloved mentor John Calvin read out. "From Ephesians," he said. Margaret handed me the volume of sermons. But Master Knox signaled with his hand. "Margaret, read it to me, so I can hear your voice." And so again I sat back, listening to the clarity of Calvin's words and the thrumming lyric of her voice.

It is not lawful for us to indulge in loose living with the excuse that God has elected us before the creation of the world, as though it were right for us to give ourselves over to all manner of evil, because we cannot perish, seeing that God has taken us for his children. For we must not put things asunder which he has coupled together. Seeing then that he has chosen us to be holy and to walk in purity of life, our election must be as a root that yields good fruits. For so long as God lets us alone in our own natural state we can do nothing but all manner of wickedness, because there is such great corruption and perversity in man's nature that all that men ever think of doing is contrary to God's righteousness. Therefore, there is no other way but to be changed by God. And whence comes this change but only through the grace that we spoke of, namely, that he elected and chose us for his children before we were born into the world.

She read on for more than an hour. The only other sounds were the hissing of burning candles, and John Knox's feeble breathing.

At last Margaret's reading of Calvin was interrupted. "Now, it comes," said John Knox, his voice barely audible. He paused, heaving a deep sigh. "Come, Lord Jesus, sweet Jesus; into thy hand I commend my spirit."

Then all was silent. We all of us looked intently at his pale face. In the silence that followed, Richard Ballantyne spoke. He asked him to give some sign that he was dying in the promises of the gospel. John Knox lifted a hand heavenward, sighed again, and without any struggle, as one falling asleep, departed this life.

I cannot explain the raging of my emotions when the last breath parted from my master's body and he lay still, no moving, no feeling, devoid of life, all vitality gone. There were tears, James Lawson's, Richard Ballantyne's, John Knox's children's, Margaret's—and my own.

Two days later John Knox's body was laid to rest near St. Giles. Though a raw wind swirled about the kirkyard, a vast crowd braved the elements and filled the streets of Edinburgh to pay their respects. There is numbing reality to a burial: the assortment of spades, the mound of muddy soil, the gaping hole in the earth, the coffin, the ropes, the creaking as the deceased is lowered into the yawing blackness of the hole, the chinking of the spades and the dull clunk of earth and gravel on the coffin, the sobs of women and children, the skirling of wind in the crown spire of the kirk, the gaping emptiness in one's insides.

My father had come to pay his respects, and though he could not say anything—perhaps *because* he could not say anything—I was grateful that he was there with me. Spade full after spade full, I watched the grave fill up with dirt. He tenderly placed a hand upon my shoulder.

After a moment of silence, the Earl of Morton, the Regent of the boy king, James VI, staring at the grave, said, "There lies one who in his life never feared the face of man."

Near-freezing rain lashed at my face as I stared at the new grave of my master. After another silence, Thomas Smeaton, one of the young men trained by John Knox for ministry, said, "I know not if God ever placed a more godly and great spirit in a body so little and frail."

It was true, though I could find no words to express my heart that day.

53

The Fatherless and Widowed

THE MONTHS THAT FOLLOWED the death of my master, John Knox, were ones of great turmoil in my heart. I was Deacon Douglas, called by the kirk to care for those in need, to care for the fatherless and widowed. Never before had my calling been so tormenting to me. I confess to my shame that far too long did I neglect John Knox's widow and his five fatherless children. Yet did I feel that neglecting them was the lesser sin.

While I was in my misery, I was not entirely idle on her behalf. I had learned that my master had kept nothing for himself of his pay, but after feeding his family, he had made so free with his means by contributing what little he had to those who had still less, that he had died nearly penniless. I presented a proposal before the diaconate that John Knox's salary of 500 merks annually be given to his widow. My fellow deacons, after much discussion, agreed to support Margaret with 500 merks for one year, or until she remarried. That qualifying proviso tormented me: *Or until she remarried.*

A motion was proffered that a deacon be appointed to care for the new widow and her children. As the discussion developed,

I felt a rising panic in my bosom. At last they reached a decision. "And we appoint over the care of the widow and bairns of our beloved John Knox," said the moderator, "Deacon George Douglas."

I felt like a stag in a thicket. As the meeting adjourned, this much was clear: I was no longer at liberty to neglect my duty to her.

I shall never forget that first morning that I called at Trunk Close. Five times I slowed my steps, then briskly walked on down the street. Once I exited the Netherbow, fully resolved to head for home and draft my resignation from my calling. It was too cruel. How was I to administer the love and grace of Christ to a widow, knowing my heart as I did?

"George Douglas!" came a cry from the house. Margaret had thrown open a window and was smiling down at me in a way that looked like she thought I'd gone daft. "George, have you gone and lost something? You've passed before the house like you've lost something. What is it, then?"

My mouth felt like I'd just taken a great spoonful of oatmeal. I opened it to speak but nothing at first came out of it. I wondered if my eyes had taken to their old ways of wagging too wide. My stomach had certainly begun its old churnings.

"Nae, nae," I managed at last. "Aye, and you, you're doing well, then?"

"Aye, I'm doing well and grateful," she said, placing one hand on a hip. "Well, indeed, by the grace of God. Though Elizabeth's gnawing on everything, and Margaret fell and skinned her knee, again. Martha does her best to help me with the little ones, but she's making efforts to teach herself the Latin. Och, did I mention, the boys need a tutor?"

I was smitten low with feelings of guilt and shame. Certainly I could manage to take up again being tutor to the sons of the man who had been my tutor. But could I be safely thus?

"George, do you think it best for us to be conversing," she said, "by all this yammering in the street?"

"Aye, and what of your larder, Madam?" I called back up to her.

"My what?"

"Your larder," I repeated. "Victuals and the like."

"Victuals?" she said, musing upward at the goat's hair clouds scudding above the street. "I'm scraping bottom on oats, and could use a bit of sausage, some cabbage, a bit of cheese, and some wine, if you can manage. And I'm a wee bit low on time, these days. Do you have any spare of that lying about?"

I had never met a more maddening female specimen in my days. I stepped near the wall of the house directly beneath the window so as not to have to be shouting above the folks walking along the Mile. "There's a wee break in the clouds, just now," I said. "Would you care to bundle up the bairns and take a bit of fresh air?"

She poked her head farther out the window and looked up at the sky. Looking down at me, her face brightened. "I'll be down in less time than it takes to stuff a haggis."

So it was that I fulfilled my diaconal duty to John Knox's widow by spending an afternoon walking on the hillside above the city with his family. I was pleased with myself. It did them all good. It did me good, romping with the lads, being pony and bouncing Elizabeth on my shoulders. I was not at all certain, however, that it did me good talking with Margaret, being with her, she walking at my side, and I at hers. I tried not to look at her as I spoke, the sparkling blue of her eyes, the delicate turn of her nose, the rosy flush on her cheeks, the fine cut of her dress, her cheerful patience in affliction as the lonely mother of my dead master's bairns—everything about her awakened all my old longings. It was like murky clouds dumping a foul gandiegow upon my bruised emotions.

I diverted my attention toward the splendor sprawling beneath us, the gothic spires, crenellated ramparts, and rigid towers of the ancient city on the dun. Meanwhile, Margaret set out for her children a meager luncheon of bannock and smoked fish on the summit.

"You'll pray then for us?" she said, grasping the children's hands in her own.

So it had always been when her husband, their father, had been living. Always he wrestled in prayer. Hence, I could think of no better prayer than one prayed often by their own father. "Be merciful, O Lord, to our offences; and seeing our debt is great, which thou hast forgiven us in Jesus Christ, make us to love thee and our neighbors so much the more." His words, so familiar to my mind and to my lips, smote like a blacksmith's hammer upon the unforgiving iron of my own heart—unforgiving, that is, toward Alexander, the scoundrel. I knew not how to overcome such stony heart winds. So I prayed on. "Be thou our Father, our Captain, and Defender in all temptations." There it was. This much was sure, I was helpless against my unforgiving heart and against my unholy desiring. But my Defender, he was not helpless. I paused, feeling afresh in my soul the hope of my master's prayer. I reached over and placed my hand upon hers and the bairns'. "Hold thou us by thy merciful hand; that we may be delivered from all hardships, and end our lives in the sanctifying and honoring of thy holy name, through Jesus Christ our Lord and only Savior. Amen."

There's not much left to say. After our luncheon, we descended the summit and reentered the city. I made free to suggest that we enter by the West Bow gate and make a stop at the Grassmarket so as to refill the Knox's larder with food.

"Perhaps we'll find a fat haddock for your supper," I said.

"Och, man," she said with a wink. "I'll not pay a farthing more than one groat!"

THE END

John Knox and the Reformation

Timeline of Events

1512	First Reformation martyrdom takes place in Paris
1514	John Knox born in Haddington
1516	Erasmus's Greek New Testament published
1517	Luther's 95 Theses issued
1518	Zwingli in Zurich; Swiss Reformation begins
1525	Tyndale publishes English New Testament
1530	Creation of the Augsburg Confession
1534	Henry VIII's Act of Supremacy; break with Rome
1534	Ignatius Loyola founds Jesuit Order to renew Roman Catholic Church
1536	Calvin publishes first edition of *Institutes of the Christian Religion*
1536	Knox ends university studies; ordained a priest
1540	Knox works as notary and private tutor
1543	Likely date of Knox's conversion to Christ
1545	Knox works as supporter and bodyguard to George Wishart
1546	Council of Trent; Catholic Counter-Reformation, begins

1546   Death of Martin Luther

1546   Wishart martyred; retaliatory killing of Cardinal Beaton; Protestants gather at St. Andrews Castle; Queen Regent places castle under siege

1547   Knox joins Protestant Castilians; preaches first public sermon; castle falls to French

1547–   Knox spends nineteen months as French galley slave
1549

Preaching in England

1549   Knox released and preaches before Edward VI; preaches in Berwick, England

1549   Cranmer's first *Book of Common Prayer* published

1550   Conversion of Mrs. Elizabeth Bowes and daughter Marjory

1552   Knox disputes kneeling at Lord's Supper; declines bishopric of Rochester

1553   Death of Edward VI and ascension of Catholic Mary Tudor

Refugee in Europe

1554   Knox flees to Calvin's Geneva; pastors English congregation in Frankfurt

1555   Pastors English refugee congregation in Geneva; commando preaching crusade in Scotland; marries Marjory Bowes

1556   Condemned as heretic in Scotland; returns to Geneva with wife and mother-in-law; contributes to translation and commentary in Geneva Bible

1558   Writes *The First Blast of the Trumpet Against the Monstrous Regiment of Women*

1558   Elizabeth I made Queen of England

Reformation Years in Scotland

1559   Knox returns to Scotland; preaches sermon in Perth condemning idolatry of Mass; revival and iconoclasm

1560   Reformation Parliament adopts Scots Confession; first wife dies

1561   Helps write *First Book of Discipline*; Mary Queen of Scots returns; ministers at St. Giles's Edinburgh; first interview with Mary

1563   Foxe's *Book of Martyrs* published

1564   Knox marries Margaret Stewart

1566   Writes *History of the Reformation of Religion in Scotland*

1567   Mary Queen of Scots forced to abdicate; coronation of James VI

1572   St. Bartholomew's Day Massacre in France

1572   Knox dies in Edinburgh; buried near St. Giles High Kirk

More from Doug Bond

Told from the perspective of a sworn lifelong enemy of John Calvin, this fast-paced biographical novel is a tale of envy that escalates to violent intrigue and shameless betrayal.

"Anything Doug Bond writes is, almost now by definition, a fascinating read. But to have his skills attached to the life of John Calvin is a double treat."
—**Joel Belz,** founder, *WORLD* magazine

"An exciting read, almost effortlessly and implicitly undoing caricatures about Calvin along the way ... Calvin and his times brought to life in a page-turner!"
—**Joel R. Beeke,** president, Puritan Reformed Theological Seminary

Half Saxon and half Dane, misfit Cynwulf lives apart from the world in a salvaged Viking ship, dreaming of spending his life with the fair Haeddi. When he is accused of murder, he must clear his name before he loses everything to the vengeance of the community that has already rejected him.

"What could be better than an intriguing mystery, a little romance, and a short sojourn in a place and time that's little known and less understood? Douglas Bond shines a light on the past in a way that's as entertaining as it is informative."
—**Janie B. Cheaney,** senior writer, *WORLD* magazine; blogger at RedeemedReader .com